# VERBAL
# ORDERS

# VERBAL ORDERS

# LARRY CARELLO

Braveship
BOOKS

*Aura Libertatis Spirat*

**VERBAL ORDERS**

Copyright © 2017 by Larry Carello

**Braveship Books**

www.braveshipbooks.com

Aura Libertatis Spirat

**Cover Design by Max von Reinhard, 99Designs**

**Book layout by Alexandru Diaconescu**

www.steadfast-typesetting.eu

ISBN-13: 978-1-64062-011-7

Printed in the United States of America

*For Mom and Dad*

# ACKNOWLEDGEMENTS

Like most writing projects, this book could not have been created without the help and support of several people. First, I extend my sincere thanks to fellow writer, good friend and shipmate, George Galdorisi, for serving as my mentor. George, you are the consummate professional and I'm most fortunate to be a recipient of your counsel. I also want to recognize my editor, Kevin McDonald, for his patience and diligence while "dissecting" my manuscript. Thanks, Kevin, for your incredible work. Likewise, a special thank you goes out to Jeff Edwards for having confidence in my writing and adding me to the list of outstanding authors at *Braveship Books*. It's an honor and privilege to be associated with such a fine organization.

I'd be remiss if I didn't single out another shipmate and good friend, John "Mac" McLaughlin, president of the USS *Midway* Museum, for providing whatever I needed while conducting research aboard his magnificent ship. Also, a heartfelt thanks to Mike Reeber for his sage advice and keen perspective on naval aviation.

And finally, to my devoted wife, Connie, for always being there to support me, no matter what. You are the love of my life!

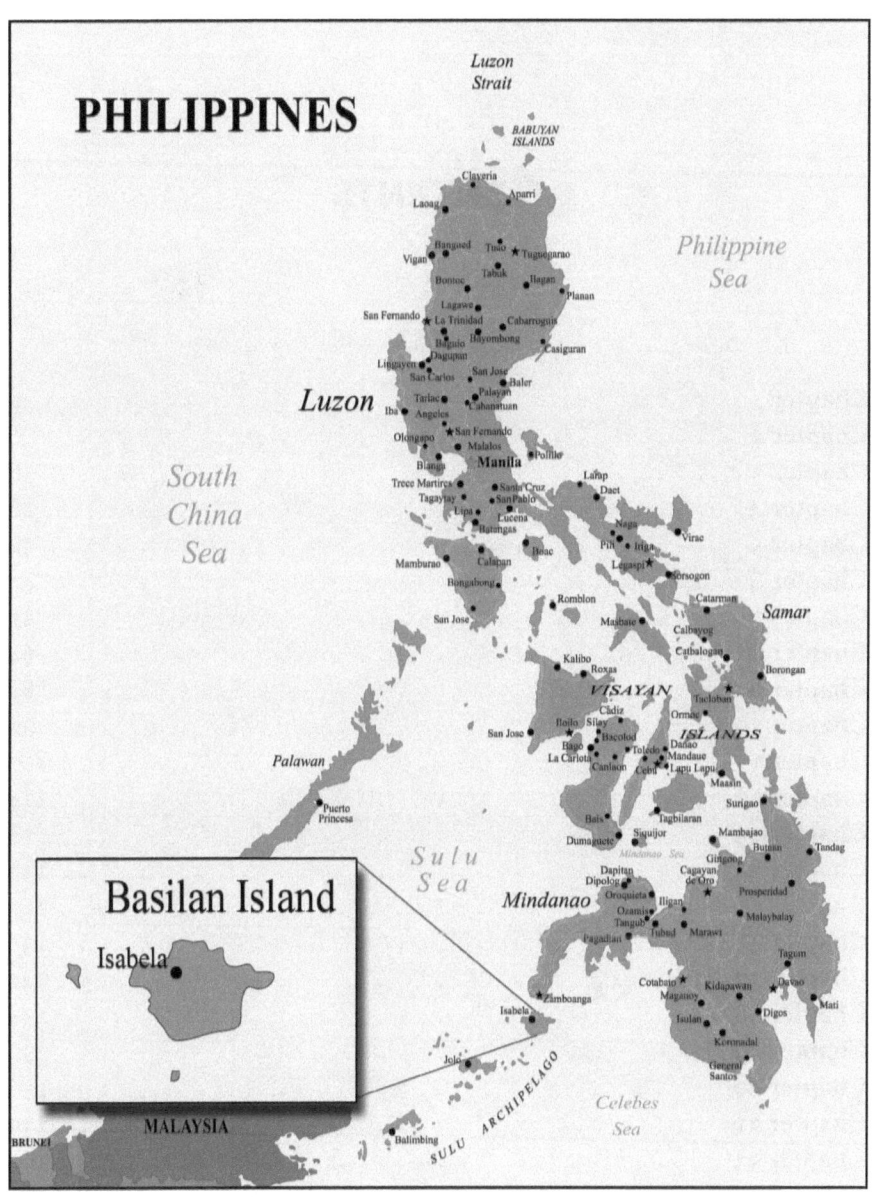

PHILIPPINES

Luzon
Strait

BABUYAN
ISLANDS

Claveria

Laoag

Aparri

Bangued Tuao ★ Tuguegarao

Vigan

Bontoc Tabuk Ilagan

San Fernando

Lagawe Planan

La Trinidad Cabarroguis

Baguio Bayombong Casiguran

Bagupan

Lingayen San Jose

San Carlos Baler

Tarlac Palayan

Iba Angeles Cabanatuan

San Fernando

Olongapo

Malolos Polillo

Bataan Manila

Trece Martires Santa Cruz Lamon Daet

Tagaytay San Pablo

Lipa Lucena

Batangas Naga

Mamburao Calapan Boac Iriga Virac

Legaspi ★

Bongabong Sorsogon

San Jose Catarman

Romblon

Masbate Calbayog Catbalogan

Kalibo Borongan

Roxas Tacloban

VISAYAN Ormoc

Cadiz

San Jose Iloilo Silay Bacolod Danao

Roxas Toledo Mandaue

La Carlota Lapu Lapu

Canlaon Cebu Maasin

Surigao

Bais Tagbilaran

Dumaguete Siquijor Mambajao Tandag

Gingoog Butuan

Dapitan Cagayan Prosperidad

Dipolog de Oro

Oroquieta Iligan

Ozamis Malaybalay

Tangub Marawi

Pagadian Tubod Tagum

Cotabato Kidapawan Davao

Zamboanga Maganoy Digos Mati

Isabela Isulan

Jolo Koronadal

General
Santos

SULU ARCHIPELAGO

Balimbing

BRUNEI MALAYSIA

Luzon

South
China
Sea

Philippine
Sea

Samar

ISLANDS

Palawan

Puerto
Princesa

Sulu
Sea

Mindanao

Mindanao Sea

Celebes
Sea

Basilan Island

Isabela

# CONTENTS

Chapter 1 . . . . . . . . . . . . . . . . . . . . . . . . . . . . . . . . . . 1
Chapter 2 . . . . . . . . . . . . . . . . . . . . . . . . . . . . . . . . . 10
Chapter 3 . . . . . . . . . . . . . . . . . . . . . . . . . . . . . . . . . 18
Chapter 4 . . . . . . . . . . . . . . . . . . . . . . . . . . . . . . . . . 28
Chapter 5 . . . . . . . . . . . . . . . . . . . . . . . . . . . . . . . . . 32
Chapter 6 . . . . . . . . . . . . . . . . . . . . . . . . . . . . . . . . . 42
Chapter 7 . . . . . . . . . . . . . . . . . . . . . . . . . . . . . . . . . 47
Chapter 8 . . . . . . . . . . . . . . . . . . . . . . . . . . . . . . . . . 64
Chapter 9 . . . . . . . . . . . . . . . . . . . . . . . . . . . . . . . . . 81
Chapter 10 . . . . . . . . . . . . . . . . . . . . . . . . . . . . . . . . 92
Chapter 11 . . . . . . . . . . . . . . . . . . . . . . . . . . . . . . . . 107
Chapter 12 . . . . . . . . . . . . . . . . . . . . . . . . . . . . . . . . 114
Chapter 13 . . . . . . . . . . . . . . . . . . . . . . . . . . . . . . . . 118
Chapter 14 . . . . . . . . . . . . . . . . . . . . . . . . . . . . . . . . 122
Chapter 15 . . . . . . . . . . . . . . . . . . . . . . . . . . . . . . . . 127
Chapter 16 . . . . . . . . . . . . . . . . . . . . . . . . . . . . . . . . 135
Chapter 17 . . . . . . . . . . . . . . . . . . . . . . . . . . . . . . . . 141
Chapter 18 . . . . . . . . . . . . . . . . . . . . . . . . . . . . . . . . 144
Chapter 19 . . . . . . . . . . . . . . . . . . . . . . . . . . . . . . . . 152
Chapter 20 . . . . . . . . . . . . . . . . . . . . . . . . . . . . . . . . 156
Chapter 21 . . . . . . . . . . . . . . . . . . . . . . . . . . . . . . . . 159
Chapter 22 . . . . . . . . . . . . . . . . . . . . . . . . . . . . . . . . 166
Chapter 23 . . . . . . . . . . . . . . . . . . . . . . . . . . . . . . . . 170
Chapter 24 . . . . . . . . . . . . . . . . . . . . . . . . . . . . . . . . 182
Chapter 25 . . . . . . . . . . . . . . . . . . . . . . . . . . . . . . . . 186
Chapter 26 . . . . . . . . . . . . . . . . . . . . . . . . . . . . . . . . 191

Chapter 27 . . . . . . . . . . . . . . . . . . . . . . . . . . . . 199
Chapter 28 . . . . . . . . . . . . . . . . . . . . . . . . . . . . 208
Chapter 29 . . . . . . . . . . . . . . . . . . . . . . . . . . . . 214
Epilogue . . . . . . . . . . . . . . . . . . . . . . . . . . . . . 221
Author's Notes . . . . . . . . . . . . . . . . . . . . . . . . . 223

# CHAPTER 1

McGirt had seen that look before: the surprised, sinking expression of a man trapped somewhere between panic and denial. The young aviator seated to his left, Lt. Tim Worley, wore that look now.

Worley, sitting in the copilot seat, had noticed the amber warning light on the helicopter's caution panel first, as it flickered, disappeared from view, and then came back on with the irrefutable certainty of a cold-fisted punch in the gut. The words escaped, in the form of a reluctant murmur, from Worley's pursed lips. "Chip light."

He waited for McGirt, who continued flying the aircraft in silence, to acknowledge his succinct call to action. When no response was immediately forthcoming, he cleared his throat, keyed the intercom, and stated again—this time with measured authority—"Skipper, we have a transmission chip light."

McGirt had seen the light a nanosecond after Worley, but he'd kept quiet. Unlike the rookie instructor pilot, he'd experienced countless similar warnings that had ultimately proven false. Old pros like Johnny Jack McGirt knew that, given a few moments, the venerable CH-46 had a habit of shaking itself free of electrically sensed glitches. But not today; not this time.

The glaring Southern California sunlight shone through the helicopter's windows at an odd angle, which cast a masking shadow on the aircraft's instrument panel, so McGirt reached up with his left hand and raised his dark-tinted helmet visor, hoping to see more clearly. Much to the disappointment of both men in the cockpit, the chip light was still illuminated.

"Tim, we gotta handle this," McGirt said flatly. "Emergency checklist, please." He pointed to the warning light.

From a flight suit pocket located below his right knee, Worley dug out a small laminated binder. He leafed through the yellow-colored pages and began reading the procedure aloud, "Reduce power to minimum … Slow to sixty-five knots … "

McGirt had already begun carrying out the first two steps from memory as he pushed down gently on the two-foot-long black steel shaft—called the "collective"— adjacent to his left side and eased back on the cyclic control stick between his knees. Through a complex set of rods and actuators, the pitch angle of the helicopter's six rotor blades flattened out, reducing lift, which caused the aircraft to begin descending and decelerate to a slower speed.

Worley called out altitude and airspeed. "Two hundred feet, one hundred ten knots … " He made brief eye contact with McGirt and hoped that his own anxiety would be disguised. The words "chip light" might sound innocuous to the layman, but short of a raging inflight fire, there were few quandaries with the potential for more ruinous consequences. Both McGirt and Worley had read past accident reports and understood the simple mechanics: a chip light was a signal that one of the helicopter's two transmission gearboxes might be coming apart and would ultimately freeze up. Without power from the transmission, the rotor blades would stop turning, and their aircraft would assume the flight characteristics of a baby grand piano.

McGirt scanned the instrument panel again as he made a slow ninety-degree turn toward the shoreline. Engine readings appeared normal, but his optimism faded when he realized that the small white needle on the aft transmission oil temperature gauge had begun rising into the caution range. The metal shavings that the chip indicator had detected were more than just a few microscopic particles in the transmission's cooling oil—the gearbox was indeed starting to fail.

"Skipper, we need to land *immediately*," Worley said forcefully after seeing the temperature increase.

McGirt was already making a beeline for the Silver Strand State Beach, located halfway between their base in Coronado and the outlying practice field at Imperial Beach.

Johnny Jack McGirt had never flown with Tim Worley, but now Worley, even as a spanking new instructor pilot, had drawn the undesirable task of administering the mandatory proficiency check to his boss. This was a check required by all Navy pilots regardless of rank, and McGirt, the desk-bound Navy captain and commanding officer, had struggled performing some of the prescribed basic flight maneuvers. Embarrassed by his sloppy airmanship, he'd sheepishly apologized to Worley for his lack of proficiency. "Too much time in the office and not enough in the cockpit," he'd lamented, shaking his head in disgust. During the course of the ninety-minute sortie, however, McGirt had shaken off the cobwebs, passed the exam, and with the mission nearly complete, both pilots had welcomed the short, scenic flight along the coastline back to Coronado and the North Island Naval Air Station.

Worley finished reading the emergency checklist and got off a quick radio call on the "guard" frequency, letting the world know their position and status.

McGirt leveled off at an altitude of 50 feet and slowed to the prescribed speed, placing the aircraft in the most desirable condition for a possible ditch into the water. They were now less than two miles off the SoCal coast, with the grayish-beige sands of the state beach clearly in sight.

An emphatic voice shot through the pilots' headsets. "Skipper, this ain't lookin' real good back here."

Worley turned and looked over his right shoulder, down the helicopter's long, empty passenger compartment. He saw the tall, rangy silhouette of their crewman, Chief Petty Officer Ralph "Guido" Sartelli, shrouded in a misty, smoke-like haze. Sartelli appeared to be pawing at the faulty aft gearbox situated just a few inches above his helmet.

"Mother f---er! I think she's starting to come unglued, sir! Hot as a whore's breath, and rattling like a lopsided honey wagon!" Sartelli hollered.

Worley watched him pull an ungloved hand away from the titanium gearbox like someone who'd unsuspectingly grabbed a sizzling fajita platter.

"Shouldn't have done that, dammit," Sartelli moaned to himself. Then, stammering, he shouted "We, we, gotta get this … this thing on the ground pronto, sir!"

The sight of the smoking transmission gearbox, coupled with the angst in Sartelli's voice, provoked a wave of emotions unknown to Worley. He'd never dealt with an actual—potentially fatal— situation like this. He suddenly realized that he wasn't in the safe confines of a flight simulator or partaking in a bullshit session with fellow instructors over a cup of coffee—this was the real deal.

McGirt saw "the look" return on Worley's face. "Hey, Tim," he said, "why don't you take the controls and I'll work with the chief." Secretly, Captain McGirt knew that, as the more seasoned aviator, he could direct the event better as the non-flying pilot, and by engaging Worley with the task of flying the aircraft, that arrangement would best serve them as a crew. "Keep us low and slow, and continue heading straight for that beach." McGirt noted that the transmission's oil pressure gauge was still in the safe range, but its temperature was now clearly in the red zone and headed to the pegged position. He felt droplets of sweat forming over his eyebrows and dripping into his eyes; he dabbed them with the sleeve of his flight suit. "How we looking, Guido?"

"Ain't no better, Boss," Sartelli said in his hurried, New Jersey accent. "Paint on the gearbox casing looks like it's about ready to blister."

Just a few hundred yards away, the sands of the state park beckoned the disabled bird and her anxious crew to continue forging ahead. McGirt could see its parking lot crammed full with vehicles. He knew that a critical decision was imminent: either press on to the beach—or ditch the helicopter off shore and hope for the best. McGirt looked down at the ten-foot swells; the rough sea state would make a successful water landing very difficult, he quickly surmised, and would likely cause the H-46's top-heavy airframe to quickly capsize and sink.

"Sir, I think we should ditch and get out while we can," Worley said firmly.

Steadiness had returned to Worley's demeanor. McGirt's intuition had panned out correctly; the act of manipulating the controls had helped the youngster regain his composure. The senior aviator looked down again at the heaving water below, then shifted his eyes to a large fishing trawler located a short distance away. The vessel rolled and bobbed erratically in the powerful swells. The thought of his aircraft plunging to the ocean floor, even if only a few dozen feet deep, roiled McGirt's innards. The squadron, *his* squadron, had an unblemished safety record. Even though he figured that he and his crew would probably get free of the aircraft before it sank, a controlled ditching was not his first choice from the list of available options.

"Chief, give me an update, will ya?" McGirt asked.

"Well, she ain't no worse, Skipper, but I'm about ready to jump out of this giant egg beater if we're not on terra firma soon."

McGirt had known Sartelli for over twenty years. The two of them had cruised the Western Pacific and Philippines together during the fledgling enlisted man's first overseas deployment. He understood the sailor's sharp, direct speech and knew that Sartelli would do just as he'd threatened if so inclined.

McGirt glanced over his shoulder and saw that Sartelli had strapped himself into the crew chief's jump seat, located just aft of the cockpit, in preparation for a ditch. McGirt scanned the transmission oil temperature gauge again; it had stabilized in the bottom of the red arc and had still not pegged out. Likewise, the tranny's oil pressure remained stable. With the aircraft less than a solid nine iron golf shot's distance from the beach, the lure of being safely on the ground was now stronger than the specter of the gearbox seizing—a thought that had dangled ominously over McGirt's head like the sword of Damocles for the last several minutes.

"You're doing fine, Lieutenant," McGirt reassured Worley. "Looks like a break in the crowd at ten o'clock, there just left of that lifeguard tower." He motioned with his left hand about forty-five degrees off the helo's track. McGirt looked down and to his right and saw that the aircraft was about to overtake a surfer, who was paddling furiously to grab a wave. The dude had just stood up and steadied himself when he caught sight of the lumbering helicopter passing overhead. McGirt watched as the startled guy kicked his board to one side and fell back awkwardly. He popped to the surface, thrust both arms in the air, and flipped McGirt a double bird.

"How's this look, Skipper?" Worley asked as they crossed the water's edge. He'd zeroed in on the vacant swatch of sand that McGirt had picked for landing.

"Perfect. As soon as we touch down, I'll chop the engine throttles and hit the rotor brake."

Worley nodded as he established the helicopter in a rock-solid ten-foot hover, then carefully lowered the collective lever with his left hand. The aircraft "planted" firmly on the soft sand in a slightly nose-up, wings-level attitude.

McGirt reached down to the center console and shoved the two engine throttles to their fuel-cut-off position.

Sartelli, as if on cue, had leapt up from his station and yanked on a lever near the throttles to arm the rotor brake.

McGirt then reached up to the overhead panel and flicked a switch that released a solenoid-activated puck, which in turn squeezed against a metal plate attached to the forward transmission, much like a car's disc braking system. In unison, the forward and aft transmissions, together with their respective rotor heads, shuttered to a jerky stop. McGirt looked to his left at Worley. The front of the lieutenant's flight suit was soaked with sweat that had dripped from his face.

Worley looked outside for a second and then back at McGirt. His tensed facial muscles began to relax as he called out at the top of his lungs, "Thank you, Jeezus!"

Sartelli followed with a relieved laughing whoop; the grizzled salt slapped both pilots on their shoulders affectionately. "Now let me see what the hell we got to deal with back there," he said. His flight boots clopped loudly as he walked aft over the H-46's decking to the scene of the crime—the rear transmission and gearbox. His verdict came quickly: "She's fried pretty good, Skipper." Sartelli had unscrewed a small plug-like device from the gearbox, taking careful pains not to burn himself with the overheated oil. The plug, or chip detector, was loaded with metal fragments that had grinded away from the disintegrating gears. Sartelli shook his head dejectedly, looked up at the failed component and mumbled, "Gotta change the whole frigging thing, dammit." He casually peeled off his oil-soaked gloves, tossed them on the deck, and then unzipped his sleeve pocket and fumbled blindly for the pack of cigarettes tucked snugly inside.

Worley had removed his helmet and began unstrapping the five-point shoulder harness that had secured him in place for the last long hour and a half. McGirt did the same and perched his helmet atop the control stick between his knees. He wearily rubbed a hand across the top of his closely cropped graying hair.

The younger, lesser experienced lieutenant took a deep breath and continued to focus on regaining his cool. He held two shivering hands in front of his face and inhaled fully again in hopes of calming down. When he realized that his CO was staring at him, he quickly folded both hands into his lap, his face reddened with embarrassment.

"You did a fine job, son," McGirt said with a smile. He gave the young helo jock a fatherly tap on the arm. Worley giggled a tired, relieved sigh. McGirt knew that the lieutenant's wife had delivered the couple's first child, a baby girl, just weeks ago. He could only imagine what had been going through Worley's mind during the last several minutes. McGirt had seen many challenging emergencies during his twenty-eight years as a Navy pilot. He knew that one could talk about it, study the aircraft manual inside and out, and sit through endless training sessions; but there was nothing that could truly prepare a pilot for a critical situation like the one they'd just experienced—nothing.

Worley had exited the aircraft and was inspecting the bird's fuselage as a curious crowd of onlookers began to assemble around the site.

McGirt looked outside and saw a chubby female park ranger plodding laboriously over a sand dune in the direction of the helicopter; she appeared to be chattering fervently into a hand-held radio. McGirt gave her an easy wave to signal things were okay now. Unlike Worley, his hands were steady as he started unstrapping. He'd mastered the art of stifling his emotions and nerves in critical situations. What did the Navy flight surgeons and aviation shrinks call it? … *Compartmentalizing.* Whatever—McGirt relished the learned knack of blocking out fear and anxiety in order to get the job done. Having watched Worley confront his first actual, life-threatening aviation event, he felt confident that the kid would build on this experience and develop into a cool-headed decision maker. Johnny Jack McGirt had seen his share of officers and pilots, ranging in dispositions from the stoic calmness of his close friend and mentor, Bud Lammers, to the sniveling unctuousness of the despicable Thomas Rayburn III, whom, thankfully, he hadn't seen since their deployment to the Western Pacific over twenty years ago.

As he sat gathering his flight gear, McGirt saw the surfer that they'd startled moments ago. The fellow, who looked barely out of his teens, stood a few feet away from the aircraft's right side, a turquoise-colored surfboard tucked securely under his arm. As the two of them made eye contact, a brilliant white smile erupted from the young dude's deeply tanned face. His thick mane of sun-bleached hair glistened with salt water in the mid-day sun.

McGirt watched as the boy raised a fist, pumped it in the air, and shouted joyfully, "Awesome, man; totally awesome!"

McGirt returned a half-hearted wave and grinned. As he wriggled his body out from the smallish cockpit, he thought to himself of all the close calls from which he'd managed to escape while flying Navy helicopters. "Just dodging another bullet," he'd laughingly say. Maybe his old pal, Lammers, had made the smarter move years ago—when the bullets they'd dodged together in the Philippines Islands were more than figurative. McGirt had neglected to return Bud's phone call yesterday after an admin petty officer had dropped the memo on his desk while he'd been at the base gym. As always, Lammers's message had been succinct, reading simply: *Call Bud.* It had been late afternoon, and after considering the time difference between San Diego and the CIA headquarters in Langley, Virginia, he'd chosen to let it slide.

McGirt stepped down from the aircraft's boarding ladder and plunked his boots on the warm sand. Some more onlookers had gathered: additional surfers, a group of sun-burned senior citizens, and a handful of darting children—unsuccessfully corralled by their parents. Beyond the sand dunes and parking lot, he spotted a white van speeding up the Silver Strand Highway toward the beach park. Emblazoned across the vehicle's side was an orange, yellow, and blue logo that read "Channel 7 News."

The TV crew had been reporting the endless saga of raw sewage seeping into wetlands near the border city of Tijuana, Mexico, and the inherent threat of the effluent flowing into the Pacific Ocean and fouling Southern California's coastline. The news station's programmers had apparently heard Worley's distress call over an emergency radio scanner and had decided to reroute the news crew from just a few miles away. The van's driver picked his way through the crowded lot, drove through an empty handicap space, and parked directly on the sand.

A tall, bearded cameraman dressed in cut-off shorts emerged, followed by a slender, blond reporter-ette wearing a dark blue blouse and cream-colored, skin-tight jeans.

McGirt saw a microphone clutched firmly in her hand. A spark of apprehension shot through him as he thought, *Christ sake, now this?* He found a cool area to stand, next to the helicopter, within the aircraft's shadow. The reporter and cameraman were deftly jogging through the soft sand toward the crowd. As they drew closer, McGirt noted that the girl's lightly bronzed, perfectly made-up face had the satisfied expression of someone who knew she'd scored a major scoop.

McGirt leaned lazily against the aircraft's fuselage; he overheard Sartelli holding court with Worley inside.

The chain-smoking lifer was relaying a sea story about the last time he'd had an emergency similar to this one. Much like an uncle giving sage advice to his adolescent nephew, Sartelli began pontificating. "Sometimes this shit just happens, Lieutenant. Ain't nothing we can do but be ready when it does."

The reporter and cameraman settled a few yards away and were discussing something as they readied for their spot. McGirt joined with the crowd and watched as a telescoping antenna rose ominously—up, up, up—from the news van while the driver established communications for the live segment. Confident that all was in order, the man waived both arms over his head, signaling the news crew that the station was standing by.

The reporter walked slowly toward McGirt and removed her dark, wrap-around sunglasses, revealing a piercing set of blue-green eyes that beamed through him like lasers when McGirt caught her glance. She zoomed in on the eagle-like insignia embroidered atop McGirt's shoulders, which signified him as a Navy captain.

"Hello, sir, may I talk with you?" the girl asked softly, almost in a whisper. McGirt nodded a "yes."

She turned toward the cameraman, who held out a wide spread hand in preparation for giving her a countdown with his fingers. She then returned her attention back to McGirt, this time focusing on the leather nametag over his left breast pocket that read: *Captain J.J. McGirt, Commanding Officer.* The girl broke from her well-rehearsed pose and gushed, "So you're the *squadron commander* ... oh my, I've got the Big Kahuna, today, don't I!"

McGirt smiled sheepishly as the reporter turned away again toward the camera and fidgeted daintily with the earpiece tucked beneath her flaxen hair.

McGirt stood erect and prepared for the interrogation. He'd quickly formulated what he was going to say: nothing overly telling—the standard boiler plate stuff giving credit to his crew and apologizing to the good folks on the beach whose pleasant day they'd disrupted. But what he'd say on live television was a comparatively minor blip on the radar screen of his mind right now. His thoughts flashed to the endless amount of paperwork and the phone calls he'd have to make when he returned to his desk at the squadron. He could hear Bud Lammers's prophetic words: Bud had once told him that he'd know when it was time to quit the game. McGirt realized that he'd probably miss it someday, just as Bud said he did: the flying; the excitement; the unparalleled sense of accomplishment that came with leading the brave, talented men and women of an aviation squadron. Deep down inside, though, in the place where only truth can reside, he knew that Bud was right—it was time.

The cameraman gave his countdown as the eager crowd closed in to witness the live broadcast. McGirt stood motionless and listened while the female reporter began her brisk introduction. She quickly shed the quiet, demure façade, lowered her voice a half octave and began gesturing emphatically—first pointing out the helicopter and its crew, then graciously recognizing the inconvenienced beachgoers. She then sauntered toward McGirt, all the time maintaining eye contact with the camera and the thousands of viewers watching on their television sets.

McGirt waited patiently as she positioned herself close to him—so close that he felt her body heat and could smell the flowery, tropical essence of her perfume. He gave a faint, humble smile and leaned forward to hear the girl as she held the microphone tightly and launched into a rambling question. He snuck a peek at the camera and thought to himself, *This is one hell of a way to bow out, McGirt, ... one hell of a way.*

# CHAPTER 2

"A blue safe, a blue safe," the old man seemed to say.

Karlena strained to hear his voice over the rat-tat-tat clatter of the boat's pinging engine; his words sounded unintelligible to her. She was seated, facing aft, and when she looked behind the small vessel, she saw only the frothy wake as their boat plied its way steadily through the dark, indigo-colored Sulu Sea, within the southernmost reaches of the Philippine Islands. The waters had been eerily placid since they'd left their last refueling stop at dawn.

As Karlena rotated her head and shoulders forward, the driver, who'd first introduced himself simply as "Duke," abruptly shoved the craft's rusty engine throttle to its forward limit causing Karlena to lose her balance. She came to an uncomfortable resting position on top of a backpack stuffed with cameras, extra lenses and film. She hurriedly inspected the gear, praying that nothing was damaged. It was all that she had left to her name—the two grand worth of professional photo equipment and a pittance of American money, of which she'd have even less after paying Duke.

She'd pawned the few clothes that she'd brought on this journey, keeping only a handful of toiletry items and roughly sixty dollars in cash that she'd tucked inside a sweat-stained money belt, hidden beneath her crumpled khaki shorts. She unconsciously rubbed a palm across her waist, found the loop of fabric that secured the belt to her shorts, and, for the umpteenth time, reassured herself that the money was still there.

"A blue safe," Duke repeated, this time shouting the words for Karlena to hear above the engine noise.

Their twenty-five foot tub of a boat began to rock gently as it traversed the wake of an early morning fishing vessel that had crossed their path moments ago. Duke raised his right arm and pointed silently to the two o'clock position.

As he did, an ash from his unfiltered cigarette flew back and hit Karlena squarely in the forehead; she brushed it away quickly.

She ran a pair of chapped fingers through the snarled mop of brassy hair on her head, thinking how much it felt like the coarse rope she'd held when learning to wrestle down a steer at her father's ranch. It'd been over a week since she'd taken a shower, although nobody in this part of the world seemed to notice or care—certainly not the weathered, mahogany-skinned Malaysian seaman she'd hired.

By now, she could see what had triggered Duke's reaction. The bright, early morning sun made the task difficult, but after shielding her eyes and squinting, she saw it: a black speck of a boat hurtling directly toward them, its low profile dwarfed by the foamy-white wake peeling away from its bow and a monstrous rooster tail spraying from its stern like a ruptured city water main. Karlena looked straight ahead and saw a smattering of emerald-shaded bumps materializing on the horizon. She pulled herself a few feet forward into the boat's tiny wheelhouse.

"Duke, what is it?"

"There," he pointed again at the rapidly approaching vessel to starboard as it zoomed closer toward them. "No good, no good," Duke said in broken English. He shook his head apprehensively and mumbled something in his native tongue.

Karlena instinctively placed a hand on his shoulder; she felt Duke's small, taut body sag in defeat. He had the look of a person who'd been through a painful event and realized he was about to experience it again. Karlena felt a shudder in her legs, followed by a scraping, thud like sound. She turned aft and saw a sickly plume of smoke sprouting like an oily, black weed between warped planks that housed the boat's inboard motor. She tapped Duke's arm. He turned and noted the smoke, but appeared unfazed by it. Karlena watched as his face took on a stone-like, almost possessed expression of someone aware of his impending fate, yet blindly refusing to acknowledge it.

It was obvious to the both of them that they were being intercepted. By now, Karlena could clearly see her destination: the southern shores of the Philippine island of Basilan, no more than a few hundred meters ahead; a thin line of rippling surf brushed against the island's craggy coast. They were so close ... *so* close. When she turned back in the direction of their pursuers, she was shocked to see that the speedy vessel had closed the gap and was a mere shouting distance away, lazily paralleling their course. The boat's sleek profile reminded Karlena of the racers she'd seen off the beaches of Corpus Christi, Texas during a college spring break. The craft looked more like a long, floating bullet, rather than a boat. Its shimmering white hull glided effortlessly alongside their clumsy scow, like a fleet-footed lioness loping confidently beside its plodding water buffalo prey.

Karlena felt another thump. Their ailing vessel shuttered again, then made a screeching, metallic grinding noise.

Duke shook his head mournfully and pulled the throttle lever back to idle as he reached down and slapped at the engine's ignition switch. The engine wheezed a short death rattle and fell silent. The boat's following stern wake pushed it gently up and forward as the craft drifted to a stop, dead in the water.

Karlena hadn't planned for an event like this when she began her odyssey through Southeast Asia. During the four months that had since passed, she'd lived among Vietnamese, Burmese, Laotians, and Malaysians without incident; she'd given away most of her personal possessions in acts of friendship and had immersed herself in native cultures while compiling a photographic journal of her travels. She'd painstakingly shipped her undeveloped film and essays to her father's address in Central Texas for safe keeping while she continued her journey. Once she could complete it, Karlena planned to submit her work to *National Geographic* magazine in the hopes they would publish it.

On this final segment of her trek, she'd scheduled a rendezvous with her on-again, off-again college boyfriend, Mitchell Castella, a native Filipino. After spending a few days of photographing on Basilan, she and Castella would travel a short distance by ferry boat to the adjacent island of Mindanao, where he'd promised to introduce her to Mindanao's mountain people, a unique sect of Muslim farmers and woodsmen. From that point, Karlena would terminate her expedition and hop another ferry to the bustling capital city of Manila, where an open-ended Northwest Airlines ticket awaited. She would fly to Tokyo, then Los Angeles, and ultimately to her home in the Lone Star State.

Karlena and Duke watched cautiously as two Filipino males rose up slowly from inside the speedboat. She noted a third person—a small, young looking, shirtless boy—sitting upright behind the steering wheel. The other two were grown men, dressed in black tee shirts and camouflaged trousers. Each of the men carried what looked to her like an automatic rifle, slung loosely over his shoulder. All three wore dark, olive-colored commando-style caps with wavy brims that shaded their eyes, ears, and foreheads.

Duke hadn't moved an inch from his station in the wheelhouse; his head hung low as he gazed suspiciously at the interceptors' boat, now positioned just a few meters off their starboard side.

Karlena attempted to stir the old man, but he seemed to be frozen with fright. His eyes met hers, and once again, more softly this time, he said the words that sounded like, "a blue safe."

Karlena, by watching his lip movement closely, now understood what Duke was actually saying—it was *Abu Sayyaf!* Terror stricken, she remembered that Mitchell had mentioned the rebel group in passing during the phone call she made to him from the nearby island of Jolo, where she'd slept a couple of nights before. Mitchell had quickly followed up, however, by assuring her that the men he had hired to meet her would provide safe passage to their planned rendezvous spot, the city of Isabela, on the north shore of Basilan.

Karlena steadied herself against the swells, nervously faced the two men, and put together a couple of Tagalog phrases Mitchell had taught her. *"Na kayo ay? Anong gusto ninyoung?"* (Who are you? What do you want?).

Both men stared at her for an awkward moment before the one on the right threw back his head and laughed. In near-perfect English he said, "My dear lady, we don't speak that piggish word of the north here. Our native language is Chavacano, and I doubt that you are familiar, so let us communicate in English."

The other man smiled nervously as his eyes darted between his partner and Karlena.

Their young helmsman had risen from his place behind the wheel and dangled two plastic fenders over the side to protect the boats' hulls from scraping. The youngster then walked to his boat's sharply tapered bow, turned his back to the group, and began relieving himself overboard. The man who'd so eloquently spoken to Karlena, spewed out a fierce order to the boy, who self-consciously finished the job and zipped up his baggy shorts. The youth turned toward Karlena and whined what sounded to her like a weak apology.

The man on the right said, "Please excuse my protégé's rudeness. It was a bumpy ride earlier when we left Isabela City." He paused and glared at the boy.

The enraged look in the man's eyes terrified Karlena.

The man broke his stare, faced her, and said unemotionally, "He needs to learn better manners."

Karlena watched silently as the boy slouched behind wheel.

"My name is Jameel, but you can call me Spider, like everyone else does," the man continued, adroitly shifting back to a more congenial mode. His partner, still speechless, had taken a seat beside the sulking young driver. Spider motioned the barrel of his rifle toward his cohort. "He goes by Blister."

Karlena looked to Duke for some guidance, but the old man provided nothing; he'd retaken his seat and was smoking a fresh cigarette with shaking hands. She then turned her sights to Blister, who'd unstrapped his weapon and was toying with his black, droopy mustache. Spider said something to him in their native tongue. They both laughed and nodded their heads in agreement.

"Miss Brandt, I want to reassure you that you are safe with us," Spider said. "Mr. Castella has requested that we escort you to a waiting place in Basilan. He has been detained in Manila and might not arrive for a few more days."

Karlena was taken aback that Spider knew her last name. At the same time, however, she began thinking to herself, his story just might reconcile with what Mitchell told me on the phone: that he's hired someone to guide me during the final part of my trip. Maybe these men are legit—and not rebels. She began quizzing the men for details, hoping to determine the veracity of their claim.

"But Mitchell didn't tell me that he had business in Manila." Karlena realized that her voice had taken on a pleading tone. She'd learned that standing her ground was the only way that a woman could stay on track with her goals in this heavily male-dominated part of the world. She shook her head defiantly. "Mitchell never mentioned Manila when I spoke with him on the phone," she persisted—this time speaking in a terse, deliberate tone. Hoping that Spider would sense her resolve, she consciously clenched her jaw and tightened the glaring look in her eyes.

Spider and Blister exchanged a few serious words in Chavacano. Blister dug his hands into a pocket, pulled out a cell phone, steadied himself, and then carefully tossed it to Spider.

Spider raised the phone toward the sky, pulled it back down, pushed a couple buttons, and said, "Please understand that we do not have the benefit of such rapid communications that you Americans are accustomed to. We could call Mr. Castella, but the satellite coverage seems to be quite weak this morning." He shook the phone dramatically, held it over his head again, and then shrugged apologetically.

Karlena felt helpless. She'd lost her own phone weeks ago at a restaurant in Vietnam. A seemingly sweet waitress there had promised that she'd guard

Karlena's backpack while Karlena was in the ladies' room. After paying the bill and seeing that her things appeared undisturbed, she'd returned to her room and gone to sleep. It was a full two days later, after a turbulent, propeller-driven plane ride to the Malaysian city of Brunei, that she'd realized that the phone was gone. She'd been forced to call Mitchell from a pay phone that last time they spoke, diligently plugging coins into the ancient-looking device every five minutes after being prompted by an operator. The incident in Vietnam had been the only occasion during the journey when she hadn't kept the backpack close by her side.

"Miss Brandt," Spider said earnestly, "may I suggest that you allow us to tow you to shore. We will locate another phone, and then you can call your friend to confirm his delay."

Karlena saw Duke as he sat dejectedly on his shabby cloth-covered seat. He turned to her and said, "No choice."

Spider chanted a few sentences; the boy rose from his seat, quickly grabbed a hemp line, and began lashing it to the bow of Duke's boat. Karlena had hired the old man out of desperation after she'd missed the last ferry bound for Isabela City the previous night; the next one wasn't scheduled for three days. Duke, who just happened to be at the dock when Karlena realized she'd missed the ferry, had assured her that he was an able seaman and could easily navigate the voyage north, while only stopping a few times for fuel.

Spider transferred over to her boat and sat spread-eagled on the bow as Blister and the boy began the tow. He peeled away the rifle from his shoulder and set it to one side. Throwing Duke an expressionless glance, he pulled up a pant leg, revealing a revolver strapped to his right ankle. He feigned retightening its holster and made sure that Duke saw the pistol.

Karlena asked stoically, "Why do you carry the weapons?" She'd managed to suppress her anxiety long enough to ask the question calmly.

Spider raised up from his sprawled position, looked her in the eye, and said solemnly, "There are many bad people that roam these waters: pirates, rebels, and the like." As he spoke, his eyes shifted briefly to Duke, who remained passive with both arms in his lap. "Your friend, Mr. Castella, must have warned you of that threat."

Karlena allayed her fears, realizing that there wasn't much she could actually do other than go along with what was unfolding. She began to hear the rush of surf as the two-boat convoy approached the shore. Prior to this leg of the voyage, she'd studied a map of the island chain to the south of Mindanao and had noted the major features of the roundish Basilan. The position of the sun clued her that they were about to make landfall on the island's remote southern coast, not near Isabela City, on Basilan's northern side.

Blister stood up in preparation of docking; he placed a hand on the young-ster's shoulder in a fatherly fashion and pointed to a ramshackle pier, barely visible inside a tiny, deeply shaded cove.

The boy silently nodded and prudently steered in that direction. The tow line began to tighten and slacken as they drifted over a reef where the small swells broke into foam.

Spider hung his legs over the bow as a precaution to prevent the two boats from colliding. They cleared the reef and entered the placid, inky water of a remote lagoon.

Blister jumped from the speedboat onto a decrepit, wooden dock. His feet found a couple of safe looking timbers as he secured a mooring line to a post. Spider quickly did the same and tied up Duke's lifeless craft. He re-shouldered his rifle, grabbed Karlena's backpack, and silently motioned her to disembark.

"What are we doing?" she asked. A lump had formed in her throat, and she felt her underarms start to dampen through the soiled white tee shirt she'd been wearing for the last three days. "Why aren't we going to Isabela City?"

Spider set her backpack on the dock and reached inside a pants pocket for a cigarette. "So sorry, but my little assistant needs to return this boat to its owner. The two giant outboards hummed softly as the boats bobbed gently in unison. "We'll travel by land the rest of the way."

Karlena looked around the small cove that was shrouded by dense jungle; she could not see a vehicle. Spider seemed to read her mind and spoke up, "Just a short hike to our jeep," he said, pointing to a freshly cut opening in the brush that looked to Karlena like the entrance to an abyss.

"What about Duke?" she asked. He was still seated inside of his disabled boat.

"Don't worry, we'll send someone to help the old fellow," Spider replied. He and Blister started walking toward the path's entrance. Spider stopped and looked back at her impatiently.

Karlena reached for her money. "I have to pay the man first."

Spider came back toward them and grabbed her arm forcefully. He sensed her fear, released her, and said soothingly, "Not necessary—Mr. Castella will take care of that."

Karlena looked at Duke apologetically as he sat motionless. Duke's caged anger finally erupted as he jumped from his boat and onto the dock. He shook his fist violently and cursed at Spider in another language that Karlena didn't understand. Spider and Blister never broke stride and continued walking toward the path.

The young driver quietly untied the line from Duke's boat and eased the speedboat out of the lagoon.

Karlena stood immobilized between the dock and the jungle. She felt a stream of sweat dripping down her spine; it caused her body to quiver with a fearful chill. Karlena realized that she had no other option but to follow these two strangers and to hope that Mitchell Castella would be waiting for her at the other end—she could only hope.

# CHAPTER 3

The steaming cup of black coffee tasted like it always did at this hour: strong and bitter. McGirt took another careful sip as he watched the events unfold below his office window, located on the second story of the hangar that housed *The Rat Pack* of HSC-30.

Chief Sartelli had taken charge of the disabled helicopter moments after the news crew had finished their segment, and he'd continued supervising the aircraft movement from that point forward. He'd phoned the squadron's maintenance control and had respectfully told a young lieutenant what he thought should be done. The officer, cognizant of Sartelli's twenty-five years of experience in the aircraft repair business, had wisely gone along with the senior enlisted man's requests. A half dozen sailors were dispatched to stand guard around the disabled bird while plans were made to extract the aircraft from the shoreline and return it to home base, ten miles away at NAS North Island in Coronado.

McGirt spotted Sartelli talking to the crane operator who'd been assigned the task of lifting the helicopter from a large flatbed truck and placing it on the tarmac, adjacent to the squadron's hangar. He watched as Sartelli ranted on as only he could: hands and arms flailing and words flying out of his mouth faster than a carnival sideshow barker.

The crane operator—an enormous hulk of a man, who could have passed for a member of the San Diego Charger's offensive line—appeared to have given up trying to participate in the conversation; he sat quietly in the crane's control cab, arms folded across his chest—listening intently. Every few seconds, he patiently bobbed his hardhat-covered head in agreement with Sartelli's instructions.

"I'm gonna walk downstairs, Skipper. Want to join me?"

McGirt turned to see that his second-in-command, Frank Taswell, had joined him at the window. Like McGirt, Taswell—the squadron's executive officer—gripped the first of his day's many cups of java. He and McGirt laughed in unison at the site of the wiry Sartelli attempting to school the crane operator.

"Boss, that guy must be twice Sartelli's size, but it doesn't seem to faze him one iota. Do you think there's any subject a Navy Chief Petty Officer isn't an expert on?" Taswell asked.

"Probably not, at least not in their own minds, anyway. Guido's got to be running on fumes by now; the caffeine and nicotine can only keep a guy going for so long. When I arrived this morning, he told me he grabbed about an hour of sleep on that ratty sofa in the chief's lounge last night—that's it. You'd better take him aside before he blows a gasket. Go on down without me. I've got some business to tend to."

"Got it, Skipper," Taswell said; he started making his way toward the door.

"Hey, Frank, one more thing. Not to take your thoughts too far off the plan of the day, but how would you feel about sliding into my job a few months early?"

Taswell turned and said, "Why, what's up? You doing okay, Johnny?"

"Yeah, nothing like that. Just passed my annual flight physical with flying colors—like the Doc said, 'not bad for an old guy.' No, something may be brewing that would pull me away from the squadron earlier than we'd planned—in fact, possibly as soon as the next week or two. What would you think about an office change-of-command?"

"You know me, Johnny. Never been much for big ceremonies with all those jangling medals and parading around with swords. If the needs of the Navy call for it, I'd be happy with the two of us simply reading our orders, exchanging salutes and a friendly hand shake."

"Good," McGirt said. He walked a few steps closer to where Taswell was standing and took his voice down to just above a whisper. "Can't tell you all the details, but I'm expecting to talk with someone in Langley today."

"Copy that, Skipper. This chat won't go any further than your office."

Taswell had known McGirt since the two first met at the Navy Postgraduate School, in Monterey, California, years earlier—where Taswell studied engineering, and McGirt earned a master's degree from NPS's School of International Graduate Studies. Taswell knew that his boss had subsequently lived in Manila for two years while serving as naval attaché to the U.S. ambassador to the Philippines. McGirt would sometimes, over a beer at the O'club, share stories with Taswell about the assignment that "had him tap dancing in the political arena more often than dealing with anything military." Taswell figured the conversation with "someone in Langley" had something to do with McGirt's former assignment.

As his XO left the room, McGirt returned to his viewing spot at the window and pondered the events of the last twenty-four hours. After their emergency landing and fifteen minutes of fame on local television, he and Lt. Worley had hitched a ride in the Navy van that had hauled the working party to his stranded aircraft. The pilots had filled out their required post-flight paperwork, which had included a detailed maintenance write-up of the circumstances surrounding the failure of the aircraft's rear transmission gearbox. They'd then spent a solid hour with the Boeing Aircraft Technical Rep, Mr. Lloyd, along with the unit's Safety Officer, who had the task of compiling a lengthy incident report that would be disseminated Navy-wide. After that, McGirt and Worley had both gone home.

Senior Chief Petty Officer Ralph Sartelli, had not been so fortunate. Within a few minutes of McGirt's landing, Sartelli had made a half dozen calls from his cell phone—first to the squadron maintenance office, and then to a bevy of fellow chief petty officers on the base. The CPO network sprang into action, cutting through government red tape and stretching Navy regulations to their near-breaking point.

The resulting chain of events had unfolded, beginning around sunset. First, a convoy of vehicles comprising a massive industrial crane, an equally impressive-sized flatbed truck, and two pickups—full of government workers authorized to remove McGirt's aircraft from the beach—had been dispatched. The notion of performing repairs on site had been quickly scuttled due to the severity of damage to the helicopter. The detail had decided to wait until after dark, when traffic began to taper off, before they began the methodical process of transporting the oversized load. The convoy had moved slowly up the Silver Strand Highway, then travelled along the western perimeter of Coronado Village, through the air station's back gate, and, finally, all the way across the base to HSC-30's concrete tarmac. The truck carrying the ailing aircraft had reached its final destination a few minutes past one o'clock in the morning.

Standing at the window in his office, McGirt continued to observe the final phase of the ordeal as the helicopter was being prepared for hoisting. The aircraft's six long rotor blades had been folded neatly within the width of its airframe's dimensions, making it just narrow enough to legally travel on the public highway. The blades flexed lazily in the midmorning breeze like giant fronds on a palm tree. All hands cleared away from the flatbed as the crane operator slowly took up slack on the lines attached to the helicopter's hoisting points; the lifting machine's engine strained as the lines grew taut.

The crane operator paused for a moment, then smoothly increased power as the helicopter began to slowly rise from the flatbed. A gust of wind caused the airframe to start a gentle oscillating motion, not unlike a rookie pilot trying to stabilize in a hover over the rolling, pitching deck of a destroyer.

Sartelli hollered out, "whoa!" and bolted toward the flatbed.

The operator waived a reassuring hand to the chief while never taking his eyes or concentration away from the multi-ton suspended mass of aluminum. He waited for the breeze to subside, which it did as quickly as it had stirred up. The operator then deftly manipulated the crane's control levers like a surgeon, maneuvering the helicopter a few yards up and away from the flatbed; the aircraft now dangled precipitously a dozen feet above the pavement. He freed one hand from the controls and mouthed a shrill whistle to get Sartelli's attention. He held out his palm, silently gesturing the question, "Is this okay?"

Sartelli gave a double thumbs up, signaling his approval. A few seconds later, McGirt's aircraft was resting peacefully on the cold concrete tarmac. Sartelli motioned a working party to turn-to; the young sailors quickly detached the hoisting lines.

The operator withdrew the crane's thick steel cable and then slowly rotated the machine's boom well clear. Another crew began to prepare the aircraft for towing into the squadron's hangar. The helicopter would remain in a "hard down" status indefinitely and would require hundreds of man-hours in labor and many thousands of dollars in parts before becoming airworthy again.

McGirt turned away from the window, set the coffee cup down, and looked at his watch: *twelve-fifteen on the East Coast.* He recalled that Bud usually took a late lunch; *this might be a good time to return Lammers's call,* he guessed. As he waited for the phone call to go through, he rose halfway from his desk chair and watched as his disabled aircraft slowly, but steadily, disappeared into the cavernous, domed hangar. He felt a pang of regret as the poignant fact registered once again, just as it had while standing next to the pretty reporter on the beach: he'd made his final flight as a Navy pilot. There'd been no fanfare or popping of champagne bottles like in the movies—but, instead, a harrowing ride in a tired, failing helicopter, a helicopter quite possibly destined to become a "hangar queen," the ignoble title bestowed on airframes that are cannibalized for parts.

McGirt sat back down as Bud's phone started to ring. The old phrase, *"So go the breaks of naval aviation,"* flashed through his head.

The phone sat on the left side of a small desk, in a cramped corner office that overlooked a densely wooded tract of land from the third floor of the Central Intelligence Agency headquarters in Langley, Virginia. Doctor Bud Lammers had earned the cushy perk of a private office with a view after twenty-three years and six different job titles. Along the way, he'd occupied an equal number of claustrophobia-inducing office cubicles—over the course of five presidential administrations. The thin, block letters stenciled on the full-length frosted-glass door to his office spelled out "DR. C.T. LAMMERS." Just below his name, in smaller print, were the words "Asian Operations."

The phone rang four times and then channeled McGirt's call directly to voice mail. Despite the room's two floor-to-ceiling windows, the space appeared crowded to most visitors. Two compact cloth-covered chairs faced Lammers's dark-stained wooden desk. Bud had procured a pricey, high-backed leather chair for himself last month, complete with an adjustable lumbar support. He'd paid his own money, figuring that he'd take it with him when he retired next year. Besides the cheap, government-issued blotter, only three items occupied the surface of his desk: the phone, a dated picture of his two adopted Korean children, and his favorite portrait of his deceased wife, Jill.

McGirt always got a chuckle from Bud's coldly drab greeting: "This is Doctor Charles Lammers. Please leave a brief message, and I will return your call." Then there was a pregnant pause, followed by the words, " … When I get a chance." Lammers had told McGirt a few months ago that, shortly after 9/11, his division had received a wordy memorandum requiring all employees to ensure that their message greetings were short, to the point, and devoid of any facts or emotions that might give the caller a hint of the CIA agent's personality. The pithy zinger, "When I get a chance," had been a dig at his boss, who—by Lammers's judgment—was a "sad, witch-like excuse for a female," who had too much time on her hands.

Lammers heard the faint sound of his phone ringing after he had closed the glass door and walked a few steps toward the elevator. It was too late for him to turn around and answer it; this meeting took priority. Bud passed through the large, open office space, where his subordinates sat inside partitioned eight-by-eight foot workstations. He nodded "hellos" to a couple of them who'd looked away from their computer screens long enough to make eye contact. He filled a plastic cup from the water cooler and then pressed the elevator's "down" button. He admitted to himself that he really wasn't very thirsty; nonetheless, he'd promised his daughter that he'd keep himself hydrated and had made it a habit to get a drink every time he passed by the cooler.

As a third year medical student at Johns-Hopkins, his daughter, Lisa, seemed to always know what was best for him—although the only thing he felt from being "hydrated" was the need to spend more time staring at the white tiles on the men's room wall while patiently straddling a urinal. He drained the cup and tossed it underhand to a trashcan, ten feet away, as the elevator door opened. He got inside, slid his ID badge into a slot below the elevator's control panel, and pressed the button labeled "LL."

It took less than a minute to travel from the third floor to the building's basement. The elevator door creaked open, and Lammers walked a short distance to the end of a narrow, brightly illuminated corridor, where he was confronted by a plain, unmarked door. The gray-painted slab of metal had a single six-by-six inch, one-way window centered at eye level. Bud swiped his badge through yet another card reader, positioned his face in front of the window, and waited. A few seconds later, he heard an electric buzzing sound and the door began to slide open horizontally from Bud's right, disappearing neatly into a wall pocket to his left.

"Hey, Bud, welcome to our creepy little shop of horrors," Joe Voss said. Voss reached out to shake Lammers's hand and then made an arm motioning gesture, signaling Lammers to follow him.

"The pleasure's all mine, Giuseppe. Thanks for taking me in on such short notice."

"No problem, Doc. Glad we could help out. I'm hearing through the grapevine that this situation is rocketing up the priority chain," Voss said, hoping to get a morsel of information as to why the project had fallen into his lap with such urgency.

Lammers dodged the probe by patting Voss on the shoulder and asking, "You losing some weight, big guy?"

"Trying to. Mama wants me to cut back on the beer and cheese twists. I'm doing okay with that until a Redskins game comes on the tube; that's when it's really hard. Sort of like lightin' up a cigar on the golf course. Some things just seem to go together."

"I hear you," Bud said as they made a sharp right turn into a dimly lit area. "My daughter's been after me, too. Dropped a quick fifteen pounds at first, but seem to have reached a plateau. Tough getting old, ain't it?" They both nodded dejectedly.

"Damn, that stuff smells awful," Lammers said. They'd reached their destination: a black-painted, low-ceilinged photography development lab.

"You get used to it," Voss said. They stepped inside the cave-like space, where Voss and his partner, Leonard Dickle, had spent most of the morning. Two large architect-style worktables sat facing each other in the center of the room. The room's walls were ringed with an assortment of enlarged, glossy eight-by-eleven-inch developed prints. Dozens of snake-like strings of negatives hung from thin metal brackets mounted to the ceiling. Dickle, a late-twenties looking guy, sat on a stool, his head and shoulders slumped over a black and white print.

"Hey, Lennie, how they hanging?" Bud quipped to Voss's assistant.

Dickle never looked up from his work. "Please call me Leonard, Doctor Lammers."

Bud had an ongoing battle over names with the recently hired whiz kid from the University of Maryland's graduate engineering school. Unlike Voss, with whom Bud had enjoyed a casual, ball-busting relationship since first meeting him several years prior, Voss's younger partner seemed to approach both of the older men as if they were his father. Lammers and Voss crowded next to Dickle as he peered through a large, handheld magnifying glass.

"Yup, just as I'd thought at first," Dickle said. He sat up and removed a pair of dark-rimmed eyeglasses. "That's an M-4 carbine, not your standard-issue M-16 rifle."

Bud and Voss crouched down lower to see for themselves. "How do you know that?" Bud asked.

"Shorter barrel; M-4's barrel is five point five inches shorter—better suited for special ops. Army Rangers and some of the Navy SEALS use this weapon." Dickle stood up and neatly slid the stool under his desk. He set the eyeglasses down and began massaging the bridge of his nose. "Excuse me, sirs, but I need to take a short break from this." Dickle walked out of the room.

Lammers and Voss studied the photo. "Well, what do you think, Joe?"

Voss looked down again at the photograph of Karlena Brandt. He and Dickle had received a fragmented copy of the digital image a couple of hours ago. They'd enhanced it the best that they could without risking any errors of distortion, but neither of them were one hundred percent confident that the image wasn't a fake.

"Whoever gets their hands on the original will have a much better shot at authenticating this," Voss said.

Bud focused intently on the image of Karlena, who was holding a three-week-old edition of *Stars and Stripes*, a military themed newspaper read by service members around the globe.

"From her eye positioning, she actually looks as if she's reading it, Bud. Can't really tell from her expression if she's under any type of duress—face and hands appear normal, as does her overall body language, other than the frazzled hair and dirty clothes. Could be simply a photo of some bored rich kid seeking thrills in an exotic foreign land. Other than the partial view of a rifle tucked in the frame's corner, I'd have to say this thing looks innocuous."

Bud pursed his lips and nodded. "I agree with you on that point, Joe, but she's been missing now for about four weeks. Our folks down in Texas confirmed that fact with her father. We corroborated the times with the Malaysian boat driver who transported her to Basilan; Army Rangers stationed there interviewed the fellow. They reported to us that he was pretty zip-lipped, except for admitting that he'd taken the girl to the south end of the island where some people who looked like friends were waiting for her. Said he had trouble starting his boat for the return trip, so he'd hoofed it into the nearest village to get some help. That's where the soldiers spotted him."

"You think he's lying?" Voss asked. He realized the question wasn't germane to his work as a photo analyst. Nonetheless, Voss knew Bud well enough to ask anyway, figuring that Lammers would stonewall the inquiry if he'd swayed into a sensitive area that neither he nor Dickle had a need to know.

"Quite possibly. The rebels have a tight grip on the natives over there. Plenty of cash to pay them off to keep quiet. Those who talk either disappear or get killed. You have to understand that most of the locals are dirt poor, and their biggest concern is how they'll get another day's ration of rice into their bellies."

"Hmm... kind of makes you think, doesn't it?" Voss said as he glanced down at his own stomach.

"You ever heard of some bad guys that go by the name Abu Sayyaf Group?" Bud asked.

"No, can't say that I have."

"The words basically mean 'bearer of the sword.' They're one of several Asian organizations splintered off from al-Qaeda. Many of them trained and fought alongside their Muslim brothers in Afghanistan. A few of the ASG leaders have been college educated in Cairo—all paid for, ironically, by the Philippine government."

"Sounds like it's getting hard to tell the players without a program over there," Voss said.

"You know it. And I'm not that confident about where the Armed Forces of the Philippines' loyalties lie in that region of the country either." Bud realized that he was drifting into his professorial mode. He cleared his throat and refocused on the photograph. "Why do you think your protégé has such a hard-on about the rifle?"

"He's more up to speed with firearms than I am. The little bit that I do know from the other images we've processed is that our fighters have been doing some work on that island, Basilan. After what you just told me about the Filipino army's allegiances, I suppose that, for the right amount of money, one of these type rifles could grow legs and walk off an army base, so to speak."

"Or be scavenged from a dead AFP soldier's body," Bud said. "Tell me again who sent you this picture."

"Spooks on board a Navy communications ship in the South China Sea intercepted an email routed to an address in Malaysia. Nothing we could pin down really from the photo. Dickle thinks the original has to be somewhere else, maybe part of the ransom note. What we got was a digital picture of a picture. We've computer enhanced it the best that we can. If we had the negative from the original shot, we'd have better chance at identifying the surroundings and the girl's location." Voss pointed down to the picture. "Difficult to make out what kind of structure she's in. I see a window, a few generic pictures hanging on the wall, but that's about it."

"What about the newspaper?" Bud asked.

"That threw me a little too. Not sure why they chose to have her hold a military paper as the dating stamp, rather than one of the local rags. We could have extrapolated that data just as easily. This paper could have been taken from any one of several military camps, or filched from the garbage. The kidnappers may have been too lazy or too cheap to go out and buy their own."

"Okay. Well, I'm on my way to California to hook up with someone who knows more than me about the culture in this area of the Philippines."

"Hey, Bud. Anything you can share about the ransom? I hear that the girl's old man is loaded. Just wondering."

"Sorry, Joe. Can't go into that. Pretty sensitive stuff—especially up on the Hill."

"Gotcha."

"Pardon me, sirs, but anything I can help with?" The two men turned away from the table to see Dickle standing in the doorway, holding a huge sub sandwich that he'd brought back from the CIA commissary. Tucked under his arm were a half-liter bottle of Mountain Dew and a party-sized bag of potato chips. Bud and Voss stared resentfully at the youngster. Dickle stood well over six feet tall, and by Bud's estimate, probably weighed less than one hundred sixty pounds.

Voss pointed angrily at Dickle and said to Bud, "Do you believe this guy? If I ate like that, I'd probably weigh three-fifty."

Lammers pictured the low-fat cottage cheese and baggie of raw vegetables waiting for him upstairs in the break-room fridge. "Yeah, me too, Joe," he lamented. "Me too."

# CHAPTER 4

Dr. Gina DeCarlo, Commander, U.S. Navy Medical Corps, rearranged her silverware on the starched white tablecloth, took a tiny sip of Chablis, and then gently set down the long-stemmed glass.

"Okay, McGirt, so what is it this time?" she asked.

"Huh?" her husband said while he avoided looking into his wife's large, dark eyes. He smiled at a passing waiter, then gulped down half of the phoo-phooey spring water he'd ordered.

"Well, you hired a limo driver, made a reservation at this pricey steak house, and are wearing a sports jacket—which, after fifteen years of marriage, I know that you abhor doing. And it's neither our anniversary nor my birthday." Gina held the wine glass to her lips and furrowed her brow inquisitively, all the while keeping her gaze firmly on his every reaction.

McGirt realized that his time was running out, and he'd eventually have to fess up. He smiled and nodded with the look of a man who was painfully aware that this woman knew him all too well. "Well … it's like this, honey," he began. "After my excitement with the helicopter on the beach and the news bimbo, I spoke with Bud on the phone." He paused and took another gulp of expensive water.

"And?"

"How can I put it?" he asked rhetorically while staring out at the lights of San Diego's harbor. "There's a chance that I may be packing my suitcase and leaving for a few days."

Gina chuckled to herself and shook her head. "So where to this time, Captain Wonderful?" A sarcastic smirk had formed on her mouth like that of a Mom trying to hold her resolve with an adolescent son—even though what she actually wanted to do was burst out laughing at his predictable hedging.

She deliberately looked away from him and fiddled with the dangling golden earrings she'd decided to wear for the evening.

McGirt earnestly studied her graceful movements before saying, "Did I tell you how beautiful you look this evening, dear?"

Gina could no longer contain herself. She threw her arms back and laughed heartily. "Yes ... yes you did," she repeated between giggles. "At least a dozen times and we haven't even been served our salads yet." She knew that it was futile: it was impossible for her to maintain anything close to anger at this man; not since the day they'd first met. What had started out as a doctor-patient relationship when she'd rebuilt one of his failing knees had quickly evolved into a short, passionate courtship between two single adults whose careers had never provided either of them with the right opportunity for marriage. That fact had changed almost instantly after they'd laid eyes on each other years ago in a Washington military hospital.

He joined in with her laughing and added, "Well, you do. No, I take that back; you *always* do." A tuxedoed waiter silently appeared and set down their salad plates.

"Thank you, Johnny Jack. This middle-aged, Italian girl from Jersey never gets tired of hearing that. You are truly an officer and a gentleman."

Happy with himself, McGirt dove into his food. They took a few bites before he spoke up. He saw that whatever peevishness Gina had shown was now in the "rearview mirror," as he liked to say. She nodded, sipped some more wine, and quietly signaled for him to go on.

"As soon as early next week—that's when Bud wants to leave."

"Should I be concerned, you know, about where you'll be going?" During their time together Gina had watched as her husband's career had shifted mercurially between aviation, duty at sea, and "secretive operations." She was usually very good at finding answers to questions—after all, she was an accomplished orthopedic surgeon. Even as smart as she was, however, Gina could never figure out how her husband was able to carry on so effectively. She never, ever heard him complain about what the Navy or government asked him to do.

McGirt stared up toward the ceiling for a moment. "Well, let me put it this way, we're not exactly jumping into a hot frying pan, but we'll definitely be in a warm kitchen."

Gina was well versed in deciphering what she'd coined, "McGirtisms," but she needed more. "Okay. Anybody involved that I would recognize if they walked into this place and sat down next to us?"

McGirt wiped his mouth with a napkin and finished chewing. "Not the actual person in jeopardy, but 'yes' to one of the other players. Let me just say they're a proud member of the Magnificent 535, and you've seen their face on the boob-tube many times; a big-time player."

"Oh, really?" During one of their joint tours in D.C.—she at Bethesda and he at the Pentagon—she'd met many members of Congress, or as McGirt called them, the "Magnificent 535." She'd found some to be down to earth, charming personalities—others not so much. She sensed, however, that because of their present public location, McGirt needed to be cautious about how much he said. Nonetheless, she pressed on. "Well then, let me try this avenue," she said while pushing her half-eaten first course a few inches forward. "What kind of food will you most likely be eating next week?"

McGirt stabbed the last shed of the iceberg wedge and waved it lightly above his plate like a prop. "Let me put it to you this way: not the type of cuisine you'd enjoy."

"I see," Gina replied. She'd never considered herself a fussy eater except for one line of food: anything Asian. She'd attributed her dislike to the time when her father—an immigrant mason from Sicily—had taken her and her younger brother on an outing to the Big Apple one summer afternoon. They'd boarded the ferry at the Paulus Hook Terminal in Jersey City and crossed the Hudson River on their way to have lunch in the Little Italy section of Manhattan. During their walk to her dad's favorite restaurant, they'd skirted the edge of the City's bustling Chinatown, where the pungent aromas wafting from street merchants' caldrons had caused her to gag. Since then, she'd been repulsed by any dish that resembled Asian cuisine.

"Can you be a little more specific, or would you have to kill me if you told me?" she said.

McGirt laughed at her use of the overused expression. "No, it's not that clandestine, really. By the way, do you care for lumpia?" he added as a clue. She contorted her mouth disgustedly at the mention of the popular Filipino staple.

"The capital again?" Gina asked, referring to Manila.

"No, south of there. Way south."

A chill went through her; she knew how unstable the Philippine's Muslim dominated region had become and she'd seen the graphic news reports about the latest round of Western hostages being held captive for ransom. The one story that had distressed Gina the most was how an American missionary couple and several others had been taken hostage while vacationing on a tropical island on the western edge of the Philippine archipelago. At first, her Catholic upbringing had been an impediment as she struggled to understand how the issue of one's religion could result in such violence. But after years of reassembling the shattered young bodies of men and women returning from war in the Middle East, she'd developed a disdain for anyone's war in the name of their so-called God. Their main courses arrived: fresh, broiled sea bass for her; the biggest steak on the menu for him. The conversation halted while they both dug in.

"How's your steak, honey?"

"Terrific; like it always is. You know I love this place," McGirt said with a mouthful.

Gina decided to forego her usual admonishment about watching his cholesterol levels and how he should consider eating more healthily. After tonight's revelation about what might lie ahead for him, she just wanted to enjoy the pleasure of her husband's company.

McGirt had been upfront from the beginning about the nature of his work. He'd had to dodge most of her pointed questions for security's sake. Nonetheless, he'd been quite open about how his life as a Navy helicopter pilot had effectively served as cover for the many covert tasks that he'd been asked to do. His close association with former-Navy pilot-turned-CIA guy, Bud Lammers, left little doubt in her mind that someday her husband's name might be broadcast nationwide just as that poor missionary couple's had been. McGirt's recent fifteen minutes of fame on San Diego's airwaves would pale by comparison, she feared.

Their waiter reappeared, politely handed them each a dessert menu, and cleared their plates. McGirt anxiously eyed the list. He knew that his wife rarely cared for sweets and didn't want to live with the guilt of eating one of the delectable treats by himself. He rubbed his belly and said, "You know, Babe, I'm pretty full." He set down the menu and differed to her.

Gina knew he was lying. *You could probably down half the items by yourself,* she thought to herself. "Well, I'm not. Let me see what they have," she said while scanning the list. "Ah there; get the waiter's attention and tell him you'd like the tiramisu. And ask him to bring two forks."

McGirt snapped to attention in his seat, smiled broadly and said, "Sure!" He turned to find their waiter, but the man was tableside before he could raise a hand.

# CHAPTER 5

*Biblical.* Otto Brandt could find no other word to describe the miracle that had unfolded before his eyes as he watched the setting sun. In his soul of souls, he believed that no entity but a divine God would have the power to create such a spectacle. The bursts of pink, orange and powder-blue colors that filled the evening sky might serve as an omen that his daughter, Karlena, could still be alive. He set a tumbler of straight-up bourbon on the small wrought-iron table that sat beside his bentwood rocking chair. He'd been nursing the drink for the last thirty minutes in the same way he did every evening—slow and easy. Next to the bourbon were an unwrapped cigar and a square, stainless steel lighter. Otto took his signal from the suns' position, which had now dipped below the colorful, thin strands of clouds like a fading fireball sinking into the flat, hardpan plains of West Texas. He held the cigar in one hand, carefully placed the smoke's tip inside the guillotine cutter and snipped. He took his sweet time, enjoying this little ritual before lighting the full-bodied Dominican Robusto that he'd come to favor over the last several years. He lit the stogie, drew five quick puffs and settled back in his chair. Sunrise and sunset: the two defining events of Otto Brandt's day; so much so, that they'd defined the manner by which he'd designed and built his home. The long, single-story, brick, ranch-style building was oriented north and south, with two oak-plank verandas running the full sixty-five-foot length of the structure. The house's layout allowed Brandt to observe the sun's rising and setting each day from its east and west facing sides. He'd placed duplicate rocking chairs and tables on both verandas. The harsh West Texas weather was rarely a factor that influenced Otto's twice-per-day ritualistic custom. He'd track the sunrise and sunset times from his Farmer's Almanac and faithfully take his solitary position each day, regardless of the sky's cloud cover. It was the same routine everyday: a cup of black coffee in the morning; bourbon and a Dominican cigar before evening meal.

Otto tapped the cigar's smoldering end into the empty aluminum tomato can that he'd converted to an ashtray. He took another sip from his drink glass, puffed again and savored the mixing of the fiery caramel-colored whiskey with the mocha-laced aroma of the aged Caribbean tobacco.

The sun had sunk halfway below the horizon as a light westerly breeze swept across the landscape's scrub oak and cholla bushes. Otto looked beyond the low-lying foliage and caught sight of the tumbling dust trail that had kicked up behind a vehicle traveling quickly over the gravel road leading to his house. He lowered his feet from the wobbly wooden crate that he used for a stool and placed his boots firmly on the deck. Otto stopped rocking, set down the cigar and drink, and then slid a hand up his right pant leg to the leather holster that held a nine-millimeter pistol. He rested his fingers on the holster's brass safety latch and watched as the vehicle made its way closer; it appeared to be an unfamiliar, older-model SUV.

The car slowed to a crawling pace when it passed through the property's open, chain-link gate; its headlamps were pointed squarely at Otto's spot on the porch. Otto remained seated, but he'd stiffened his muscles like a coiled rattler sensing its domain was under threat. Blinded by the car's lights, he cautiously unbuckled the holster and rested his grip on the pistol's handle.

The car's driver spotted Otto on the porch and switched off the headlamps.

Otto held an opened hand above his brow and squinted as the car approached from an angle directly in line with the setting sun. The vehicle appeared to be a tattered, brown Jeep Wagoneer with wood-grain siding; its sole occupant was a middle-aged-looking male. Still seated, Otto slid the handgun halfway out from its holster and braced himself. The driver eased the vehicle close to the building and parked parallel to the porch.

The man cranked down his window, leaned his head out and said, "How you doing there, Otto?"

Brandt exhaled a silent, relieved breath, removed his hand from the pistol and re-buttoned the holster. He recognized the man; it was Congressman Clayton Gantry.

"You oughta be a might more careful about barging up on someone like that, Claytie," Otto said. "Fella's likely to get his head blown off doin' that around these parts."

Gantry eased out from the car and stretched his lanky frame. "My apologies, Otto. Should have called you first, but my gal up in D.C. couldn't locate your phone number. Mind if I join you up on the stoop?"

Otto pictured a buxom young secretary feverishly pawing through a Rolodex for his name. *I reckon most of Gantry's crowd would have trouble finding their butt cheeks with both hands,* he thought to himself.

Otto nodded his head and motioned with a thumb toward a steel folding chair propped against the entryway's wood-trimmed door jamb.

Gantry unfolded the chair, set it close by Otto's table and sat down. They sat silently and watched as the early chapter of nightfall unfolded. The sun had disappeared below the horizon; its rays now struck the underside of a rippling strand of clouds from such an angle that the sky's muted hues had transformed into a clash of flaming orange and intense strains of cold, vibrant turquoise. The prismatic display cast a peaceful glow against the ranch house's brick and stone façade.

Otto reclaimed his cigar from the tin can and slid the wooden crate back into position with his feet. He leaned backward, plunked his dusty boots onto the crate and commenced a slow, rhythmic rock.

"What'd you do, Claytie, commandeer that jalopy from a couple of Mes-kins? Thought you'd moved up to a stretch limo or at least one them 'Beamers by now."

Gantry coughed a subdued laugh and said, "Naw, my pilot has a buddy who drives the fuel truck over at Midland airport. Loaned me his spare car for the night."

"Sorta goin' in-cog-neato while slumming with us common folk, eh?"

Gantry shuffled uncomfortably in the metal chair and cracked a weak smile. The temperature still hovered near ninety degrees, and if his memory served right, it wouldn't venture much below that throughout the midsummer night. He undid a couple more buttons from his heavily starched white dress shirt, removed the garment's diamond-studded cufflinks and rolled up its sleeves nearly to his elbows. Beads of sweat formed on his forehead and trickled down from the sideburns of his meticulously coiffed salt-and-pepper hair.

Otto glanced inside the car and spotted Gantry's dark suit coat and silky necktie draped neatly over the passenger's side front seat. "Thirsty?" he asked.

"Could use a drink of ice water, if it's not too much trouble."

Otto leaned back in his rocker a few inches farther and called out over his shoulder, "Hola, Maria, come on out here, will ya?"

A few seconds later, the tapping sound of footsteps grew louder as Otto's housekeeper/cook/maid approached the arch-shaped door on the home's west side. Otto felt a gush of refrigerated air spill out from the entryway as she opened it. The matronly, dark-skinned woman stepped back, startled, when she recognized Congressman Gantry.

"Ol' Claytie here'd like some aqua fria. Seems he ain't much used to our climate anymore."

Maria nodded her head slightly, went back inside and returned promptly with a tall, clear glass of ice water. She set the drink on a square paper napkin next to Otto's bourbon.

"Thank you, ma'am," Gantry said. "Thanks so much." Maria drifted quietly back inside. "Hard-working folks, aren't they?" he said while tilting his head in Maria's direction. He stroked a hand across the glass' pebbly coat of condensation, then rubbed the cool moisture over his forehead and down the sides of his neck. He took a long, gulping draw of the cold water.

"Yup. Ain't nobody puts in a harder day's work than a Mes-kin." Otto said. He leaned forward, placing his chin a foot away from Gantry. "But more important to you, Claytie, they vote."

Gantry smiled politely and took another, shorter sip. The men turned their heads to the sound of a motor laboring to turn over; its worn starter moaning and clicking alternately before the engine finally fired after three attempts. A small pickup truck swung out from behind a corrugated steel barn adjacent to Otto's house. Maria's truck disappeared down the driveway as quickly as she'd delivered the ice water. Her truck's headlights cut through the dusty air like twin lanterns from the back corner of a darkened barbeque smoke shack.

Otto gripped the brim of his tan colored Stetson, then reached over his left shoulder and hung the hat on a square-edged spike that he'd pounded into the wall. He ran a weathered hand over his short, neatly parted, crop of gray hair. He'd never let it grow out any differently than from the day he'd been discharged from the Army. He crossed both arms across the front of his pale-blue, western-styled shirt. A yellow tinted security lamp at the far end of the veranda automatically switched on; its gleam gave Otto's shirt a greenish tinge.

"She's gone now. So tell me, Gantry, what the fuck do you want?" The folksy, bantering tone had vanished from Otto Brandt's demeanor; the look on his face showed only harshness.

Likewise, the cordial politeness that Clayton Gantry had displayed toward Otto and his housekeeper had melted away faster than the ice cubes in his drink. "I think you know why I'm here, Brandt—it's about your daughter."

Otto's body tensed as if he'd accidently backed into a barbed wire fence. He stared straight ahead, past Gantry's car—through the ranch's gateway and over the bobbing oilrigs that dotted the darkening horizon on the far reaches of his land. His chin jutted out defiantly as if to project himself the eight thousand miles that separated West Texas and the Philippines. "I already spoke with those two FBI agents that came by last week, but I'll tell you the same thing that I told them: She's an independent spirit who can take care of herself—that's how I taught her. Not unusual for her to go a few weeks without checking in."

Gantry lowered his eyes to the floor as he spoke. "Otto, I know that our families aren't on the best of terms, but there's not much that you or I can do to change what's happened in the past…" He rose slowly from the rigid chair, and then walked a few steps toward one of the veranda's wooden pillars. He leaned up against the pillar, crossed one highly polished cordovan loafer over the other and casually folded his arms. He'd known Otto Brandt since grade school and understood that the man's disposition could be tougher than a two-dollar steak. He held out the palms of his hands and asked, "Listened to me, please. We have good reason to believe that people over there have tried to contact you about a ransom. The Navy intercepted part of a transmission that depicts your daughter, and our intelligence folks are working around the clock to pin down her location. I'm here to make a personal appeal to you to not pay a ransom. Let the United States and Philippine governments handle this without your interference."

Otto shook his head disgustedly. "Okay, like they did with that kidnapped missionary couple that I read about? Sounds like the guy got shot to death by friendly fire and his wife barely made it out alive."

"Otto, try and be—"

"Or how 'bout that poor fella from California on vacation that got his head lopped off? I read how them savages paraded it around on a pole like a bowling trophy." Otto had come out of his chair and had worked his way across the veranda; he stood face-to-face with the congressman.

Gantry prayed that Otto wouldn't get physical. Despite his towering height over Brandt, he remembered from his youth that he'd be no match for the powerful, stocky rancher.

Otto sensed Gantry cowering away from him. "Don't worry, Claytie, I don't plan to start wompin' on you. I didn't go to Princeton like you, but I'm not that stupid." He now stood just inches from his adversary. "You know," he said, "I truly can not recall which committee it is you work on up there in that big puzzle palace."

"Appropriations… I've chaired the Appropriations Subcommittee for Defense the last three years."

"Hmm, I see. Well, I'd wager there are some smart folks working for you, and they're doing their best to help. But you have to understand what it's been like for me. That girl's all I've got left." He regretted saying the words as soon as they'd come out of his mouth; he had no intention of tipping his hand, and he feared that even a hint of reasonableness might do just that. He backed away a few steps and said, "We've both spoken our pieces, and I appreciate you taking the time to come down here. I know that you mean well." Otto had lowered his hands to his side and stood rigidly, like a proud soldier at attention.

Congressmen Gantry nodded graciously and paused for a few seconds as he searched for the right words to conclude their meeting. He cleared his throat, mirrored Otto's upright pose and said, "I'd be negligent if I did not remind you of the United States government's policy against private citizens paying ransom money to suspected terrorist organizations. It's my duty as your representative to bring up that fact."

Otto took a deep breath through his nostrils and exhaled. He took hold of Gantry's extended hand. There was no compassionate pumping of their arms, but rather a resolved connection between two middle-aged men who had held firmly to their convictions.

Gantry pursed his lips and grinned from one side of his mouth as he squeezed Otto's hand and said, "When this ordeal plays out like I'm confident that it will—in a good way—maybe the two of us can finally sit down and talk some real business. He turned this head in the direction of the oilrigs and then looked back at Otto. "But this isn't the time nor the place, is it?"

Otto felt Gantry's grip tighten slightly before releasing his hand. He stood motionless on the veranda's plank flooring as Gantry got into his vehicle and backed away from the porch. The evening's blazing sunset had dulled into charcoal darkness as Gantry eased the car through the gateway, kicking up gravel as he sped away toward the faint glimmer of Midland's city lights. Otto let out a sigh.

By the time Gantry's car had reached the county road and its taillights had faded from view, the edge of night had completely swallowed up the sky. As if on cue, the din of chirping crickets rose up through the humid night air like a creaking symphony. Otto turned away from the black, pulsating noise and went inside. He sat on a stool next to the door and pulled off his pointed-toe, snakeskin boots one by one. The day's dust had filtered down into the boots and had spread a thin, brownish ring on the instep of his white athletic socks. He wiggled the toes of his aching feet, stood up and walked gingerly across the home's leathery, terra-cotta tile floor.

The big, sprawling ranch house was silent except for the gentle, steady hissing sound of air flowing through its cooling vents. Otto Brandt dreaded this time of the day, when he was alone with only his thoughts and worries. He'd followed his usual, structured daytime routine: up before dawn to welcome the morning's sunrise from his spot on the eastside veranda; then breakfast, followed by driving an open-air four wheeler to inspect the twenty-seven active oilrigs he owned, making it a point to have a personal conversation with every roustabout that might be on site; then embarrassing himself with his clumsy Spanish while Maria served him a large, midday meal. But after he'd witnessed the sunset, it was if the darkness of night would descend on him, through his head and shoulders and finally coming to rest inside his heart.

Otto walked in his stocking feet from the high-ceilinged foyer, transitioning to a long, wide-plank pine hallway. He stopped halfway down the corridor in front of a credenza that was tucked inside a small alcove that served as his bar. He took hold of the bottle that held his drink of choice, Jim Beam bourbon. Otto twisted the bottle top free, grabbed a crystal studded tumbler and poured—one, two, three seconds. He needn't measure it out—he could gage the perfect amount by simply counting. Above the bar's countertop was an oak paneled wall that ran up the hallway's ten-foot ceiling. The wall was covered with dozens of photographs, tracing the Brandt family's history, beginning with Otto's German-born great-grandfather, Herman, who'd led his family to a new world, free from the famine and political abuse that his countrymen had endured for decades. During that same period, America had offered free, vast tracts of fertile soil to the waves of Europeans who longed for a better way of life. Herman Brandt had been what was later termed a "dominant personality" within his community—a strong willed individual who was admired, trusted and respected by his neighbors. Once Herman had made the long voyage and set foot on the newly annexed Texas territory, he'd written letters to friends and family members extolling the seemingly endless virtues that came with living in the Lone Star State. More and more citizens of the Fatherland had followed dominant personalities like Herman, which led to the formation of ethnically named Texas towns like Fredericksburg, New Braunfels, Bergheim and Boerne.

Below the faded picture of his great-grandfather hung a portrait of Otto's immediate family—his mother Gerda, father Karl and two older brothers. He reached up and held the picture frame in his hands. Karl Brandt had followed in his father's footsteps as a farmer in the rich, rolling fields of the Central Texas hill country, near Austin. Working the land had provided three generations of Brandts with a sufficient way of life as they grew and sold produce to local markets and canneries. It had been a comfortable life for Otto as a young man, so when Karl Brandt had been captivated by the dream of making a quick fortune, Otto had resisted the move to what had become known as the "West Texas Oil Patch." Karl shared many of the same risk-taking traits of his grandfather, Herman. Farming had not made him wealthy, yet he'd accumulated a sizable financial reserve, enough to purchase a section of land in the petroleum-rich Permian basin, near Midland.

The Brandt Oil and Gas Exploration Company had flourished during its early years, which enabled Otto's family to rise up the community's economic and social ladders. But Karl Brandt was a gambler, who lived by the creed that "if a person isn't moving forward, then they are actually moving backward." He leveraged the family's growing fortune to the hilt and obtained a remote fifty-acre stretch of land south of Midland's sister city, Odessa. The geologist that Karl had contracted had provided a seismology report that showed the land held "great potential" for gas and oil exploration.

But Karl Brandt's big gamble had failed. After investing huge sums of borrowed dollars to purchase drilling equipment, the acreage proved to be no more than worthless, hard-packed dirt littered with dwarf shrubs and rattlesnakes. By the time Otto had returned from fighting in Vietnam, the Brandt family was penniless. Two years later, Karl Brandt had passed away from a heart attack; his mother had remarried and moved to Dallas; both brothers had left the state; and the family's homestead in Midland had been auctioned off.

It wasn't until Otto had moved in with his Mexican-American friend, Alejandro, that he'd learned what had actually caused Karl Brandt's financial collapse. According to Alejandro, the geologist who'd filed the land survey had deliberately forged his report. Alejandro's cousin had been a laborer on the site when seismology readings had been taken, and he'd witnessed that the tests showed the land had little potential for exploration—but the geologist had reported the exact opposite.

It was later discovered that Clayton Gantry's father had bribed the geologist to steer Brandt away from a more valuable adjacent plot that the elder Gantry wanted to buy. Shortly after Brandt's transaction had been consummated, the seismology company folded its tent, and its owner disappeared. Clayton Gantry's father had greased enough palms along the way to protect himself from being prosecuted. The Brandt family had been left with no recourse—they were flat broke and unable to pursue the case in the Texas court system. What had been a rags-to-riches story evaporated faster than a splash of water on a West Texas highway in July.

Otto Brandt had refused to leave the area. He used the GI Bill to obtain a two- year degree from a local community college while working whatever job he could find to support himself. He'd worked as a dishwasher and gas station attendant, peddled magazine subscriptions and sold vacuum cleaners door-to-door. However, the most humbling employment had been as a grounds keeper at the posh Midland Country Club where the Gantry clan had been founding members. Otto had worked as a grass cutter on the course's lush fairways and greens. He'd frequently pass by Clayton Gantry's foursome while the ivy-league undergrad was home on break. Clayton had attempted to reach out to him, but Otto would respond with only a hand wave or simple "hello," nothing else. His insides burned with resentment, not from a jealousy of Gantry's privileged lifestyle, but rather his rage over how Clayton's father had surreptitiously caused the demise of Otto's family.

A lifetime's worth of memories flashed through Otto's mind as he gripped the gilded-edged picture frame that held the four-decade-old family portrait. He gently hung the frame back in its place, drained the last drop of his drink, and allowed his eyes to drift to a bank of portraits and snapshots of his only child—Karlena Jane Brandt. He'd painstakingly arranged a chronological display of the girl's life: birthday parties; soccer games; prom night; and her high school graduation. But the pictorial timeline ended abruptly with a snapshot of Karlena's commencement from the Texas Woman's University. Otto had placed the five-by-seven-inch photo on the far corner of the credenza. Only three people were in the shot—Karlena, Otto, and his brother Edgar, who'd flown in from Louisiana for the occasion. Otto and his brother flanked Karlena with their arms placed affectionately against her lower back.

That snapshot was the last photograph that Otto had of his daughter. Ten days later, she'd left for graduate school at the University of California at Berkeley. Other than a handful of infrequent phone calls or emails, Karlena had virtually disappeared from his life over the last four and a half years. She'd gained complete access to a generous trust fund that he'd set up for her, and as she'd told him with resolute conviction shortly after moving to California, she had no intention of ever returning to the harsh lifestyle and climate of the Texas oil country.

Otto walked away from the pictures and continued down the building's long central corridor. He entered the home's kitchen, where he spotted a dinner plate that Maria had prepared and left for him on the butcher block island: a vibrant array of beans, peppers, onions and shredded chicken, tightly sealed in plastic wrap. He tucked the plate inside the refrigerator for tomorrow—he'd lost any appetite after the confrontation with Clayton Gantry.

Otto then left the kitchen and passed by his darkened office. He stood in the doorway, mesmerized by the colorful image of his computer monitor's screensaver as it tumbled and swirled psychedelically. He thought about sitting down to check for any news about his daughter, but decided against it.

The small, tabletop reading lamp cast a soft glow against the bedroom's walls. Otto sat down on the bed's edge, slid open the table's top drawer and removed the large, rectangular envelope that he'd found wedged inside his mailbox, located at the end of his driveway along the county road. The envelope carried no postage or return address. He reached inside and removed the photograph of his daughter; she looked tired and disheveled as she held the newspaper in front of her. Behind Karlena stood a man dressed in commando-style gear; a black bandana masked his facial features except for his coal-black, determined-looking eyes. The barrel of his weapon drooped lazily to the floor.

Otto had re-read the ransom note until he could nearly recite the words verbatim. It was clear in his mind what he had to do to save his daughter.

# CHAPTER 6

"You bastards *lied!*" Karlena cried out. *"Why are you treating me like this?"* Blister had removed the gag to give her water from his canteen. He allowed her to gulp a few ounces before placing the rag back between her teeth. Karlena had felt an unexpected kindness in Blister whenever it was his turn to feed her or offer sips of water. He'd always finished the task by tapping her on the cheek—not a slap, but more like a parent would do after gently scolding a child. Spider, on the other hand, had carried out the same ordeal by crudely yanking the rolled kerchief out from her jaw and then jamming it back into place when she'd finished.

Karlena had realized that she'd been duped soon after the military helicopter buzzed overhead in the predawn hours during her first night of captivity—when she repeatedly begged Spider to explain what was happening; and he finally lost patience with her persistence, swatted her across her face and said, "I thought a college person like you would have figured this out by now. You are my prisoner, and you will stay so until your rich daddy gives us what we want."

She had slumped into the jeep's back seat and rubbed her smarting, swollen lips. Then, as Blister had driven them through the darkness that early morning, her anger subsided and she allowed her mind to focus on two questions: *How could these evil men have known that her father was a wealthy man, and where the hell was her "friend" Mitchell Castella?* Karlena's heart had sunk at the thought that someone whom she'd come to know and love could have possibly let her down.

Now, this latest outpost was much like the others where she'd been moved: a smoky, primitive fire pit; sporadic comings and goings of sinister-looking young men; and the praying. At first, she hadn't paid much attention to the men's prayers, but as her feelings of boredom and isolation had grown, she'd become more attentive to the five-times-per-day ritual, with the recitations serving as a form of time keeping for her. Karlena had become particularly fond of waking to the sound of the predawn prayer—not because of its unique melodic chant, but rather that it marked the fact that she'd survived another day.

Shortly after her captors had kneeled to offer the noon-hour devotion, Karlena gave the signal that she needed to relieve herself: she placed her bound wrists over her crotch and rocked her head from side to side. She'd been lashed loosely to a tree with a rope tied snuggly around her waist; a small, tent-like tarp had been suspended over her for shade. A few meters away, Blister and a half-dozen others were seated on the ground, eating. Blister acknowledged her request with a wave, then spoke to the youngest looking one of the group. The boy mumbled something in protest, but quickly backed down when Blister repeated the order more forcefully. The petulant youth rose up and shuffled toward Karlena while the others laughed.

He untied Karlena from the tree and then led her several meters away from the camp. He yanked on the rope communicating for her to stop, then bent down, turned his head to one side and abruptly yanked down her drawers. The other men began to howl as Karlena unashamedly squatted and did her business. After she'd finished and the boy had helped her with her garments, she heard a rustle of commotion; the rebels began gathering up their rifles and belongings.

Blister was in the lead as the group jogged toward her. He shoved her empty backpack under one of her arms and said flatly, "We must go now." The backpack had been stripped of her photo equipment, but Blister had allowed Karlena to keep a few personal items.

She followed Blister and his crew to a thickly wooded area a few hundred meters from their campsite. He found a cluster of dense bushes and motioned for the group to hide inside for cover. He pulled Karlena to the ground and kept her close at his side.

Minutes later, Karlena heard the sound of muffled footsteps and low voices coming from the direction of the area they'd vacated.

Blister whispered something to the others and then placed his mouth next Karlena's ear, so closely that she could smell the garlic-laced food he'd just eaten.

"You need to be still," he said while jabbing the barrel of his rifle against her ribs. He set a hand on the shoulder of her trembling body and said, "Shhh…be very calm, and you won't be hurt."

Karlena strained her eyes to see what was happening. She watched as a dozen or so uniformed men slowly emerged through the trees and approached the campsite. They appeared more regimented than the paramilitary rebels who'd been holding her. Unlike her rag-tag captors, these men wore helmets and were dressed in combat-style garb. They all carried at least one rifle slung over their shoulder—some appeared to be carrying two.

The leader waved an arm above his head in a circle, directing the unit to fan out. Karlena closed her eyes and prayed that one of them would find her, and she'd be rescued. She heard tentative footsteps crunching softly against jungle floor as one of the soldiers inched his way toward her position. He was near enough to see her if she'd been able to stand, but Blister's arm pressed hard on her shoulder, holding her down.

She and the rebels were well camouflaged; Blister had located an excellent hiding spot, deep inside the dense bushes. The soldier edged closer, using the tip of his rifle to separate tangles of vines and branches as he plodded forward.

Karlena could see his face clearly. Like the members under Blister's command, the man appeared very young. He came to a sudden stop less than ten meters away, slowly scanned from side to side and then tilted his head back as if searching the trees. Gradually, his eyes lowered and focused directly on the thicket where Karlena and the others were huddled.

Karlena felt Blister's grip tighten around her.

The soldier held his gaze for several seconds, but he didn't move any closer to the thicket. She saw the corner of his mouth twitch, ever so slightly, before he abruptly spun around and double-timed back to the campsite. The soldiers regrouped there and then retreated swiftly in the direction from which they'd come.

Karlena didn't need an interpreter to comprehend Spider's rage; he was furious when Blister told him what had happened. He pulled Blister away from the others and began reaming his cohort up one side then down the other.

After the close call with the AFPs at the last campsite, Blister had led her and his crew on a long, tedious march, terminating at a location that resembled the hilltop setting where he and Spider had held her that first night. Karlena gauged that the camp was due west from where they'd been; it was late in the day, and

Blister had led them on a track straight into the setting sun. She'd struggled to keep up the last several hundred meters when the terrain had risen sharply.

One of Blister's men shoved a stale piece of bread at her and offered a drink from his canteen. She swallowed a slug of the tepid water and then nibbled on the bread before her stomach began to rumble and she felt the urge to relieve her cramping bowels again. The same man who'd "assisted" her with the duty the last time was assigned the task. After she finished the humiliating ordeal, he led her to a spot next to where he'd stowed his gear, tied her to a tree and had left her undisturbed. Karlena slid the backpack under her head and dozed off.

Spider eventually cooled down. He led Blister to a place far enough from the others where they could talk in private. "That girl is starting to be a royal pain in the ass," he began. "This was supposed to be a snap, but it's turned into a hassle; we're wasting too much time with her."

"Tell me about it," Blister said. He lit a cigarette, handed it to Spider, and then lit one for himself. "What do you think the holdup is with the money?"

"Beats me. Apparently, it's being wired from the States, but I think it has to pass through some other hands first. I'm not too swift with that side of the operation. I'll leave those things up to our smart little friend in Isabela City."

"Yeah," Blister added. "He may be a prick, but he's *our* prick." They both laughed and took a few more puffs.

Spider looked at his watch. "You know, we might want to revise our plan and just stash her some place so we can move on with other business. I've hired another ten guys who we've got to get trained on the weapons; I doubt if any of them have ever even touched a gun. Also, there's a group of Germans supposedly staying over near Lamitan. I want to meet with our people over there to see if there might be an opportunity."

"Let me guess, another bunch of do-gooders who want to drill more wells for fresh water?"

"Probably. Either that, or some nurses running around vaccinating everyone in sight. I don't really give a shit why they're here. But if they're connected to any money, that's a different story."

Blister crushed out his smoke in the dirt. "What do you hear from Castella?"

Spider smirked and said, "Nothing, and that's just the way I want it; he's served his purpose."

"Right. So what's the plan, Spider? What do you want to do with her?"

Spider took off his cap, rubbed the top of his head, and then wiped the sweat from his brow with a rag. "I think I know the perfect place. Remember that old shack on the east side, south of Maluso?"

"Yeah, uphill from where we've been keeping the boats. That spot might work fine. It's remote, and we wouldn't have to tie up so many resources moving her around so much."

"Exactly," Spider added. "Besides, those dipshit AFPs have been spending most all their time on the other side of the island lately."

They turned at the sound of a vehicle approaching. An open-air jeep weaved along a narrow trail that passed a short distance from where they were standing. "Okay, my friend," Spider said. "You take it from here. Bed down tonight with your crew, and then get that bitch over to the shack in the morning." Spider jogged to his ride and hopped in.

Blister watched as the four-wheeler slowly meandered out of view. He suspected that Spider had found a new lady friend and was on his way to spend the night with her. He lit another smoke and started walking back to the campsite. When he got there, he found his men roasting a couple of rodents they'd trapped. One of the guys yanked off a leg and offered it to him, but he turned it down—he wasn't hungry.

Blister looked over at Karlena—she was curled up and snoring. He pulled a ratty blanket from his pack, rolled it out on the dirt and prepared to spend another depressing night in the woods.

# CHAPTER 7

"Sir, I've thought it over long and hard and decided this is the course I'd like to take," McGirt said.

Admiral Willard Truckee slid his chair back a few feet, grabbed the lower sash of the wooden-framed window and pushed it up. The motion took an extra boost from Tuckee's good arm: the office walls and window trim had been repainted so many times during the last forty years that the fleshy-beige colored enamel had a tendency to bond like glue during Coronado's warm summer days. Truckee switched on a small, circular fan that sat on a table next to the window and then reached inside his desk for a pipe and a canister of his favorite brand of loose tobacco: Prince Albert.

"Don't mind, do you, McGirt?" he asked as he opened the can and began filling the pipe bowl.

McGirt smiled politely and shook his head. He sat directly across from the admiral's big mahogany desk, or "BMD" as Truckee liked to cynically boast he'd been flying for the last two years of his twilight tour in the United States Navy. The celebrated fighter pilot held the pipe in the hand of his battered left arm and methodically tamped-down the leaves with his right. He lit the tobacco, then paused and drew three rapid puffs. He blew the aromatic smoke into the fan's airstream, which vented the fumes cleanly and completely out the second story window, thus—at least in spirit—putting him in compliance with the government's latest NO SMOKING policy.

Truckee tilted his head back toward the open window, exhaled again and said, "You've had an extremely unique career path, McGirt, unconventional to say the least. But somehow you always seem to land on your feet. I may never understand what really motivates you." He tapped the pipe against the corner on his desk. "Gina onboard with this?"

"Yes, sir, she is. One hundred percent."

Truckee grunted and continued puffing. He suspected that, like his own wife, Gina had decided long ago to go along with her husband's career choices even when she didn't agree with them. As Truckee's spouse had once told him, "It's easier to maintain the strain and follow wherever you decide to go—otherwise, you'll just act like a gloomy old bastard."

Truckee glanced away and nodded his head like a parent silently showing approval of a child's homework assignment. He looked back at McGirt, made eye contact for several awkward seconds, and then craned his neck to look down into the building's parking lot. "That your Harley parked in the visitor's spot next to my car?"

"Yes, sir."

More puffs, then silence and another grunting acknowledgement. "Well, enough with the pleasantries." He picked up a thick, dark-red binder labeled *Top Secret*, paged through it nonchalantly and set down his pipe. "I trust that you've studied this report as well?"

"Yes, Admiral. Spent the last hour and a half in your building's communications locker. Everything seems to be in line with what Dr. Lammers and I spoke about yesterday, as far as the non-classified items that we're allowed to cover over the phone. With your endorsement, sir, I'll just need my discharge orders and to be formally relieved by Frank Taswell."

"Sure. I'll get on the horn to the detailer this morning and see what I can do to speed up the process. Can't make any guarantees, though," the Admiral bemoaned. "I doubt if things have changed much from when we both served at Navy headquarters. Probably easier teaching an elephant to tap dance rather than make that bureaucracy run more efficiently."

McGirt chuckled at Truckee's way of phrasing things. He peeked over at one of the room's walls, where a colorful array of squadron plaques and photographs had been arranged, tracing the senior naval aviator's career. On the table that held the fan was a single black and white snapshot of Lieutenant Willard "Tarzan" Truckee being greeted by his wife after five years captivity as a prisoner of war in Hanoi. McGirt had seen pictures and videos of the homecomings of other P.O.Ws, but he'd never known any of those men like he'd come to know his boss.

Truckee noticed McGirt staring at the snapshot of him walking away from the stairway of the Air Force C-141 transport aircraft and into the wide spread arms of his young, attractive-looking wife. Truckee's left arm was still encased in a shoulder-to-wrist plaster cast at the time.

"That was one happy day for me. All that misery from the past eighteen hundred and seventy three days was swept away when I walked across that tarmac. Some guys were never able to shake it off, but I was one of the lucky ones." Truckee paused as he stared at the photo of him and his wife. "Sometimes I wonder why in the hell we ever set foot in that crap-hole of a country." His eyes blinked a few times as if he'd been snapped back to the present from a forgotten bad memory. He took a deep breath and absently repositioned some files on his desk. There was a clamor of talk and laughter from below as a group of sailors transited the parking lot on their way to their unit's hangar. Truckee slid his caster-wheeled chair back toward the window and slammed the opening shut.

"Captain McGirt, I don't have all of the gouge on your mission, only what was in the same dossier from Langley that you read, and the conference call that I had with Bud Lammers and the CIA director. They both told me unequivocally that, because of your education and experience with the Philippine people, you'd be the best man for the job."

McGirt sat motionless and vigilantly concentrated on Truckee's words. He couldn't help but recall how over twenty years ago he and then-Lieutenant Commander Bud Lammers had narrowly escaped with their lives while rescuing a squadron mate who'd been kidnapped by a couple of Filipino thugs. McGirt knew that the undertaking that lay before him and Lammers would be vastly different—it'd be even harder to differentiate between the good guys and bad guys. The rules of engagement had been turned upside down and scrambled since that fateful, sun-drenched Tuesday morning on September 11, 2001.

Truckee glanced over to the closed door that separated his office from the anteroom where his secretary, Phyllis (or the "gatekeeper," as he affectionately called her) sat.

"I'm not sure if you and Lammers will be in harm's way as you were in Luzon back when Marcos was running the place. Regardless, I don't have to remind you how sensitive this job will be. It goes way beyond the fact-finding tasks. Both you and Lammers, but especially you, have had a unique exposure to the culture when you were stationed in Manila. I've read through your service record and made a few phone calls to satisfy my own curiosity about your past endeavors. That said, I suspect that, like most things of this nature, there'll be a few surprises."

McGirt nodded and sat up a little straighter in his chair. He extended his right leg in hopes of relieving the cramping muscles that surrounded his twice-rebuilt knee joint. "Sir, what can you tell me about this congressman, Clayton Gantry?"

"Well, he's chairman of the House Appropriations Subcommittee on Defense. Besides having both hands firmly on the purse strings of our military budget, he carries a boatload of horsepower when it comes to funding the CIA."

McGirt swallowed back a muffled chuckle. "Somewhat incestuous, in my opinion," he said offhandedly. He hoped that he'd not taken the liberty of speaking out of line with one of the Navy's most senior officers. Truckee tilted his head in a curious manner that reminded McGirt of his pet Jack Russell terrier, who, on rare occasions, struggled to understand a command. Truckee set down his pipe and frowned as if to brush off McGirt's comment.

"Well, that sort of overlapping power distribution is far too common," Truckee said. "I'm confident that you saw that during your tour in D.C. Our political system reminds me of when the enlisted troops go through the chow line during rough seas —the food on their trays all runs together: mashed potatoes and gravy slide into the ice cream, etcetera. Everything gets mixed up in a way that's difficult to keep separate. You get the picture. The fact that this missing girl's father lives smack in the middle of Gantry's district carries more than a little weight. It's an election year, and I suspect the honorable congressman's push for her return won't hinder his chances for another two years ensconced comfortably on the Hill. The skinny I get from my friends cruising the Beltway Bandit circuit is that he's a player on the rise who'd more than welcome the opportunity to hang his name on a good cause like saving a constituent's loved one. But the director made it clear to me that you and Lammers are not on a rescue mission: keep the scope of the job on track with what the director wants. Leave the John Wayne stuff to the SEALS and Army Rangers."

"Got it, sir. Bud and I are both getting too old for that kind of excitement."

"Tell me about it," Truckee lamented. "This is my last tour of duty for the U. S. Navy. I'll turn sixty-two in a couple of months and I'm looking forward to spending my Navy pension on spoiling my grandkids. Just hope that I live long enough to enjoy it. Too many of my roommates at the Hanoi Hilton haven't been so lucky."

He unconsciously massaged his crippled left arm and groaned softly. McGirt saw the sad look of a man who'd done his best to recover from the horrendous treatment he'd received decades ago in a North Vietnamese prisoner of war camp. McGirt realized that even a hard-as-nails warrior like "Tarzan" Truckee had his limits.

Truckee stood up and stared across the building's parking lot and spotted a navy destroyer, slowly making its way through San Diego harbor and out to sea. Instead of a gallant, combat-hardened fighter pilot, McGirt saw a hunched-over, burned-out old man who'd given his entire adult life in the service of his country. Truckee's physique, once the lean, taut frame of a cross-country runner, had taken on the image of a sloped-shoulders senior citizen. The admiral's khaki uniform didn't fit properly anymore—too big in the chest, too small in the midsection. The old man's stomach appeared to be pushing the buttons of his shirt to their breaking point. McGirt felt guilty that he had lost the desire to follow Truckee's career path for the next decade—only to end up flying a BMD while counting down the days until his retirement. Truckee turned away from the window and walked around his desk. McGirt stood up to meet him.

"Johnny Jack, wish I could talk you into turning down this assignment and staying on board with us. Your detaching fitness report will be filled with remarks explaining how your unit has consistently outperformed all other squadrons under my authority. That's something no one can take away from you." He inched closer and faced McGirt squarely.

"When I proposed bringing you, a senior O-6, back to rescue your former command, I went straight to the top and called Vice Admiral Chambers at BuPers (Bureau of Naval Personnel). I explained how your old squadron had slipped into a death spiral: major mishaps, poor readiness and unit morale in the shitter. Chambers didn't hesitate: He said, 'I know all about McGirt; he's a proven winner. If you want him, he's yours.' Most of your contemporaries would have considered it a big step backward. But you never complained; you worked your tail off and resurrected that unit from the grave." Truckee grabbed McGirt's right hand and held it firmly. "You made me proud, son. If you have a change of heart, I'll personally see that there's a spot for you."

McGirt felt a lump in his throat as his mind retraced what he'd endured during his naval career: the thrills, jubilation and excitement—all intertwined with the perils and stress of military service. He composed himself before speaking. "Sir, I can't thank you enough for the offer. But I've made up my mind and have to carry through with my decision."

Truckee released his grip, placed a hand on McGirt's shoulder and said, "When you came in here, I told you that I've never quite been able to understand what makes you tick." McGirt began to feel uncomfortable—until he noticed that Truckee's expression had changed from dour sternness to a boyish grin. The man's tired-looking eyes seemed to suddenly twinkle with the piss and vinegar of a young, virile flyboy. "But, the more that I think about it, the more I see myself twenty years ago: someone who sticks to their guns, regardless of how others might judge him. No, McGirt, we may come at life from different angles, but I'd suspect that we're both cut from the same cloth."

As McGirt made his way out of the Truckee's office, the admiral said, "Be careful over there, and if you can remember, bring me back a case of San Miguel, will ya?"

McGirt heard the window sash slide open. He turned and saw that Truckee had turned on the fan and had resumed meticulously repacking his pipe. McGirt responded by flashing the thumbs up signal and said, "Aye aye, sir. Will do."

McGirt motored across the air station to his squadron's hangar, where he parked his two-wheeler in the close-in, reserved location known as the "king's spot." Directly next to his parking spot sat Frank Taswell's road-worn, wood-paneled station wagon. The car's back section was overflowing with soccer balls, tennis rackets and crumbled fast food wrappers. McGirt knew that Frank's pending pay bump, precipitated by his promotion to captain, was probably already spent. The family man and his stay-at-home wife seemed to be constantly juggling their time and resources as they raised four children.

"Good morning, Skipper," Chief Yeoman Aaron Blake said as McGirt entered the squadron's administration office. McGirt's own workplace was strategically located adjacent to Blake's, in effect making the chief petty officer McGirt's own gatekeeper. Plus, the arrangement promoted an easier flow of the endless paperwork and message traffic that seemed to prevail at every aviation unit.

"Any word on the inbound flight, Chief?" McGirt asked as he opened the door into his private office.

Blake pulled the yellow memo from where he'd paper-clipped it to his inbox. "Yes, sir. I spoke with the tower supervisor, who told me that your visitor's flight is running late. Some bad weather over the Midwest forced the crew to make a deviation from their original flight plan." Blake handed McGirt the chit and then looked up at the big government-issued clock on the office wall. "They're still an hour or so away."

"Thanks, Chief," McGirt said as he stepped inside and closed the door. He peeked through the small, waist-level sliding window located on the wall that separated his space from Taswell's. The opening allowed the pair to shuffle paperwork between one another. He saw Taswell's khaki uniform hanging neatly on the side of the man's locker then remembered that his XO had gone flying. McGirt then glanced out a window and saw that the squadron's flight line was deserted—the morning launch had already departed.

McGirt sat down and looked around the space that he'd occupied during the last eighteen months. It had been the best time of his professional life. But this would be his last day. He'd announced his stepping down as commanding officer at yesterday's all hands meeting, and later in the afternoon, he and Taswell would make it official by exchanging a few formal words and a salute. From that point forward, Captain Johnny Jack McGirt would embark on his new life as a civilian.

"Boss, ceiling and visibility just went down below visual minimums. With your concurrence, I'll change the ATIS, get the rabbit running and set us up for instrument approaches."

The tower supervisor looked out over the air station's tarmac at the thick wall of fog rolling in from the Pacific. "Yeah, we've held off for as long as we can, go ahead and do it," she said. "Looks like we'll be in the soup in a few minutes."

The petty officer pressed a button to record North Island's weather update. The recording, or Automatic Terminal Information Service (ATIS), would relay to inbound flight crews the airport's deteriorating weather and the requirement for an instrument approach. He then flipped a switch that illuminated the primary runway's sequenced, flashing white lights, or "rabbit," which would assist the pilots as they switched their vision from the cockpit's flight gauges and lined up visually for landing after they'd descended below the cloud layer.

"How we doing recovering the rotor-heads?" the supervisor asked.

"No problems yet. Most of them are still special VFR; a couple are requesting radar guidance, though."

"Good," she answered.

The station's helicopters operated under a completely different set of guidelines from their fixed winged counterparts. By flying lower and slower, the "special visual flight rules" allowed rotary crews to skirt below low clouds and to navigate by eyesight down to one-half mile visibility.

In a darkened space below the tower cab, another sailor sat behind a radar screen that displayed an aircraft's position relative to the runway. The specialized array, or precision approach radar, permitted him to "talk down" pilots by relaying their distance to touchdown, plus vertical and lateral deviations from the proper glide path and course. The procedure was formally dubbed a "ground controlled approach;" pilots referred to it as simply a "GCA."

Satisfied that her crew was ready to receive inbound traffic, the tower supervisor took a seat at her desk. She slid her landline close by in anticipation of the calls she expected to start pouring in to complain about noise. The station's primary instrument runway was in direct line with a fifteen-story high cluster of condominiums located to the east. When the weather was good, like it normally was in Southern California, aircraft inbound to the station would fly on an offset track to avoid passing over the tall structures. However, when the ceiling or visibility dropped down as it had today, the aircraft's radar monitored approach path crossed directly above the condominiums, clearing the top floor by just a few hundred feet.

"Got one helo lined up on short final, boss, followed by that government Gulfstream jet inbound from D.C.," the petty officer reported.

His supervisor spotted the H-60 helicopter as it broke out of the clouds and came to hover over the end of the runway. Its crew air-taxied clear of the runway to make room for the next arriving aircraft.

Three minutes later, the sleek biz-jet carrying Dr. Bud Lammers came into view and made a gentle touchdown. Seconds later, the supervisor's phone rang loudly.

"North Island tower, Chief Miller speaking. May I help you sir or ma'am?" Miller held the receiver a couple inches from her ear and braced for the inevitable.

"That airplane almost crashed into my apartment!" a panicky female voice shouted.

"No ma'am, I can assure you that all aircraft arriving at the air station are flying well within prescribed legal limitations. Because of the degraded ceiling and visibility, they are unable to offset their flight tracks like they'd normally do when the weather is better."

Chief Miller's subordinates watched as she diligently repeated the same spiel to the flood of similar callers. Eventually, her patience wore thin and she'd dispensed with her extended, courteous greeting.

"Tower, go ahead," she answered abruptly after the tenth call. The usual irate complaint spilled out at her, but this caller—a fast-talking man with a grating, upper-East-coast-sounding accent—was different from all the rest she'd handled earlier. He cut her off repeatedly as she attempted to explain the reason for the increased noise level over the high rises. After over a minute of silently listening to the man's tirade, the line went quiet.

*"Hey, lady, are you still there?"* he barked.

"Yes, sir, I'm still here—and giving you *every* ounce of my undivided attention," Miller said.

He resumed his rant, unfazed. "What the hell am I supposed to do if one of those things gets too low and smashes into my penthouse, huh? Tell me, what am I supposed to do?"

Chief Miller took a deep breath to help calm her nerves. "Well, sir, at the very least, you'll have to redecorate." The next sound she heard was that of a definitive "click" as the man hung up on her.

"Chief, looks like the sun is starting to burn off this crud," a subordinate reported. "Ceiling and visibility are coming up rapidly, and I think we'll be able to terminate the GCAs and go back to the offset visuals."

Miller refilled her cup with another dose of strong coffee and said, "Thank God."

McGirt had Frank Taswell's car to pick up Bud. He parked in the spot marked by a sign that read, "Visiting Dignitary," adjacent to the flight line. He figured that after his colleague's wartime service in Vietnam, followed by the man's long career at CIA, Lammers deserved the perk of a short walk. Once the jet came to a stop and its engines wound down, McGirt approached the aircraft. He met Bud with a big hug as Lammers stepped onto the tarmac.

"Hey, old timer, how was the flight?" he asked.

"Bumpy as all get-out until we got clear of some thunderstorms over the Midwest. After that, pretty smooth."

McGirt took the large suitcase from Bud's hand and led him toward the car. He looked over his shoulder and saw that the Gulfstream's two pilots were in the process of securing their aircraft for its overnight stay. "Those guys need a ride?"

"Nah, I set them up with a rental car and rooms out in town. They should be fine," Bud said. "One of the bennies of being a deputy; I get a nice budget for things like this."

McGirt lifted the tailgate of Taswell's wagon. He pushed a boogie board and a knotted mess of soccer shoes out of the way to make room for Bud's suitcase.

"So nice of you to roll out the red carpet," Bud quipped as he climbed into the old car.

"Sorry about this, but Gina's Lexus is in the shop, and we've downsized to just one car and the Harley. Frank was nice enough to lend me his wheels." McGirt backed out of the parking spot and drove slowly past the station's air terminal where a C-9 transport plane was on-loading a gaggle of passengers.

"How'd he take the news about an office change of command?"

"Actually, I think it took a monkey off his back. You met Frank last time you were out here, remember? Pretty basic guy and not a big fan of pomp and circumstance. Plus, I know he's happier not having to ante up for the after-ceremony reception."

"Yeah, best for everyone to just do it low key."

"Yes, I agree," McGirt said as they passed through the main security gate. He made a sharp right turn onto Alameda Boulevard. "I'm going to drop you off at our place and then head back to the office. When Frank returns from his flight, he'll relieve me and we'll be done with it."

"Sounds good." Bud leaned back against the seat's headrest. "I could use a nap, anyway."

Gina DeCarlo handed the taxi driver his fare plus a nice tip. He'd made great time maneuvering through San Diego's snarled rush-hour traffic by taking a short cut through one of the city's Chicano districts, Barrio Logan, before getting on the ramp for the San Diego-Coronado Bridge. It had been a long day for the Navy orthopedic surgeon. She'd reconstructed a retiree's knee, performed a hip replacement on a fifty-eight year old vice admiral, and sadly, had assisted with the heart-rending task of amputating the lower leg of a nineteen-year-old female Marine. The girl had received the tragic injury when the transport she was driving had triggered a land mine in Afghanistan. DeCarlo and her team had performed three previous surgeries in an effort to save the young woman's leg, but after the mangled limb had refused to heal properly, their only alternative was to remove it. During Gina's taxi ride home, she couldn't get the brave girl's pretty face out of her mind.

"Hello there, McGirt," she said as she wearily deposited her briefcase on a living room chair. "Bud get in okay?"

McGirt held an index finger to his lips. "Yeah, he's fine. In the guest room sleeping."

"You go for a run?" Gina whispered.

"Yes. After the change of command I felt like putting in a few miles on the beach. Just got back."

Gina spotted a trail of sand that led from the front door of their casita-style home, through the living room and into the kitchen where he was sitting. She glared at him.

"*I know, I know.* Forgot to leave my shoes outside again. I'll vacuum it after he wakes up. Sorry."

She motioned to a side door that led to the home's tiny yard. McGirt rose from the table and followed her outside where they could talk more freely. "Tell me, how was your day?" he said.

"I've had better." She ignored the sweat of McGirt's damp tee shirt and hugged him tightly while tucking her head up under his chin. "First part of the day was routine and then..." McGirt felt his wife begin to sob, but she choked the emotion back and gently pushed herself away from him. "That young Marine I've been telling you about? We had to take her leg today."

"Oh, Gina, I am so sorry."

"Thanks," Gina said while dabbing her eyes with the sleeve of her scrubs. "It was a shame, but there was no other option, really."

"How's she doing?"

Gina could no longer contain herself; the tears began to flow freely. "I was with her when she came out of the anesthesia. She opened her eyes and managed a faint smile for me." Gina's speech began to stutter as the grief overwhelmed her. "She...she actually thanked me...and...asked how soon before she could go back to her unit."

There were no words that McGirt could conjure up to help his wife. He drew her into his arms again. As he rocked her lazily, they both heard a soft, thud-like noise followed by the rapid patter of dog feet scurrying across the home's hardwood floor.

A small, black and white Jack Russell came skidding around the corner and bolted out into the yard to join them. He began bouncing excitedly at Gina's feet. The sight of their beloved pet, Arnie, immediately lifted her spirits. She crouched down and cupped the dog's little head in her hands.

"How you doin' today, fella?" she said while tousling his whiskered face. "Did you miss your mama?"

McGirt laughed at the comical sight of the rambunctious terrier as he continued gyrating crazily and licking at Gina's hands. "What is it about these animals?" he said. "They always act like they haven't seen you in years, don't they?"

Gina wiped away the last of her tears. "And they seem to know when you're feeling down too." She tenderly stroked the dog's back. "I think Arnie and I could both use a good long walk. I'll put dinner in the oven and be back in about an hour, okay?"

"Take your time," McGirt said as he followed her inside and headed for the shower.

When McGirt came out of the bathroom, he found Bud channel surfing in the living room. Lammers had helped himself to a can of beer and was cranked back in McGirt's favorite easy chair. "Nice digs you got here," he said. "What'd you pay for it, a couple million?"

"No, but you're close. Wish I would have snapped up a place when we were stationed here twenty years ago, before home prices went through the roof."

"You and me both. We sold our place out in Bonita when I went back East with the Agency. Made a nice profit, but wish we'd kept it as a rental." Bud switched off the television and said, "I heard Gina go out the door with the dog. Friendly little guy, isn't he? Jumped up onto my bed while I napped."

"Yeah, he does that, but only with people he thinks like him. Some sort of sixth sense."

"Huh…go figure," Bud said. He glanced at his watch. "Do we have a few quiet minutes to talk before they get back?"

"Sure. Let me grab a coke. But I outrank you, so you'll have to move you rear end out of my chair."

Bud grumbled something, got up and moved over to the sofa.

"I could use a little more gouge before we leave tomorrow, what do you have for me?" McGirt asked as he cracked open the soft drink and sat down.

Bud hoisted a leather briefcase onto his lap, removed a laptop computer and inserted a disc. After a long series of passwords, the computer's disc drive came to life and a word document displayed on the screen. He rotated the laptop so they both could see.

"Here's our itinerary," he began. "I would have preferred to avoid the two days of 'haze-gray and underway,' however, everyone in my shop suspects that it'd be just too damn obvious for us to fly into the Zamboanga airport on Philippine Airlines. Plus, the Director had a run-in with State over getting diplomatic clearance for our Gulfstream to land there. Anyway, after we get dropped off at Cubi Point, we'll have to activate our sea legs on the way down to Basilan Island."

"Wonderful. Did you request VIP staterooms for us?"

"Of course," Bud deadpanned. "Hey, we'll be lucky to get a couple of cots and box lunches." He scrolled down through his notes. "Yeah, there it is: USS *Lansing*— commissioned in the late sixties. I see the old girl is slated to be decommissioned and transferred to the Military Sealift Command, whatever that is."

"That's a sign of the times, pal. Most all of the supply ships you and I served on are going that route," McGirt said. "Same with the H-46. Navy's dumping all of them in a couple years."

Bud pulled up another page from his classified notes. "This is all subject to change, but we'll be hosted by the Commander of the Army Ranger unit that's garrisoned on Basilan, a Colonel Woodbridge. He and his men are part of a joint unit headed by his Filipino counterpart, Colonel Felix Romolo. Romolo is the guy who is setting up our meetings with the Muslim kingpins on the island."

McGirt paused for a moment before asking, "So cut to the chase, Bud, what's the likelihood that one of those local honchos knows where this missing girl is?"

"My folks have predicted that as a 'high probability.' But, so many of them are on the take, it's been difficult to ascertain fact from fiction. That's why I wanted you to go with me; you've spent a hell of a lot more time, both in the northern and southern islands, than I ever have." Lammers tapped a finger on his computer to emphasize the point. "You bring the knowledge, and I bring the figurative horsepower." Bud finished his beer and then said, "But as I told you when I first offered my proposal, there's always some risk involved with these types of negotiations."

McGirt chuckled to himself at the irony of what was unfolding. Like most things in his Navy career, none of this latest chapter had gone as he'd expected—starting foremost with Bud Lammers's initial query about McGirt's plans after he had decided to leave active duty. His promised job at the Central Intelligence Agency had, at first, seemed very appealing. Gina had massaged the system for a set of orders to the D.C. area—plus he'd be able to start drawing a pension from the Navy. But the reality that this string of life-changing events had now been set in motion struck him with the impact of Tim Worley's abrupt landing on the beach a few days ago.

"You're much more in tune with the political side of this operation," McGirt said. "What degree of influence does the congressman from Texas, Gantry, carry?"

"Trust me—a bunch," Lammers responded without any hesitation. He saw Gina and Arnie turning onto McGirt's street and walking toward the house. He closed the program he'd opened, removed the disc, shut down the laptop and locked everything in the briefcase. "This girl, Karlena Brandt, is getting more attention than several other hostages being held by the same sect in the Philippines. There are two simple reasons: she's from Clayton Gantry's congressional district, and her old man is loaded. The FBI dug back and uncovered there's a history of bad blood between the Gantry and Brandt clans; some squabble over land and oil. That being said, Gantry has made a personal appeal to the girl's father not to pay any ransom. But Otto Brandt has the reputation of a stubborn mule that likes to carry grudges. We suspect that he might find a way to pay a ransom not just to free his daughter, but also as a way to tell Gantry to shove it where the sun don't shine."

As Gina approached the front door both men stood up. Bud concluded by saying, "Remember when JFK's son crashed his plane into the ocean?"

"Yeah?"

"There was a gigantic search and rescue operation that was deployed to recover the bodies of him and his two passengers. Do you think if the poor kid had been some nobody, the government would have spent that amount of time and resources?"

"Probably not," McGirt said.

"Well, on a much smaller scale, that's why you and I are flying on a private jet to the Philippines tomorrow."

Gina's casual lasagna dinner provided her and McGirt the chance to catch up with the events of Lammers's life. She and Bud shared a bottle of wine, while McGirt, a life-long teetotaler, sipped his soft drink. Their conversation began with Bud giving them the rundown on his two children and how the adopted Korean kids, now both college graduates, had been so successful in their endeavors. He gave all of the credit to his deceased wife, Jill, claiming that his career with the CIA hadn't allowed him to be much of an involved father.

Talk had eventually turned to a "remember when" session as McGirt and Bud relived the time they'd spent together on the USS *San Angelo* during a deployment to the Western Pacific. Though the cruise had marked the involuntary end of Bud's Navy career, Gina enjoyed listening to the two men as they shared information about what they knew of the other sailors who'd served as part of *San Angelo's* air detachment.

McGirt began by relaying that the "det's" maintenance chief, Irvis Jenks, had started a fishing charter-boat operation based out of San Diego's Mission Bay, and that he and Gina saw the big man regularly whenever they needed fresh fish, "right off the boat." Both men were aware that the det's junior-most officer, Robert Bright, was now head of the Aerodynamics Department at the Navy's Postgraduate School in Monterey, California. Bright had tried unsuccessfully to regain his medical clearance after the crash in the Philippines that had resulted in crippling his left arm. With his flying career ended, Bright had turned his energies to academics.

The detachments other two copilots, Paul Uker and Ron Carbone, had essentially dropped off the radar. Uker, who'd turned in his aviator wings during their West-Pac, had transferred to surface line duty. Neither Lammers nor McGirt had heard from him since the day the ensign had walked down the ship's gangway in Subic Bay, Philippines. Carbone had kept in touch briefly, but had been bounced around from duty station to duty station and had happily retired once he'd accumulated twenty years of service.

Gina had sat quietly while her husband and Lammers swapped sea stories. With neither of them mentioning one particular officer, she spoke up.

"What about that guy who crashed up in the mountains?" she said. "What was his name?" She turned to her husband.

A pall set over the dinner table. "Oh, that was Thomas Rayburn, honey." McGirt gently touched her arm. Gina read his gesture as a signal to say no more.

Bud smiled and poured himself another glass of wine. "Nah, that's okay; we can talk about Thomas Rayburn III."

Gina's eyes darted between Bud and her husband. McGirt had told her how Rayburn's misconduct had been a major reason for Bud's fall from grace as a naval officer. What he had not told her, however, was how Rayburn's "crash" had nearly set off an international incident.

Bud faced Gina as he began to explain. "Well, I'm sure that your husband has told you how Rayburn got himself involved in a scam reselling goods from the Navy Exchange system to civilians off base in the Philippines."

Gina nodded.

"As far as the crash goes, the official record shows that his aircraft had suffered an engine failure and was unable to maintain level flight in the thin mountain air."

Gina had studied human psychology enough to sense that Bud was becoming uncomfortable. She adroitly tried to change the subject by rising from her chair and asking cheerfully, "Who's up for dessert?"

Bud laughed and politely waved his hand for her to sit back down. "No, that's alright. I'll finish," he said. "What I have to tell you is important."

McGirt knew that Lammers never cared to bring up the subject, so, like Gina, he was anxious to hear the rest.

"Got a call a few months ago from another old Navy buddy who got out of the service and went to law school. The guy now works as a federal prosecutor in New York City. He told me that he was doing an investigation into insider trading on Wall Street and asked what could I tell him about one of the defendants: a former naval pilot by the name of Thomas Rayburn III."

McGirt's jaw dropped. "No *shit*."

"Yup, seems that our former shipmate finally crossed the line and got his cajones in a ringer."

"How'd it turn out?" McGirt asked.

"Not so good—at least for him. Ole Tommy Boy was fined a shit-load, lost his broker's license for life, and he's now serving six to ten in federal prison. Not the kind filled with rapists and murders, unfortunately. He ratted out a whole slew of other people and plea-bargained himself into one of those 'Club Fed' places down in Florida. You know, the joints for nice, respectable white-collar criminals."

A wide grin spread across McGirt's face. He raised his glass dramatically. "Here, here. To Thomas Rayburn. Justice has been served!"

Gina and Bud raised their glasses and repeated: "To Thomas!"

# CHAPTER 8

She was "The Woman of the Woods," yet people on the island had come to know her simply as "The Woman." Nobody knew her real name, or if she'd ever actually been given one by the unknown pair who'd brought her into the material world. She would appear indiscriminately throughout Basilan—mostly at small, out-of-the-way Muslim villages—where she would share her knowledge of herbal remedies and render mystic prophecies about the Day of Judgment. She lived off of the earth, and by the generosity of her followers, who'd offer up what little clothing or food she needed as repayment for the spiritual healing and sense of consciousness she'd provide to them. She never carried any form of money, nor would she accept it from anyone—never, ever. The Woman never stayed more than a day or two in one spot, preferring instead to slip back into the rejuvenation of her true home—the woods—once satisfied that her obligations had been fulfilled.

She'd been living in silent solitude for nearly a week's time in an area along Basilan's secluded southeastern coast. The distinctive smell of a campfire had perked her senses while she was foraging the tropical forest's greenery for new, natural medicines. Her sense of curiosity had prompted her to climb the steep hill without trepidation and to explore who else might be sharing nature with her today. The Woman lacked fear of strangers or of the unknown; she'd decided at an early age that fear was a useless, wasteful emotion embraced only by those of no faith.

When she reached the isolated shack, she stood for a moment and studied it from a distance. She wondered what purpose the run down structure would serve to anyone. She balked at the sight of food wrappers and plastic bottles that surrounded the shack's perimeter, then bent down and methodically placed the litter onto the fire's smoldering embers.

But as she crept closer to the tiny building, the smoky aroma of the fire was overtaken by something else—the stench of decay and human waste. The smell became more intense as she tried to peek over the bottom of a shattered window. She heard the sounds of breathing and muffled groans beneath her, but the window was positioned too high for her short legs to stretch far enough to see what was below. Her inquisitiveness grew as she walked around the shack and discovered a way inside.

The thick, wooden-plank door had been barred shut from the outside with a crude but effective device—a thick steel pipe that had been dropped into two slots on either side of the doorway. She knocked, waited a moment and then dislodged the pipe and stepped slowly inside.

The Woman had been witness to a variety of startling sights during her years of wandering the woods: the deaths of humans and animals, both natural and unnatural, and more recently, the acts of man's inhumanity to man brought on by the armed, nefarious-looking men she'd seen prowling the villages. Nonetheless, those experiences hadn't prepared her for the image of Karlena Brandt. What struck her most was the scared, helpless look of Karlena's eyes—like those of a dying animal.

The Woman quickly surmised what had taken place; the stories had spread throughout the island by word of mouth. A chill passed through her body at the thought of being caught helping their hostage, but the angst was soon overshadowed by her sense of compassion. She knew that she'd have to do something to help this pathetic creature.

Karlena's greenish-blue eyes widened as The Woman bent down to touch her. Her jaw was frozen in place when the stranger slid the cloth out from between her teeth. The Woman slowly and gently untied the spittle-and-blood-coated rag and set it aside.

After the muscles had loosened, Karlena spat out, "Oh, thank *God* you're here!" But Karlena saw that her words were not understood by the sweet-looking, round-faced woman standing over her; she might as well have been pleading with one of the mango trees that she could see from the lone dirt-crusted window in the tiny shack where she'd been held. The corners of her mouth had been rubbed to a raw, oozing redness by the handkerchief that Blister had used to gag her.

The petite, brown-skinned woman had appeared out of the haze of Karlena's crumbling psyche, a gossamer-like image, swaying between reality and hallucination inside of a tired mind. The Woman said something to Karlena in her native tongue and then lightly stroked her face.

"Please help me, *please...*" Karlena begged.

The Woman's eyes ran over Karlena's cowering body as if she were inspecting a farm animal before purchasing it. Her diminutive hands plied Karlena's knotted hair, carefully separating the sticky strands from her scalp as if she were searching for something. She smiled approvingly and made a walking motion with her fingers, moving them in a quick, creeping motion across her own arm.

Karlena surmised from The Woman's actions that she'd been grooming her and searching for bugs. "Are there lice?" Karlena asked, hoping she understood.

The Woman smiled as she lightly touched Karlena's head; she waived an index finger signaling "no."

Karlena eased her head and shoulders back into the corner of the sordid, one room hut—the latest place where she'd been relocated during her captivity. She'd sat in the same spot on the roughly-hewed plank floor for over a day, during which time the she'd been given only water to consume. The teenage-looking boy, whom she'd recognized as Spider's boat driver from the day she'd arrived in Basilan, had appeared carrying a rusted bucket and a wooden ladle. She'd gulped the lukewarm drink hungrily until her belly was overfilled, then promptly wet herself. She'd relieved her bladder again, twice, during her sleep.

Karlena's last meal had been three days ago, when she'd wolfed down a bowl of coconut milk and tepid rice, mixed with some sort of greenish, stringy vegetable; but the food had not set well in her stomach. Minutes after finishing, she had been dragged outside the hut, where her captors turned their backs disgustedly while she groaned as her bowels convulsed.

Spider had cursed and stormed away angrily after ordering her to *"do it quicker!"* Taking pity at her distress and humiliation, Blister had loosely attached a makeshift collar of nylon rope around her neck and anchored it to a tall pine tree. He tightened the line that lashed her hands behind her back, said quietly in plain English that he was "sorry," and then followed behind Spider.

She'd listened to the muffled pat of his footsteps across the jungle floor as she squatted like a sick, tethered dog. After finally relieving herself, she had rolled to one side and prayed tearfully as her pulsing innards slowly calmed. She'd remembered her father's claim that there was some good in every man, even the most devious and vile ones—but as she lay half naked on the bare soil, alone and in pain, she'd struggled to find truth in those words.

Later that day, after sunset, Spider had returned. He'd dragged her emaciated body back inside and restrained her again without saying a single word.

The Woman began humming a soft melody as she continued the inspection; she slid her hands along Karlena's shoulders, arms, lower ribcage and hips. But the humming stopped as she got closer to Karlena's midsection. Karlena hadn't bathed or changed clothing since the morning that she'd boarded Duke's small boat, weeks ago. The woman backed off, sniffed lightly a couple of times and then reached for Karlena's wrists, which were folded in a defensive manner across the front of her shorts. The Woman relaxed her grip, looked deeply into Karlena's eyes and said a phrase in her native tongue.

Karlena couldn't understand the words, but she did not need to—The Woman's eyes silently conveyed what she felt: that there was no reason to be afraid. Karlena turned her head and began to sob as The Woman removed her bound hands and dropped them passively to one side. The Filipina's face cringed and she initially winced at the sight. But after a few seconds, she continued humming, unfazed. The mess had partially dried into an oozy form that clung to Karlena's skin and stuck to the hut's wooden floor like a scabby adhesive.

Karlena felt The Woman's tiny, calloused hand brush tenderly across her cheek. She made a light, song-like noise that sounded like "Amen" and patted Karlena compassionately on the top of her head.

"*Please* help me, *please*," Karlena begged. Her voice carried a thread of strength; the Woman's kindness seemed to have fostered a renewed sense of hope in her heart. "There, over there," Karlena said. She nodded her head and thrust her lashed hands in the direction of the opposite corner of the rickety hut.

The Woman pointed expectantly to a mounded pile, shrouded by a hole-riddled piece of green canvas.

"Yes!" Karlena acknowledged.

The Woman rose from her kneeling position and walked a few steps. She looked back at Karlena for approval then pulled away the tarp, exposing a tangled collection of rusty tools, and several meters of spooled, yellow nylon rope, similar to what Spider had used to tie up Karlena's wrists and to lash her body to a wall. He'd wrapped the line tightly under her armpits and then knotted the other end to a large steel eyelet that was screwed deep into a stud. Using a cigarette lighter, he'd then fused the ends of the knots into a tight, melted blob, making it impossible for her to unravel and break free without a sharp knife.

The Woman peeked outside through the hut's partially opened door: there was no sign of anyone else. With a furtive expression, she tossed the tarp aside and began pawing through the cluttered heap. At the bottom was Karlena's teal-colored backpack; its newness stood out plainly against the other tattered, dusty items.

Karlena bent her bound wrist in a back and forth motion, signaling the woman to bring the backpack to her. The Woman smiled obediently and complied with Karlena's command.

When Spider and Blister had abandoned Duke at the dock, they'd covetously eyed the bag, hoping that it held some form of value: cash, jewelry, credit cards—anything that could be bartered for more practical goods. During the drive inland from the lagoon, Blister had stealthily rummaged through the bag while positioned in the jeep's rear seat. He'd deftly removed the paltry sum of currencies, composed of U.S. Dollars, Malaysian Ringgits and Indonesian Rupiahs. He'd frowned disappointedly at the small amount before stuffing the cash inside a pocket of his fatigues. He'd decided, at least for a while, to leave Karlena's photography equipment intact.

The Woman squatted next to her while Karlena began eagerly going through the bag as best she could with her still-bound hands. The Filipina's dark, almond-shaped eyes followed Karlena's hands as she carefully unzipped each compartment; Karlena was not surprised to see that, in addition to her camera gear, the captors had pilfered everything, even her most personal items.

The Woman sensed Karlena's sadness and mumbled something in a soft, sympathetic way.

The diminutive Filipina appeared to be in her fifties; her long, ebony hair was twisted neatly into a compact bun, secured tightly on the back of her head with a thin, intricately woven narrow band of fabric. She wore a shoulder-to-ankle, flowery blue and green dress. The roughness of her palms and fingers were a stark contrast to the smooth, ageless looking skin of her face. Even while cast into such a dire circumstance, Karlena found it difficult not to admire the female's raw, natural beauty.

Karlena leaned back against the wall and said, "You have to help me, please." The Woman smiled again and nodded as if she understood, but Karlena wasn't sure that she did. Karlena then unzipped a large pocket, reached inside and rubbed her fingers carefully over the pocket's inner lining until she located what she wanted. "Yes!"

Most all of her fingernails had broken off, but for some reason, the one on her right thumb had stayed intact, in effect serving as a crude marker of the length of her captivity. The woman leaned in closer from her crouched position and helped hold the bag steady while Karlena diligently waggled her thumbnail into a section of the lining where the color of the seam's stitching was a shade different. She gritted her teeth and shoved hard. The thread finally gave way as her thumbnail snapped halfway back and tore jaggedly down to the nail bed. The Woman winced at the sight as blood oozed from the wound, but Karlena was undeterred by the pain. A broad grin erupted across her dirty face as she bit down on her lower lip and slid an index finger into the ripped opening.

"There!" she shouted. She wriggled a finger carefully, plying deeper, then gingerly removed a tightly folded one hundred dollar bill. When she'd packed for the journey months ago, she'd conceived the idea of hiding a small amount of money—a secret stash for some unforeseen emergency.

Karlena's hands trembled as she extended the money to the little Filipina. Tears flowed from her eyes. "I know you probably don't understand my words, but please do something to help me." She made a desperate attempt to communicate by focusing on The Woman's eyes, hoping the Filipina would somehow grasp what she was saying.

The corner of The Woman's mouth flinched as if she were about to smile again, but she didn't. Instead, she snatched the bill from Karlena's hand and tucked it back inside the bag. She then walked over to the pile of tools and rope, buried the bag inside the rubble, and then diligently re-covered the mound with the canvas tarp.

Karlena began to weep. "No, no. Don't do that!" she pleaded. Her trust that this caring person had come to her aid quickly vanished as the Filipina took hold of the rag, raised it swiftly over Karlena's chin and pressed the rolled cloth firmly in place between her teeth. Karlena shook her head in defiance, but the little woman was too strong and too quick as she pushed Karlena's head forward, held it down with her forearms and then re-secured the gag. Strands of Karlena's red hair were entwined painfully in the snug knot.

The Woman spun abruptly and moved toward the door. She opened it and stood motionless, as if torn between staying and leaving. Her eyes darted nervously between Karlena and the vast, dense woods. Finally, she stepped outside and quietly closed the door behind her. Karlena heard a scraping thud as the door's locking bar dropped into place. Her head fell back against the wall as she concluded that the Filipina had been just another cruel player in the confusing conspiracy of holding her prisoner. She began to sob uncontrollably.

Karlena tried to reason: *Why doesn't somebody come to my aid? My father... anyone. And where is Mitchell? How could he have allowed me to be led into such a calamity?* She'd always considered herself a strong person. Being raised without the kind affection of her mother, she'd been forced to find her own way so many times, despite her father's genuine efforts to make up for being a single parent. This adventure that she'd chosen to undertake by traveling halfway around the world to explore exotic lands and to document native cultures had been so close to being completed.

The trip had been more than just a wealthy college kid's fantasy—it had been her chance to finally prove herself without the hovering presence of her dad. She pounded the back of her head against the wall and trembled with rage: *How could I have been so stupid and so gullible to have allowed this to happen!*

This journey would have been her release from the well-intentioned bonds of her father and an escape from the flat, dusty nowhere that, in her mind, was West Texas. But that same tired vision had been enough to buoy her spirit and to endure the maltreatment of whatever devious ends her captors were pursuing.

Again, she tried to shout for help through the spittle-soaked rag, but her energy was depleted; all that emerged were a series of pathetic, muted croaks. The rough-edged nylon rope that Blister had strapped around her wrists, ankles and waist had rendered her no better off than a hogtied steer trapped inside a barn stall. After several minutes of fading in and out of listless stupor, she felt her heartbeat speed up. She made one more convulsive flailing act of her arms, legs and back muscles in an attempt to somehow free herself—but it was pointless. She sank back against the wall, totally defeated.

As her pulse and breathing began to slow, Karlena sensed an odd calmness. The clamor of jungle life began to ebb, leaving her with just the sporadic growling of her empty stomach. She closed her eyes and let her mind float to a place back home, where she hadn't been since her early teens—just before her mother had left: a small Baptist church, set on a lonely, two-lane road that traversed the West Texas hardpan, east of Midland. Her head began to sway involuntarily, keeping time with the imaginary voices of the choir as they sang a lilting hymn. The peaceful sounds reverberated off the old brick building's plastered walls and stained glass. Karlena began to drift off. Nothing troubled her now: not fear, hunger or thirst; not even the humiliation of wallowing in her own filth. Her thoughts traveled deeper and deeper into the past as she quietly surrendered to her dreams.

*She stood motionless on the hard-packed dirt that surrounded their home as a cool, morning breeze brushed over her body, blowing unruly strands of hair over her eyes. Karlena reached up and pushed them away. She saw her father's compact figure standing, tall and proud, on the eastside veranda, several dozen yards away; the tips of his fingers were tucked snuggly into the tops of jeans pockets. He was wearing his favorite plaid, long-sleeved, western-style shirt, buttoned neatly at the top—the way he always did. He raised his right hand as if to waive to her, but instead, began moving it back and forth in a beckoning motion. A faint, relieved grin rose across Otto Brandt's face as tears began to fill his eyes; Karlena had never seen her father cry—never. But as she moved closer, she saw that the stream of tears were dripping freely from his cheeks, making small, wet stains on the starched cotton shirt. The grin changed to a wide smile as he allowed his tears of happiness to fall unashamedly. Karlena walked slowly across the hard-packed dirt, closer to Otto, as he spread his arms out wide, ready to embrace her. The front of his shirt was now soaked with tears. He opened his mouth and in a soft, trembling voice said, "Come home."*

### Three Weeks Earlier

After Duke's boat had been towed and docked at the remote cove on the southern shores of Basilan Island, Karlena was driven to a location near the center of the island's densely forested, mountainous terrain. She was told by Spider—Blister continued to remain tight-lipped—that she'd be able to speak with her college friend, Mitchell Castella, once they were closer to the island's most populated region, Isabela City, and could receive a better cell-phone signal. Karlena felt reasonably confident that the two men who'd intercepted her onboard Duke's boat were legitimate. Despite her initial impression, she'd ruled out that the Filipinos were on some sort of underhanded mission. After all, she thought to herself, Mitchell had told her that someone would meet her when she arrived in Basilan; that part was correct. What confused her, however, was the abrupt, pirate-like way that she and Duke had been chased down: Mitchell hadn't given a clue that her "welcoming committee" would carry out their duties with such vigor.

The drive to their first destination had taken nearly four hours from the secluded mooring point where she'd said goodbye to Duke. Sitting in the front seat of the open-topped jeep she'd been treated to one of the most captivating series of views since she'd arrived in Southeast Asia. Along the pothole-riddled way, she'd snapped nearly three full rolls of film on the one 35-millimeter reflex camera that she'd kept for the final phase of the expedition.

"We stop here for a while and try to call your friend, Mr. Castella," Spider said after he'd parked their vehicle in front of an isolated, clapboard-sided cottage, perched on a heavily wooded ridge overlooking Isabela City. The teeming port, located on Basilan's north coast, appeared only a few kilometers away from the elevated vista.

Karlena got out of the jeep and lazily bent forward at the waist in an effort to stretch the lower muscles of her back that had endured the long, bumpy ride.

Spider mumbled some words to Blister who silently acknowledged and went inside the building.

Karlena watched him spring up two steps onto a narrow porch and then walk through a door-less entryway. The structure appeared in desperate need of care: its paint, which she guessed might at some point have been robin's egg blue, was peeling off wooden clapboards in large swatches; the buildings foundation and walls canted noticeably to one side, but the metal roof looked solid with a minimal amount of rust.

"So where is Mitchell?" Karlena asked. The smoky, acrid aroma of Isabela City filled her nostrils as she looked down at the smog-shrouded cluster of humanity.

Without hesitation Spider pulled his cell phone from a thigh pocket of his cargo pants and began pressing buttons. "Three bars reception. We should make a successful connection this time."

Karlena peeked around Spider and saw that Blister was standing on the building's porch, holding a briefcase-sized green metal box—it was a camping stove. He set it on top of a dilapidated wooden end table, opened the stove's lid, gave a couple of pumps on the handle of a cylindrical fuel bottle, then lit the unit's single burner with a plastic cigarette lighter. He placed an ancient-looking steel pot over the flame, then filled the pot halfway with water from a plastic jug. At his side was a large burlap sack from which he scooped a few handfuls of uncooked rice; he sifted them carefully into the pot and then rubbed his hands together briskly to get the last few morsels into the heating water. He stared at the burner's flame briefly. Satisfied, he nodded contently and went back inside the building.

"Ah, finally, the call goes through!" Spider said. He grinned at Karlena and held the phone loosely away from his ear so she could hear.

Karlena set her camera aside and moved closer to him. As they stood overlooking the city, she surmised she was facing north. She heard the ringtone—a muffled buzzing sound—at the other end of the call. After what seemed like a dozen or so rings, a male voice answered. Karlena yanked the phone away from Spider. "Mitchell!" she shouted. "Finally...where are you?" There was an exasperatingly long period of silence that followed; she strained to hear a tinny, echoing version of her college friend's voice that sounded as if he were standing at the bottom of a well.

"I made it out of Manila, but I'm still stranded on the Mindanao mainland; the ferry is delayed."

Karlena stared out across the channel that separated Isabela from the city of Zamboanga on the southern tip of Mindanao. She guessed Zamboanga to be no further than a dozen miles from where she was standing.

"Well, I'm already here on Basilan; it's been quite a journey, but I made it." For the first time in over twenty-four hours she began to feel more secure. A smile came across her face as she heard Mitchell's familiar voice. She shifted her eyes to Spider, who nodded approvingly and appeared equally happy that the couple had connected.

"When will you get here?" she asked. Their connection began to fade as she waited for Mitchell's reply. Karlena pressed the phone closer and covered her other ear with her free hand as she strained to hear him.

After another long pause, Mitchell answered. "They tell me the next ferry will leave in two hours."

The connection quickly deteriorated, and Mitchell's voice was barely understandable. Karlena made out the garbled words "meet you there" before the hissing static grew in volume, and then the call abruptly went dead. She pulled the cell phone away slowly from her ear, looked down dejectedly at it, and then handed it back to Spider.

"Why would the call drop off so suddenly like that?" she asked him. Spider saw the bewilderment in her expression. He shrugged his shoulders. "Is your phone coverage really this bad?"

Spider laughed nervously as he shoved the phone back into his pocket. "You must understand, Miss Brandt, our technology has not been so good like you have in the U.S." He pulled a crumpled pack of cigarettes from another pocket then lit an unfiltered smoke effortlessly without taking his eyes away from her, as if he could have accomplished the habitual task in a darkened room. He motioned an arm to the West as he drew in a long, forceful, first drag, exhaled and said, "Besides, it's a big storm approaching. Sometime that hurts the phone calls."

Karlena turned to see a darkening wall of clouds creeping ominously over the ocean in their direction. If she were in Texas, Karlena thought, those type skies would have most likely triggered tornado sirens. The approaching weather front pushed a cool gust of wind against their faces. She felt a smattering of rain driblets on her arms.

"We should be inside now," Spider said. The wind had picked up dramatically as the storm bore down on them.

Karlena removed her backpack from the rear seat of the Jeep while Spider grabbed his rifle and an old-looking canvas bag from beneath the driver's seat. They both scampered onto the porch for cover as a steady rain began to fall.

Blister joined them from inside; in his hands he held two small, opened food cans. He gingerly removed the pot's lid and emptied both cans into it, then stirred the concoction with a makeshift spoon, which looked to Karlena like a sliver of wood torn from the cottage's siding.

The storm's force continued to build, causing a flapping, whistle-like noise through the dense array of palm trees that shrouded the cottage on three sides. There was a single clap of thunder, and then it was as if God had taken a giant saber and ripped open the angry clouds from above. The sky unloaded a violent deluge of water that outmatched anything Karlena had ever seen before, even the most powerful gales along the Texas Gulf Coast, as the sideways-driven rain pelted their bodies like wet needles. They exited the porch for the dry confines of the one room building.

Once inside, Karlena's first thought was, *Where's the bathroom?*—before realizing that, in addition to lousy cell phone coverage, indoor plumbing— or most any other Western convenience for that matter—was virtually non-existent on this primitive part of the planet.

The room measured roughly twenty by twenty feet square. The flooring and walls were constructed of similar wide-plank wood that reminded Karlena of the knotty pine inside her father's hunting cabin, only more weathered and faded to a blanched gray hue. There was a bent rattan rocker and dilapidated end table in one corner, a round card table without chairs centered in the room, and twin cots pressed up against one wall. The building's lone door had been removed from its hinges, allowing random splatters of rain to swirl in through the opening. On each of the four walls was an identical square-shaped window, about eighteen inches wide and placed exactly in the wall's center at eye level.

"I think time to eat now," Spider said to Blister. He had to nearly shout over the relentless roar of downpour against the structures tin roof. Blister inched his way back onto the drenched porch where raindrops splattered and sizzled against the rice pot. He wrapped a rag around its handle, walked back inside and placed the hot pot on a chunk of plywood that he'd laid on the floor. Karlena watched curiously as Blister reached for a long banana-tree leaf that he'd chopped while she was talking to Mitchell; he sliced it with a pocketknife into three equal sections and set them on the floor. He then slowly removed the pot's lid, taking pains to let the content's steam release without burning his hands and arms. A deliciously pungent aroma instantly swelled inside the tiny building.

"Eh, eh, eh!" Blister sounded off proudly as he began distributing the meal onto the glossy leaves. Spider immediately attacked his portion, plying the teeming mixture gingerly with his fingers in an effort to cool the food before shoveling it down. Both men ate ravenously while Karlena stood by silently.

She mimicked their squatting position and examined her food. The brown rice was laced with an assortment of peas, carrots and what she believed to be diced chicken. She pawed at the mixture inquisitively and glanced up at the two men who were too engrossed with eating to pay any attention to her staring.

She scooped a meager portion off her leaf, smelled it briefly and placed it into her mouth; it tasted divine. Whether it was relief at finally arriving at a spot where she felt safe, or the fact that she hadn't eaten in nearly a day's time—it didn't matter. She quietly joined in and devoured her ration.

The storm ended as abruptly as it had begun. After an hour of torrential rain, the clouds dissipated, and slivers of bright sunshine beat down upon the soaked earth. Humid moisture hung in the air like a heavy cloak as forest creatures emerged from their chosen methods of shelter and resumed their chirps, grunts and whistles of life.

Sated by the food, Karlena, Spider and Blister had all given into fatigue and crashed. The relentless pounding of rain on the building's roof had lulled them all into a long, deep midday slumber, Karlena and Spider each laying on the cots and Blister curled up on the cottage's floor with Spider's canvas bag tucked under his head for a pillow.

Karlena rolled to her side and saw that Spider had gotten up; she heard his footsteps clopping over the porch as he returned from outside. He stepped over Blister's sleeping body and extended a folded newspaper toward her.

"Greetings from America!" he said cheerily. "Blister found this yesterday and saved for you."

Karlena accepted the paper, opened it and saw that it was a three-day-old issue of the military daily, *Stars and Stripes*. She eagerly started paging through it. It had been weeks since she'd last read, heard or seen any news from the States. She found that defense related headlines comprised much of the paper's content, yet was pleasantly surprised to find articles of world and national interest. She sat on the edge of her cot and began reading the front page's lead story about the grisly salvage project at the World Trade Center site.

Karlena had just followed the article's "jump" to *page two* when she heard a sharp "click" sound. Looking up, she saw that Spider was focusing a tiny Instamatic camera on her. He snapped another shot.

"Not a big one like you have," he said as he tucked away the camera in a pants pocket. "But I practice to make photographs too."

Her initial reaction was a feeling of confusion at why this stranger would want the picture, especially with her appearing so grungy and worn out. Nonetheless, she smiled back at him and felt a tinge of affection at his clumsily worded attempt to establish the connection with her photography.

After she finished reading the article, Karlena refolded the paper and then walked out on to the porch. With the bad weather now cleared, she was able to look out over Isabela and across the wide channel that separated Basilan Island from the much larger metropolis of Zamboanga, located on the Mindanao mainland. She noted a large number of boats—some large commercial-looking vessels, others miniscule sampans—traveling in both directions between the two cities.

Spider brushed by her side and jogged a short distance to the center of an open area in front of the cottage. "Maybe we get a better signal now with storm gone," he said to her. "Mitchell can answer our call from the ferryboat." Karlena watched anxiously as he began dialing. The sun beat down on the wet, grassy earth causing the ground to emit a dank, swampy smell. She saw a layer of humid mist hovering around Spider's ankles as he pressed vigorously on the phone's buttons. But after several failed attempts to complete the call, he shook his head dejectedly. "Not so lucky."

Karlena returned to her spot on the cot and settled back into reading *Stars and Stripes*. She felt in desperate need of a hot, soapy shower and her bottom was still sore from the long ride over bumpy dirt roads. Nonetheless, her stomach was full, she felt reasonably rested, and she'd actually spoken—albeit briefly—with Mitchell. Spider and Blister had terrified her when they'd commandeered Duke's boat, but they'd kept their word and taken her to what seemed like a safe place, and Spider had earnestly made contact with Mitchell Castella. She remained faithful that he would appear soon.

The day lingered on as Karlena's hopes of seeing her friend started to vanish faster than they'd eaten Blister's savory pot of rice. After reading most of the newspaper, she passed time by alternately napping and walking outside to gaze at the landscape. During one of her naps, the two men disappeared silently into the woods and shot two wild chickens in addition to a fat squirrel-like critter. She woke up to the men's laughter as they emerged from the brush with dinner in hand.

Blister was busy dressing out the animals while Spider appeared to be tinkering with something under the jeep's hood. Karlena decided to kill more time by reading the rest of the paper, this time concentrating on every word, including the classified ads, which served no purpose other than to occupy her thoughts. But it didn't help. She was growing bored, worried and more anxious.

As the sun continued its graceful descent toward the horizon, Spider rose up suddenly from under the hood and shouted excitedly in his native tongue. Karlena followed Blister as he ran out from behind the cottage to join up with Spider, who shifted his position to the open area where he'd dialed the previous calls. He pointed toward Isabela City, laughed happily and said, "The ferry boat, there." Karlena estimated it to be only a few kilometers off shore; the sleek passenger vessel stood out against the other boats like a big, shiny pearl surrounded by dirty pebbles.

"I know the captain's number," Spider said as he started punching buttons on his phone. He switched the phone to speaker mode and waited for the call to go through; the connection was perfect this time with a loud, clear ring tone. When he heard the man's voice answer, Spider immediately spouted off a mixture of English, Chavacano and Spanish sounding sentences. "Mitchell Castella" were among the handful of words Karlena understood. "I ask him to check all people," Spider said to her.

Karlena heard the captain reading names under his breath as he went down the ferry's manifest. Spider nodded his head nervously and continued holding out the phone for all to hear. After a few seconds of silence, she heard the captain's raspy voice: "Castella, Meechel? Ah, no."

Spider turned slowly to face Karlena and repeated the bad news; "My friend Captain Robani say no Mitchell aboard. "He also tell me that this was the last ferry for today." The threesome stood motionless and watched as the large boat finished its approach to a mooring spot along Isabela's crowded wharf.

Blister quietly drifted back to behind the building were he'd built a small fire pit to roast the wild game. Karlena returned to her cot, sat down and pawed absent-mindedly through the paper.

With nothing else to do and nowhere to go, Karlena sprawled out on the cot and fought back tears as the daylight faded; the two men joined her inside. She heard some rustling as Blister held a canvas bag out in front of him while Spider rummaged through it.

He removed two swatches of rolled cloth, then dug his arm down deeper into the sack. "Ah..." he said softly as he pulled out a small, round device and held it up for his partner to see.

Spider shined a flashlight to better see the compass-looking instrument, reoriented his body, and then silently raised and lowered his extended arm like a policeman signaling traffic in a specific direction.

Karlena surmised that he was pointing toward the West and then remembered from her class in Middle East history the proper name for the compass: it was called a *Qibla*. She shifted her position on the cot and watched as Blister obediently spread the two prayer rugs in the line that Spider had pointed. The men removed their shoes, stood side by side at the eastern end of the rugs, then dropped to their knees in unison and began chanting evening prayers. After a few minutes of bowing and reciting, they rose up silently. Blister put away the rugs and compass.

"Tomorrow to be another day, Miss Brandt," Spider said. "Much better chance of Mitchell being on morning ferry, okay?"

Lacking anything thoughtful to say, Karlena answered with a simple reply of, "Okay." She didn't share Spider's optimism; she was exhausted, uncomfortable with her sweaty, grimy body, and increasingly peeved at her college friend for not being there when she'd landed on Basilan. She smelled their dinner roasting over the fire that Blister had built, but she had no appetite. She lay back and stared out a window at the thin sliver of a crescent moon as it rose above the treetops.

"Wake up, now!" Spider repeated for the third time. Karlena felt his hand shove her shoulder forcefully. "We go now."

She propped herself up on her elbows and tried to focus in the dim, pre-dawn light. "But what about Mitchell? We need to wait for him."

Spider didn't answer; instead, he barked an order to Blister who'd already risen from his sleeping spot on the cottage's plank floor and had headed outside to start the jeep.

Karlena watched as he pulled the vehicle out from a secluded nook behind the building; he'd left the vehicle's headlights off. Karlena turned to see Spider gather up his rifle, sling it across his shoulder, and then aim a flashlight at the canvas bag, from which he retrieved a full clip of bullets. The foreboding metallic "click" sent a chill through her tired body as he shoved the magazine into place.

Spider shined the light at her face. When he saw the fear in her eyes he moved the beam to one side. "Go now," was all he said as he motioned toward the door with the rifle's barrel. She heard the muted ring of a phone inside the jeep and watched as Blister reached inside a pants pocket to answer it—until now, she hadn't realized that he too possessed a phone.

She slipped on her hiking shoes without lacing them and grabbed her back-pack. As she scurried across the porch, she heard the unmistakable "thump, thump, thump" of a helicopter in the distance. She looked toward the approaching sound as the aircraft seemed to be bee-lining straight to their position. When she hesitated between the cottage and the jeep, Spider tapped her firmly on her buttocks with the barrel of his rifle.

"Get in, *now!*" he growled impatiently.

She tumbled into the back of the jeep while Spider hopped up front. Blister was talking rapidly on the cell phone in his native tongue; the only words Karlena understood were a panicky sounding string of "okays."

She sat sprawled haphazardly in the back seat as Blister jammed the gas pedal down. As they accelerated over the bumpy trail, the force knocked her to one side. Her neck and shoulder ached as she struggled to sit upright and steady herself. She saw Spider turn toward the thwapping noise of the incoming helicopter; it sounded as if it were only a kilometer or so away from their position.

Spider silently motioned toward the side of the trail. Blister obliged and steered the jeep a few meters off the path and under the protective canopy of the forest. Spider held up a hand, signaling all to be still as the sound of the flying machine grew deafening and the ground began to shake. They looked up in unison as the dark silhouette of a helicopter dashed overhead.

# CHAPTER 9

When McGirt settled his body into the cushy tan-colored Gulfstream's copilot seat he felt as if he were relaxing in his favorite easy chair rather than behind the controls of an aircraft currently hurtling at nearly six hundred miles per hour, or eighty-five percent of the speed of sound. He snapped the seat's five-point harness into place over his shoulders, lap and crotch, then looked forward at the glittering display of digital instruments and square-shaped black computer screens. He mouthed the words—thinking that no one would hear him—"man, this is the way to go."

Dr. Bud Lammers slid himself into the narrow gap that separated the two pilots seats and looked up at McGirt smiling and said, "See, I told you." McGirt rotated his head to the left, nodded and flashed a grinning thumbs-up.

"You're lucky to do this and get paid at the same time," McGirt said to the flight's captain, a dark-haired, late-thirties-looking bachelor named Rick Haley.

The pilot's tanned forearms made a striking contrast against his crisp, white shirt and gold-piped epaulets. Earlier in the flight, while seated back in the cabin, Bud had revealed to McGirt that Haley was a CIA legacy whose father, grandfather and uncle had all been "agency lifers," working in a variety of departments throughout the government's huge intelligence network. But Rick had been the only one of the clan to pursue flying. Despite the appearance of nepotism, he'd come up through the aviation food chain the hard way. Following an Army ROTC scholarship at Penn State, he'd served with valor as a combat helicopter pilot, flying an AH-1 Cobra during Desert Storm. He'd chosen to leave the service in the mid-90s, had initially bounced around between various rotary and fixed-wing instructing gigs; been furloughed from a commuter airline; been married briefly to a flight attendant then divorced, before finally landing a job at the CIA. Rick Haley freely admitted that his family connections were the only reason that he'd even gotten an interview for the job, but everyone around him knew that's where the favoritism had stopped. After five years of patiently sitting in the copilot position, he'd finally upgraded to the captain's chair.

Prompted by Lammers, Haley had bumped the flight's normal copilot, a retired Air Force fighter jock named Dowdy, who'd grumpily retreated from the cockpit and taken his place in the aircraft's passenger cabin. Captain Haley had flown the previous leg of their long journey and this would have been Dowdy's turn to fly and make the landing at Subic Bay Airport in the Philippines. But not today; LtCol James Dowdy's USAF (Retired) prior status meant nothing to Haley; this was *his* aircraft, *he* was the captain, and *he* would decide who was to sit in the copilot's seat.

The sleek, unmarked business jet had carried the four of them smoothly and swiftly from their last refueling stop at Naval Air Station Agana, Guam, over sixteen hundred miles of open ocean to the shores of the Philippine Island of Luzon. The area's usually portentous tropical weather had cooperated, yielding nothing more than soft, puffy white clouds that dotted their path below.

The trek had begun two days ago with Bud's arrival at McGirt's home base in Coronado, California. A delicious lasagna dinner prepared by Johnny Jack's wife had capped off the first leg of Bud Lammers's journey from D.C. to the Philippine Islands. The evening had passed too quickly for Bud, who'd not visited with McGirt's vivacious spouse in over a decade. Food, wine and a spirited debate over the insanely exorbitant price of Coronado real estate had made for an enjoyable evening of "catching up" by old friends.

Haley clicked a button on his control yoke that disengaged the aircraft's autopilot. He leaned forward and squinted through his darkly tinted sunglasses and started searching for the airport, now less than thirty miles away. He'd programmed the machine's flight computer to create an engines-at-idle descent profile from their cruising altitude of 48,000 feet. McGirt watched as the ship's two engine controls advanced magically from their full aft position to a place mid-range on the throttle quadrant, located just beneath the plane's instrument panel and between the two pilots' kneecaps. The ambient noise inside the Gulfstream transitioned from a whisper-like, graceful swooshing sound to a soft, throaty rumble as the jet's motors spooled up.

Haley pulled slight backpressure on the yoke and leveled off at exactly ten thousand feet. He pressed a switch located on the "W"-shaped control wheel and said into the microphone attached to his headset, "Roger, Subic Tower, X-ray Five-Niner cleared for low approach, Runway Two-Five."

McGirt instinctively looked for his own headset. After some fumbling, Bud came to his aid and placed the headset/mike combo onto McGirt's head and adjusted the volume. McGirt nodded an appreciative "thanks."

The young-sounding male controller in Subic Tower said slowly, and in near-flawless English, " Ah, sir, weend light and var-ee-ible on Roonway Two-Five." McGirt raised the volume level slightly in his headset and chuckled to himself at the man's enunciation: the melodic, singsong accent that he'd come to know during his two year tour at the U.S. Embassy in Manila.

Haley nosed the aircraft over and gingerly pulled back on a lever that deployed a set of wing-mounted flight spoilers; the aircraft entered a steep descent that caused McGirt's body to rise slightly and press up against his seat belt. He glanced out the copilot's window and took in the stunning view of the rugged, verdant Zambales Mountains that guarded Subic Bay on three sides. He then shifted his view to the left, over Haley's shoulder, and sighted the smog-drenched skyline of Manila. But the sky was brilliantly clear to the northwest, where Subic lay roughly twenty miles in the distance.

Haley closed the throttles to their idle position and yanked, this time more aggressively, on the speed-brake lever. "Yeh, that's more like it," he said as the aircraft began to drop from the sky like a cheap safe. The approach end of Subic's westerly runway seemed to be racing toward them, far below.

McGirt thought to himself, *There's no way in hell this guy's going to pull it off; he's too high and too fast.*

But the career rotor-head was wrong. Haley had coaxed the sleek jet into a stabilized glide path as if he were seducing a wary sparrow to eat from his hand. McGirt was in awe as the jet's flight instruments—basic to any flying machine—eased into conformity: airspeed bled off slowly, and descent rate settled at a manageable 2000 feet per minute.

"You've done this before, haven't you?" McGirt said over the intercom.

A sly, satisfied grin edged from one corner of Haley's mouth as he said, "Captain McGirt, we'll make a low pass over the runway, then head west, out over the bay, climb to four thousand feet and then reverse course to come back for a landing, in the opposite direction, on Runway Seven. "

McGirt groped for his mike switch, found it and replied, "Sounds good to me." He continued to be struck by the young aviator's graceful calmness at the controls of the multi-million-dollar government jet. McGirt easily recognized the aircraft's basic flight instruments: airspeed gauge; attitude indicator and altimeter. Despite his own limited time in fixed-wing aircraft, those three primary flight instruments, located from left-to-right in front of each pilot, were as common to all types of flying machines as two wheels and handle bars were to all bicycles. He saw the altimeter unwind rapidly through 5000 feet as they skimmed over the ragged, densely wooded terrain. Haley was flying strictly by the seat of his pants now—the way nearly every aviator who McGirt knew loved to do—unencumbered by regimented approach procedures dictated by air traffic controllers who issued course vectors and instructions to climb or descend while staring at blips on a radar screen, as if the ordeal were a video game.

Haley gently pushed forward on the jet's speed-brake lever, which re-stowed the drag-producing surfaces on the Gulfstream's slickly designed wings. McGirt saw that their airspeed had hovered around 250 knots until Haley inched up the throttles, causing the machine to lurch forward and, in what seemed a like a few seconds, accelerate back up to 300 knots.

As they closed in on the airfield, McGirt recognized the red and white array of lights on the runway's left side that indicated the jet was established perfectly on the proper three-degree descent angle, or glide path. Haley had placed the aircraft "in the groove" for a high-speed approach—albeit purposely much too fast to land, but rather—to make a fly-by; McGirt noted the altimeter unwinding below 1000 feet.

They were traveling over three times faster than the speed to which Johnny Jack had conditioned his reflexes while piloting the lumbering H-46 helicopter during the last twenty-five years. He began to feel uncomfortable at the sensation of traveling so fast while so close to the ground. Further to his left, he caught sight of a light-gray-painted helicopter parked idly on the airport's tarmac. McGirt reached down and squeezed the edge of his seat firmly, as if to brace himself as they raced, low level, over the pavement; the plane's altimeter was "wired" at a mere 50 feet above the ground; airspeed locked at 300 knots. McGirt's eyes darted from side to side as he struggled to see something familiar on what had once been the U. S. Navy's largest overseas facility—but it was too late. They'd passed the airport in a blur and were now heading quickly out over Subic Bay, bee-lining toward the South China Sea.

McGirt was able to spot the familiar recreation spot, Grande Island, just ahead. As he craned his head for a better view, he heard Haley's voice on the intercom. The young pilot laughed in a gamesome way and simply said, "Hold on." McGirt felt his head snap back and his butt sink deeper into the plush seat as Haley pulled the jet into a climbing, turning maneuver to the left. McGirt heard Dowdy holler something profane and Bud's joyful yelp as Haley continued the impromptu airshow, settling the aircraft into a tight, 90-degree-banked attitude. He rolled wings level and adjusted the engine throttles; the plane was established precisely at 4000 feet and a comparatively slow speed of 210 knots on a south, southwesterly heading. McGirt realized that a bead of cold sweat had formed above his eyebrows and upper lip.

Haley turned to him, removed his hands from the flight controls and said, "Okay, Captain, you've got it!"

McGirt's face blanched. He felt his arms and legs go weak, but he instinctively placed both hands on the control wheel and glanced down at the jet's instrument panel. He feared that he'd taken on the same bewildered, "what-do-I-do-now?" look that he'd seen flash across Tim Worley's face a few days ago when the gears of the helicopter they'd been flying started grinding themselves into metal chips off the coast of San Diego.

This aircraft felt rock solid, though, as he held its control wheel lightly between his fingertips. Confident that this unfamiliar aircraft was not going to suddenly flip upside down and plummet into the sea, he calmed his nerves and said coolly to Haley, "Okay, I guess you need a real pilot to land this thing, don't you?" McGirt's bravado was met with a roar of laughter from Haley and Bud Lammers, who'd returned to his previous inflight station, hunched over and wedged between the two pilots' seats.

McGirt's heart rate began to rise as he suddenly realized that he'd have to put up or shut up. Nonetheless, he refused to show the inner fear that started to overwhelm him; he had no idea what to do next. He hadn't flown any type of fixed wing aircraft, let alone a complex business jet, in over a dozen years. He could feel Bud's body next to him, heaving with stifled chortles.

"Lammers, you son of a bitch, you put Haley up to this, didn't you?" Lammers and Haley were still choking back their laughter as Bud wiped away the tears from his eyes and simply nodded his response.

With the prank conceived, well executed and complete, Rick Haley nonchalantly switched back on the Gulfstream's auto flight system.

McGirt relaxed his dampened hands from the wheel, and then took a long, relieved breath. The aircraft had traveled another ten miles on the southwesterly heading. An endless blue horizon filled the cockpit, as nothing but empty ocean lay between their position and the next landmass—the coast of Vietnam, nearly a thousand miles away.

"I've got it back, Captain," Haley said as he reached up and twisted a small dial that caused the aircraft to enter a gentle bank to the right. "Seriously, though, wanna take the landing, sir? I'll talk you through it."

McGirt looked over his left shoulder and saw his longtime pal still hovering over him. Bud had the joyful expression of a father waiting eagerly as his child was about to open a spectacular, unexpected present. McGirt shrugged his shoulders. "Sure, Rick, why the hell not? It's your tail if I screw up." A sly grin erupted on his face.

Haley shook his head. "Don't worry, that's not going to happen. I'll ride through the controls with you all the way." He then made a radio transmission to the Subic control tower and requested a long, straight-in approach to the airport's easterly runway, in the opposite direction from which he'd made the high-speed, low pass. Haley fidgeted with a set of buttons on an unfamiliar-looking radio. McGirt saw the bold-print symbol "ILS," which he recalled from his flight school days stood for "Instrument Landing System"—a device that he and his brother rotor-heads rarely had installed on their aircraft.

"Okay, sir, here's the drill. We're going to fly the ILS localizer and glide slope to Runway Zero Seven. All you need to do is to keep the flight director's two yellow bars, located on your attitude indicator, centered. Don't look up at the runway until I tell you, just focus on keeping the horizontal and vertical bars lined up like crosshairs on a rifle scope. I'll take care of the landing gear and flaps and set the power to keep you on airspeed."

McGirt guessed by Haley's tone that he'd done a fair amount of flight instructing during his comparatively short civilian career. The confidence and firmness of his voice gave McGirt a reassuring sense of security.

The dark green landscape of dense trees and jungle foliage grew larger in their sights as they continued to descend and close in on the airport. Haley switched off the auto flight system and turned the controls over to McGirt. "Sir, just keep those yellow vertical and horizontal bars centered the best you can. And stay light on the yoke—don't over control. There's minimal crosswind today, so you shouldn't need to use much, if any, rudder," Haley said.

McGirt nodded and recalled the similar advice he'd received from his first flight instructor when learning to fly the tiny T-34 nearly three decades ago in

Pensacola. He continued making finger-light corrections on the control yoke to keep the plane's course and descent path within a safe, stabilized limit. Haley acknowledged the Subic tower operator's radio transmission clearing them to land.

McGirt broke his scan away from the two yellow bars for a nanosecond to sneak a peek at their altitude; they'd already descended to just 1500 feet above the ground. At this rate, he thought to himself, they'd be on the ground in barely a minute or two. Things were happening much faster than he'd grown accustomed to while flying the slower, twin-rotor H-46 helicopter.

"Okay now, she's going to balloon up a little when I lower the gear and flaps," Haley said with a warning inflection.

McGirt felt the aircraft shudder slightly as the landing gear dropped into place, followed by a rising feeling in the seat of his pants, and just as Haley had predicted, the aircraft "ballooned" and drifted slightly above the programmed vertical path. McGirt followed the flight director's yellow horizontal bar and nudged the yoke forward.

"You're doing great, Captain. Go ahead and steal a look at the runway, but go right back to the flight director."

McGirt glanced quickly over the nose of the aircraft and saw that the jet was aligned nicely with Subic's long, paved easterly strip.

Haley's right hand reached up and rotated another button. "Setting our final approach speed. Stay on the flight director."

Out the corner of his left eye, McGirt saw the two engine throttles slide back in perfect unison as the aircraft began slowing to its proper landing speed. He removed his right hand from the yoke briefly to wipe his damp palm against the side of his trousers.

"Captain, place your left hand on the throttle levers, please. I'll leave the auto throttle system on until two hundred feet, and then talk you through the flair and tell you when to pull them back all the way back to idle."

"Got it," McGirt said. A bead of sweat dripped from his nose onto his sport shirt. He sensed his forearms and wrists tightening up, but remembered Haley's caution to not over control the nimble biz-jet. Its light, sporty feel reminded him of the first new car he'd bought as an ensign: a swift little British convertible.

"Okay, start to bring the runway into your scan but keep most of your attention on the yellow flight director bars," Haley said. His tone was firm, but not condescending.

McGirt felt Haley's light grip pressure on the controls as they passed through 200 feet. "Now shift your sights just to the runway and fight the temptation to pull up as the runway gets closer; hold the nose over." Despite Haley's warning, McGirt did in fact feel the urge to start pulling back on the yoke as the pavement seemed to rise up quicker than he had anticipated. Haley pushed gently forward on the yoke to keep the jet on the correct glide path.

"Flare, *flare now*," Haley said firmly.

McGirt obliged and increased backpressure slightly; the aircraft seemed to be suspended just above the runway surface.

"Throttles to idle," Haley commanded.

McGirt complied. The two jet engines unspooled with a faint whine—like the sound of a dying wind through cracked window glass.

"Keep the nose up, don't let it drop!" Haley said more forcefully this time.

McGirt was simply following instructions now, but the longer he was at the controls, the more comfortable he became. All the fundamentals he'd learned as a primary student flying a basic propeller-driven aircraft came rushing back to him. The motions felt like riding a bike: Once learned, it was a skill never forgotten.

*Thunk.* The aircraft skipped once, got a few inches airborne, and then finally settled smoothly back onto the 9000-foot asphalt runway. The Gulfstream's automatic braking system took hold and slowed the graceful machine to an easy taxi speed.

"Not bad for a rotor-head!" Haley said as he took back control and steered the jet clear of the runway and onto Subic's expansive parking area.

McGirt wiped his wet palms over the sides of his trousers again. He took a deep breath and looked outside; the place seemed to be deserted. On the far western edge of the concrete ramp he saw just one other aircraft—a nondescript cargo plane buttoned up and tied down securely; there was no activity around it. The former bustling Naval Air Station's sweeping layout appeared way too oversized for its present condition as a more sedate, less used civilian facility. But as Haley steered the jet toward Subic's modest passenger terminal, McGirt saw the familiar sight of a Navy CH-46 parked smartly in front of the building.

"There's our connection flight," he said, pointing emphatically. He heard Bud talking with Dowdy, and the rustling sounds of the two men gathering their personal effects. Haley sighted a small, dark-skinned Filipino, wearing shorts and a reflective orange vest over a white tee shirt. On the man's feet were a pair of faded pink shower shoes.

Haley silently followed the marshaller's signals and parked a short distance away from the H-46. Within seconds of the aircraft stopping, Bud had opened the ship's boarding door and lowered it carefully. Steps unfolded automatically from the door, which came to rest a few inches off the pavement.

McGirt heard the familiar *twap, twap twap* sound as the H-46's rotor blades began spinning up in preparation for the next leg of this journey with Bud. Haley finished reading the shutdown checklist and both men started to unstrap.

"Thanks for the landing," McGirt said as he extended his hand. "Hell of a lot different than the big eggbeater over there." He tilted his head toward the waiting helicopter.

"Hey Captain, you did great! Flying is flying, and you took to handling this thing like a duck takes to water."

McGirt laughed and just shook his head. He knew he would have probably smacked the pristine jet onto the runway had it not been for Haley's superb coaching.

McGirt and Lammers said their goodbyes to the two CIA pilots, who'd booked hotel rooms in the former infamous sailor town, Olongapo City. McGirt followed Bud down the steps and onto the ramp, where another airport employee had already taken their luggage and was scooting toward the whirling helicopter. McGirt took one last look around him: At first glance, the landscape hadn't really changed that much. Absent however, was the bevy of U.S. Navy ships crammed into Subic Bay's port facility and the gaggle of fixed wing and rotary aircraft departing and arriving at the Cubi Point Naval Air Station, now known as Subic International.

The hot, stifling air draped over him like a wet blanket slung over his shoulders in a sauna. McGirt took in a deep breath of that familiar air—what smelled like a mix of charcoal fires and rotting vegetables, with a trace of raw sewage. His wife had once described the experience as "an assault against one's olfactory senses that alternated between revulsion and addiction." McGirt knew that any sailor or Marine grunt who'd ever spent time in this place would probably never rid their memory of that unique aroma: It was the P.I.!

As he and Bud approached the waiting helicopter, McGirt recognized the aircraft's insignia, which tied it to its home squadron in Guam. He then read the name of the detachment's current at-sea address, stenciled in small black lettering on the side of the aircraft: *USS Lansing*, the same ship that he'd cut his teeth on as a rookie vertical replenishment pilot twenty-odd years ago. And that's when it hit him—the reality of why he and Lammers had travelled so far from their homes. Fatigue from the long flight began to set in as he boarded the helicopter. He poked his head into the cockpit, hoping he'd recognize either of the pilots; he didn't. He then absent-mindedly took his position on one of the bench-like canvas troop seats that planked the sidewalls of the noisy aircraft.

One of the aircrew handed him a life vest and a pair of sound-suppressing headphones, then motioned toward a jack box where he could plug in to listen on the aircraft's intercom system. McGirt donned the gear but declined to hook up the headset.

Bud had eagerly accepted the offer, adjusted his mike and had started chatting up the crew as the helicopter taxied across the ramp and into position for takeoff. McGirt wondered where Lammers, who was nearly eligible to receive Social Security payments, had found the energy. He tilted his head back against the aircraft sidewall and had begun to doze when he felt a firm slap on his shoulder. He looked up and saw the vaguely familiar face of one of the enlisted crew. He searched for the man's nametag, but it was obscured by the sailor's bulky survival vest that engulfed his body from shoulder-to-waist. They shook hands. McGirt strained to hear the man's voice, but the roar of engines and rotor blades drowned him out. The only words that McGirt caught were *San Diego* and... *a half hour to the boat.*

McGirt's thoughts flashed back to the last helicopter ride he'd taken, just a few days ago—his final check flight, which had ended with a dispiriting emergency landing on the beach and his fifteen minutes of fame on a San Diego television station. He peeked out a side window and watched the shoreline fade from view as the aircraft accelerated rapidly and shuffled over the water at a mere 100 feet above the surface. The rush of cool air through the cabin felt nice against his perspiring skin and dampened shirt.

Seated across from him, Bud Lammers had opened his weathered, brown leather brief case and appeared to be reviewing a dossier stamped "CLASSIFIED." As Lammers thumbed through the folder, McGirt recognized the photo of the red-haired girl from Texas; he'd studied both the classified and unclassified files during their long flight segments on board the Gulfstream. Bud caught a glance from one of the aircrew, smiled at the guy and discreetly closed the folder and placed it back inside the briefcase.

McGirt glanced down at the big-faced watch on his wrist: It read ten thirty-five in the evening, San Diego time. He knew that his wife would most likely be putting the final touches on her pre-bedtime routine of laying out clothes for a zero-dark-thirty wake up and the drive to the Naval hospital, where she'd spend the day reassembling the shattered limbs of Gulf War veterans and mending the aches and pains of other active and retired service members. Johnny Jack McGirt hoped that he would live long enough to make up for the scores of times when duty had called and he'd left Gina alone to deal with household emergencies, car repairs and the other tedious tasks that he normally handled without hesitation.

The ambient air temperature inside the cabin dipped from cool to cold as the rotorcraft continued climbing to an altitude of several thousand feet. He pawed around inside his suitcase and located a thin, non-insulated khaki jacket; he hadn't bothered to take anything heavier when he'd hurriedly packed for this trip to the tropics. He removed his life vest, donned the jacket and then cinched down the flotation gear back over it. The stiff, bench-style seat led to his backside hurting, and he found himself squirming constantly to stay comfortable. McGirt laughed to himself at how quickly he'd grown accustomed to the plush comforts of Haley's luxurious biz-jet. The H-46 helicopter was near and dear to his heart. Nonetheless, he'd concluded early in his career that the venerable rotary aircraft wasn't the most occupant-friendly machine for extended flights, especially when seated in its cabin.

The crew chief leaned toward him once more, this time at closer range, and shouted, "five minutes out, Captain." McGirt nodded a thank you and glanced across the aisle to Bud, who was writing diligently on the pages of a spiral-bound notebook.

The aircraft buffeted as the pilot guided it through a puffy cluster of clouds; the air grew hot and humid again as they descended to a lower altitude. McGirt sensed from the change in engine noise and pitch angle of the aircraft that the pilot was slowing the aircraft to approach speed for its landing on the ship. He unconsciously snugged up his seatbelt and looked down through a cabin window; the frothy, turquoise colored wake of USS *Lansing* came into view, and he could smell the unmistakable, oily fumes of the big vessel's stack gas.

As the pilot brought the helicopter into a hover above *Lansing's* rolling deck, McGirt felt a pang of anxiety at being so far away from home again. He questioned if he'd made the right decision to come on this strange mission.

# CHAPTER 10

The rolling, pitching flight deck of the *USS Lansing* felt oddly good and familiar underneath him.

McGirt hadn't been out to sea for years, after a desk-bound stint in the Pentagon (a.k.a. the Puzzle Palace) followed by a string of other assignments that included a couple of years in the U.S. Embassy in Manila, and then his tour as XO/CO of HCS-30 in San Diego. As much as his wife had cherished the uninterrupted, relatively peaceful time in their tiny Coronado home, he'd secretly longed for the action and drama of being part of the sea-going Navy. Or in swabbie vernacular, "Haze gray and underway."

After the cockpit crew had received the hand signal to 'cut' from the LSE (Landing Signal Enlisted personnel), they shut down fuel to the helicopter's twin turbo-shaft engines and applied the aircraft's rotor brake system, which brought the counter rotating hubs and rotor blades to a swift stop.

With the engines unspooled and rotors now static, the only sound present was the shrill droning of the aircraft's auxiliary power plant; a stark contrast to the deafening ride McGirt and Lammers had tolerated on the half hour transit from the Subic airport to *Lansing*.

McGirt strolled up to the cockpit, tapped both pilots' shoulders and thanked them for the ride, then followed Bud down the aircraft boarding steps. As they walked forward into the aircraft hangar bay, a youngish-looking ensign sprang toward them and introduced himself, while two even younger-looking enlisted sailors snatched their bags.

The ensign guided them through *Lansing's* hangar—a cramped garage-like compartment capable of housing the ship's two helicopters, but only after the aircraft's rotor blades had been folded tightly within the dimensions of its fuselage. McGirt maneuvered gingerly around a tow tractor and a stack of empty wooden pallets, then dodged a couple of large upright toolboxes. After stubbing his toe against a pile of tie-down chains, he was painfully reminded of how precious every square foot of space was on board a naval vessel. *Lansing's* second H-46 was parked on one side of the hangar, chained down securely, and appeared to be undergoing some sort of repairs. McGirt saw two sets of dungaree-clad legs visible on the aircraft's aft ramp; he surmised by their position that the mechanics were working on one of the aircraft's engines.

Both he and Lammers paused at the sound of one mechanic's hollering curse, followed by the clanking thud of a long, slender metal piece of piping and a ratchet tool that had fallen from the engine compartment. A head dipped down into view to retrieve the dropped items. Both sailors' faces reddened when they made eye contact with Lammers and McGirt.

"Carry on, men," McGirt said authoritatively.

Bud looked at him strangely, then tugged at the fabric of his shirt as a silent reminder that neither of them were in uniform; McGirt, now on terminal leave and awaiting his discharge papers, wore dark trousers and a pastel blue polo shirt; likewise, Bud was dressed casually in chinos and a long-sleeved white dress shirt, its cuffs rolled up to his elbows.

As they followed their escort out of the hangar and into a narrow passageway, Bud nudged him and said in a whisper, "You are what you do, until you don't, then you aren't."

McGirt stopped and stared at his friend for a few seconds until Bud's words finally set in: He, Captain Johnny Jack McGirt, had absolutely no charge over anyone but himself while on this vessel. When he'd declared the phrase, "I stand relieved," to HSC-30's new skipper, Frank Taswell, during their hastened change of command, he'd relinquished his final grasp of authority over his subordinates. His concurrent assignment to this "special project" had transformed him, from the vaulted position of a commanding officer, to the seemingly unglamorous, mundane role of a civil servant. He shrugged his shoulders and replied, "You're right, Bud. Guess I'll have to get used to that."

They filed forward and up through *Lansing's* labyrinth of corridors and snug spaces, en route to the commanding officer's stateroom. The dank smell of fresh paint, soap and urinal cakes greeted them as they passed by a head. McGirt noted a placard that read, "MEN," on the compartment's steel door. Old notions seemed to die a slow death as he thought to himself, *Who the hell else would be on this ship?*

Just then, a short, perky African-American female sailor glided past him from behind and shouted, "By your leave, sir!" The faint, flowery scent of the enlisted girl's perfume provided a stark contrast to the whiff of the male bathroom facilities and reconfirmed that this was no longer the "rocks and shoals"-style Navy that he'd joined long ago.

The ensign, whose name McGirt had already forgotten, looked back over his shoulder and said, "Skipper's waiting for you in her stateroom, sir."

McGirt turned to Bud with raised eyebrows and silently mouthed the question, *her?*

Bud frowned apologetically. "Forgot that when I briefed you. Just let me do most of the talking, okay?"

McGirt rolled his eyes and raised up his hands, as if surrendering. He thought to himself, *Why not? What other surprises do you have for me Mr. PhD-CIA- smart guy?*

Their extended trek required steps over the knee-knocking bottoms of hatch-like doors and ascents up a series of steep, narrow steps that more closely resembled ladders rather than stairways. Finally, they'd reached their destination: the stateroom/private office of the ship's commanding officer.

McGirt extended his hand to thank their escort while at the same time scanning the junior officer's nametag. "Much obliged, Ensign... *Bul-in-ski.*"

"My pleasure, gentlemen," the youngster replied. "She's expecting you, sir. I recommend that you go ahead and knock."

McGirt heard Bud's wheezy, heavy breathing from behind as the sexagenarian struggled to catch up. Lammers shot him a peeved glance, stepped in front and then rapped twice on the gray, windowless, steel door.

A firm, feminine voice called out, "It's open. Please enter."

Once again, Bud took the lead and filed ahead to introduce himself to Captain Katherine Marie Torres, Commanding Officer, USS *Lansing*.

McGirt followed suit and reached out to shake hands; the woman's tight, no nonsense grip surprised him. He'd encountered many female officers—including a few squadron commanders—Torres, however seemed to immediately define herself as someone unique. She stood eye-to-eye with him at nearly six feet tall and had a trim, yet curvy, athletic build. Her satiny, raven hair was perfectly coiffed and cut just above the collar of her short-sleeved, khaki uniform shirt. McGirt found her attractive, but not particularly pretty.

"Please have a seat," she said while gesturing to a long dark-leather sofa and two pastel-colored easy chairs.

Torres joined McGirt on the sofa, while Bud claimed one of the chairs. McGirt flashed back to over twenty years ago, when he'd paid a couple of visits to another captain's stateroom on board the USS *San Angelo*, while he was a new lieutenant, under the tutelage of the air detachment's officer-in-charge, Lieutenant Commander Bud Lammers. As he scanned Torres's living space, he was struck by the juxtaposition of its spotless, antiseptic-like layout against that of *San Angelo's* skipper, Walter "Big Lug" Lugansky. Absent were Lugansky's overflowing roll-top desk, decrepit coffee maker and the quiet hum of Big Lug's small, concealed refrigerator that housed his favorite "beverages." Absent too was the instant warmness he'd felt in Lugansky's presence.

"So I see from yesterday's message traffic that the two of you will be hitching a ride south, down to Basilan Island," Torres said. She turned to McGirt for a response; he followed Lammers's advice and let Bud speak first.

"That's right, captain. We sure appreciate the ride." Bud leaned back in his chair and continued. "It's been a long haul from San—"

Torres cut him off. "Tell me more about your mission." She'd put on a set of thin reading glasses and started paging through a folder stamped boldly with the word "SECRET."

Bud sat upright and placed both palms on his knees. "Well, Skipper, not sure what you've been briefed on, but our mission is to make behind-the scenes inroads to track down a large sum of ransom money, and to gain some intel about a young woman who the Agency suspects is being held captive by a Filipino sect of al Queda; a group of bad guys known as Abu Sayyaf."

Torres peered over the top of her glasses and said, "So what makes this little debutante so important?" She pointed to the folder in her lap. "I see that we've already lost a handful of special forces chasing down other hostages. What gives with her?"

McGirt saw that Bud's jaw muscles had begun to twitch nervously; he'd seen this occur before and sensed that his former shipmate, being long-removed from active duty, had been set back by Torres's aggressiveness and her apparent need to control the conversation. McGirt shrugged off Bud's advice and prepared to speak up. "Skipper," he said, "as you might presume, there's a strong political link here. The girl's father is connected to congressman Clayton Gantry, chairman of the House Appropriations Committee. The usual procedures employed during hostage negotiations have failed miserably up to this point, and our sources believe that the girl's father, a Mr. Otto Brandt, is pursuing his own avenue to buy her freedom. As you're well aware, the United States highly discourages private citizens paying ransom to terrorists. Bud and I plan to intervene and short-circuit a release of that nature."

Captain Torres removed her glasses and placed the folder of messages on a glass-top coffee table in front of her. She rubbed her chin reflectively. McGirt sat close enough to note the nails on her long fingers were short, yet perfectly manicured, and, as per Navy regulations, painted with a clear, neutral color. He also caught sight of a faded scar that ran jaggedly along her left forearm, from elbow to wrist. The pinky and ring fingers on her left hand appeared partial clenched and rigid.

She leaned in and said, "Captain McGirt, Mr. Lammers, my crew has spent the last seven months parading around WestPac, supporting every Tom, Dick and Harry mission that Washington can dream up: everything from what we've been trained to do—servicing the fleet by conventional and vertical replenishment ops—to typhoon disaster relief and transporting Navy SEALs to islands that my navigator could barely locate on a chart. My men and women miss their families and want to go home. We were slated to out-chop back to San Diego last week when we got word of your pending arrival. Now, we've been directed to remain in the South China Sea until further notice." She took a deep breath and tucked her glasses into a breast pocket. "I've requested some replenishment operations with other vessels transiting the area, just to keep these kids busy and waylay their homesickness. Nonetheless, as you probably remember, word travels very fast on a ship and everyone is aware that right now, you two are the only obstacle between us and the sight of Southern California peeking over the horizon."

McGirt simply nodded and looked over to Bud, who said, "Captain Torres, it's been quite a while since I've been deployed at sea, but I remember the feelings like it was yesterday—the long, demanding hours, not to mention the time away from loved ones. I speak for Johnny Jack and myself when I tell you how truly grateful we are for *Lansing's* support."

Torres sat motionless and looked both men squarely in the eye for several seconds. She stood up abruptly and said, "I'll do what I can to support your mission, gentlemen." She then glanced down at her watch. "XO should join us any minute now; he'll show you to your stateroom. Please excuse the cramped accommodations, but you'll be sharing a space. Unfortunately, we've had to hot-rack a couple of my junior officers in order to make room for you."

McGirt and Lammers followed Captain Torres as she guided them toward the door in anticipation of the ship's executive officer. As they passed the moments reviewing *Lansing's* itinerary, Bud noticed a small, neatly arranged collage of photographs pinned to a corkboard on the bulkhead. Pictured were snapshots of two young children—a boy and a girl—in different stages of play and athletics. A crayon-written note, adorned with pink hearts and a primitively drawn gray ship, dangled from the display's edge. Located in the center of the collage was a larger, more formal group portrait of a uniformed Katherine Torres, the two kids, and another woman who appeared close to Torres's age.

Bud motioned to the photos. "Family?"

For the first time since they'd arrived in her office, Torres's iciness seemed to thaw a bit. She stared at the photos, smiled and said softly, "Yes...I guess you could say that." Her eyes glanced between the two men, and then lowered slightly to the carpeted floor; her smile faded as quickly as it had appeared.

McGirt looked at Bud for a reaction and saw an impish grin on his face. He was sure that he and his old pal were thinking the same thought: *Don't ask, don't tell.*

"Gentlemen, welcome to your home away from home," said *Lansing's* executive officer, Commander Bill Draper as he pushed open the stateroom's door. The berthing space seemed about the same as the one they'd shared years ago—musty and claustrophobic. Smaller than most walk-in closets, the compartment necessitated the three men to stand shoulder to shoulder once they'd all wormed their way inside. "The gym is open 24/7, pool and room service shuts down at 2200 hours." Draper turned to see McGirt's and Bud's reaction; both men had an unfazed look on their face.

Two racks (bunkbeds) were stacked up against one bulkhead; a stainless steel, round sink sat in a corner next to the doorway; for storage, there was a thin array of metal lockers and drawers positioned against the opposite bulkhead, less than four feet from the racks. Bud hadn't spent a single night on board a ship since his final days in the Navy, when he'd been a detachment officer-in-charge. McGirt, though he'd logged several years' time at sea following the tour when he'd roomed with Bud, had not set foot in what was known as the "J.O. jungle" since he himself had been a junior officer.

"I pity those poor bastards having to hot-rack in a space like this," McGirt said, referring to the custom of sailors rotating use of the same bed after standing duty at alternating time periods.

Bud pounced firmly on the lower rack. "I'll take this one; don't think my back can handle maneuvering up and down to the top." He looked up sheepishly and asked, "Your knees okay with that, Johnny?"

"Yeah, that's fine," McGirt said. He spun around one of the compartment's two unpadded, steel chairs and sat. Draper did the same while Bud sprawled across the lower rack—half on, half off—with one foot resting on the tiled deck.

"I guess Captain Torres already apologized for having to double-up you guys. We're staffed full and had to hot rack—"

"Hey, no worries," Bud interjected. "Just grateful for the ride." He undid the top three buttons of his shirt in an effort to cool down. The tiny space had one round-shaped air vent protruding from its low ceiling. Despite its powerful gush of damp, semi-cool air, Lammers struggled to get comfortable.

"I know, I know," Draper said to him empathetically as he pulled a crumpled white handkerchief from a pocket and dabbed the beads of perspiration from his forehead and upper lip. "After seven months, you'd think that I'd get used to this. The ship's chief engineer does his best, but given this ship's age and, well…" His voice trailed off as if he'd given up adapting to the tropics and its steamy climate.

McGirt sat quietly while the two other men commiserated about the venerable ship, built before most of its crew had been born. He felt sorry for Bud, who'd battled carrying extra body weight ever since kicking a life-long smoking habit.

Draper took a seat next to McGirt. He scanned his watch hurriedly as if he had an imminent meeting, then swiped his forehead again. "Fellas, Skipper and I were wondering something: Why didn't the government fly you someplace closer to Basilan, say into Davao or Zamboanga? I understand not being able to jet you into Basilan's airport; we downloaded a satellite image and the island's only strip looks to be no more than a short, scraggy collection of weeds and busted-up pavement. But sticking you on board us for a couple of days? What the heck?"

Bud sat up and moved his head more directly under the air vent. "Our orders call for us to arrive under the guise of the disaster relief *Lansing* has been tasked with providing after the last tropical storm that hit the P.I.'s southern islands.

Our story is that we're part of a civilian group going in to build freshwater wells and get food and medicine to Basilan's inhabitants."

"Thanks. Our ops plan didn't get into all those details," Draper said. "One of our choppers is scheduled to drop you at an A.F.P. base where a group of U.S. Army Special Forces is stationed." Draper smirked and shook his head derisively. "Good 'ol Uncle Sam…always the first to help out those in need. Guess that's why everyone around the globe likes us so much."

"Let's hope that the Armed Forces of the Philippines genuinely share your sentiment," McGirt added. He knew from his political dealings as an attaché in Manila that the state of the Philippines' government and its armed forces had been volatile ever since Ferdinand Marcos had been ousted from power in 1986. Likewise, after U.S. forces had withdrawn totally from its former colony in the mid '90s, the two countries had carried on a love-hate relationship fraught with mistrusts, resentments and old dependencies.

"Our helo crew inserted groups of Navy SEALs and Army Rangers into the big island of Mindanao last month," Draper said. "Intelligence folks tell us that radical extremists have been establishing a foothold with other sympathetic Muslims in the area. Sounds like Basilan might be turning into a snake pit of bad guys as well."

"XO, this mess isn't going away anytime soon," Bud said rhetorically. "Public opinion appears to be focused on what's happening in the Middle East while this caldron keeps slowly simmering to a boiling point."

McGirt stood up and stretched his arms overhead. As he did, the wedding ring on his left hand struck an overhead pipe with a "clink." He laughed to himself at the crude accommodations that he and Bud had been assigned. "XO, not to put you on the spot, but what's the general mood about the ship taking us down there? No disrespect intended to Captain Torres, but she didn't seem too pleased to have us aboard." McGirt had a hunch that there might be more to the fact than, as Torres had said, *Lansing's* crew was burned out and just wanted to go home.

"Well, sir, you read her correctly," Draper began. "Since 9/11, we've been on a whirlwind of training work-ups and long at-sea periods. I can't say that I agree with all the actions that we've been involved with over here. Some of it seems downright mickey-mouse, if you ask for my off-the-record opinion." He paused and bit down lightly on his lower lip. "Captain Torres has had her hands damn full. I've done what I could to ease the load. Nonetheless, she keeps pretty much to herself." A cold-stone seriousness emerged on Draper's facial expression. "But from my experience as her executive officer, I can say unequivocally that there is no finer officer afloat, man or woman. I've known Katherine Torres since my plebe year at the Naval Academy, when she was an upperclassman in my company. She may not be the most charming person, but she'll always get the job done—and get it done right the first time."

McGirt saw the emotions well up in Draper's eyes as he spoke. There was an uncomfortable silence in the compartment as Draper rose from his chair. He impulsively wiped his forehead again, hiked up his trousers and cracked open the door a few inches.

"Wardroom is one deck directly below; chow's served at 1730." Draper opened the door fully and continued, "Scuttlebutt has it that, in another life, you were both H-46 drivers. You and the rest of our rotor-heads should have plenty to jaw about over dinner. How that thing manages to fly, I'll never understand. What do they say: 'ten thousand moving parts flying in close formation?'"

McGirt and Bud laughed loudly at hearing the old adage. They welcomed the XO's light-heartedness after enduring his take on *Lansing's* arduous deployment and the skipper's aloofness. As the door closed behind him, they heard Draper break out into a comical mimicking of a helicopter: "Thwop, thwop, thwop, thwop!" he chanted while strolling away down the corridor.

With Draper gone, McGirt and Bud began unpacking their bags and settling in for the several-hundred-mile, two-day journey paralleling the Philippine archipelago's western flank. McGirt had packed spartanly, filling his shoulder-slung leather bag with bare essentials. He filled his side of the compartment's locker space in a few seconds. He looked on in amazement as Lammers labored to do the same.

"Jesus Christ, Bud, where do you think we're going, on an around-the-world cruise? McGirt stood baffled as Bud plied through layers of garments stuffed into his big, hard-sided suitcase; he methodically hung up a variety of shirts and slacks. When he reached a folded blue blazer, he took extra care to press out wrinkles.

"Can't come unprepared for the unexpected," Bud retorted. "This will be my final trip overseas before retirement. You never know what type of event we may need to attend."

McGirt stared down at the measly array of slacks and golf shirts he'd brought. "Like what, a dinner dance or something?" He shrugged his shoulders at the quirkiness his former shipmate had developed since losing his wife, Jill, to breast cancer three years ago. He decided to back off with his razzing. "Well, guess life in D.C. has its own ways," he said. "Ever get tired of sitting at your desk all day?"

Bud sat back down on his rack. "Not really. Between dodging bullets flying a Huey in 'Nam and then our fiasco with Rayburn and the New People's Army in Luzon, I was ready for a change."

McGirt rarely heard his friend bring up either of those events from twenty years past. He'd gotten his own naval aviator wings just months before the Vietnam War concluded and had, luckily, avoided serving in the "conflict." But he'd been at then Lieutenant Commander Charles "Bud" Lammers's side during their deployment to the Western Pacific that had led to Bud being relieved for cause as the detachment's officer-in-charge. The official record was more than any officer's career could have survived: two aircraft crashes; an entanglement with a criminal, insubordinate officer; and the hushed political event that had put a huge strain on relations between the U.S. and Philippine governments. McGirt was one of the few who actually knew the truth behind Bud's fall from grace and subsequent tagging as the scapegoat to cover up a terrorist event. The tragedy had been buried like a dead dog at the Pentagon, White House and CIA headquarters.

The passage of time hadn't erased McGirt's anxiety from his tour as one of Bud's aircraft commanders on board the USS *San Angelo*. During a long, tedious night of vertical replenishment operations. McGirt had allowed his shaky copilot to settle their CH-46 helicopter into an insidious descent while flying low-level on a black, stormy night in the South China Sea. Under other circumstances, his heroic recovery and miraculous shipboard landing might have earned him an air medal. Instead, it seemed to be the impetus that had pushed Bud Lammers's career into an abyss.

Contrary to Bud's decline, McGirt's naval career had ascended like a Fourth of July rocket, culminating with his assignment as the commanding officer of his original unit, Helicopter Combat Support Squadron Thirty (HSC-30). Among McGirt's other achievements was the earning of a master's degree in Asian Studies and a two-year stint as naval attaché to the U.S. ambassador to the Philippines in Manila. When he'd taken Bud's phone call and accepted this special assignment, he'd, in effect, thumbed his nose at his boss, Admiral Truckee, and a long line of other brass who'd placed him squarely on an accelerated track to flag rank. But, as Bud knew, McGirt had never really been a conformist. Something had changed inside of him after his scary ordeal along San Diego's Silver Strand Beach and the fifteen minutes of fame that had followed. He'd had enough of the rat race of service life, and despite the golden specter of future career advancement, in his heart, he knew that it was over. Bud's call had come at the perfect time. McGirt was ready for a new adventure.

Bud finished unpacking, and then plopped back down on the lower rack. McGirt crawled gingerly up a set of rungs that led to his upper rack. He was sandwiched less than two feet below the compartment's overhead (ceiling) of clustered, dusty pipes, wire bundles and ventilation ductwork. The hard-mounted fluorescent light fixture buzzed obnoxiously and cast an inhospitable glare across their surroundings.

*Lansing* began to rumble as the ship's officer of the deck rang up the engine room to fire all boilers and set maximum speed. The sea was relatively calm, which allowed the big, lumbering cargo vessel to crest the waves in a powerful, gently rocking way.

"Cozy, isn't it?" Bud said. McGirt heard his friend's unmistakable giggle, most likely triggered by the bizarre circumstances that had reunited them at sea: one man nearly eligible for social security, the other a retiring senior naval officer "on loan" to the Central Intelligence Agency.

McGirt glanced at his watch: evening meal was still a couple of hours away. He felt the jet-lag-induced fatigue begin to shroud his body like a snug, down comforter. His eyelids grew heavy, and his muscles loosened as he gave way to slumber.

"Yeah…cozy," he mumbled lazily.

The next two days on *Lansing* rekindled some memories for McGirt and Lammers. Bud hadn't been out to sea on a Navy vessel since his abrupt termination as the officer-in-charge of a West Pac helicopter detachment twenty years ago. After the extended "land-locked" period at his desk in Washington, D.C., he welcomed the opportunity to spend time riding the waves.

In contrast, McGirt had endured six long deployments during his career: four to the Western Pacific, plus one each to the Atlantic and Mediterranean.

His last sea assignment had been as the Air Officer on one of the Navy's massive amphibious assault ships, where he'd overseen flight operations for an entire Marine air group. Next to commanding his own Navy helicopter squadron, the assignment as "air boss" had been the most demanding and rewarding tour of his career.

During their transit to Basilan, there wasn't much for the two retired pilots to do other than, what McGirt called, the *big four*: breakfast, lunch, dinner and the evening movie. Nonetheless, he and Lammers used the idle time to get acquainted with the pilots who'd been scheduled to fly them ashore. McGirt vaguely remembered one of them from when the guy had gone through H-46 training in San Diego. When someone else queried about the details of his legendary emergency landing aboard *San Angelo*, McGirt scuffed it off as ancient history. Thankfully, the topic of Thomas Rayburn's crash never came up.

Bud Lammers had a fitful night before their early morning launch to Basilan. On the return from his third trip to the head, he'd stubbed his toe on a chair in their darkened stateroom. He cursed under his breath and did his best to navigate inside the pitch black compartment without making any further disturbance.

"What…what's going on, Bud?" McGirt said sleepily. He switched on the tiny fluorescent reading lamp above his rack.

"Ah, you know, the usual routine," Bud bemoaned. "Wake up and pee, wake up and pee. Another one of the perks of getting old." Lammers slid back into the lower rack and tried to get comfortable on the stiff mattress. "Back in the old days," he lamented, "I'd just smoke a cigarette and fall back to sleep. Can't do that anymore."

McGirt turned off the light; their stateroom returned to its abyss-like darkness. "Well, look at it this way, you'll probably live longer. And besides, you can't smoke inside navy ships now. You have to go outdoors, just like with government buildings."

"I know, but the down side is I've gained thirty pounds since giving it up. How come all the fun things are bad for us, anyway? What's up with that?"

McGirt had known Bud Lammers for over twenty years; he sensed that there was something else gnawing at his friend besides being frustrated about quitting smoking and trying to lose weight. He wasn't in the mood to spend another hour of the night chitchatting over drivel. "You nervous about tomorrow?" he asked.

"Maybe a little. This really isn't much different than the other negotiations I've been involved with. A few surprises along the way, but…" Lammers paused as he if he were searching for the right words.

"But this one's in the Philippines," McGirt interjected. "Lots of old demons for the both of us over here, aren't there?"

"Well, yeah, but that's all water under the bridge, or as Rick Haley likes to say, 'runway behind you.'"

"Call it what you want, Bud, but that was some scary shit we went through last time you and I cruised in Westpac. That kind of stuff doesn't just go away."

They felt the ship begin to take on some gentle rolls. McGirt heard Lammers's slow, heavy breathing above the *whooshing* din of their stateroom's ventilation system. He waited a few seconds before asking, "You finally dozing off?"

"Not a chance," Bud answered as he shifted in his rack. "McGirt, can I ask you something personal?"

"Sure. Go ahead."

"You ever think about dying?"

McGirt paused for a long time before saying, "Only once—and I think you know when that was."

"Had to be after you and Uker pancaked on the water that night, right?"

"No, not then. I was a little scared at first when we hit the water, but once I realized that the rotors were still turning and we had enough gas to get back to the ship, I settled down."

"Hmm, I would have thought that was the time. Okay, then when was it?"

McGirt rolled to one side and propped himself up on an elbow. As he did, the top of his head brushed against the stateroom's low-hanging pipes. "After Rayburn had crashed and then left his crew alone to die, remember how we chased those two commie bastards up the hill, after they'd taken Lincoln hostage?"

"Sure, how could I forget that?"

"Well, I remember feeling like John Wayne running way ahead of you after those guys. When I'd finally caught up to them and found myself unarmed and looking down the wrong end of a rifle—that was when. I thought for sure that I was going to die. It was just like you hear people say, my whole life flashed before me: my house in Michigan, my mom and sister and how I never got a chance to say goodbye to my dad before he killed himself. I've never felt that sensation again—not ever."

"Wow, it still bothers you, even after all these years?" Lammers asked.

"Yeah, sometimes. But then I'm able to dig myself out of the rut and rationalize that there must have been a good reason that everything unfolded the way it did."

"Like what?"

McGirt glanced at the illuminated dial of his watch; it was still a few hours before he'd need to get up for their flight to Basilan. He laid his head back down on the rack's musty pillow. "Well, in simple terms, me bolting up the hill way ahead of you ended up serving as a distraction. Those two dirt bags were focused on me and that allowed you time to catch up and get a good shot at them. Sort of like a divine intervention, you know?"

Lammers laughed. "Or maybe just blind luck."

McGirt felt himself drifting off, but he bolstered himself to stay awake. "What about you—you know, ever think about dying?"

"A couple of times when my chopper had taken fire in Vietnam. Except after being over there for a while, I think I just latched onto the idea that I was already dead. That way, I figured that it wouldn't be a big shock if I bought it, I wouldn't be so surprised."

McGirt laughed. "I guess that's one way to look at it."

"But I'll tell you what's worse is watching somebody else die. You ever had to witness that?"

"No, I never have. They'd already hauled my dad's body away when I got home from school. Lucky that I didn't have to witness something like that."

Bud sat up and set his feet on the stateroom's hard tile floor. "I saw many men die during the war. Whenever we'd extracted the wounded from a battlefield I tried not to look back at them in the cabin. It wasn't the blood and gore that bothered me; it was the look in their eyes. Not so much a look of fear or pain, but an expression of bewilderment as if they were wondering, *Why is this happening to me?* I thought I'd seen the last of that until I watched my wife slowly fade away. The doctors had her pumped up pretty good with drugs, and they convinced me that she wasn't feeling much pain. But when she'd open her eyes, sometimes she had the same baffled look on her face as those young soldiers and Marines. She couldn't speak anymore at that point, but I swear I could tell what she was thinking, you know: *Why me?*

McGirt and Gina had purposely avoided bringing up Jill's recent passing during Bud's night with them in Coronado. They both knew how hard her death had been on him. "I'm sorry, Bud. I truly am."

"Thanks, McGirt. You guys have been great through it all. And so have the kids. But you know what really smacks me as unfair? After all the things I did, hanging my ass out on the line—in the Navy and with the CIA. After all of that, she'd be the one who dies first."

"I know, man," McGirt offered. "It just ain't fair."

"Yeah, and I'll tell you what else ain't fair: having to take a leak so many times during the night." He stood up and groped his way toward the door. "Sorry to keep waking you up. You have my permission to go back to sleep now."

"Gee, thanks," McGirt said with a chuckle. "That's mighty big of you."

# CHAPTER 11

Eight seconds—that's the length of time Ahmad Jalil had calculated it would take for his body to free fall fifty-five stories. He'd had to get online to dig up the formula—the "splat equation" as his physics professor at the University of the Philippines had so gruesomely coined the algebraic computation. Considering the drag coefficient applicable to his lean, five-foot-seven-inch frame, he would accelerate to slightly over one hundred miles per hour during the eight-second plunge before impacting the sidewalk that paralleled Manila's busy Ayala Avenue. Ahmad figured that his death would be quick and painless, but he couldn't prevent his sleep-deprived, unsound mind from conjuring up the same metaphorical image over and over—the visual replay of a huge bag of tomatoes being tossed from the top of a skyscraper. *Splat!*

He maintained a trance-like focus on the horizon and the blazing orange sun that had just started to dip below the ragged peak of Mt. Mariveles on the Bataan peninsula, some thirty miles across Manila Bay. Gaining access to the rooftop of one of the city's tallest buildings had been easier than he had expected. His security badge had allowed him into the building and its elevators; a stealthy reconnaissance run the day before had revealed a faulty door lock into a top-floor utility closet. The space included an ample-sized window for access to the outside. From that point his trek to the rooftop had been, as the professor would have said, "elementary."

He'd used a mop handle from the closet to train the lone westward-facing camera away from his intended dive point. Ahmad had correctly guessed that the bored watchman would most likely be eating dinner and fixated on a television show rather than scanning the myriad of flickering screens that monitored the building's integrity.

He drifted slowly to the roof's edge while maintaining his sight on the furthest point away, the mountains of Bataan. The only sounds were that of his feet crunching against the roof's pebble coated surface and the muted din of cars, buses and taxicabs as the Makati district's business people made their way home. Ahmad's peripheral vision signaled that he'd nearly reached the roof's edge when he came to a sudden halt. He'd stubbed the toe of his glossy Armani loafer on the knee-high guard wall that encompassed the roof's perimeter. He paused and glanced down at the scuffed shoe, one of the many pairs that lined his wardrobe closet. With his concentration broken, he felt his heart begin to pound; he began to pant uncontrollably. It would take only two more strides: one to step up onto the guard wall and then one more to the pavement, eight hundred feet below.

A breeze swept across the rooftop. He'd worked up a sweat maneuvering through the narrow window and the cool air felt good. He cinched up the necktie that he'd loosened and redid the top two buttons of his suit coat. He hadn't worn a Western style suit in years, and it felt stiflingly uncomfortable compared to a barong Tagalog—the sheer Filipino dress shirt worn sans tie or jacket. But Ahmad figured that today he would go down, literally, in grand style; he'd chosen the most pricey, classiest-looking suit from his closet. His heart now raced as he gathered the strength and nerve to execute the abrupt act of finality. His surroundings grew eerily quiet as the surface traffic thinned out and the breeze fluctuated between calm and a gentle bluster.

The major events of his entire life flashed through his brain, in the way he'd always heard was the case just before a person dies. In a nanosecond he thought of the most recent chapter of his thirty-eight years. It had all gone so wrong in a short manner of months: an affair that had ended his marriage; failed investments in the high-tech industry; then a foolhardy drive in the fast lane of drugs, hookers and gambling. His tragic unraveling seemed to have gained momentum like a granite boulder hurtling down a steep incline.

He took a deep breath and was beginning the first step when his cell phone rang. It rang seven times, the preset number before the call would go to voice mail. Ahmad's face contorted in a ghoulish smirk at the idea of another person actually trying to contact him during his short act of self-destruction—an ironic twist of humanity reaching out too late.

But the call never triggered into voice mail. Instead, the caller had immediately redialed and the phone began another countdown of pulsating rings from inside his jacket's breast pocket. He ignored it and stepped onto the wall. *Three rings, four rings...*

Something—something outside of his earthly consciousness—made Ahmad reach for the phone on the sixth ring. He unfolded it and held it blindly out to his side.

"Hello...hello...is this you Ahmad?" The voice came across as tinny and unfamiliar until Ahmad realized who it was.

"Ahmad, can you hear me?" This is Malik. Malik Abbas."

The sound of his friend's voice, though muffled and scratchy, caused Ahmad's legs to freeze. He brought the flip phone to the side of his head. His tensed jaw unlocked as he managed to eke out a feeble, "Yes, this is Ahmad." He heard his old college buddy laugh a sigh of relief, followed by the question of, "Where are you? It sounds like you're outside in the wind or something."

"Yes, I am outside and...it is slightly windy," he slurred. His eyes had drifted away from the horizon, where the sun had set below Bataan. He scanned the dim lights of Manila's harbor.

"Man, you sound a little off. Are you okay?" Malik asked. Ahmad's gaze had meandered lower, finally focusing on the tiny figures scurrying along the sidewalk directly below him. His knees buckled, and he swayed forward. He steadied himself briefly and then lost his balance when the heels of his shoes snagged the ridge of metal trim attached to the guard wall's edge. He fell backward onto the roof's stony surface; the phone flew out of his hands.

"Ahmad? Ahmad? Are you still there?" Malik persisted.

Ahmad rolled to his side and picked up the phone."Malik...I...I," He looked down at his expensive shoes, which had been badly scuffed from the spill. The right pant leg of his suit had a tear over the knee.

"Is this a bad time to talk?" Malik said. "I can call back, but I have a business proposal that could be beneficial, *very* beneficial to both of us."

Ahmad sat up and brushed away the pebbles that had adhered to his palms after he'd fallen. His panting had subsided, and the act of conversing with another person seemed to help clear his thinking. "No, no, I'm okay." He feigned a laugh in an attempt to reassure his friend. "Just having one hell of a day; you know how it goes."

Malik reciprocated with a laugh. "Yeah, I sure do. Listen, this deal is somewhat complicated, but I think you can come away with a lot, and I mean a lot, of money. It involves you coordinating the shipping of some heavy machinery from Mindanao to North America."

Ahmad first thought was that he was dreaming. But when he realized that he wasn't, he began to sob joyfully while Malik summarized the plan. The words cascaded from his friend's mouth in rapid order: *Mindanao; pipes, pumps and motors; Mexican seaport; and finally the unfamiliar name of a city in the American state of Texas.* His sobbing changed to lighthearted, relieved chuckles as he felt the deadweight burden of defeat lifted from his shoulders.

He simply responded with cadence-like strings of "yes…a huh…yes" as Malik cut him in on the details.

The events that unfolded over the following days felt like gifts from heaven. Ahmad's floundering import/export firm had received enough quick cash for him to keep it solvent. Rent, living expenses, and bookies could be paid, and he'd be able to feed the circling loan sharks with whom he'd dealt before they began to move in on him. Malik had sent an electronic advance, labeled craftily, "For consulting services rendered," directly to Ahmad's bank account with promises of more to come once the transaction was completed.

Ahmad heard Ling's dainty knock at his office door. "May I come in please, Ahmad? I have something I'd like to discuss with you."

As his attractive, young secretary opened the door, he looked past her at the vacant space where a half-dozen employees used to sit before he'd let them go and then pawned off most of the office furniture. The solitary lamp atop Ling's desk cast a dingy shadow across the otherwise-empty room.

Ahmad stood at the window, looking over Manila Bay. It was an unusually clear day that allowed him to pick out the tiny island-fortress of Corregidor, the historic spot from where General MacArthur had fled shortly before Japanese forces overpowered the island's defenses and forced Allied fighters to capitulate early in the Second World War. He held his stare to the west and replied, "What is it, Ling?"

"Well, I've studied the invoices that you provided me, and I'm not sure if these figures are correct." Ahmad knew that, despite the Chinese-Filipina's lack of higher education, she had a hawk-like eye for calculations. She held out a file stuffed with papers. "What I see is that the total price you've negotiated with the company in Mexico is way, way over what the equipment is actually valued. I checked several comps with other distributors and they all come up much cheaper, nearly by a two thirds."

Ahmad turned to face her. "Yes, I know, we were most fortunate to come upon a deal like this. Our contact in Mindanao has an excess of this equipment and is willing to let it go just to clear out their warehouse. That, coupled with the Mexican's eagerness to purchase, led to a windfall."

Ling looked down again at the numbers before her. "But can we let this stand? Is there risk of an audit?" She walked closer, close enough for Ahmad to smell her essence and to feel the warmth of her slender body next to his. Her dark, almond-shaped eyes looked up at him, not with passion or affection like the scores of times when they'd made love, but with concern; this was business, and she didn't want to jeopardize her job.

Ahmad placed a hand on Ling's shoulder and rubbed it gently. He felt the tendons and muscles that ran to her graceful neck loosen beneath the shear, silk dress that she was wearing.

"I must confess something to you," he said. "Before this opportunity came to us, I was about to give up on this business. I'd cursed the day that I decided to leave the engineering field and go off on my own."

Ling's worrisome look changed to a more inquisitive expression as she wondered to what purpose her boss's explanation was leading. Their affair, combined with the rapid decline of the import/export firm Ahmad had established—dubbed *Quality Expeditors*—had contributed to the collapse of Ahmad's marriage and estrangement from his two children; she still harbored guilt for her part in the downfall. Though not religious herself, Ling had been raised by devout, working-class Christian parents who had imbued in her a sense of right and wrong.

Ahmad leaned in and kissed her gently on her forehead. "This will prove to be what saves our company, my sweets." He dipped a hand into his jacket and removed a small, thin box, elegantly wrapped.

Ling opened the gift and found a shimmering diamond necklace.

"That's just a small token of my appreciation for you sticking with me these last several months."

Her expression softened as she fondled the jewelry. Any suspicions about the authenticity of this international transaction were swept away like a cooling breeze that follows after a humid thunderstorm.

"I don't know what to say," she whispered. "I..."

Ahmad touched her lips with a fingertip. "Now we can pay our hungry creditors and get back on our feet; maybe even hire a couple of office assistants. Would you like to become my business partner and not just serve me as a secretary?"

Ling's face erupted into a broad smile. "Oh yes, of course I would!"

"Fine," Ahmad proclaimed. "It is done. We will have official papers drawn up immediately. You are no longer 'Ling Chin, administrative assistant at *Quality Expeditors*.' Consider yourself my new vice president."

Ling beamed at the thought of finally holding an esteemed position rather than simply being hired help. She hugged Ahmad and gave him a long, passionate kiss.

"Thank you," she said. "I will not let you down, *partner*." They both laughed at hearing her say the word. Ahmad put his arm around her waist and guided her tenderly to the window. Manila's sky was crystal clear after morning rains had cleansed the city's characteristic grayish-brown, turbid air. He massaged her hip and then slowly slid his hand lower. He squeezed her compact buttocks in a playful, loving way.

"There's a thought that just came to me," he said. Her eyes widened as she signaled him to go on. "I've been away from my faith for so long that, at times, I've lost my way. But my faith has found me. It is only proper for me to recognize what I must do." When he saw Ling's doe-eyed expression, he knew that he now had her in the palm of his hand.

"Yes?" she asked.

"My good friend in the south, Malik Abbas, heads a charity that helps needy people: people who those of us far away in the north have all but forgotten. Malik is a good man. I've known him since the University, when I was an engineering student and he was studying law." Ahmad looked away from the bustling cityscape and harbor. He turned again to Ling and gripped her lightly by the shoulders. "We must share our good fortune with Malik's charity. We must share in a *big, big* way."

"Would you like me to put a check in the mail for him today?" Ling asked. Her eyes perked again.

"*No, no.* I don't trust the mail, especially going down to such a primitive place like the southern islands. We should wire him the funds. I'm quite sure there's a branch of the Philippine National Bank in Isabela."

"How much should we donate?"

Ahmad sensed that the warm affection they'd just shared was beginning to fade. He inhaled deeply and breathed out. "We must donate half of what we've reaped," he said flatly.

"But that would be a couple of hundred thousand..."

"Yes, I know," Ahmad interrupted. He removed his hands from her and redirected his sights back out over the bay. "You must trust me on this. The old adage that 'it takes money to make money' should be our best form of guidance during this endeavor. If all goes as expected, I have confidence that my associate, Malik, will steer more transactions our way."

Ahmad saw a rising look of distrustfulness in Ling's eyes. He held his breath and waited for her reaction. She calmly raised a hand to toss back a long, errant strand of her glossy black hair. Her response surprised him.

"Then if that's what it takes, we must do it." A stern, resolute expression fell over her pretty face.

Ahmad let out a relieved sigh and gave her another affectionate hug. "Excellent! Now that we have a business plan, we'll need to sit down and make things right with the creditors, starting first with our landlord. A company as successful as *Quality Expeditors* can't be evicted out into the street, can it?"

Ling laughed in agreement and then backed away slowly from the window. She folded her arms and said coyly, "Perhaps Mr. Jalil should consider taking his new partner out to lunch. We can't pay the bills on an empty stomach, can we?"

"Why, of course not." Ahmad acknowledged her request with an exaggerated bow.

Ling returned to the empty office space to retrieve her purse. She sat down briefly at her desk and smiled as she envisioned the bright, shiny nameplate that she planned to have made.

It would read, "Ms. Ling Chin, Vice President."

# CHAPTER 12

Malik shuddered when he heard the eerily familiar sound—a distant rattling, thumping noise that he felt in his bones. He shielded his eyes from the morning sun's glare and looked high above; his instincts served him well as he recognized the helicopter's distinctive profile and twin sets of twirling wings. He hadn't seen one like it in over twenty years. The helicopter was painted a different color than the AFP helicopters that he'd grown accustomed to see flying over Basilan and other parts of the Autonomous Region of Muslim Mindanao (ARMM). He watched as the aircraft flew south and then disappeared behind the mountains. He took some deep breaths to calm himself down from the painful memory from long ago that seeing the aircraft had triggered. After he'd parked his motorbike in the alley by his office, he passed by the two other shops that shared the shabby, one-story commercial building with him: a fish market and a beauty salon. He waved to the fishmonger, who regardless of the time of day, always seemed to be busy or surrounded by people and engaged in conversation. Nonetheless, the gregarious, heavyset fellow never failed to interrupt what he was doing to greet Malik, chat for a moment and to wish him a pleasant day.

Malik was glad to see that the beauty salon had not yet opened, thereby relieving him of the duty of acknowledging the two women who worked there. He particularly disliked the younger one; the smell of her overpowering perfume made him nauseous and the girl's heavily made-up face reminded him of a circus clown. He'd never met the other beautician, but she appeared to be a much more respectable lady.

The fifteen-minute drive to work had provided Malik time to clear his mind and to stop worrying about the declining condition of his invalid mother. He'd risen early to prepare their breakfast, taking pains to not disturb the old woman until he was sure she was awake.

He'd asked her the same question every morning: "How would you like your eggs this morning, Mama?" She'd always answered his question with the same sentence: "Whatever way is easiest for you, son."

Malik cracked the three eggs that he'd purchased at the morning market and dropped them into a sizzling pan: one for her, two for him. It had been virtually the same routine since his father, Hashim Abbas, had passed away nearly ten years ago. After breakfast, he'd guided her to the toilet again and assisted with the common morning rituals. The embarrassment they'd both experienced after she'd lost the ability to tend to her own hygiene had faded, and those private duties were now merely that—just *duties*. Once they'd both eaten and he had dressed her, Malik would guide her to an easy chair, where she'd spend the morning reading, listening to music, or napping. He'd return for lunch and repeat the cycle of cooking, helping her onto the toilet and making the elderly woman comfortable until he returned in the evening. The cell phone he'd purchased for her would sit at the ready, on the table next to her ancient-looking AM radio. Their four-room flat was well furnished, but not plush.

He navigated the meandering drive, through Isabela's bustling streets, to his office at the *Basilan Betterment Foundation*: a charitable organization he'd established after he'd stopped practicing law. The work he performed at the foundation was rudimentary for a man of his credentials: an honors graduate from the University of the Philippines Law School and a rising star with one of Mindanao's largest firms. But, after his father had died, life had taken a series of fateful turns for the Abbas family. His mother could no longer run their little *sari-sari*, or variety store, by herself. Malik was a bachelor and her only child, so he left the law practice to help out his mother. Ultimately, Elham Abbas sold the store, and the two of them moved from her home in Cotobato, on the Mindanao mainland, first to Zamboanga and then—so that Malik could avoid the daily ferry boat ride—to Basilan's provincial capital, Isabela City.

Though Malik and his mother lived comfortably, they both longed to some-day return to their roots—the lush, fertile river valleys of Central Mindanao. Malik dreamed of purchasing a spread similar to the farm where he'd been raised. When his parents had abruptly sold the property, he was too young to comprehend why his father had let it go for a fraction of its actual value. But as he became more educated, it became painfully clear how such an unfair transaction could have occurred.

From the moment of his birth, Malik had been considered a "golden child." After his sister died tragically at a young age, his parents had celebrated him as a divine gift from Heaven; he could do no wrong. Malik exceeded his peers in grammar school and was promptly singled out for a scholarship at an elite, private school in nearby Cotobato City. As a teen, he'd diligently taught his illiterate parents to read and write. When then-President Ferdinand Marcos established a special program for Muslim students from the southern islands to obtain a college education, Malik was chosen as a candidate from his region. He left home at the tender age of seventeen and travelled to Manila, where he enrolled as a freshman at the University of the Philippines.

Despite the benefit of his scholarship, Malik was too poor to afford the common pleasures, such as eating out or going to a movie, that college students enjoy. His parents had no money to spare. Malik's father made a meager living by growing produce and raising livestock, while his mother kept their home and helped her husband on the farm whenever she could. In order for them to send him any significant money, their sole option was to cash in the only asset that they owned—their farm. But the choice to do so had been a relatively easy one; they were getting too old and worn out to effectively maintain the property any longer; plus they were confident that their college-educated son would never wish to return home to a life of rural, physical labor. With the profit they expected from the sale, Hashim and Elham Abbas would provide their gifted child with the lifestyle they thought a young man of his stature deserved. They decided to relocate closer to the city, where they'd open a small convenience store and live the remainder of their years more comfortably. Hashim and Elham prayed that Malik would someday return to Mindanao and build his life near them.

But their plans fell apart. Shortly after Malik left for Manila, Hashim became aware that the land his family had worked for over a century was not properly titled in accordance with modern Philippine law. When a consortium of Northern developers discovered that he—and scores of others like him—couldn't provide suitable documentation, their land was either seized outright or purchased for a meager fraction of its true worth. Droves of native Muslims were evicted from their homesteads while savvy investors swooped in like vultures to gobble up the resource-rich lands.

The sad event seemed to spark more bad luck for Malik and his parents. When Malik learned of his parents' unfortunate loss, he panicked and tried to do something to help them survive their hardship. He unwittingly took a part-time job in Manila for an outfit that served as a front for a communist-based faction known as the New People's Army. The NPA had conspired to bring down a U.S. aircraft as a display of their hatred toward Philippine president Marcos and the country's most generous ally, the United States of America. During a terrorist attack against U.S. Forces, Malik had been caught in the crossfire. One of his legs had been severely wounded by gunfire when he attempted to flee the scene. But he survived the ordeal, went to law school, and then on to pass the Philippine bar exam. With high hopes, he moved back to his native Mindanao and lived near his parents. He never married.

Malik heard the helicopter again; this time it sounded much closer. The noise grew louder as the aircraft approached Isabela City and then boomed directly overhead in a thunderous roar of turbine engines and spinning rotor blades. It then banked sharply toward the coastline and descended out of sight. Only a handful of commuters debarking the Zamboanga-Isabela ferry bothered to look up at it. Many were busy texting on their smart phones, and most had become numbly immune to the frequent stream of military aircraft patrolling the island's rugged terrain.

Malik's contact had informed him of the American helicopter's expected arrival time. He looked at his watch and saw that it was nearly thirty minutes early; his guests would be here soon. He hurriedly began to clean up his cluttered office and unfolded a couple of extra chairs. When he came across a folder labeled, "Ahmad J. Donation," he smiled and tucked it away, deep inside a desk drawer.

# CHAPTER 13

*Whoever said that money can't buy happiness never spent anytime flat broke.* That poignant old phrase had passed through Mitchell Castella's mind as he yanked open his duffel bag and began searching the pockets of every shirt and pair of pants for spare change. Earlier that morning, he'd convinced the one-star hotel's desk clerk to accept a personal check, even though he knew that it would bounce. The old lady had reluctantly gone along with his alibi that he'd lost his wallet while out to dinner the previous night. Between stiffing his hotel bill and the few pesos he'd scrounged out of his clothing, he'd tallied enough money buy a round-trip ticket on the ferryboat from Zamboanga City to Basilan Island.

The long walk from his seedy hotel had worn him out, both mentally and physically. Despite his one hundred percent Filipino lineage, somehow, every beggar, pimp and hustler along the way seemed to tag him as just another foreign tourist—an easy mark, who wouldn't have traveled to their city unless he had plenty of cash. He'd patiently waived off the first few by simply saying "no," but as the pestering had become more intense, he'd resorted to the handful of Chavacano curse words he'd learned and, at times, had to push forcefully to shove them away. He wasn't sure if it was the look of his clothing or simply the way that he carried himself, but these omnipresent street hustlers hadn't left him alone since the moment he'd stepped off the plane at the Zamboanga airport.

By the time he reached the ferry ticket window, his short sleeve white shirt was drenched with sweat. He sheepishly doled out the required amount—the equivalent of a couple of American dollars—to pay for the hour-long economy-class trip. He found a seat on the boat's open-air upper deck. Once the boat got underway from Zamboanga's crowded pier, the cooling breeze felt good against his dampened shirt. Mitchell managed to calm himself down and tried to gather his thoughts in preparation for what he would say to the intense little man to whom Spider had introduced him.

Traveling on the low-rent boat to a fourth class city like Isabela was about as far away from Mitchell Castella's privileged upbringing as he could have ever imagined—both literally and figuratively. Until recently, he'd led a pampered life. Mitchell Castella and his four older siblings were raised in a posh Palo Alto, California, neighborhood by virtue of their father: a self-made millionaire who'd diligently climbed the steps of the American dream ladder by seizing every opportunity that came his way after moving from the Philippines to America.

Anding "Ding" Castella had begun his journey to America as a Navy cook, part of the Philippine Enlistment Program, which allowed a few select Filipinos to join the U.S. Navy each year. Once the program was expanded to permit those sailors to pursue ratings other than mess steward, Ding Castella took a test that would qualify him for more challenging work—that of a data processing technician. His new job exposed him to the nascent fields of computerization and digital technology. After completing a twenty-year career in the Navy, Ding branched out to establish himself in San Francisco's Silicon Valley where he made a fortune developing software for business computers. Ding was very proud of the way he'd risen from poverty to provide for his family. He'd often say to Mitchell and his other children: "You'll never have to worry about money like I did, growing up in Manila; just pay attention and work hard. That's all it takes to be successful in this country."

But Mitchell had been the classic youngest child—the "baby" of the family, who seldom chose to follow a conventional path in life. While his brothers and sisters had taken advantage of their privileged upbringing by getting an education, holding down good jobs and starting their own families, Mitchell was content with being a slacker. Bored and unmotivated, he dropped out of community college. His father insisted that he get a job, but Mitchell never lasted more than a few weeks in the menial work that he was able to find.

Ultimately, Ding Castella grew tired of bankrolling his lazy youngest child. He gave Mitchell two choices: either go back to school and finish, or risk being cut off completely. With the aid of his father's business connections—plus a hefty donation to the school—he was accepted into the University of California at Berkeley, where he discovered an interest in graphic arts and photography. During a study-abroad program to the Far East, he became fascinated with the plight of the Philippine Moro, or Muslim, population. From his time spent with them and experiencing their culture, he'd found a new purpose in life and something that he'd never felt before—a sense of belonging.

When he returned from the Philippines, he informed his parents that he'd decided to convert to Islam. They were devastated by his proclamation. Like the majority of Filipinos, they'd been raised as Christians, and though they tried to convince Mitchell to abandon his plans, their pleas only bolstered his resolve. Despite the news of his son's decision, Ding Castella kept his word and continued to fund Mitchell's education.

Mitchell met Karlena Brandt while she was doing a graduate project in the same building where he was taking an art class at Berkeley. They became fast friends—initially because of their shared interest, but the relationship soon developed into something much more than that. Mitchell moved in with the pretty redhead and they began to share a life together.

But a few months into their cohabitation, Mitchell became restless again. He drained his bank account and made plans to leave school for good. When he informed Karlena that he wanted to move to the southern Philippines, she was hurt. But she wished him well and said that she hoped they'd meet again sometime "down the road."

They stayed in contact after Mitchell left for the Philippines, through emails and sporadic phone calls. But the spark between the two young adults seemed to have been rekindled when Karlena announced that she'd be in Southeast Asia on a photojournalism excursion. He offered to be her de facto tour guide and to show her the sights of what he had described as an "unspoiled tropical isle" called Basilan. Karlena leapt at the opportunity to explore the remote island and to add images of its people and untouched, natural beauties to her portfolio.

Mitchell had drifted around the sprawling archipelago, half-heartedly taking photographs, before ultimately setting down roots in Zamboanga City, where he'd taken a job as a bartender. But his funds were beginning to run out.

The ferryboat tapped gently against the pier. Mitchell draped the duffel bag over his shoulder and joined the queue as it crowded around the boat's hatchway. Once off the boat, he was again assaulted by a swarm of people who wanted something from him. He concluded that no matter what steps he took to appear "Filipino"—by learning the language or trying to dress like a local—it just wasn't working. *I must have "American" typed across my forehead*, he thought to himself.

He plied his way through Isabela's teeming street, en route to the *Basilan Betterment Fund's* office. He'd done his part in the agreement, he reasoned, and it was now well past time for him to be paid.

# CHAPTER 14

Leonard Dickle washed down his third slice of pizza with a gulping slug of Mountain Dew. Dickle loved the second Wednesday of every month at the CIA cafeteria: all you could eat pizza day. He coaxed down the last wad of saucy dough, cheese and pepperoni, taking care not to speak before the food had descended past that part in his throat that divides the passageway between the stomach and lungs. Confident that the last of his lunch was headed down the right pipe, he spoke.

"Joe, I think I've got something here." His supervisor, Joe Voss, rose slowly away from his desk where he'd been analyzing satellite images of a suspected Abu Sayyaf training camp in mountainous Central Mindanao, Philippines.

"What's up, Lennie?" Voss asked as he sauntered his hefty frame across the room to Dickle's station.

"Remember our briefing with Dr. Lammers last week before he left for the P.I.?"

Voss frowned in disgust. "You know, *Leonard,* just because I'm twice your age doesn't qualify me as a candidate for Alzheimer's; of course I remember the briefing. Why do you think we've been doing follow-up most of this week?" Voss and Dickle had been trading passive aggressive insults ever since the youngster had come aboard at the CIA's imaging lab earlier in the year: Dickle hated being called "that other name"—*Lennie*—and retaliated by continually ragging Voss about his age.

"This just came across." Dickle spun his laptop around for Voss to see. "It's an audio with transcript from a field agent in Basilan. Cortez, over at the FBI, got someone to translate the conversation. It's a little muffled, but with the transcript, you pretty much get the gist. Cortez says it's a mish-mash of English, Tagalog and Chavacano."

"*Cava-what?*" Voss asked.

"You know, *Chavacano*. That's a Spanish-Creole dialect that originated in the Southern Philippines during the seventeenth century. I believe when the Spanish imperialists began to—"

"Okay, okay, I get it, Einstein. Geez, just play the damn thing!"

Dickle fumbled inside a desk drawer for another headset so Voss could hear better; he also handed his boss a copy of the translated script.

Joe Voss thought how one of the few positive consequences of 9/11 was the improved sharing of intelligence data between the FBI, which handled most kidnapping cases, and his office. Back in the day, it had been like pulling teeth when he needed to get sensitive information from other government departments. Each sector and its hierarchy seemed to guard their turf with bullheaded stinginess—as if their jobs depended on it. Joe was thankful that newbies like Dickle would not be subjected to such handicaps.

"The good part only lasts a few minutes. You ready?" Voss nodded and Dickle triggered the "PLAY" icon on his laptop.

After less than one minute, Voss's eyes widened. "Christ sakes, we've got to push this to Lammers. And *quickly*."

### Six Weeks Earlier

When Nina Acala received the phone call from a person claiming to be at the American embassy in Manila, she thought it might be a prank. Had she not been a former employee of the U.S. government, she would have simply told the guy that she didn't want what he was selling and to please remove her from his call list. But the official-sounding man persisted by beginning his spiel with a sobering reference to her previous home in California, along with stating her current address in Basilan. He continued by reciting the location of the FBI satellite office in Oakland, where Nina had worked for nine years. A chill went through her body when she realized that the caller was somebody more worthy of her attention than an annoying telemarketer.

Nina scanned her surroundings to see if anyone was nearby and said matter-of-factly, "Oh sure, yes. I'm at work right now; can I call you back within the hour?" Her part-time job as a cashier at the Basilan Ferry Terminal allowed a ten-minute break every couple of hours; it would be another twenty minutes before she'd be able to step away from the ticket window.

The sequence of events that followed would transform Nina Acala's life. When she returned the call, a man who identified himself as an assistant to the United States ambassador promptly set up a time and place for Nina to meet with his female associate. He advised Nina to pick a public spot, so she chose the bar at a beachfront hotel along the sands of Basilan's northern shore, not far from her apartment.

The woman proved to be a Filipina-American, employed by the FBI. She carried a file that detailed Nina's past as a secretary with the Bureau and documentation of her freshly renewed security clearance. What surprised Nina the most, however, was when the women allowed her to read through another file that essentially told her life's story: growing up as a naturalized Filipina-American and military brat; her marriage to a Caucasian who'd been killed in an auto accident; and finally a short bio of her two adult children—a daughter in Jacksonville, married to a sailor, and a son, who worked as a lifeguard in San Diego.

The FBI agent suggested that, for privacy, they take a stroll on the beach. The agent continued to recount details of how Nina had left the Bureau and had moved to Zamboanga in order to spend time with her aging parents. Her dad had retired from the U.S. Navy as a chief petty officer disbursing clerk and had fulfilled a life-long dream of returning to his homeland to live out his days. Nina chuckled as the agent quoted a line from her tape-recorded FBI job interview, when she'd quipped, "the old guy is convinced that his Navy pension will let him and ma live like royalty back home." Retired Chief Acala had been correct: His government stipend—modest by U.S. standards—had provided for a very comfortable standard of living on the southern Philippine island of Mindanao. But after Nina's folks had passed, she'd been forced to rent out their waterfront condo on the mainland and take a job across the channel, on Basilan Island. She had eventually moved to an apartment there to avoid the commute between Zamboanga and Isabela City.

As she'd expected, the pleasantries ended when the FBI agent got down to business. She offered Nina the opportunity to triple the money she was making at the ferry terminal if she'd agree to serve as an informant. In return, a generous retainer would be deposited each month into her bank account. She'd be placed as a cosmetologist—a skill she'd acquired before her first FBI job—at a salon in downtown Isabela. On one side of the salon was a fish market—on the other side, the office of a charitable organization. Besides cutting hair, doing nails and makeup, Nina was to keep alert for any suspicious activity around the building, especially those at the charity known as the *Basilan Betterment Foundation*. It was an offer that Nina could not refuse.

She was at the salon for less than a month before she discovered a few things about the foundation. First, the small Muslim man who worked in the office was not very friendly. He'd nod and say hello if they met, but that was the extent of his sociability. However, the salon's bathroom was adjacent to the man's desk on the other side of the building's flimsily constructed walls, which allowed her to eavesdrop whenever she had to use the toilet. But she rarely paid much attention since his conversations seemed boring and were usually over the phone. Plus the fellow spoke in such a soft, quiet voice that he was difficult to understand.

But on the day when she spotted the rusty, white contractor's van parked across the street, her interest perked. What caught Nina's eye were the two thug-looking youths leaning against the vehicle and another older fellow, who sat in the front passenger seat chain smoking. After an hour had gone by, a pile of cigarette butts began to stack up on the pavement as the man appeared to nervously burn one smoke halfway down, then use it to light a new one.

Nina glanced up at the van every few minutes from her chair; it was a slow day at the salon and she'd spent most of it cleaning her utensils and reading gossip magazines. Then she saw something even more curious. The two thugs had changed their position and seemed to be talking excitedly about something. One of them pointed discreetly to a neatly dressed, college-aged man as he walked determinedly by the salon, stopping in front of the foundation, where he commenced pounding on the door. Nina saw that the smoker had tossed another butt onto the street and was now talking on his cell phone.

Her heart began to race. She stood up and turned to her coworker: a gum-snapping tart named "Pinky," dressed in leopard-print yoga pants and a too-tight halter-top. "I'm going to the lady's room," Nina said. The girl never looked up from filing her own nails as she mumbled, "Whatever…"

Nina closed the bathroom door behind her and pressed an ear to the wall-board, but the sounds were muted and not understandable. She then stood on top of the toilet's lid, dug out her cell phone from the back pocket of her shorts and pressed the device's 'record' icon. She held the phone against the grill of the ventilation ducting that the adjoining suites shared. Nina strained to hear the voices; they were weak but discernable.

"No, Mr. Abbas, *you* listen to *me*!"

"Keep your voice down, Mitchell. These walls aren't very thick."

"I don't give a shit! You told me she wouldn't get hurt. Now I don't even know where she is. When can I—?"

"Settle down. Like I told you before, she will be fine, and this will all be over soon. You'll be proud of how you've helped your new brothers and sisters. Many good things will come of this; trust me."

"But Spider told me that he's done stuff like this before, and this would be a quick and easy task. Why is this taking so long?"

"The girl's father has the money. It's just a matter of the transaction being layered properly to protect our interests."

"What do you mean? You told me that the ransom note was received and the money was on the way."

"Yes, that is true, but he can't just drop a check in the mail and send it from Texas to my office. We must follow a strict protocol with these matters."

There was a long pause, and then the younger-sounding man said flatly, "I want my money and I want it now. This wasn't our agreement." There was another period of silence, followed by what sounded like a cabinet or drawer opening then closing.

"Here, take this. Now get out of here and stay away until I call you. You're being much too visible."

"Ok, but I'm not very happy about this, Mr. Abbas. I'll be back." She heard the shuffling of a chair against the floor and then a door slam.

Nina nearly fell from the toilet when she was startled by Pinky's beating against the bathroom door. "Hey, grandma, what's going on?" she said. "Did you fall in or something? Get your chubby butt out here; we finally got some customers."

Nina flushed the toilet, feigned washing her hands and went back out into the salon, where three middle-aged women were chatting merrily in the waiting area. She quickly readied her styling chair, smiled and signaled for one of them to come forward. As the lady sat down, she looked outside and saw that the van and the men were gone.

# CHAPTER 15

"Reveille! Reveille! All hands heave out and trice up. Now reveille!" USS *Lansing's* crew began their day the same way they'd done since leaving San Diego, seven months ago: to the shrieking sound of the boatswain's whistle and wake-up call, piped through the ship's main circuit, or "1MC."

Unlike his first two mornings at sea, though, McGirt had risen two hours earlier and had already performed the traditional "triple S": *shit, shower and shave.* He'd hung out alone in the officer's wardroom, arriving at the darkly paneled space a full hour before the cooks had fired off the kitchen's griddle and had begun preparing gobs of eggs, sausage and bacon. He'd taken advantage of the quiet time to sip a couple cups of coffee and to review his notes about the mission. McGirt had spent extended time in the Philippines, both as a sea-going aviator and in the quasi-diplomatic role as naval attaché to the United States ambassador to the Philippines in Manila. While in the attaché position he'd accompanied the ambassador on several trips to the country's southernmost islands, though he'd never actually set foot on Basilan.

He and Lammers had sat attentively through a zero-dark-thirty briefing with the CH-46 helicopter crew that had been assigned the mission of transporting them. The details were straightforward: the POD (plan of the day) called for them to launch from *Lansing's* flight deck at 0730 for the thirty-minute flight to a Philippine Army outpost located on the northern coast of Basilan, near the island's provincial capital, Isabela City.

Lammers had spoken up at the briefing and proposed that the crew allow time for a short aerial tour of the island before dropping off him and McGirt. Captain Torres had initially balked at the idea; she wanted her aircraft back on deck ASAP in preparation for the day's other major event—a lengthy replenishment operation involving three other ships. After some bickering between all parties, the mission's aircraft commander offered the obvious solution: just get airborne earlier. Word was passed to the air detachment's maintenance chief to push the aircraft out of the hangar as quickly as possible and to prep the bird for flight. All hands "turned to," which resulted in the flight lifting off forty-five minutes earlier than originally scheduled.

McGirt shrugged off the last minute scramble as just another early morning "crisis du jour."

Bud's staff at Langley—along with his contacts in the Pentagon—had greased the skids for McGirt and him to be met by a U.S. Army colonel by the name of Woodbridge, who'd act as their liaison with the Armed Forces of the Philippines base commander. Once settled into their quarters at the AFP post, Bud had requested that they be escorted a few miles from the base to meet with the head of a local Muslim charity, a Mr. Malik Abbas.

During the flight to Basilan, Bud Lammers had perched himself between the two pilots and was happily chatting them up. McGirt laughed at how Lammers had managed to wedge his husky frame into the narrow opening that separated the aircraft's cockpit and cabin.

While Bud held court with the chopper pilots, McGirt took the opportunity to review the notes he'd highlighted from his graduate school files. He'd earned a master's degree in security studies from the Naval Postgraduate School as a new Lieutenant Commander in preparation for embassy duty. The course of study had concentrated on the Philippines—tracing the archipelago nation's colorful history from its tribal roots to the Spanish colonial period and subsequent domination by America, to the country's formal independence from the United States on July 4th, 1946. In more current political terms, the curriculum at Monterey had been revised to reflect how the Philippines had not been immune from the impact caused by the actions of radical Islamic terrorists.

Though thousands of miles from the Middle East, scores of Filipino Muslims had been enlisted to fight, alongside Islamic insurgents, against the Soviet Army and Democratic Republic of Afghanistan forces. Those Filipino fighters would return to their homeland to form the nucleus of an al-Qaeda offshoot known as the Abu Sayyaf Group, or *ASG*—the militant group that had kidnapped Karlena Brandt. Abu Sayyaf, meaning "Bearer of the Sword," had begun creating havoc by first migrating swiftly throughout the Muslim dominated states of Sabah and Borneo, then infiltrating the Southern Philippine islands and establishing a stronghold on Basilan.

A voice inside McGirt's headset interrupted his reading. "Ten minutes out, Captain," one of the pilots told him. McGirt double-clicked his mike switch to acknowledge. He'd noted how the crew had been cordial yet, at the same time, almost overly respectful toward him and Lammers since they'd arrived onboard *Lansing.* He suspected that they'd heard the stories—most likely embellished over time—of the pair's exploits during their earlier years in the Western Pacific: McGirt's heroic shipboard landing (after slamming into the water and nearly sending his helicopter to the bottom of the South China Sea) and then-Lieutenant Commander Bud Lammers's pistol-wielding rescue of a sailor (who'd been taken hostage by a band of rebels in the northern Luzon town of Baguio). Seemingly, even after a couple decades had passed, the duo was still worthy of legendary status.

McGirt stood up, walked up to the cockpit, and peeked over Bud's shoulder through the aircraft's windscreen. The smallish tropical island of Basilan—no more that forty miles across at its widest point—stood out on the horizon. He wondered how such a picturesque looking spot could be the location for the mayhem that had erupted on its soil over that last several years. Tarzan Truckee's advice to "be careful over there" resonated in his thoughts. Regretfully, after being fully briefed on Karlena Brandt's grave situation, and considering the complexity of the mission that he and Bud had undertaken, he wondered how the hell he'd remember to bring back some of the Philippine's national brew, San Miguel beer, to the Admiral.

The helicopter aircraft commander turned toward McGirt and said, "Sir, Dr. Lammers wants me to make a quick recon run around the island's perimeter, concentrating on the eastern side."

McGirt knew from his reading that the island's eastern and southern regions were where most of the bad guys, the Abu Sayyaf Group, hung out. He gave a silent thumbs-up to the pilot. From the corner of his eye, he saw one of the aircrew saddling up an automatic weapon; the man cooked off a few test rounds into the water. McGirt stiffened. Until now, he hadn't devoted much thought to the bulletproof vests that he and Bud had been issued on the ship and had tucked inside their baggage. Bud had insisted that carrying the gear was only a precaution since they'd be under the vigilant care of American and Filipino soldiers. Regardless, the rat-tat-tat of machine gun fire jarred him into the reality that he wasn't in tranquil Coronado any more.

McGirt felt the aircraft begin climbing. They'd been cruising over the water at 500 feet and at a speed of 120 knots. He'd heard the aircraft commander tell the copilot, who was flying, "Let's get above any small arms fire; make it five K." The junior man complied by pulling up on the collective on his left side, which increased the pitch angle simultaneously on each of the aircraft's six rotor blades. He then tugged back gently on the control stick, or cyclic, located between his legs. A cooler, less humid breeze swept through the cabin as they leveled off at 5000 feet.

McGirt looked down at the shimmering strait that separated Zamboanga City and Basilan Island. He saw a large ferryboat and a plethora of smaller vessels transiting the cobalt-tinted channel; to the east, cast against a bright, cloudless sky, stood the rugged mountains of Central Mindanao.

Bud had done his homework and commenced as the sortie's de facto tour guide over the aircraft's intercom, or ICS. "That's Isabela City, where McGirt and I will be meeting with one of the influential locals today." Bud knew that the crew was smart enough to not ask "why," although *Lansing's* mess deck rumor mill had correctly swerved into the truth that the pair's mission was related someway to an American hostage. "Just east of that is Lamitan," he continued. "The Abu Sayyaf Group operates surreptitiously over the entire island, but they seem to be concentrating more to the south of Isabela."

The aircraft entered a gentle bank to the south as McGirt shifted to the cabin's right side for a better view. The eastern coast of the island appeared far more remote than the clustered burgs of Isabela and Lamitan. Inland, its densely wooded terrain reinforced what Bud had told him: It was the ideal place for terrorists to hole-up and to hide a hostage.

Bud ran off a string of Arab-sounding words denoting towns where the ASG and the Moro Islamic Liberation Front (MILF) had established a presence. "That's Akbar directly to our right and Hadji Mohammed Ajul on the peninsula that juts out to the east. "Lieutenant, please make a wide pass around that peninsula then take up a southwesterly heading." The copilot acknowledged with a nod and complied. "Gentlemen, all of this real estate is part of the Autonomous Region of Muslim Mindanao, or the ARMM for short. Other than the Isabela City area to the north, the rest of the island is a nation within a nation—a different culture and, most importantly, a starkly different set of rules that its inhabitants live by."

The copilot piped in, "That sounds like a recipe for disaster, sir, if you don't mind me saying."

"You got it, son," Bud replied. "Makes you wonder if something like that will ever happen back in the States, doesn't it?"

The ICS banter fell silent as everyone on board seemed to digest his words. Bud broke the quiet. "Okay, that's enough here. We'll fly over Tipo-Tipo next and then head back toward Isabela and land. The only thing I'll say about Tipo-Tipo is that, unless you're packing some big-time firepower, you don't want to wander anywhere near that place on the ground." He turned around to face McGirt and the two enlisted crewmen, then made a devilish throat- slashing gesture to further emphasize his point.

Karlena Brandt opened her crusted-over eyelids when she heard the thumping sound in the distance. It was a different rhythm and tone from the other aircraft she'd heard flying in the area. But the helicopter was not what weighed on her now: It was the screams and horrific visualizations that she'd endured the evening before that had caused her body to wretch with fear and revulsion. Ultimately, her stamina was sapped and she had passed out, but not before her innards had convulsed with dry heaves that had filled her mouth with bile.

Gagged and unable to spit, she was forced to swallow the bitter liquid. She'd clamped down hard on the spittle-soaked rag upon hearing the dreadful, howling bellows of a human as he was slaughtered like a farm animal. She thought she recognized the voice that she'd heard pleading and begging, but the conversation had been at a distance from the building where she was held, and the words were difficult to comprehend. There had been no response to the man's pleas, only the rap-rap-rap sound of a chainsaw as it was started and revved up to its full, most effective operating speed. But the short-lived shrieks that had followed overwhelmed the grinding buzz of the power tool's motor.

Unlike the times when Karlena had trimmed an unruly branch from one of her dad's prized bur oaks, the pitch of the saw's motor deepened only briefly as it began ripping its way through. The man's brief screams changed to a wet gurgle, and then ceased all together. As quickly as the butchery had started, it was over. After the saw's motor had wound down, Karlena heard a few muffled words, some laughs, and then the unmistakable sound of Spider's voice as he shouted orders. There was trampling of footsteps, followed by the fading rumble of a vehicle as it sped away. No more screams; no more chainsaws; only dark silence and nightmarish sleep.

McGirt looked out a cabin window as the teeming, ramshackle waterfront of Isabela City whisked by in a speedy blur. Seated in back as a passenger, he suddenly became aware of how much he already missed being at the controls. The scenery below changed quickly from a sea of cloistered rooftops to unpopulated, thickly vegetated fields. McGirt felt the aircraft's drive system unload as the pilot lowered the collective to its bottom stop, thus killing lift on the helo's six rotor blades. The aircraft went into a very steep left bank, then spiraled down rapidly. As the ground rushed up at them, the pilot rolled to a level attitude, pulled back on the cyclic and yanked in an armful of collective. The helicopter stabilized in a hover and then touched down softly.

The crew chief quickly lowered the aft ramp while his cohort stood by with the automatic weapon tucked stealthily along his side. McGirt and Bud grabbed their gear and hustled off the aircraft. Once clear of the helicopter's rotor wash, McGirt turned and watched as the H-46 rose up and departed as quickly as it had arrived; the aircraft had been on deck for less than one minute.

McGirt felt a firm tap on his shoulder as he fixated on watching the helicopter accelerate and climb, headed back out to sea.

"Captain McGirt, I am Colonel Felix Romolo, base commander."

McGirt spun around to face the barrel-chested, stout AFP officer. "With all the noise, I guess you couldn't hear Dr. Lammers and me hollering your name," the colonel said with a friendly laugh; but Romolo's vice-grip handshake conveyed that the dark-skinned warrior was all business.

Bud shook his head and chuckled at McGirt's apparent absent-mindedness. "Must be the jetlag, Colonel. He's normally not this foggy."

"Please join me in the mess. Have you eaten breakfast?"

Lammers and McGirt acknowledged that they already had and followed the colonel across the acre-sized open field where the helicopter had landed. Romolo led them into an elevated pavilion that served as the military outpost's eating facility. McGirt heard the clucking and purring of wild chickens nested under the building as he climbed the half-dozen steps into the open-air structure. Inside, a handful of AFP enlisted men were finishing up their morning chow. McGirt peeked into the kitchen as they walked by. He noted clean, modern-looking appliances and well-stocked shelves. Romolo guided them toward the facility's beverage station, where there was a tall coffee urn and a cooler chocked full of bottled water and soft drinks.

"Thank God," Lammers said as he grabbed a water.

McGirt poured himself a cup of black coffee.

Romolo took a seat at the banquet style table across from McGirt and Lammers. "Gentlemen, we can leave at any time for your appointment with Mr. Abbas; or would you prefer to get settled in your quarters first?"

Lammers spoke up. "Colonel, if it's all the same to you, we'd like to meet with Abbas ASAP. But I'm a little concerned; wasn't one of our Army Rangers, a Colonel Woodbridge, supposed to meet us here today?"

Romolo shuffled in his chair and cleared his throat. "The colonel phoned me earlier this morning and said he was delayed in Zamboanga. His second in command, Captain Travis Banks, will be available later today."

Bud's affability disappeared faster than the eight ounces of cold water he'd gulped down. He turned to McGirt with a peeved look, then faced Romolo. "Okay, then why isn't Banks here now?"

Romolo sat up a little straighter and paused before answering. "He and his men are on a reconnaissance training mission with one of my platoons. They've taken a pair of vehicles south to Lamitan and will then patrol near the Tipo-Tipo region. It's about a three hour round trip."

"Fine. We'll meet with Banks after lunch, if Woodbridge is still AWOL," Lammers snapped. An awkward pall descended over the group as McGirt took another sip from his coffee cup. Romolo looked down and began fiddling with his wristwatch.

McGirt noticed that Bud had begun sweating profusely. He wasn't sure if it was a sign of Bud's anger at being stiffed by Woodbridge, or a physical reaction from downing the ice cold drink so quickly. He leaned over and half-whispered, "You okay, pal?"

Bud waved him off and ignored his question.

Romolo stood up. "Okay, very well. My men will take care of your bags if you'd like. I have you billeted in your own huts, adjacent to one another, a short walk from here." He barked some words in the direction of two young soldiers, who'd been straightening up tables and chairs on the other side of the building. The pair double-timed over to their commander. Romolo must have read the American's minds when he said, "Your things will be safe and secure, gentlemen;

I give you my word." With that, he then turned very slowly to the soldiers and seemed to silently communicate: *Don't even think of tampering with their stuff.*

McGirt and Lammers followed the colonel to his personal vehicle—a bland-looking, beige-colored minivan, devoid of any military markings. Other than the officer's compact holstered revolver, there were no other weapons aboard the vehicle.

They drove through a guarded gate and onto a dirt road that zigzagged by endless rows of pineapple plants and coconut trees. Once off the base, the contrast was dramatic—from the clean, well-provisioned efficiency of the military, to a world of abject poverty and dilapidation. Romolo maneuvered carefully between rain-carved potholes and roaming farm animals. The stench of garbage and raw sewage was pervasive.

"Colonel, is this type poverty prevalent on most of the island?" Bud asked.

"In some areas, yes, especially the further you get from the cities, or away from the Christian regions." Romolo slowed the van to a crawl to allow three women clothed in long skirts and white headscarves to cross in front.

The women's eyes followed them in unison as they passed by. McGirt, who was riding in the front passenger's seat, looked back at the group through his side window. He saw one of the women pull out a cell phone and begin texting. "Looks like the locals can at least afford phones. How about cable and HBO?" he quipped.

Romolo laughed. "No, not yet, Captain. The cell coverage is fair, but needs much improving. Maybe our beloved leaders in Manila will take pity on us poor southerners someday and spread the wealth, so to speak." The steering wheel jerked violently between his hands. "And to fix this damn road," he added. "My sincere apologies about the rough ride."

The van jolted as they made a ninety-degree turn, drove over a steep curb and merged onto a paved highway. Romolo pounded down the accelerator. "Gentlemen, we're now on the island's main thoroughfare: the Basilan Circumferential Road. We'll be at our destination in less than ten minutes."

The colonel's graciousness seemed to diffuse the tension that had followed Bud's display of indignation back at the mess pavilion. McGirt decided to go with the flow and offered, "Your English is flawless, Colonel. Spend any extended time in the States?"

A slight grin formed on Romolo's leathery face. "Yes, I lived there for a while."

# CHAPTER 16

Neither McGirt nor Bud Lammers were fully prepared for the onslaught to their senses when they stepped outside of Romolo's air-conditioned van. The oppressive heat and humidity that had somehow gotten worse during the thirty-minute drive was no surprise; some memories never fade. But what startled them the most was the swarming clusters of vendors hawking their wares; rattling motorbikes careening through crowded alleyways—and then there was the smell: that fishy, rotting-vegetation aroma woven like slippery strands through untreated human waste. Although they'd often been exposed to it during their cruises to the Western Pacific and Philippine Islands, it was something to which they could never grow accustomed.

Colonel Romolo parked across the street from the *Basilan Betterment Foundation's* office.

Again, Bud Lammers took the lead before the colonel had the chance to speak. "McGirt and I would prefer to meet with Abbas alone, if it's all the same to you, Colonel. Would you mind just keeping an eye out for anything that looks suspicious?" Bud realized that his request had been ill worded, as if he'd been talking down to the professional soldier. "*My* apologies this time, sir," he offered. "That didn't come out just right. Thank you for getting us here safely."

Romolo appeared to understand Bud's misstep and nodded. He undid his seatbelt and shuffled the 9- millimeter handgun's holster to a more comfortable position.

Though neither man was wearing any type of military garb—they'd dressed in khaki pants and golf shirts—they stuck out from the crowd like a couple of white-collared clergy at a topless bar. There were no other Caucasians, or "round-eyes," to be found in any direction. A few panhandlers started to approach them, but after sighting Romolo glaring at them from his van, they backed away. Most of the civilians on the narrow street appeared too busy, or too afraid, to bother the Americans. McGirt followed Bud as he navigated through the horde.

"Just like Olongapo on its worst day," Bud quipped as he sprung over a mud puddle and onto the sidewalk.

"Smells about the same, too," McGirt added.

"Well, this is step number one, my friend. Like I said at the briefing: let me do the initial talking until Abbas asks you something, okay?"

"Got it—loud and clear." McGirt had struggled a bit with Lammers's assertiveness when they'd met with Captain Torres; had they not gone back so far, he'd probably have been pissed at Bud's bossiness.

The door swung open at Bud's second knock. A meek-looking, stone-faced little man held it open just wide enough for the two of them to pass through. "Welcome," Abbas said. No handshakes or gestures of hospitality; instead, a curt motioning of an arm toward a couple of folding chairs as he closed the door. Abbas returned to his place behind a non-descript, gray metal desk, the kind that seemed to occupy most military and government offices back in the states. Behind Abbas was a huge, floor-to-ceiling wooden bookcase, crammed to its limit with thick tomes and stacks of notebooks and folders.

"So what can I do for you today, gentlemen?" The Filipino's English was good, but more measured and deliberate than the colonel's. He leaned back and stroked his wispy goatee nonchalantly.

"Mr. Abbas, my name is Dr. Charles Lammers, and this is my associate, Mr. John McGirt. First off, thank you for meeting with us today. Our country respects and praises the outstanding work that your foundation is doing to help the Muslim citizens of Basilan."

Abbas nodded gratefully, raised a small, dark-skinned hand. "We assist *all* of Basilan, not just those of my faith. Please remember that." The tone of his voice was not hostile, yet neither McGirt nor Lammers failed to pick up on the man's intended condescension.

"Well, of course. From the input that I've received, your foundation has done wonderful things with bringing fresh well water and improved sanitation to the residents—*all* residents—of the island." Bud unzipped the tan-colored canvas valise that he'd brought along and removed a thick, business-sized envelope. He set it in front of Abbas.

"The citizens of the United States would like to offer a modest contribution to the *Basilan Betterment Foundation*, to be used in whatever way that you see fit."

Abbas reached out, deftly slid the envelope across the desk and dropped it into an opened drawer, all the time maintaining a locked eye contact with Lammers. He closed the desk drawer firmly and simply said, "Thank you."

McGirt had been sitting idly as Bud had instructed him to do, but he could not mask his surprise any longer. His eyes widened at what he'd just observed: *If I've come all the way over to this third world cesspool to simply be part of a 'pay-to-play bribe,' then I've just wasted several days of my life*, he thought. What unfolded was an exchange that his three decades of military training and experience hadn't prepared him for; he felt about as confident as a ballerina who'd been entered in a kickboxing tournament.

Bud seemed to have shifted gears at the sound of Abbas closing the metal drawer after accepting the money. McGirt noticed how he now sat up a little straighter and had stopped sweating. Dr. Charles 'Bud' Lammers, PhD.—game face firmly in place—appeared ready to get down to business.

"I've read that you are a highly educated man, Mr. Abbas," Lammers began. "Magna Cum Laude from the University of the Philippines Law School and all. But we didn't just travel nine thousand miles to simply line your pockets and pat you on the back."

McGirt watched as Abbas, for the first time since they'd arrived, showed a tinge of emotion as he began to blink rapidly. He then reached up and straightened the snow-white skullcap, or kufi, that rested on his neatly trimmed black hair. His eyes darted quickly to McGirt and then back to Bud. A smirk crept from the corner of his mouth.

"By the tone of your voice, Doctor, may I assume that you wish to gain some information about one of your Americans who is assumed to be *missing*?" The manner in which Abbas had pronounced the word '"missing"—with an awkwardly drawn-out inflection of the first syllable—left no doubt to either McGirt or Lammers that he was well on his way to being torqued. Abbas started pawing at his goatee again.

"Like I've told Colonel Romolo and the FBI agents before you, my charitable organization, as its name implies, focuses solely on the betterment of living conditions for all Filipino residents of Basilan. Neither my staff in the field nor I have the time or resources to track down missing people." Abbas's disdainful snicker transformed effortlessly to a mildly sincere grin.

"I understand everything you're saying, Mr. Abbas. That being said, I'd be less than honest if I didn't tell you that my government is fully aware of the contacts that your group has had with Abu Sayyaf."

McGirt saw that Bud seemed to have again struck a nerve with the little Filipino. Up until this point, Abbas had, for the most part, appeared coolly stoic—much like a professional poker player who held a good hand yet chose to sit back and let his competition defeat themselves.

Abbas shifted erratically in his chair and commenced tapping his fingertips on the desk. His grin expanded slowly into a half smile. He glared at Lammers and held his focus for several seconds; Lammers neither flinched nor blinked. The standoff was broken when the Filipino rose from his seat and walked from behind his desk to a credenza on the other side of the room. As he did, McGirt noticed the man's hop-like limp. One of Abbas's legs appeared to be shorter than the other, and he wore an elevated shoe to compensate for the abnormality. Once at the credenza, he opened a compartment and removed a square wooden plaque that displayed a mounted handgun; he held it out for the Americans to see.

"Are either of you gentlemen familiar with this weapon?" he asked.

McGirt turned to Bud with a "what the hell?" shrug of his shoulders as Lammers quickly spoke up. "My guess is that's one of the early single-action Army Colt 45s. Looks like possibly the Peacemaker model."

His smile seemed more genuine now as Abbas responded, "Very good, sir. I sensed that your training at the Central Intelligence Agency has exposed you to some firearms history."

McGirt concluded that he was no longer an active participant at this meeting. He crossed his legs, sat back and could only guess at what was about to follow. He waited for his colleague's next move.

"That weapon was designed in the late 1800s and was used primarily during the Spanish-American and Indian Wars."

"Correct!" Abbas said enthusiastically; he appeared fully engaged in the discussion.

"But if you're going to fully test my knowledge," Bud continued, "I'm reasonably well versed in its significance during the Philippine-American War just after the turn of the century."

Abbas took on the demeanor of a patronizing professor as he turned to McGirt . "Mr. McGirt—or would you prefer that I call you *Captain?*—during your studies in Monterey and time at the U.S. Embassy, were you ever schooled in the magnitude that this weapon was used against my fellow countrymen?"

"Nah, you got me there, pal," McGirt said. He felt Bud's elbow strike firmly against his side. "But I have a feeling that you're about to tell me."

Abbas continued the dissertation unfazed. "It seems that while Filipino freedom fighters in the northern provinces had decided to accept their fate by surrendering into another long period of colonialism—first to the Spaniards and then to the Americans—my ancestors, or Moros, as commonly referred to, continued to do battle with a fervor unknown to Western soldiers. The 38-caliber pistol carried by your fighters at that time proved to be unsuccessful in its stopping power against the Moro guerrillas. Unless struck with a headshot, those brave jungle warriors were able to continue their charge. Thus your army, many of whom had fought to tame your country's Native Americans, was forced to revert to using the larger caliber 45, with its heavier bullet."

Bud shook his head and stood up. He joined Abbas at the credenza. Though Lammers wasn't an exceptionally large man at just under six feet tall, he towered over the miniscule Filipino. Lammers took hold of the plaque and ran his fingers across the antique firearm. He turned to Abbas. "Why do I think there's more to this history lesson than meets the eye, and you're not just bloviating?"

For the first time, Malik Abbas seemed to show a sense of humor. "Very good, Dr. Lammers; I admire your choice of descriptive verbs. I will cut to the chase, as you people like to say. My grandfather captured this revolver from one of your fallen soldiers during a battle on the island of Mindanao, across the channel, near Zamboanga City. I've kept this weapon as more than just a souvenir; it reminds me of all the senseless violence between the "haves" and the "have-nots" that has taken place on the soil of my homeland."

Lammers acknowledged with a polite bow as he handed the gun back to Abbas. "With all due respect, sir, may we take our seats and continue with the heart of why McGirt and I flew all the way over here? And for the record, yes, those Moro tribesmen were fearless, but in large part because they were so hyped-up on narcotics that a sledge hammer to the head might not have brought them down."

Abbas looked sternly at Bud. "As they say, Doctor, in wartime, whatever it takes to win, whatever it takes." He returned to his seat behind the desk.

McGirt wasn't sure, but he thought he detected Abbas's caramel-colored complexion turn a slight shade of red from anger; the glare on the man's face left no doubt.

"Gentlemen, I will keep my eyes and ears open for any news from my people about missing Americans. Occasionally, some of our volunteers cross paths with the rebels you referred to, the ASG. Many townspeople have maintained a cordial relationship with that faction."

Bud extended a business card. "My phone number can be reached world-wide. There are some very influential people in the United States that would be *most* grateful for your assistance. Please call me if you can offer anything at all."

"If that does happen, I will most likely contact the Colonel first," Abbas said. He rose a few inches off his chair to peek out a window. "Who I see is still waiting patiently for you."

"Thank you," Bud said as they concluded. Unlike when they'd arrived, Abbas shook their hands as they left.

McGirt and Lammers paused at the curb as a burst of cars, buses and motorbikes sped by in a noisy, exhaust-spewing flurry. Romolo started the van's engine while they waited for the stream of the vehicles to pass by.

"How much did you give him?" McGirt asked.

"Not much. The Director only authorized ten grand this time."

"I was surprised that you didn't bring up those NPA guys in the North; you know, those commie bastards that brought down Rayburn's aircraft."

"Nope. Wouldn't have served any purpose in this case," Bud shot back. "Trust me, Abbas knows more about that whole movement than either of us."

"Huh?" McGirt said as he started to cross the street once traffic had cleared.

Bud pulled him back before they got within earshot of Romolo. "Do you remember our debriefing after Rayburn's shoot-down, when that federal agent mentioned a young boy who'd been hit in the crossfire?"

McGirt raised his eyebrows. "Gee, that was twenty years ago, but yeah—some Muslim college kid who'd been at the wrong place at the wrong time. Right?"

Bud tilted his head toward Abbas's office. "That was him."

# CHAPTER 17

Otto Brandt was sure that someone was watching him. He'd noticed a white panel truck parked in the same spot for the last several days—in a dirt lot across the highway from the diner where he went for coffee every morning. The truck had no significant markings other than its Louisiana plates. What had stimulated Otto's interest was the fact that the truck was in direct line of sight and with a clear view to his ranch about a mile away. He'd considered calling the Odessa police, but after conferring with his life-long friend, Harvey Durst, he had decided against it.

At Otto's urging, Harvey had cautiously approached the vehicle and peeked inside through the driver's side window, but there wasn't much to see; a plywood partition had been installed directly behind the truck's cab, preventing him from scoping out what was inside the back of the vehicle. Likewise, the small windows on the truck's bi-fold rear doors had been blacked out. The day after Harvey had performed his reconnaissance run, the truck had mysteriously disappeared.

Harvey's kin had also migrated from Germany during the late 1800s to form what some had dubbed, "the Texas Reich." Like Herman Brandt, his great-grandfather had travelled west and found life in Texas to be far superior to the conditions he'd experienced in the motherland. The Brandt and Durst clans had begun their new lives in a similar fashion: as farmers in the Texas Hill Country. Otto and Harvey had struck up a friendship there, as children, and remained close after both families had sold their properties to seek fortunes in the oil-rich Permian Basin of Odessa/Midland. After everything that had gone down since Karlena's disappearance, Harvey Durst was about the only person left whom Otto really trusted.

The ransom note had been tucked inside the *Odessa American* newspaper that was delivered every evening to a roadside box at the end of Otto's long, gravel driveway. The note—typed in the stiff, OCR-style font used by financial institutions and government agencies—had been unmistakably direct: what to order; dollar amount; account and routing numbers. The icily terse sentence, "Do this within forty-eight hours or Ms. Karlena Louise Brandt will die," had concluded the group's demand.

Otto had immediately phoned Harvey after reading the note. They'd met outside the diner where they put their heads together and discussed what to do. Clayton Gantry's earlier admonishment that the U.S government forbids the paying of ransoms by private citizens replayed in Otto's head. Despite the warning, he and Harvey had agreed: He was going to ignore Gantry's advice and pay the money.

The amount was substantial, but easily within Otto's means. A few keystrokes had moved the funds from his stock brokerage trading account to a money market that he held with a Dallas bank. From that point, he only knew that the funds were to be electronically transferred to an Arab-owned company, located in Mexico, in the form of a purchase order for "oil exploration machinery." Otto had done business with other Mexican firms, but not this one. His computer search of the outfit's name—MexErig—hadn't yielded much. *Yahoo Finance's* web page had devoted just a few words in summarizing the company's affairs: "An oilrig component distributor conducting business in Mexico, Asia and the U.S."

Otto had paused after discovering that the company was actually based in Riyadh, Saudi Arabia. He'd suspected from the start that Karlena's disappearance had been tied, in some way, to "those damn A-rabs." And Harvey Durst had warned him that, "These ain't a bunch of dumb jungle monkeys you're dealing with. I think it goes much deeper than what appears on the surface." After reading where MexErig was headquartered, Otto realized that his friend was probably right. What neither of them knew for sure, however, was to where the money would flow after being wired to the Mexican firm.

MexErig would not directly provide the machinery to Brandt's oil and gas exploration company, but would instead—after extracting a ten-percent fee— forward the order to *Quality Expeditors* in Manila, where Ahmad Jalil would purchase, at a huge markdown, used equipment from a drilling company in Central Mindanao. The order would then be shipped to the Mexican port of Lazaro Cardenas, and from there, the grossly overpriced goods would travel, via rail and highway, across the Mexican border to Odessa. Ahmad would take his hefty cut, and then make a large "donation" to Malik Abbas's charity. Once her captors had been notified that the transaction had been completed, Karlena would be released.

It had been over twelve hours since he and Harvey had laid out their strategy. Otto had spent the early evening hours in a sweaty, sleepless state, eventually surrendering to the grip of insomnia by getting out of bed and walking into the kitchen. He flicked on the "BREW" switch of the fancy automatic coffee maker that Karlena had given him a couple of birthdays ago, then stood by and watched it go through its gyrations as it magically refilled its water tank, ground beans and ultimately brewed them all in one smooth motion. He fondly recalled how his daughter had guided him through the gizmo's instruction manual before reluctantly turning him loose with the modern appliance. "Guess I'm just a low-tech guy in a high-tech world," Otto had confessed sheepishly. "Getting oil out of the ground is easy compared to workin' this darn thing."

But Otto's affection for the coffee maker only reminded him of Karlena and served to deepen the aching sadness brought on by her disappearance. Harvey had recommended that, in order to avoid arousing suspicions, he should wait until after the Dallas bank opened before executing the transaction—that way, he'd reasoned, "it won't stick out so much." Otto occupied the last several hours by mindlessly surfing the Internet as he waited for night's dark solitude to pass. The only sound in the room was the rhythmic sound of his fingers as he pecked away on the keyboard. As with the automatic coffee pot, Karlena had purchased and taught him how to use the computer.

His forth cup of coffee made the normally tight-lipped, stoic Texan feel punch-drunk and giddy. He began chuckling as he scrolled through tabloid news stories, outrageous advertisements and other nonsense that seemed to magically pop up on the computer screen. He figured that somebody—maybe whoever owned that white truck that had been parked over by the diner—was probably monitoring his every move as he typed. But he didn't care; it was worth the risk and he had nothing to lose.

He prayed that once this whole ordeal was completed, his little girl would be freed and she'd return to where she belonged: safe with him at their West Texas ranch.

# CHAPTER 18

The drive back to the AFP camp was tedious and hot. The air-conditioning unit on Romolo's van was valiantly trying to combat Basilan's oppressive midday heat, but it was losing the battle: The vehicle's little high-revving four cylinder engine just could not produce enough umph to power both its drive train and cooling system effectively.

Bud finally capitulated and said, "Colonel, go ahead and kill the A-C if you'd like; maybe she'll go a little faster." He looked at McGirt in the back seat and rolled his eyes in frustration as Romolo complied and switched off the air conditioner's compressor. "Why prolong the agony?" he added rhetorically.

The van lurched forward at a noticeably faster clip. Bud mumbled something under his breath as he swiped an already-soaked handkerchief across his face, then tilted his head out the opened passenger's-side window in hopes of snatching some additional breeze. He glanced over at Colonel Romolo, who looked to be unfazed by the steamy climate; the soldier's face and body appeared bone-dry.

"You get used to it," Romolo said. "I had the same reaction both times after returning home from my years at the Academy."

McGirt leaned forward to hear Romolo's words better. As he did, he noted the big, ornate ring on the colonel's hand as the soldier steered the van. "If you don't mind me asking, sir, is that a West Point ring?"

"Yes, it is; Class of 1978."

Bud rallied from his uncomfortable grouchiness. "Ah ha. That explains it! So you're a 'ring-knocker!'"

A big smile erupted across Romolo's face. "Did four years there as an exchange cadet, and then a two-year tour as a literature instructor in the nineties."

Bud looked back at McGirt with a surprised expression. They seemed to be having the same thought: This rugged looking warrior didn't come across as a man of letters.

"Wow, would not have guessed that," McGirt piped in. "Colonel, you seem more suited to be the engineering type in my humble opinion."

Romolo laughed. "Many people have said that to me as well. All things considered though, West Point was the best thing that ever happened to me. Most of my classmates compared their time at the Point to being in jail, but not me. I loved the discipline and challenges. God willing, when my career ends here in the P.I., I'd like to go back to the Hudson River Valley. Maybe buy a small farm or something like that."

The traffic surrounding Isabela City began to thin out, and Romolo was finally able to coax the underpowered machine to a speed that allowed the van's interior to cool off. With all of its windows lowered, the ride was noisy, but bearable.

"Gentlemen, I did not want to share this until after your meeting with Mr. Abbas, but Colonel Woodbridge will not be available during your stay—in fact he was recalled to your Special Operations Command in Hawaii."

"Oh?" McGirt said. He noticed that Romolo's grip on the wheel had tightened, and the soldier's expression had returned to its stern, all-business state.

Bud pressed the situation and demanded, "So what the hell is up? Shouldn't we have been briefed before we arrived?"

Romolo took a deep breath and appeared to be laboring as he searched for the right words. "His second-in-command, Captain Banks, can fill you in on the complete story. What I do know is that Colonel Woodbridge was relieved for cause. He seems to have developed a problem with alcohol. Again, I'm not the best one to convey all the details. Banks can do that."

Bud Lammers sat back and shook his head at the news. His pre-mission briefing had explicitly stated that Woodbridge would be his point of contact as he and McGirt sought intel on the whereabouts of Karlena Brandt.

Colonel Romolo proceeded. "But I can tell you that, from what I've seen so far, Captain Banks is a capable officer whom I've known for some years. He was an honors student in the modern literature class that I taught back at the Point."

"Well that's just dandy," Bud sniped. "Maybe he can bring us up to date with the latest bestsellers list." Bud's anger and frustration at this new development threw a damper on the otherwise congenial conversation.

McGirt tried to temper Bud's moodiness. "I'm confident that we'll adapt, Colonel. Anyway, this is merely a fact-finding mission for us." He tapped Bud affectionately on the shoulder and laughed. "Nothing too risky for these old swabbies, eh, Bud?"

"Yeah…that's right," Lammers groused. "Guess we'll be okay with Banks." Bud noted the digital clock centered on the van's console. "How about we get some chow, meet Banks and regroup back at camp?"

"My thoughts exactly," Romolo said. His grip loosened on the wheel. He appeared relieved that the news about Woodbridge was finally out. "Banks and his men should arrive with my guys around noon. You gents should have sufficient time to eat, unwind and get settled into your quarters. Work load permitting, I normally let my men stand down and take a short siesta after lunch." The van bounced as they turned off the paved highway and onto the pitted dirt road that led back to camp. "One of the few worthwhile customs the Spaniards left behind," he quipped.

McGirt and Lammers made their way to the quarters that Romolo had set up for them at the AFP camp. They found their hut to be a surprisingly well appointed, duplex-like unit, constructed on six-foot long bamboo stilts. The structure was powered with electricity, but like all other quarters except Romolo's, lacking its own bathroom.

After a quick shower in the camp's community head, the men walked back to the compound's open-air mess hall. As they did, a convoy of armored, all-terrain trucks filed past them.

"Must be Banks and his crew," McGirt said as the group came to a halt and unloaded.

Through the dusty spectacle of soldiers, weapons and diesel exhaust, it was easy to distinguish the Americans from their Filipino counterparts: they stood out like a group of Big Ten football players alongside junior high schoolers. The U.S. Army detachment was part of the first wave of *Exercise Balikatan* or "Shoulder-to-Shoulder," a joint forces engagement tasked with routing out terrorist from Basilan Island and restoring social order to its citizenry.

A strapping African-American emerged from the crowd and double-timed toward McGirt and Lammers. "Let me guess, you're the dudes from Langley who are here to aggravate me?" he said. The officer flashed a magnetic smile and extended his hand. "Captain Travis Banks, U.S. Army Ranger, sir!"

Bud stepped forward, grabbed Banks's hand and shook it enthusiastically. "Name's Lammers, Bud Lammers; this is my colleague, Johnny Jack McGirt."

Banks looked at McGirt and titled his head with mocked uncertainty. "Johnny and Jack..." he said slowly. "That's an interesting combo. Should I call—"

McGirt snatched Banks's hand aggressively. "McGirt's fine, Captain. Just call me McGirt."

Banks responded by clamping down a little harder on McGirt's hand. "Understand you're a retired rotor-head. That right?"

"Yes. Bud and I both flew Navy helicopters on active duty."

"Man, we're in desperate need of a reliable aviation division here in this hell hole. Romolo has us sharing a chopper with another AFP group over on the mainland, in Mindanao. Damn thing's down for maintenance more time than it's up."

The threesome looked up at the sound of a non-descript, civilian pickup truck in need of a new muffler as it approached the camp's security gate. The vehicle was quickly waved through, drove past them and parked in front of Colonel Romolo's private quarters. A sloppily dressed Filipino emerged from the pickup; he glanced their way and then marched up to the door of Romolo's private cabin. The man wore tattered blue jeans, a brown tee shirt and a weathered ball cap. Dark, wrap-around style sunglasses shrouded his eyes.

"Who the hell is that?" Lammers asked.

Banks studied the guy for a few seconds before saying, "I don't...know. Never seen him come around before. But he seems to have an in with the Colonel."

The Americans watched as Romolo and the newcomer shared a few words in the cabin's doorway before the Colonel walked the man back to the pickup. They shook hands, and then the stranger departed as quickly as he'd arrived. Romolo joined the group and ushered them to the mess hall.

"Somebody we should know, Colonel?" Lammers asked. McGirt detected a hint of rancor had, once again, returned to Bud's tone.

"Just one of the locals that I'm dealing with; nothing really that important," Romolo answered matter-of-factly.

Lammers pulled McGirt aside as the Colonel and Banks walked ahead. He followed the pickup's movements with the distrustful suspicion of a person who'd made a living by sifting truth from bullshit. The pickup truck left the camp and drove out of sight. Lammers raised an eyebrow and then whispered to McGirt, "Yeah, right, just one of the locals—my ass."

Following the colonel's lead, they allowed every enlisted man to snake through the chow line before they did, and then found a table on the far side of the building. The American and Filipino soldiers sat at separate tables.

"I was hoping that the men would begin to intermingle," Romolo said while motioning to the seated troops.

"Colonel, I'll get on my top sergeant again about that," Banks replied. "I agree that we may need to nudge the boys a little in that direction." He swiped his fork across the rice, diced vegetables and some-sort-of-meat concoction that covered his food tray. "Man what I'd do for a good bacon-cheeseburger and fries about now." Nonetheless, he dug into his meal with a vengeance.

The group spent the next several minutes quietly eating before Romolo spoke up. "Captain Banks, I gave our two guests a short briefing on Colonel Woodbridge's status. Nothing more than the basics; perhaps you'd care to elaborate."

Banks nodded and finished chewing. He folded his hands in front of him on the table and paused for a few seconds before beginning. "Gentlemen, I was forced to initiate the recall of Colonel Woodbridge to the States." The affable manner Banks had displayed at first toward McGirt and Lammers switched to a sterner, pained expression. "I'm certainly no expert on this—I'll leave that to the shrinks—but my take is that Woodbridge may be suffering from post-traumatic stress after his tours in the Gulf during Operation Desert Storm." Banks lowered his eyes, as if he were carefully measuring his words before continuing. "It was a tough decision, but one that had to be made before he injured himself or caused any further damage to unit morale. As you both know, we've been sent over here to Basilan to advise our Filipino allies in their battle against this latest wave of bad guys. Woodbridge was in no condition to effectively lead his men in that pursuit."

McGirt glanced at Romolo as Banks spoke. He saw that the colonel was nodding in silent agreement with Banks's assessment.

Banks shook his head disgustedly. "When I had to drag his drunken ass out of a whore house for the third time early one morning, it left me no choice: He had to go home. I put him on a Philippine Airlines flight yesterday morning and just prayed that he would stay sober long enough to make his connection in Manila. It's my understanding that, ultimately, he'll be reassigned to Army Special Ops Command back at Fort Bragg for further evaluation."

An unpleasant pall fell over the group, followed by Lammers offering, "Well Captain, sometimes you have to do what you have to do, and we certainly wish Woodbridge the best; but if it's okay with everyone, can we switch the discussion to why McGirt and I are here?"

Romolo and Banks both chuckled nervously as if they were more than happy to drop the topic of Colonel Woodbridge's tribulations.

"First, thanks for hosting us. From what McGirt and I gather, this will be a significant challenge as you put together your operation—Joint Task Force Five Ten. From what my team back at the Agency has uncovered, this Abu Sayyaf group is not going away by itself. It's an established fact that many of them have deep roots back to al-Qaeda and fought with that group during the Soviet's war in Afghanistan. We're not talking about a group of rag-tag banana farmers."

Banks perked up. "Dr. Lammers, quite frankly, it's hard for me to believe that you and McGirt flew to the other side of the globe on just a fact-finding junket to learn more about a young girl who's disappeared."

"That's correct, there's more to it," Lammers replied. "The girl's father is a wealthy... no, make that a wealthy, *very-well-connected* Texas oilman. We're afraid that he may have already paid a ransom in hopes of gaining his daughter's release. McGirt and I met this morning with a Muslim community leader in Isabela City, who runs a charitable organization. In addition to his group's humanitarian efforts, our sources suspect that a large portion of the charity's budget finds its way to support the ASG's terrorist activities through recruitment of new members and the purchasing of weapons."

Lammers realized that he was monopolizing the conversation, so he turned to McGirt, hoping that his partner would take over.

Romolo, however, spoke up first. "May I add that recruiting the next batch of bad guys is not difficult for the ASG. Most of these young Muslims in the southern islands have little hope of ever improving the quality of their lives otherwise. They're faced with a lack of education, no decent jobs and abject poverty."

"Right on the mark, Colonel," Banks said. "It's no secret that, if we're to be successful down here, we'll have to establish some trust with the Islamic communities. We patrolled the Circumferential Road this morning, as far south as Tipo-Tipo. My men, along with our AFP counterparts, received some mighty mean-looking glares. But once the locals realize that we have the capabilities to offer assistance with things as basic as obtaining clean water from a new well, or that our medics can provide simple hygiene items and immunizations for their children, we'll begin to gain their trust and respect. Eventually, we should be able to obtain enough intel from the locals that we'll be better suited to overtake the thugs that are causing all this havoc."

Banks sat up rigidly. His thick neck muscles flexed as he tilted back his head and faced Colonel Romolo. "But in the meantime, I recommend a strategy of hunting down the bastards like dogs and offing them."

Romolo had sat quietly while Travis Banks was going off on his diatribe. McGirt volunteered, "Colonel, this is your native country." He paused and made brief but purposeful eye contact with Banks. "Any thoughts?"

"Well," Romolo began, "I've had the opportunity to observe what's going on from many angles: as a foot soldier in the field, staff tours in Manila and from an American perspective while serving at West Point." He turned to Banks. "Travis, there is some hesitation on my part about hunting down fellow Filipino's like dogs and then executing them. I've observed my men closely—not all of them are of the Christian faith, I remind you. Many have respectfully voiced their concerns whether or not the Joint Task Force is the most appropriate method for dealing with this situation. It goes without saying that we look forward to the arrival of your aviation units and your Navy fighters—the SEALs—but in the end, like all conflicts, there will have to be negotiations in order to provide a longer-lasting peace, and a deterrence to radical groups like the Abu Sayyaf."

Banks rose abruptly with his food tray in hand. "Colonel Romolo, I've known you for a long time, and I respect your views. What I'm saying is that, given a choice, I'd prefer to take action first and ask questions later." He then turned to McGirt and Lammers. "Gentlemen, the Colonel and I have scheduled a patrol on the island's western side, in the Maluso region; more or less to show the flag and to assuage the locals' concerns about our motives. With the colonel's permission, I'd like to offer you the chance to join us."

Romolo nodded and gave a silent "thumbs-up."

Banks looked at his watch. "Say another hour from now, around fourteen hundred?"

Lammers's mood seemed to brighten upon hearing Banks's proposal. "Damn, right—finally, something out in the field!" he said. "It'll give us a chance to get a lay of the land, don't you think, McGirt?"

Tarzan Truckee's admonition to "stay out of trouble" flashed through McGirt's mind. But, with three sets of eyes focused on him, he decided to simply go along. "Okay," he said. "See you then."

Banks dropped off his tray at the kitchen and then proceeded to the enlisted men's section of the hall. He addressed both his own troops and Romolo's while one the AFPs translated for the handful of Filipinos not fluent in English. When he'd concluded, the cadre nodded and mumbled in agreement with the news of their next mission.

Romolo sat silent with arms folded across his chest; he looked peeved.

The look was not lost on McGirt. "Colonel, who's your second in command here?"

"That would be Major Salazar. He's my deputy, and he'll be leading your patrol to Maluso. He spent the night in Zamboanga and should be arriving very soon on the next ferry."

McGirt thought to himself, *We're leaving in an hour. Salazar's cutting it a little close, isn't he?* Both he and Lammers decided to let it pass.

Romolo forced a grin. "Travis Banks was a hell of a football player during his days at the Point; a fine student as well. That said, in my opinion, his rough urban upbringing occasionally overwhelms his patience and good sense. I will be thankful when Woodbridge's replacement arrives. I'm not really in his chain of command to properly counsel Banks in the manner I believe would benefit him." Romolo paused and searched for the correct words. "Just let me say that Captain Banks is an enthusiastic *young* officer."

"You said that your man Salazar will be calling the shots on the patrol today?" Lammers asked as the trio got up from the table.

"Yes, Doctor, Salazar will have full authority over the *wheres, whens and hows.*"

Bud looked at his watch and smiled. "Well with that settled, I think it may be time for a little nap before we saddle up."

# CHAPTER 19

When The Woman returned to the shack early the next morning, she found that the place was still unguarded, but the campfire appeared to have been stoked with a new log, and the trash that she'd placed on it had burned away. She set down the burlap sack that she'd brought with her, removed the steel bar and opened the door. Karlena's eyes were open, but The Woman saw that the girl looked even more spent than she had the day before.

"Oh, thank God you came back," Karlena gasped once the gag had been removed. "I...I think they are going to kill me soon." She started to sob, but there were no tears left for her to cry.

The Woman emptied the contents of the sack. A bottle of water, three small bundles, tied neatly with string, and a crust of bread fell to the wooden floor. She held the bottle to Karlena's lips and then placed morsels of the bread in her mouth.

Karlena chewed and swallowed them quickly and then pleaded, "Cut me free, *please*, cut me free." She raised her arms in anticipation that the Filipina would have a knife to cut away the bindings from her wrist, but instead, The Woman reached for a small piece of white linen. She poured water onto the cloth, then sprinkled the contents of the bundles onto the wetted cloth. She rubbed the mixture together until the cloth was drenched in a pulp-like concoction.

"What are you doing, you have to cut me free!" Karlena begged as The Woman began dabbing her wounds with the cloth. She'd rubbed the salve over Karlena's wrist and had begun treating her ankles when there was a clatter of voices followed by the rushing sound of footsteps. Karlena cringed at the sight of Blister in the doorway. Next to him was another man and the boy she recognized as the one who'd driven the boat when she and Duke had been hijacked.

Blister burst into the shack and jerked The Woman to her feet. "You crazy old bitch!" he hollered in his native tongue. "You have no right to be here."

The Woman snapped back, "And what right do you have to keep another human being in this way?" Her angelic face had become twisted with rage; she pulled her arm free and spit at Blister's feet. "I'm not stupid enough to sacrifice my own life by letting her go; I know what you people can do. But you can't leave her in this condition—like a pig in a sty."

Although Karlena could not understand the Woman's words, she was stunned at how the peaceful Filipina had transformed into an enraged tigress.

Blister glared back at her, then turned his attention to the young boy. He slapped the teen across the face. "When Spider learns of this… how you've neglected your duties," he snarled, "Salid, what were you thinking?" Blister waited for an answer, but the boy could only slump his shoulders and whimper.

Blister turned away from the group and stared outside through the open door. After a few seconds, he shook his head disgustedly and then spun around and charged The Woman. He threw her to the floor and straddled her body. She lay passively while he pummeled her face with repeated backhands. After the beating, he stood up and confronted the man who'd come along with him and the boy.

"This is how you have to deal with these matters: quickly and with force." The man nodded enthusiastically. "You better learn fast if you want to survive in the Movement," Blister concluded.

The man looked down at the bloodied Filipina's face and smirked viciously. "That won't be a problem for me," he said. "No problem at all."

Blister went over to the tarp-covered pile, pulled out the spool of nylon rope and then took hold of The Woman.

"You two hold her still while I do this." He tied up The Woman's hands and feet in a similar fashion that he'd done to Karlena but did not lash her to the wall. Instead, he dragged her outside the building.

"Sit!" he said as he pushed her to the ground. He then yanked Salid by the neck of his tee shirt and shoved him outside next to the woman. "I'm giving you a second chance, boy; you stand guard over the American and this miserable hag while I get word to Spider; then he can decide what to do. Do you understand?"

Salid swiped the tears from his face, stood a little taller and said, "Yes, I will do that."

Satisfied that he'd solved the matter, at least for the moment, Blister re-latched the door securely and said, "Let's go." The two men hiked back to the spot where Blister had hidden his jeep. He got behind the wheel and maneuvered the vehicle out of the woods and back to the highway.

"This will be your first official duty as a new recruit," Blister said as he drove. "I want you to get word to Spider that the boy fucked up and allowed that crazy old lady to discover the girl. I'll drop you off by the main camp."

The Woman pulled up the ripped fabric of her garment to cover her exposed breast. Her face was bloodied and her knees ached from being thrown to the floor. She shimmied her body slowly across the dirt and leaned against the shack's wooden siding.

Salid had taken a seat on top of a thick piece of firewood. His fingers danced furiously over the buttons of his phone.

"What are you doing?" The Woman said through her swollen lips.

"Shut up old lady," Salid replied, never looking up from his phone as he typed.

"You know what they will do to me, don't you boy?" The Woman sat quietly and studied him. She wondered how someone so innocent looking and young could be part of the rebel group. "Your name is Salid, yes? Do you know the meaning of your name? *Do* you?"

"I told you to be quiet woman. Everyone knows you are crazy. I don't want to talk to you." He reached into a pocket on his shorts and pulled out a knife. He flicked his wrist and brandished the weapon's shining blade in front of her face. She held her stare without blinking.

"You never answered my question," she said. "Your name—Salid—means one who is *correct*."

Salid lowered his eyes. "I know what it means; my parents told me when I was little."

The Woman saw that she'd made a connection and continued. "So, if you know what your name means, what would your mother and father think if they saw you like this? Would they think *this* is correct?"

Salid looked up from his phone. Tears flowed freely from his eyes as he struggled to speak. He hung his head low. "No, old lady, what I am doing is not correct."

"And neither is what those evil men are doing to that girl, is it?"

He hesitated for a long period before answering. "No. No it is not." Salid looked at the barred door and then at the pathetic sight of the battered old lady. The Woman stared up at him and lifted her bound wrists. Salid took his knife and began to cut her free.

"Old woman…go as fast as you can to the highway and wait until you see the military men. Show them the way."

# CHAPTER 20

Ling Chin put on a pair of stylish glasses to better see the email attachment. She quickly scanned the bank document that confirmed and finalized their completed transaction with MexErig. She hit the "PRINT" icon displayed on the top of the computer monitor and then, as an added measure, wrote down the deposit's tracking number on a sheet of paper. She could no longer contain her excitement. "Ahmad, Ahmad honey, it's here; the money we've been waiting for is here. It's in our account, and we have access to it now."

Ahmad Jalil got up from his desk and ran to join Ling. "See, right there; it's ours now, all of it," she said.

"Yes it is," he said proudly. Ahmad wiped away joyful tears as he re-read the document. At last: He could finally put to rest his worries and concerns that their floundering import/export business would have to file bankruptcy. The convoluted chain of transactions that had originated with Otto Brandt's order for drilling machinery had passed all scrutinization. It had stood up to the inspection of North American Free Trade Agreement (NAFTA) regulators, who'd essentially rubber-stamped the deal and, likewise, had sailed through similar examination by Philippine officials. To the international world of business, the arrangement that Malik Abbas and Jameel "Spider" Abijon had concocted appeared to be nothing more than a relatively smallish act of trade involving three countries.

Ahmad shifted his thoughts to the transfer of funds that he'd already mentally designated as a donation to Malik Abbas's charitable organization. He reached over Ling's shoulder to pull up another page on the bank's web site that would guide him through the process of wiring the money to Basilan. Ling stopped him with a delicate wave of her hand.

"What are you doing?" she asked.

"Ling, dear, we can't hesitate with carrying out what we have promised to my friend. Don't you remember our discussion about how it takes money to make money?" Ahmad saw that a broad frown had draped over Ling's pretty face. "We have to make the donation *now*, before doing anything else; not just because Malik is expecting it, but more importantly, it's the right thing to do."

Ling's frown deepened to that of a pout. "Well, I know that's what we agreed to do, but—"

"No *buts*," Ahmad said flatly. "That was our agreement, and that's what we will do." His hands started to type on her keyboard.

"So I guess that, in reality, your new vice president has no say in what goes on at *Quality Expeditors,* does she?" Ahmad felt a chill from her tone. "You just promoted me so that I would still sleep with you."

Ahmad saw that his lover and new business partner was visibly upset. He decided to take a different tact. "Well, I guess we could wait a few hours before sending Malik his money," he said. "That would give us the time to have lunch and then visit that swanky high-rise they're building over in Rockwell Center. I read in the paper that the condominium sales office has just opened. Maybe we could take a look."

Ling instantly perked up. "Could we, really? I don't know how much longer I can take living in your run-down flat; it's so depressing." She pulled Ahmad toward her and gave him a long, passionate kiss.

Ahmad looked deeply into Ling's dark, almond-shaped eyes. "So, we're okay?"

Ling smiled and nodded happily. "And after looking at the condos, maybe swing by the Mall?" She devilishly ran her hand up Ahmad's pant leg, but stopped just short of his groin. "I could use a few new pairs of shoes, sweetie, you know?"

Ahmad laughed and gently guided her hand away from his leg. "Alright, alright," he said. "I guess we can do that too."

Inside of a warehouse several hundred miles south of Manila, near Cotobato City, Mindanao, two Filipinos sorted through a pile of dilapidated machinery and oil drilling components.

"How about this one, Fidel?" one of them asked. "It's a little rusty, but it might still work."

"Sure, Eddie, why the hell not?" his partner answered. "What are they going to do if it doesn't, send it back? I doubt if the Mexicans would bother; go ahead and toss it into the crate with the others." A clanking thud echoed through the building as the motor was deposited with the other items that they had hauled out from the company's storage locker of used equipment.

"And why would they want all of these drill pipe couplings?" Eddie said as the pair hoisted a metal box crammed full of hardware into the crate.

"Beats me. You'd think they could find most of this stuff someplace closer to where they're drilling and save on the shipping costs."

"Yeah, you'd think." Eddie added.

They backed away from the big, reinforced wooden container that would travel across the ocean to Mexico and, then, by rail and truck to Texas. Eddie pulled a handkerchief from his pocket. "Whew, glad that's done," he said while drying off his face. "I'll go get Ortiz so he can do the final inspection before we close it up."

"No need. He told me to just double-check everything myself; then for us to go ahead and seal it shut."

"Oh?"

Fidel grabbed a hammer and reached for a box of nails. "Yeah, poor bastard's nursing a doozy of a hangover. Smelled like he'd fallen into a vat of San Miguel when I went to get our work order this morning. He's been sitting in his air-conditioned office all day, just drinking coffee and staring at his computer."

Eddie joined in and started nailing. "Serves him right, the old drunk. Let's get this done and forklifted over to the loading dock so we can go home."

# CHAPTER 21

"Nice that you could join us," Travis Banks said through clenched teeth. He bit off a small chunk from the end of his cigar and spit the wet stub in the direction of Major Ramon Salazar.

Salazar glared back at him as if the American were an obnoxious, uninvited relative who'd crashed a family gathering, then mumbled something as he hoisted himself into the armored truck. Three Filipino enlisted soldiers joined him in the HMMWV, or *High Mobility Multipurpose Wheeled Vehicle*—more commonly known as a "Humvee."

McGirt and Lammers stood by outside another Humvee. Banks walked briskly toward them. "Something about that guy I don't like," he said under his breath. "I know he's Romolo's deputy, but I've never worked with another officer so…drifty."

"And he's leading us today?" McGirt asked.

"Yeah, that's the plan, sir," Banks said. "No worries, though. We're here as non-combatants." He then added with a mocking tone, "And carrying weapons only for self-defense—nothing offensive." Banks shook his head as if disgusted with the entire arrangement. He handed McGirt and Lammers each a helmet and flak jacket. "Just to be on the safe side, gentlemen. We're planning to stay on the main highway sans off-roading; that is unless Major Drifty gets us lost."

As Lammers and McGirt slipped on their gear, Bud pointed to another armored Humvee that sat near them, parked and empty; unlike Salazar's and Banks's rides, it was fitted with a sinister-looking roof-top gun turret. "What's wrong with that one?" he said. "Shouldn't it be part of our convoy?"

Banks shook his head again in displeasure. "Not the colonel's wishes, sir. He's concerned that we might project too much of an aggressive profile to the locals. We should be fine, though, cruising the Circumferential Highway south, toward Maluso. More or less showing the flag to reassure the natives that we're here to *protect* them, and we're not the bad guys."

McGirt and Lammers hopped into the Americans' Humvee, behind Banks and the vehicle's driver. McGirt acknowledged the enlisted man with a respectful nod. Despite his fierce-looking warrior's garb, the soldier appeared barely old enough to vote.

The Humvees' big diesel engines pinged and throbbed as the two-vehicle convoy began its one-hour long patrol to the Province of Maluso, a heavily Muslim-populated region, located on Basilan's southeastern coast.

"Ride's not as smooth as my old man's Lincoln," Banks shouted above the pounding engine noise. "She sucks down fuel pretty fast too with the added armor weight; but better than taking a bullet."

"Thought you said this would be a peaceful mission?" McGirt hollered back.

Banks sensed that his two civilian visitors might be growing uneasy about riding along so he replied, "We'll be okay, sir, provided we stay on our designated route. And we shouldn't have to worry like those poor bastards playing in the sandbox," he added, referring to his fellow warriors fighting in the Middle East. "We haven't had a single report of land mines exploding since I've been here. Some theft and sabotage of our equipment at times, and the kidnapping of folks like the young lady you're looking for, but no mines."

While their multi-ton vehicle plodded toward Maluso, McGirt reflected on what he'd read about the plans to upgrade Army and Marine armored fleets with a more durable, though even heavier, transport vehicle labeled the MRAP, or *Mine Resistant Ambush Protected*. During its testing, the truck's V-shaped, raised chassis and added armor was proving to be a better counter to the blast of an Improvised Explosive Device (IED).

As if on cue Banks chimed in, "That MRAP will save a lot of lives. Unfortunately, my contact at the Pentagon tells me there's already a food fight raging in Congress over the truck's cost; something like one million per copy for the tricked-out models."

"Tell me about it," Bud Lammers lamented. "I've been working in the D.C. meat grinder for twenty years. Never ceases to amaze me how bloated a well-intentioned project can become after politicians start figuring ways to bring home some pork to their own districts."

The convoy lumbered along the island's twisting main roadway through scantily populated farms, small villages, and the ubiquitous free-roaming livestock. McGirt observed an occasional curious wave, mainly from children. Most adults they encountered, however, seemed to stare warily as the military transports passed by.

After nearly an hour of travel, Banks's hand-held radio came alive with the static-laced voice of Major Salazar. McGirt peeked over Banks' shoulder and saw that they were approaching the outskirts of Maluso. Banks and Salazar traded a series of rapid transmissions—none of which McGirt nor Lammers could decipher.

When finished, Banks set down the radio and said, "Gentlemen, Major Salazar says that he has a source a few kilometers farther down the road that just sent him a text message. He's not sure of its authenticity, but the source claims to have knowledge of the missing girl's location. With your concurrence, he'd like to pursue the lead and to continue in that direction." Banks delivery of the news was flat; he showed neither enthusiasm nor dismay.

A stunned McGirt looked at Bud and saw that his partner was equally dumbfounded. He leaned forward, closer to Banks's ear. "Travis, what do you think? Is this worth going in deeper or turning around?" McGirt recalled the young officer's trepidation about the reliability of Colonel Romolo's second-in-command. He guessed that Banks's past experiences with Romolo at West Point might have obliged him to go along with Major Salazar's decisions despite his own reservations.

After a long pause Banks said, "Sir, I believe at this stage of the game, we are safe to continue on." He slapped a hand on the truck's dash to emphasize his point. "Salazar told me that he's already called back to camp and requested backups to cover us if things get out of hand."

"But without any air support, it will take over an hour for anyone to get here, right?" McGirt said. Before Banks could answer, Salazar's vehicle lurched forward in a hurried cloud of diesel exhaust.

"Well that looks like Major Drifty has already made up his mind," Lammers said sarcastically. "What the hell. I'm in if you guys are."

Banks turned to his driver. No words were needed; he saw the hunger for action in the kid's eyes. Finally, McGirt completed the poll by simply saying, "Let's do it." Banks keyed his mike and told Salazar. A few minutes later, after the sights and smells of Maluso had faded, the convoy came to an abrupt halt.

"Now what's going on?" Bud asked. As he spoke, Salazar and two AFPs bolted from their vehicle. They disappeared into the tall roadside grass where the shrouded image of another human being began to materialize through the brush.

"Looks like old Salazar's finally woke up and got the lead out. Never seen him move that quickly," Banks said. McGirt heard their driver's heavy breathing, like an overanxious pit bull that'd been penned up too long. The soldier opened his door and started to exit.

Banks grabbed him by the arm and shouted, "Soldier, get your ass back in this Humvee and stand down!" The ferociousness in his order shot a shiver through McGirt and Lammers.

"On second thought, maybe we should just turn around and get the hell out of here now," Lammers said meekly. McGirt saw that his friend had turned pale and was sweating profusely—not beads of sweat like the rest of the truck's occupants, but gushing, uncontrolled perspiration.

"Stand fast!" Banks barked a second time. He jumped out of the vehicle and headed in the direction of the AFPs. As he did, Salazar and the two other AFPs emerged from the thicket; between them, they supported a limping, disheveled elderly Filipina. Her flowery, full-length garment had been ripped half off and her face looked badly bruised.

Banks turned back toward the Americans and hollered, "McGirt and Lammers, we need you here!" It was the first time since they'd arrived that Captain Banks had not addressed the two senior Americans by "sir." Both McGirt and Lammers read the unintentional slight loud and clear: Banks was tired of the pleasantries and readying himself to do what he was trained to do—kick some serious butt.

As McGirt approached the scene, he scanned their surroundings. They were still positioned on Basilan's main thoroughfare, a few kilometers outside Maluso; the terrain was dense and jungle-like on both sides of the road. When the convoy had stopped, its presence seemed to have prompted no more than perfunctory glances from the handful of motorists who had passed by. But the flow of traffic had now eerily disappeared; not a single vehicle was in sight from either direction. *If there were ever a perfect spot for an ambush, this would be it,* he thought. As he and Lammers closed in on the group, Salazar appeared to be interrogating the woman.

"She says that she was beaten because of what she did," Salazar said as the woman jabbered on. Whatever absent-mindedness or apathy Major Salazar had displayed earlier seemed to have vanished; spittle flew from his lips as he took hold of the poor woman's shoulders and pressed her for more details.

"What's going on?" Bud asked Banks.

Banks listened intently for a moment before answering. "My Chavacano isn't that great, but I think she said she knows something about a red-headed girl."

"Jesus Christ, that has to be her!" Bud said.

Before anyone could react, Salazar grabbed the woman and shoved her into the back of his Humvee. "We're going in," he said emphatically.

Banks spun Salazar around by his arm so they were face-to-face. "Major with all due respect, are you sure you want to go in there without more firepower?"

Salazar appeared undeterred by Banks's concern. "We've already called back for reinforcements," he countered. "The longer we sit here, the more time they will have to relocate your hostage. I'm going in."

Banks turned to McGirt and Lammers. For the first time since they'd arrived, McGirt saw hesitation creep into the Ranger's steadfast demeanor. "Damn, I wish we'd just wait until Romolo sends more guns."

"*Wait?*" Salazar retorted. "Do you not think that someone along the route hasn't seen us and already sent a runner to the ASG, informing them of our presence? The old lady just told me she ran away from them after they'd beaten her up for trying to bring the girl food." Salazar's eyes welled with anger. "Do you not want to find this girl?" He looked to McGirt and Lammers, not to Banks, for a response.

McGirt spoke up. "Of course, but like Captain Banks said—"

Salazar ignored the American and shouted to his men. The Humvee's engine rattled and growled back to life as Salazar and the other AFPs joined the old woman seated inside.

Banks stared down at his feet for a long, several seconds, then faced McGirt and Lammers. "Sirs, this is supposed to be a joint exercise. My men and I are here as advisers and trainers. That said, I cannot, with a good conscience, fail to provide backup to Major Salazar."

McGirt was struggling to find the right words when Bud Lammers offered, "I propose that we proceed for a while with Salazar. If it looks like a bust, then he's own his own. We can reverse course and head back out to the highway."

McGirt saw that Bud appeared to have recovered from whatever had spooked him so badly when they'd stopped and found the woman. He watched as Salazar waved his arm in the direction of a carved out path of vegetation, highlighted by a couple of dirt furrows that disappeared into heavily shaded woods.

"Salazar told me that he knows this island like the back of his hand and that this trail snakes its way in a circle—parallel along the coastline—then it intersects the highway again after a klick or two further south. That will provide an escape route if for some reason we can't trace our way back out." Banks said. He then realized that he'd returned to his soldier's way of thinking without considering his two guests, who were unarmed and untrained for what might lie ahead. "But you don't have to do this, gentlemen. More of Romolo's men should be here in less than an hour if you're alright waiting in place for them. This wasn't your idea; I'm the one who encouraged you to ride along."

McGirt stared ahead at Salazar's vehicle. He saw the major's arm emerge from the passenger side window. Salazar signaled that he was ready to move out by waving his hand vigorously toward the trail.

After a silent pause, Lammers said, "Well, dammit! We can't let him start in there alone. Let's follow him."

McGirt agreed.

Banks signaled that they were ready, and the two vehicles began inching their way into the woods. After several hundred meters, the lead vehicle stopped, and Salazar leapt out with the woman in tow. She pointed off the trail to their right. Salazar quickly issued an order to his men. They disembarked, cinched up their gear and readied their weapons. The major then trotted back to the Americans' Humvee. "Banks, you should maneuver ahead of us and wait," he said. "If necessary, head straight down this path like I described—past the cove and keep going. It will lead you back to the highway."

Banks motioned for his driver to comply by guiding the all-terrain vehicle off the dirt furrows, over some low bushes, and then back onto the trail—a dozen or so meters ahead of the Filipino's Humvee.

McGirt squinted to focus on Salazar's team as they proceeded cautiously through the thick foliage. He could barely make out the profile of a ramshackle building in the distance. Salazar's camouflaged crew had completely merged with their surroundings when the sound of a muffled gunshot cut through the humid quietness.

"What the fuck was that?" Bud shouted.

Before anyone could respond, Banks tore out from the truck. "You people stay here, and I *mean* it! Do *not* leave the vehicle unless I give the order!" he hollered over his shoulder.

McGirt heard the driver begin to pant.

"My God…what did we get ourselves into?" Bud said. The copious sweating had returned, and the color had left his face again.

McGirt reached for a water bottle and forced it into Lammers's hand. "Better take a drink, buddy. You look about ready to pass out."

# CHAPTER 22

USS *Lansing* glided across the water at a stable speed of eleven knots, one hundred miles off the west coast of Mindanao and Basilan Island. The massive ship and her crew were wrapping up the last of a replenishment operation that had involved an aircraft carrier group composed of the carrier, two cruisers and three nimble destroyers, or "small boys."

Each ship had "come alongside" to port and paralleled *Lansing's* course, precisely matching her speed while maintaining a separation distance of approximately one hundred feet. A series of lines and cables had been exchanged between the two vessels, which had allowed towering cargo rigs to be suspended between *Lansing* and her receiving customer ships. This method of resupplying while underway at sea was called conventional replenishment, or "CONREP" for short.

While each ship took its turn alongside, *Lansing's* two CH-46 helicopters also delivered large quantities of packaged items to surrounding vessels by an ingenious method coined vertical replenishment, or "VERTREP." The airborne delivery system employed the powerful, twin-engine rotorcraft, which carried pallets of goods externally. By employing a sturdy line, or "pendant," hooked to the underside of the aircraft, tightly wrapped bundles of cargo were suspended beneath the helicopter and transported rapidly by air. Nearly every item on board *Lansing's* floating department store—with the exception of pumped fuel oil—could be moved by the ship's air detachment. VERTREP enabled the evolution to be completed much faster: While one ship came alongside, others in the group could also receive tons of supplies, placed neatly on their decks by the helos. The group of vessels had been resupplied with fuel, spare parts, armaments, food and a variety of other consumables. The seas were glassy, and the skies immaculately clear. All hands, especially the flight crews, were grateful for such ideal conditions to conduct the five-hour evolution.

At *Lansing's* main control station, or bridge, Commanding Officer Katherine Torres sat quietly in her chair. She held a white, well-used coffee mug in one hand as she oversaw the operation.

"Skipper, Supply Department tells me that the last of the CONREP pallets are going across the cables now," *Lansing's* XO, Commander Bill Draper, said as he stood next to Torres. "The helos have another half-dozen or so loads to transfer—then *we are done. Finito.*"

Torres glanced over her left shoulder and watched as the array of fuel hoses, guide cables and riggings were being detached from the last customer ship, a destroyer, and were systematically being winched back into place on *Lansing*. Over the last several hours, her ship had transferred several hundred tons of supplies and fuel. She placed her coffee into the cup holder of the big, barbershop-style chair that was reserved for one sailor, and one sailor alone, on *Lansing*: the commanding officer. Torres grasped her left forearm and gently massaged it. She looked up at Bill Draper and said quietly, "Seems to always tighten up when the weather's about to change." She slid her right hand across the nasty looking, jagged scars that ran along her forearm, and then, moved her grip into the knotted ball of clenched fingers on her left hand. Methodically, she pried each finger open from her palm, grunting softly with pain as she did.

"XO, I'll be glad to get back to Southern California where the climate is a little more consistent," she bemoaned.

Draper acknowledged with an understanding smile. He marveled at how the lady had fought off numerous attempts by Navy doctors to discharge her because of her handicap. Torres had always rallied and been able to pass whatever physical tasks the "quacks" had thrown at her as they'd challenged the strength and maneuverability of her weaker, gimpy left arm and hand.

Draper had learned the legend of Katherine Marie "Slash" Torres two decades earlier, when she was a senior, or "firstie," during his demanding year as a fresh-men, or "plebe," at the Naval Academy. The story had been embellished over the years, but he'd learned the true skinny from one of Torres's closest classmates. While on liberty at a club along Baltimore's trendy Inner Harbor, Torres had spent the evening having a good time with three other midshipmen: two males and another female. To save a few bucks, the group passed on the nearby pay parking lot and had found a spot a few of blocks away, on a dark street. On the way back to the car, a couple of local thugs had crept up on the group and demanded money. Ignoring the punks seemed to only anger them, and they kept in close trail of the Middies as they continued walking. When Torres reached into her jeans for the car keys, one of the thugs shoved her against a building wall and drew a knife. What happened from that point was where the facts got fuzzy, and the legend began. A cluster of bodies tumbled to the pavement. Torres had ripped the knife from the assailant's hands and stabbed him squarely in the thigh, but not before he'd inflicted his own damage—a deep, nine inch gash across Katherine's left forearm that required over four hours of surgery to repair.

But despite all the intrigue of the "Slash" Torres saga, her knife fight in a Baltimore alley was not what had endeared the woman to Bill Draper. Two days prior to her incident in Baltimore, Draper had marched up to her room in Bancroft Hall, stood at rigid attention, and informed Torres that he wanted to D.O.R., or drop-on-request. He'd struggled desperately during the Academy's arduous eight-week long indoctrination program and had decided to voluntarily leave. She closed her dormitory room door, sat Draper down and talked him out of quitting.

It was the first time during plebe summer that Bill Draper had seen the human side of his steely, hard-edged squad leader. She told him that he'd never forgive himself if he quit, and inspired him to stick it out for the rest of the summer and start classes when the rest of the Academy's Brigade returned in the fall. Her words of encouragement and leadership by example provided him with the spark he needed to complete the remainder of a grueling plebe year, graduate and receive a commission.

Years later, when his rotation back to sea duty came due, he jumped at the opportunity to serve as Torres's executive officer on *Lansing*. Unbeknownst to Draper, she had sought him out from a long list of other highly qualified officers; he'd been handpicked for the job. A bond that had started during a hot, humid summer in Annapolis was now playing out nearly ten thousand miles away on the South China Sea.

A petty officer from *Lansing's* communications department appeared on the bridge and handed Captain Torres a message clipboard.

"Thanks, sailor," she said while donning her glasses. She quickly summarized the classified document. "Well, what do you know…looks like the spooks back at the puzzle palace on the Potomac may have located our little yellow rose of Texas." She passed the message board to Commander Draper. On the top sheet was an unencrypted version of the intelligence that CIA agents Leonard Dickle and Joe Voss had received regarding Mitchell Castella's confrontation with

Malik Abbas. Their conclusion that Abbas probably knew of Karlena Brandt's whereabouts was a game changer.

"We need to get this information to McGirt and Lammers—fast," Torres said. She paused in thought for a few seconds before continuing. "We've got shabby, at best, comms with that AFP unit that's hosting them on Basilan. Other than CINCPAC's orders that we operate within chopper range until otherwise directed, we're sort of in the blind here. Do either of those guys have a satellite phone?"

Bill Draper stared at the close-abeam destroyer as it peeled off from alongside *Lansing*. The graceful man-o'-war sprayed a rooster-tail-like wake as it accelerated rapidly ahead of the lumbering supply ship. "Skipper, Bud Lammers gave me his cell number. I'm not sure if it has satellite capability; we can try. But we may have another option by using that AN/PRQ-7 I handed McGirt before they took off this morning."

Torres rose slowly from her chair. She put on arm on the XO's shoulder and pulled him aside from the rest of the bridge crew. "Bill, I apologize; I remember when you pushed for the procurement for that gear before we left San Diego. But for the life of me, I can't remember the details. You'll have to give me the Cliff Notes version of how it works."

# CHAPTER 23

McGirt and Lammers watched idly as Travis Banks double-timed toward Salazar and the shack. When Banks arrived at the scene, he saw an adolescent boy, lying face down in the dirt.

Blood had begun to ooze through the back of the youngster's white tee shirt; a cell phone lay beside his motionless body. Banks didn't need an interpreter to figure out what had happened: From the cussing out that Salazar was giving one of the AFP soldiers, it was clear what had gone down.

Salazar composed himself and faced Banks. "She's inside; this kid was the guard." He motioned his drawn pistol toward the boy's killer. "And this fool shot him."

Banks looked at the soldier; the man was shaking from the realization of what he'd done.

"Why did you shoot him?" Salazar said in clear English. The soldier just stared back at him with a confused expression. The major repeated his question in Chavacano, which caused the guilty soldier to simply hang his head without responding.

"The boy's name is Salid," Salazar said to Banks. "He's an orphan, who I've been communicating with for several months." He bent down and gently patted the kid's shoulder, then slipped the boy's phone into his own pocket. It was still flashing with an unanswered text. For the first time since they'd met, Travis Banks spotted a modicum of compassion in the Filipino's harsh demeanor.

Banks had heard how the Abu Sayyaf Group had recruited many young males, but the sight of the child's motionless body was difficult for him to accept. "Christ sake, he can't be more than ten or twelve years old," he said.

Salazar stared coldly at the dead body and nodded. His jaw tightened as he forced himself back into the role of a professional warrior. He turned to Banks again. "Well, there's plenty more just like him. Don't lose any sleep over it."

Banks turned his head as he heard clamoring from inside the rustic building. A moaning, feminine-sounding voice rose above the din. When he entered the shack, the old Filipina that they'd found along the highway confronted him.

She began chanting in her native tongue while bowing from the waist with hands clasped in a thankful, prayer-like way. Behind her, propped up against a wall by two of Salazar's men, Banks saw Karlena Brandt. The soldiers had cut away the bindings from her raw, bleeding ankles and wrists and removed the soaked gag from her mouth. The stench of her body was overwhelming.

Karlena's eyes were opened, but she was incoherent and unable to support her own weight as the AFPs raised her slowly from the filthy plank floor. When she'd mustered enough strength to finally stand, Banks saw that the girl's gaunt body and her clothing were caked with a sickly mix of brownish-yellow dried sweat and waste.

"Let's get out of here, right now," Banks said to Salazar. "Someone had to have heard that gunshot."

Salazar nodded his head in agreement.

"Put her in my vehicle," Banks ordered as the group scrambled back outside and toward the Humvees.

"My God, here they come," McGirt hollered. "I think they found her!"

Before anyone else could speak, there was a muffled, thud-like "bwah" noise in the distance, quickly followed by the ripping sound of torn leaves and branches. A few seconds later a thundering explosion detonated as the errant round fell about fifty meters away and self-destructed.

"RPG!" Banks screamed, as the group raced toward their vehicles.

Banks opened the Humvee's front passenger side door and flung Karlena inside. As he did, a second rocket-propelled grenade was launched. Traveling at a speed of five-hundred feet per second, the Russian-built weapon's warhead found its mark this time, striking the rear section of Salazar's unoccupied vehicle. The truck heaved to the left violently, causing both right side wheels to lift off of the ground. It then crashed back into place; a short, odd pause followed before the truck's fuel tank ruptured and exploded, blasting a towering fireball through the overhead canopy of tree branches. The detonation rocked the Americans' vehicle.

Banks's driver didn't need an order to engage—he sprang from the Humvee and assumed a prone battle position on the low side of a nearby shallow ravine; he aimed his automatic weapon in the direction from which the RPG had been fired.

"Take her, take her *now*, you and Lammers!" Banks shouted. He held his rifle to one side and swiveled his head, searching for the enemy. He then removed his pistol from its holster and tossed it into Bud's lap. "Here, take this with you."

Bud stared up at him.

"God dammit! *One* of you get behind the wheel and drive!" Banks screamed. "*Go!*" He then pointed at the trail. "Salazar said that it leads back to the highway. Now get the fuck out of here!"

McGirt felt as if everything had slipped into slow motion as he hoisted himself into the Humvee's driver's seat. With the exception of a few strange looking gadgets, the truck's cockpit closely resembled that of an off-road, all-wheel SUV. He put the vehicle into gear and pressed down on the gas pedal. The Humvee jerked forward as he, a sweating, wide-eyed Bud Lammers, and a catatonic Karlena Brandt were on their way.

Karlena had slid off of the passenger seat and was crumpled on the vehicle's floorboard.

"*You okay, Bud?*" McGirt yelled as he navigated the potholes and twists of the primitive roadway.

"Yeah, I think so," Lammers answered in a weak, hesitant voice.

McGirt couldn't hear his friend over the noise from the racing Humvee, but he could read his lips. "Stay with me, pal!" McGirt pleaded while turning his head quickly. He saw that Lammers's face had blanched and was dripping with sweat again. "Please…don't pass out on me," McGirt muttered to himself.

Salazar and his men had taken cover behind a tightly grouped grove of mango trees upwind of their torched vehicle. The limp body of a comrade, struck by shrapnel from the explosion, lay on his back, a few meters from the Americans.

Banks joined his driver in the ravine and exchanged hand signals with Salazar, indicating that they were okay.

Salazar responded by pointing to his own eyes with index and middle fingers, and then motioning them toward the shack.

Banks followed the signal to "watch." He saw several dark silhouettes advancing toward them; the invaders danced between trees for cover as they moved forward.

McGirt fought to keep the big machine on the narrow trail while still maintaining a decent speed. He was surprised that the Humvee was equipped with an automatic rather than manual transmission. *Thank god. One less thing to deal with*, he thought.

Low hanging branches slapped against the truck's windshield as they weaved through the dense woods. The trail narrowed to only a few meters wide in places, obscuring McGirt's view. *"How's she doing?"* he asked. *"I'm afraid to take my eyes away from what's ahead!"*

Bud craned his head forward, grasping the front seat for stability. Karlena's eyes were open, but their pupils had the "thousand-yard stare" of someone in shock. Bud held his gaze until he saw her blink.

"I think she's gonna make it! She just blinked her eyes! There…she moved her arms and legs a little bit too; she's coming around!" Bud remembered McGirt's advice and grabbed for a water bottle, spilling half of it on himself before he managed to get down a couple of gulps.

McGirt fought to manhandle the big, armored truck as it bounced along the rough terrain. They trudged up a steep hill that descended dramatically from its peak. On their left, in the distance, Bud spotted a grass-covered swatch that fell off steeply toward a small inlet.

*"Didn't Salazar say when we saw the inlet we'd almost be back to the highway?"* he said over the noise.

"I think so!" McGirt answered as another cluster of branches slapped against the windshield. They travelled a few hundred meters further when, again, a mass of vines and branches struck their vehicle, this time completely blocking his vision. When the clutter had cleared, he saw that they were headed straight into the woods.

"Turn! Turn!" Bud screamed as the trail took a sharp jog to the right.

McGirt struggled to execute the tight curve, but they'd built up too much inertia coming down the hill. The truck sideswiped a tree trunk, lurched left and began skidding toward the drop off.

"Hold on!" McGirt hollered. He spun the steering wheel to the right and hammered down the gas pedal hoping to reverse the truck's direction. Unfortunately, the fundamental laws of physics, specifically momentum and gravity, eventually prevailed.

"Aw *shit.*" McGirt groaned as the Humvee began sliding backwards down the grassy incline and toward the water. He took his hands off the wheel and braced for impact.

They'd slid about thirty meters—roughly three quarters of the way down the slope—before the Humvee came to rest against a large tree stump. The vehicle sat at a precarious angle, with its front end pointed straight back up the hill.

McGirt was surprised to find that the vehicle's motor was still running. He pressed gingerly on the gas pedal in an effort to regain traction and power back up the hill, but the Humvee's tires just spun on the slippery grass.

Lammers poked his head up from the rear seat. "Oh no, look up there; we've got company!"

Through a break in the foliage, they saw an open-aired jeep as it crested the big hill that they'd just travelled down. McGirt squinted to make out the vehicle's occupants; he saw what looked like three men inside. One of them held a long, ominous looking tube, straddled over his shoulder. "Those aren't friendlies," he said. "Bud, how long do you think it took us to get from that peak to where we spun out?"

Lammers's brow furrowed. "Just a few minutes. Maybe five or six, tops."

McGirt didn't hesitate. "We're sitting ducks here; we gotta move. We'll have to carry her."

Lammers got out and opened the front passenger side door. As he did, Banks's firearm fell out of his lap and onto the ground.

McGirt came around from the other side to help. He bent down and grabbed the gun. "Let me carry this," he said. He managed to release the weapon's magazine clip, saw that it was fully loaded, then shoved the magazine back into place and tucked the gun into the waistband of his pants.

Bud shook Karlena's arm and said, "Karlena, you have to get out."

She opened her eyes, said what sounded like "all right," and began to push herself up from her crouched position.

The two men hoisted the girl's emaciated body—McGirt grasping her arms, Lammers holding both of her legs.

"Now what?" Lammers asked, as they held her and surveyed their surroundings.

"I saw a couple of boats in the inlet, just before we slid down the hill," McGirt said. "If we can start one of them, we can make a run for it."

Lammers fought to catch his breath. He set down one of Karlena's legs and wiped his face. "Okay, and then...?"

"If you've got a better idea, tell me *now*," McGirt snapped.

Lammers picked up Karlena's legs and motioned his head toward the water. "I think…think I can walk," Karlena said.

"Are you *sure?*" McGirt asked.

"Yes, let me try."

The determined tone of her voice sent a signal to the men that she was regaining some strength and mobility. Bud slowly lowered her legs to the ground. Karlena wobbled a bit, but stabilized and kept her balance.

McGirt led them through a tangled batch of vines and shrubs that hugged the shoreline. From the elevated position of the dirt path, they'd had a clear view of the inlet, but not now—now, they were maneuvering in the blind. The sound of waves brushing up against the boats and pier was their only sense of guidance. As they inched closer to the water, McGirt heard the rustling of branches.

"Get down!" he whispered forcefully. He drew the pistol from his waist and searched for the weapon's safety. He wasn't much of a gun guy—the last time that he'd even held a firearm had been three years ago, when he'd completed the mandatory renewal of his Navy pistol qualification. He turned to Lammers for help.

Bud took hold of the gun, pulled the slide assembly back to chamber a round, then clicked a small metal tab on the side of the receiver and said, "She's live now. You want me to take it?" As Lammers spoke, McGirt saw that his friend's hands were shaking, and he seemed to be getting paler by the minute.

"No, you stay with her while I see what's ahead of us down by the boats." McGirt took the weapon and began crawling forward on his belly. He'd only traveled a short distance when he looked up and saw the image of a man begin to materialize through the dense bramble, about a dozen meters away from him—headed directly toward Lammers and Brandt. McGirt saw that the guy was carrying a rifle over his shoulder. He surmised that the man was one of the rebels, who'd been given the task of guarding the boats.

McGirt felt his heart beat pounding in his chest as he waited for a clear shot. But his view was obscured as the man continued plodding directly toward Karlena and Bud. McGirt realized that he needed to attract attention to himself, so he reached up and shook a low hanging tree branch.

The rebel reacted by stopping and then pivoting his movement toward McGirt. As he closed to a range of about twenty meters, the man's dark-clad body emerged slowly from the brush.

McGirt raised his weapon off the ground and pressed its buttstock firmly into the palm of his left hand. His mind flashed back to the words of the intense drill instructor who'd trained him at the pistol range in Pensacola: *Sight alignment, trigger control. Sight alignment, trigger control.* He lined up the square-shaped, front sight with the handgun's dovetailed rear sight. Like the Marine gunny had taught him, McGirt held his breath and ever so gently squeezed the trigger.

The .45 caliber round exploded from the firearm's barrel. McGirt quickly recovered from the kickback and took aim again. His first shot had struck the rebel in the shoulder.

The man cried out in agony, but was able to raise his rifle with one arm and point it toward McGirt. But McGirt never allowed his adversary to get off a single round. He followed up with a volley of four more shots, two of which stuck the rebel squarely in the chest.

The man fell to the ground.

Lammers and Karlena pushed their way through the brush and joined Mc-Girt over the fatally wounded rebel.

"We gotta get out of here fast," McGirt said. "If this asshole's pals haven't already spotted us, they sure as hell must have heard my shots." He safetied the gun, shoved it back into his pants and grabbed the dead man's rifle and bandoleer. The big, wooden-stock weapon reminded him of the bulky M-1 Garand model on which the same gunnery sergeant had qualified his aviation cadet company. *Some things, you never forget.*

McGirt and Lammers sandwiched Karlena between them and held her by the waist as they pushed their way through the dense vegetation. She tried vainly to keep her legs moving but, ultimately, gave in to letting the men drag her along. In a few seconds, they were in the clear and standing at the water's edge.

Moored in the secluded cove were two swift-looking, outboard boats: the twin-engine rig that Spider and Blister had used to hijack Karlena and, a few meters away, a slightly smaller craft, powered by a monstrous, single motor.

"Get in the closest one," McGirt ordered as he motioned toward the bigger, twin-engine boat. His brain did cartwheels as he tried to remember how to do something that he hadn't pulled off since his teenage years growing up on the outskirts of Detroit: how to hotwire and steal a boat. It was a period of his life that McGirt was embarrassed to admit—a string of joyriding stunts that he and a couple buddies had committed on boring, hot summer nights while carousing the shores of an inland lake near his hometown of Ypsilanti, Michigan.

"Jesus, this thing's beautiful," he said as he led them single file across a rickety wooden pier and onto the sleek vessel

Karlena collapsed into one of the boat's cushy seats and closed her eyes; she looked totally spent from the brief exertion.

"What can I do?" Lammers asked while McGirt ducked down below the boat's console.

He handed Lammers the rifle and gun. "Let me know when you see them, but don't fire unless we get stuck here." He then shimmied deeper below the console and yanked on a handful of wires that led to the boat motors' ignition switches. Rising to his knees, he sorted out the tangled mess until finding the colors he wanted.

"Okay...here we go," he said while touching two bare ends together. A zapping sound and sparks followed. "Shit, let's try this," he lamented while he plied a couple other wires, then connected them; one of the outboards rumbled, then quit. "Got it!" he shouted and touched the wire ends together again. This time the big motor fired and held its idle. "Bud, get us out of here! I'll start the other one on the fly."

Lammers untied them from the dock, jumped back aboard and plopped into the driver's seat. He found reverse and eased the craft away from the pier. Once clear, he shoved the working engine's throttle forward and headed for the open sea.

He scanned the craft's instruments and reported, "Right tank's full, left one's down to a half!" A rush of adrenaline filled Bud's system; other than a token few minutes at cruise in one of the Agency's jets, he hadn't gripped the controls of anything more exciting than his Buick sedan while sitting in traffic on D.C.'s Beltway. Not since his final Navy helicopter flight over twenty years ago had he felt so alive.

McGirt had prostrated himself on the deck, next to Bud's feet, while probing under the instrument panel for the second set of ignition wires.

"I'm calling Romolo!" Bud yelled. He began slapping at his pockets hoping to locate his cell phone. His heart sank when he realized that he didn't have it; somehow in the mayhem, it must have fallen out. "Christ sake, I can't find my damn phone!" he groaned. "Gimme yours!"

Suddenly, the second engine sputtered awake. "I don't have a phone, Bud. *Firewall* it, and head us out to sea!" McGirt hollered over the engine noise.

Bud pushed both throttles forward to their mechanical stops. The acceleration pushed him back into his seat as they rocketed out of the inlet and onto the placid coastal waters of the South China Sea.

McGirt got to his feet and checked on Karlena. She was sitting partially upright in the boat's rear bench seat; her eyes were wide as saucers.

*"How you doing?"* he asked loudly.

Karlena began to mouth some words, but seemed to be floundering. McGirt assumed that the young woman had gone back into shock when, suddenly, she rose from her seat and wrapped her arms around his neck. McGirt steadied himself by gripping a gunwale with one hand; he hugged Karlena with the other arm and felt the warmth of her depleted body against his chest. She let out a torment-filled cry.

"I just want to go home! I want to go *home!*" she wailed.

McGirt squeezed her a bit tighter and said, "We have to get out of here first. Now lie down and rest."

Karlena complied and appeared to promptly pass out.

McGirt looked behind them. "Here they come, Bud!"

Bud turned to see that whoever had tailed them had jumped into the other boat, fired it up and had already exited the inlet.

The seas had appeared smooth at first glance. However, the swells increased the farther away from shore they traveled. Bud looked down at the rifle and handgun. It was pointless to start shooting at their pursuers, he concluded: The range was too far, and considering the wavy ride, he doubted if either he or McGirt would be able to hold a steady aim. *"Should we parallel the coastline and look for a place to beach this thing? We can't just keep heading out to sea, can we?"* he yelled.

Bud's question went unanswered. McGirt was holding a black, rectangular-shaped instrument that he'd removed from a pocket of the loose-fitting camo pants Banks had outfitted them with before the patrol. He studied the hand-held device for second and then said, "This heading looks good, Bud. Just keep steering west on the wet compass."

Bud sighted the small, bulb-shaped compass mounted on the boat's dash and shouted, "Okay! I can keep going west, *but what the hell is that?*"

"Something Draper gave me before we flew off *Lansing*. Hoped we'd never need to use the damn thing!"

McGirt held up a Combat Survivor Evader Locator (CSEL) hand-held radio. Known to radio nerds as the *AN/PRQ-7*, the compact unit approximated the size of a sixteen-ounce cheese brick and provided users with over-the-horizon data communications via satellite. In addition to texting a variety of pre-loaded messages, the system was capable of precise geographic-positioning. Bill Draper had convinced Captain Torres to pull some strings and procure the gear for *Lansing*: Placement of the hand held receivers and their associated ship-based workstations had typically been restricted to larger aircraft-carrying vessels such as CVNs and LHAs.

When McGirt's text was received by *Lansing's* communications center, or "radio shack," Petty Officer Sheryl Briscow didn't know what to make of it. She'd been given a classified briefing on the Joint Search and Rescue Center (JSRC) network that had enabled McGirt to transmit a distress message and his geographic position. But it had been a cursory briefing at the end of a long day, while she'd been suffering the effects of jet lag—two days of air travel from her previous duty station in Norfolk to a sea duty assignment on *Lansing*.

"Chief, you better come take a look at this," Briscow said. She was afraid to touch anything on the desktop-computer-looking contraption that had sat unused and humming idly during the time she'd been aboard. The unit now beeped and flashed with an intensity that suggested something important must be happening—at least that's what her Navy training as an Information Systems Technician (IT) forewarned her.

Chief Petty Officer Bob Pescotti, strolled over to the AN/PRQ-7's base work station. He studied the unit's screen for a few seconds then reached for the closest phone.

"Yeah, Bridge, Chief Pescotti. We need the Skipper or XO in radio immediately. That's right, sailor. You heard me, *now!*" he barked to the bridge messenger.

Both Captain Torres and Commander Draper arrived in less than one minute. By then, Pescotti had pulled out the operations manual for the JSRC system, but he'd already reached the obvious conclusion.

"Sir, my take is that whoever sent this is in peril, and they're asking for our assistance."

Bill Draper focused intently on the screen and then turned to the Skipper. "That message is coded with the I.D. from the handheld that I gave to McGirt."

Torres stared at McGirt's message for a few seconds. "Well, XO, looks things are playing out faster than we'd anticipated." She recalled that Draper had given McGirt the radio. "You may have just saved their asses from the frying pan."

"I punched in our position after that first RPG was fired," McGirt shouted to Lammers. "The ship's been tracking us ever since."

As if on cue, the radio emitted a chirp, and its tiny digitized screen blinked.

"There, they just answered!" McGirt hollered over the wind stream. "Bud, help is on the way! Ship's about eighty miles away and Torres launched a helo ten minutes ago. They're doing *buster* toward our position!"

McGirt and Lammers looked behind them and saw that the other boat was still on their tail. It had faded back to what looked like a distance of a few miles.

"I can only guess how much longer we have until these motors flameout!" Bud shouted. The boat's fuel gages had dipped since they'd left the inlet, but neither man had any idea how much farther they could travel—especially with the throttles pushed up "balls to the wall."

*"Bud, how fast do you think we're going?"* McGirt asked loudly.

Bud searched for a speedometer, but found none; the boat had only been equipped with a tachometer to register engine speed.

"Pretty damn fast for a boat; I'd guess at least forty or fifty miles an hour!" he yelled. The swells had increased, causing a more-bouncy, yet manageable, ride, and the seas ahead of them still looked relatively calm for the open ocean. "Unless the waves start to build, I think we can keep up this speed."

McGirt saw that the coastline was no longer visible: Only Basilan's verdant mountain peaks protruded above the horizon. He ruled out turning back to land and then did some quick mental math. "If they launched ten minutes ago at their max speed—say a hundred and thirty knots—and us going at what you said, we should have a closure rate of about a hundred and seventy five miles an hour. My guess is the helo should be overhead in about twenty minutes!"

Lammers stared at the fuel gauges again. He couldn't resist performing the superstitious aviator's ritual of tapping a gauge to verify that it hadn't become stuck. Both glass-cased needles held their spot, confirming that they were probably accurate. "Then we should be okay with fuel," he announced. "We haven't burned that much."

"*You got any more bottles of water?*" McGirt asked.

Bud pulled an unopened one from a deep pants pocket and handed it over. McGirt took a swig for himself and then turned to Karlena, who'd awakened but was still lying flat on the rear seat. He bent down and coaxed her into taking a few sips. "Karlena, a helicopter is on its way to rescue us! We'll be hoisted aboard!"

"What…what about those… guys?" she stammered.

McGirt could only barely make out what she was saying, and the terrified expression had returned to her face. She looked even more fragile than when Banks had shoved her into the Humvee.

McGirt saw that the other boat was holding its position, still a safe distance behind. But it suddenly dawned on him that if they stopped during the helicopter pickup, their pursers would have time to close the gap and might be able to fire at them.

He patted Karlena lightly on the shoulder. "It will be okay!" he shouted at her. "Drink more water and try your best to gather some strength."

Karlena nodded that she understood.

Within minutes of the time McGirt's initial text had been received aboard *Lansing*, a game plan had been worked out: One of the ship's CH-46 Sea Knight helicopters had been refueled and launched toward McGirt's position. The ship's navigator had quickly plotted the latitude/longitude coordinates and would data-link updates to the helo pilots, allowing the crew to make a beeline to McGirt's position. Torres had also dispatched two of *Lansing's* gunner's mates to ride aboard the normally unarmed utility aircraft. The petty officers each carried automatic rifles.

# CHAPTER 24

"What's going on, Chief?" Petty Officer Briscow asked.

Chief Bob Pescotti marked the page he'd been reading in the JSRC's user guide, then set down the manual. "As far as I can tell, those two civilians that flew off this morning got their...you-know-whats in a ringer." Pescotti silently congratulated himself for remembering to clean up the language that he'd normally use around the male sailors. Having women on board ship had been a culture shock at first for old salts like the chief. The initial novelty of a rule change allowing females to deploy at sea had long since faded, though, and Pescotti had concluded that the women "swabbies" were as sharp and as hard working as the guys—in some cases, even more so.

"Chief, does this have anything to do with why we've been drilling back and forth in the same waters for the last several days? I thought we'd be steaming east by now. My quartermaster pal on the bridge told me we've been given orders to maintain a position near some island until those two CIA guys are finished with whatever they're doing."

As *Lansing's* communications center supervisor, the chief had been privy to all classified correspondence relating to the ship's support of McGirt and Lammers, tracing back to the day the pair had boarded a CIA jet in San Diego. He wasn't sure how much Briscow had learned from the ship's rumor mill, but he decided that she really didn't have a need to know much more.

He dropped all cordiality and told her, "Maintain watch on that gear, sailor, while I go to the head. And remember that not everyone on this rust bucket holds a top secret clearance like you and me."

Briscow saluted him crisply. "You got it, Chief."

Jameel Abijon, who'd introduced himself to Karlena by his code name of "Spider," cursed himself for potentially letting this opportunity slip through his fingers. Malik Abbas had sent word to him that the ransom money had not yet been wired from the U.S., and that he had to—at all costs—maintain their hostage in custody. After receiving a text from a trustworthy civilian who heard the gunshot that killed Salid, he had scrambled a group of his comrades from another nearby outpost. Nowhere to be found, Blister had not answered his phone for hours. When the battle ensued, Spider feared that Blister had either been shot or apprehended.

When he saw his hostage being shoved into the Humvee, Spider had grabbed two of his fighters, an extra box of ammo and the RPG launcher. He'd directed his driver to skirt the field of fire and to follow the Americans' Humvee along the cluttered trail that led back to the highway. Maneuvering off road to stay clear of the gun battle had cost the rebels valuable time. When they'd finally come upon McGirt's vehicle after it had slid down the grassy slope, the Americans had already commandeered a getaway boat and were hurtling out to sea.

Spider didn't know the names of the two rebels he'd yanked away from the melee. They were new members of the Abu Sayyaf, and despite the age difference, these recruits harbored the same enflamed hatred toward the Philippine government's suppression of members of their faith as did Spider. Likewise, they held an equal disdain for their country's staunch ally, the United States of America.

"You: Do not back off one inch on the throttle!" Spider shouted to the longhaired rebel he'd ordered to take the boat's helm. "And *you!*" he yelled to the other man while grabbing him by the shoulder, "I want you to fill all of these magazines and be ready to fire when I command!"

Spider's fierce orders terrified the men. They'd heard about their leader's legendary exploits while fighting the Soviets alongside their Muslim brothers in Afghanistan. Much of that had occurred before their time, however. Spider's reputation since returning from the Middle East had been equally convincing: the sabotaging of AFP troops; hijacking goods from passing freighters; the kidnappings. But what the two novice terrorists feared most was Spider's propensity for beheadings. They'd both been forced to participate in the abhorrent atrocity as part of their swearing of allegiance to the ASG. Jameel "Spider" Abijon had signaled during that grisly event that he'd have no qualms about turning the saw on them, or anyone else, who failed to carry out his wishes.

"Like I told you, just keep them in view and don't slow down!" Spider restated forcefully to the driver. He glanced at his boat's fuel gage. A faint smile sprang from his mouth at the knowledge that his craft, with its full tank and single motor, would easily outlast the slightly faster gas-guzzler, even if the Americans had started out with a full load of fuel. Plus, he doubted that his adversaries had any idea of what they had on board—a launching tube and a half-dozen rocket-propelled grenades.

When the ride became wavier and McGirt's boat temporarily disappeared behind the swells, the hesitant driver turned to his leader for guidance. Spider motioned his arm forward, encouraging the helmsman to keep going. Like the cunning, yet slower, hyena in pursuit of a wounded gazelle, he was confident that he'd eventually win out.

The firefight at the shack had lasted less than twenty minutes, with Banks and his driver escaping the brief, furious battle unscathed. Likewise, Major Salazar's troops had prevailed with relatively minor injuries: the one soldier who'd been struck by shrapnel from the Humvee explosion and another, who'd sustained a nasty, but non-critical, bullet wound to his foot. The old woman had vanished into the woods.

The paramilitary rebels of the Abu Sayyaf Group had not been as fortunate. Of its seventeen members who'd responded to the joint rescue operation, eleven of them had been killed or critically wounded; three had fled on foot.

Travis Banks stood by Major Salazar while the officer interrogated one of the ASG survivors. Banks noted that the rebel—like the dead guard—appeared to be barely out of puberty. The boy lay on the ground, wounded by a bullet to his upper arm; he was crying.

"He's not much help," Salazar concluded as he stood up from questioning the child-soldier. "What he told me is something we already know: that he'd been promised food and some money if he'd join the group." Salazar had a disgusted look on his face. "You see, Banks, this is what we're up against. These kids can be so easily recruited because they have little hope of doing anything else."

Captain Banks recalled his heated discussion about the same topic with Colonel Romolo earlier in the day. He watched as one of Salazar's men clumsily applied bandages and a tourniquet to the boy's bloody arm. Banks heard another

AFP call out to the Major from about fifty meters away. He followed Salazar to a spot deeper into the woods.

Captain Travis Banks had seen his share of macabre sights during his ten years of active duty: mangled and missing limbs, disfigured faces and horrifying burns. That being said, nothing could have prepared him for the grotesque site that was now before him.

One of Salazar's men had discovered a decapitated, maggot-riddled corpse. A few meters from the body, jammed onto a pole, was a human head. Salazar silently turned to Banks as if he were gauging the American's reaction.

"God almighty..." Banks said as he fought back the urge to heave.

Salazar issued an order to the AFP; the soldier just stared back at him. Salazar repeated his words, but this time with an angry-sounding admonition. The soldier's expression changed to one of revulsion as he bent down and began pawing through the corpse's pants pockets. He hesitated, vomited to one side and then continued. A few seconds later, he handed a black billfold to Salazar.

The major plied through the dead man's wallet, finally removing what he wanted—some form of identification.

"Ah, this is a bit surprising: a driver's license from the U.S.," Salazar said. "And where exactly in California is a place named Pa-lo Al-to?" He handed the license to Banks for inspection.

"It's near San Francisco, on the West Coast."

Banks studied the pictured face on the driver's license, and then glanced at the grisly skull on the pole—despite the gore, it was obvious that they matched. He paused and cleared his throat in hopes of conveying that he was unfazed by the grossness. "Well..." he said blandly, "I guess somebody didn't care much for Mitchell Castella, did they?"

# CHAPTER 25

The twenty minutes that McGirt had guesstimated until rendezvous with *Lansing's* helicopter seemed like an eternity. Bud Lammers had spent the time nervously shifting his eyes between the boat's compass, his wristwatch and the pursuing vessel behind them. Spider's boat was holding its position a few miles in trail, but the rebels had clearly not given up their chase.

*Lansing's* navigator had computed intercept headings for McGirt's boat and the inbound helicopter, relaying the vectors by radio to the helicopter crew and via satellite to McGirt. Chief Pescotti had relieved IT2 Briscow from her watch duties in *Lansing's* radio shack. As the shop supervisor, he'd taken it upon himself to personally type the text messages to McGirt on the ship's AN/PRQ-7's base workstation keyboard.

"Keep it steady on this heading, Bud, you're doing fine!" McGirt shouted as he read *Lansing's* last update off the handheld's rectangular gray-tinted LED screen. "We should be seeing the helo anytime now!" he added hopefully. The seas had picked up, forcing him to take a seat next to Lammers. He braced himself with one hand for the bumpy ride while gripping the device in his other. Karlena Brandt had alternated between periods of lucidity and incoherence as the boat skimmed and bounced across the South China Sea's foam fringed, cobalt waters.

Lammers steered a westerly heading by referencing the boat's wet compass. The magnetically influenced compass rose swayed wildly—plus or minus thirty degrees—leaving Bud with few options other than to split the heading differences and to pray for the best. He switched his sights from the compass, looked down at his watch, and then squinted at the horizon. "I think I see them," he yelled. His tone was tentative.

McGirt rose from his seat, shielded his eyes and joined Lammers in the search. After a long pause he called out, "There! God damn, it's them!" Karlena propped herself on one elbow and swiveled her head in vain. "There, just off to the left!" he shouted while pointing to the speck of an image racing toward them.

The CH-46 was flying low and fast above the wave tops, its fuselage inclined at an intimidating, nose-down attitude. The helicopter's six rotor blades made a distinctive, mechanical *twapping* sound as they propelled the machine at its maximum forward speed. Lammers turned the wheel slightly and aimed directly at the approaching aircraft. *Lansing's* navigator had nailed the rendezvous point: Their tracks would intersect in a matter of seconds.

"We can't afford to slow down, Bud!" McGirt declared loudly. "They'll have to pick us up on the move!"

Lammers gave a thumbs-up signal while McGirt began rousing Karlena to her feet. "You'll go first," he said. He realized that in their haste of escaping, neither he, Bud nor Karlena had donned a life vest. He looked frantically around him, but couldn't locate one. He saw that the helicopter was now paralleling their course in a close-abeam position to port. The aircraft flew in a crabbed, sideways track while maintaining roughly 50 feet of altitude and matching the boat's speed. A crewman appeared in the right-side boarding door, where the rescue boom and winch had been installed. Next to the crewman, stood a camo-clad sailor carrying a machine gun. The crewman began paying out the hoist's cable, lowering it slowly into the water to discharge static electricity that may have built as the cable had unspooled from the rig's winch. A yellow-colored, padded rescue ring, or horse collar, skipped across the water as the helicopter slowly inched its way to an overhead position. The crewman raised the horse collar from the water as the helicopter's commander—flying from the right seat—maneuvered his craft with surgical dexterity. He placed the collar in a dangling position, squarely above the boat's midsection.

McGirt held Karlena stable while Bud Lammers maintained a steady track. "Now remember," he shouted above the hurricane-force rotor wash, "When I wrap the horse collar under your arms, hold it to you with all your might!" She nodded and smiled faintly at him. "You *don't* want to go swimming!" he added.

But those last well-intention words seemed to have renewed the fear and horrors that the girl had endured over the last several weeks. She grabbed McGirt in a death grip; he felt her body shaking like a terrified animal.

McGirt peeled her away from him. "Listen, you have to do this, *now!* It will be okay!"

The crewman lowered the collar until it came to rest inside the boat, against the seat next to Lammers. McGirt quickly grabbed the horse collar, wrapped it under Karlena's armpits and secured the collar's metal latch. He didn't give her time to react, but rather flashed a signal to the crewman who engaged the winch and yanked her abruptly into the air. A few seconds later, Karlena Brandt was a passenger inside the big helicopter.

McGirt stood next to Lammers and started edging him out from behind the wheel. "You're next Bud! I'll take over from here!"

Lammers shot back a fierce look while shaking his head vehemently. "No way! I'll go last!" he bellowed. McGirt had known Bud long enough to know that it was pointless to argue with his headstrong friend.

Their tactic of completing the transfer on the fly appeared to be working; the rebel's had managed to close the gap somewhat, but by his estimate, McGirt saw that they were still at least a thousand meters away, beyond small-arms range and too far away for an accurate RPG launch.

The next phase went swiftly. McGirt was hoisted aboard the chopper in less than a minute, and the horse collar was sent down again. He stood in the doorway wedged between the crew chief, whose white helmet was emblazoned with the black, saw-tooth-lettered moniker, "Psycho," and one of the gunners. The trio watched as Bud struggled with the task of controlling the boat while, at the same time, donning the collar.

McGirt craned his head aft and was surprised to see that the rebels had somehow closed in dramatically. He glanced down again at the water and realized what had happened: While Lammers had been floundering alone in the boat, he'd inadvertently allowed the vessel to drift from its westerly track, which had resulted in the boat and helicopter tracing a lazy circle through the water. The misstep had permitted the rebels' boat to take an intercept angle and to creep up to within a few hundred meters of the Americans' position.

McGirt hollered at the gunner while pointing toward the rebels. "They've got an RPG! You guys have to do something!"

The sailor hustled back to the helicopter's lowered aft ramp, where his fellow gunner had taken a prone firing position behind the tripod of an ominous looking, long-barreled machine gun. The men immediately began firing, quickly emptying their weapons' magazines, but their bullets fell short.

While they scrambled to reload, McGirt heard one of them let out a wail loud enough to be heard above the helicopter's ear-splitting din. He peeked over Psycho's shoulder just as the smoking trail of a rocket-propelled grenade splashed less than a dozen meters behind them. Rearmed, the gunners began a vicious assault on the surface target, zeroing in by meticulously "walking" their bullet spray patterns toward the boat's bow.

*Where the hell is Blister when I really need him?* Spider cursed to himself. He'd had to grab the two closest bodies when he'd left the gun battle to pursue Karlena. After launching the first grenade shot at *Lansing's* helicopter, Spider was forced to take over driving when one of the rookies became violently seasick and acted incapable of doing anything other than hurling over the side while frozen in a pathetic, paralyzed pose on the boat's deck.

Spider reluctantly handed the launch tube to the other man and ordered him to reload while he took over at the helm and got back on course for another shot. *This wouldn't have happened with a seasoned comrade like Blister,* he lamented. *Why'd that son-of-a-bitch decide to leave me now!*

Spider pressed hard against the boat's throttle lever, and by employing the axiom that the shortest distance between two points is a straight line, he zeroed in on a spot ahead of the helicopter's arcing track. But as he raced toward the chopper, a cluster of small puffs exploded from the bird's tail section. He watched helplessly as another angry flurry of bullets danced toward him; this time the gunners had found their mark.

A fusillade of projectiles pierced the bow and ripped through the boat's left side. Shreds of fiberglass sprayed into the air like kernels of popcorn erupting from an uncovered pan. When Spider spun around to check on the guy who held the grenade-launching tube, he saw that the man had been hit.

The dazed rebel stood erect for a moment, then folded at the waist and slipped overboard like a discarded piece of trash. The launch tube went with him.

The cruel spectacle caused Spider to snap. He no longer cared about Malik Abbas's charity, the ransom money, or even the supplies and weapons that had been promised to his terrorist group. He now focused solely on one objective: to inflict revenge on these arrogant infidels who'd foiled his plot.

Streams of bullets whistled past him as the riddled vessel filled with seawater; but Jameel "Spider" Abijon had no fear. His mind became overwhelmed with the deranged illusion that he'd been ordained to carry out this valiant act for the good of his people. He reached for his machine gun and raised it into position for a desperate, final shot.

With Bud Lammers secured in the collar and ready for pickup, Psycho took up cable slack and began reeling him in. But when Lammers had removed his hands off the boat's steering wheel, the torque effect of the vessel's big twin motors caused the craft to veer sharply to the right and away from the chopper. The sudden movement resulted in Lammers being jerked overboard and disappearing from view beneath the moving aircraft. His body skimmed over the waves like a skipping stone across a pond.

The pilot immediately reacted by reducing power, and then raising the aircraft's nose in an effort to slow down.

Sensing this, McGirt shoved Psycho aside and bolted into the cockpit. He wedged himself between the two pilots and screamed, "No, dammit, don't stop! He's already in the collar—keep going!"

# CHAPTER 26

Captain Torres had assumed control of the bridge and had commanded her ship to proceed at "flank" speed to a rendezvous point with the rescue helicopter. Although plowing through the waves at barely twenty knots, the big freighter's hull throbbed with energy as her three boilers burned at their maximum temperature, vaporizing purified seawater into high-pressure steam that powered the ship's drive shaft and massive six-bladed screw.

*Lansing's* air detachment quickly "hot pumped" the ship's second helicopter and launched the re-fueled bird to a holding pattern, or "starboard delta," on the vessel's right side. Torres's decision to keep the second chopper airborne accomplished two things: it provided a clear deck for the returning aircraft, plus it made ready an additional rescue bird if needed.

"XO, what's the latest?" Captain Torres said into the phone that rested fast by her bridge chair. Bill Draper was providing her with updates every ten minutes, yet Torres had been uncharacteristically edgy since the moment after the radio shack had received McGirt's distress call via satellite.

Commander Draper had stationed himself a short distance from the bridge in *Lansing's* Combat Information Center, or CIC, where he had instant access to all communications in addition to the ship's surface and air radar presentations. "Skipper, the helo crew reports that two survivors have been hoisted aboard with one to go. They also said they're being tailed by another small boat, possible hostiles."

"Range, please?"

Draper stared down over the shoulder of a radar operator who was tracking the helicopter. "Estimate forty miles at this time. We should have a visual with them any moment now."

Torres grabbed a set of binoculars and went outside to an exterior viewing platform, known as the starboard bridge wing.

Draper left his station in CIC and joined her as they both scanned the horizon.

"There, I got him now!" Psycho hollered. After some nimble stick work by the pilot, Lammers had come back into view from underneath the aircraft. "Reeling survivor in now, sir," he reported to the cockpit.

McGirt stood by the rescue winch as the crew chief prepared to hoist Lammers the fifty-foot ascent into the helicopter. He saw that, despite the dunking, Bud appeared to be in reasonably decent condition. McGirt knew, however, that the combined ordeals of being dragged through waves and having to tread water while encased in the armored vest had to have taken a toll on the sixty-two year old.

Bud raised his head for a split second signaling that he was ready, then dropped it wearily back to his chest.

Lammers's feet had just broken the surface when McGirt heard a string of metallic pinging noises rip through the cabin, followed by the moaning sound of an unspooling turbo-shaft engine. The aircraft shuddered as if it had been kicked by a giant's foot. McGirt felt a sinking sensation in his gut as the helicopter entered a wobbly descent; he braced for impact.

But the pilot responded to the emergency exactly as he'd been trained: He manually boosted fuel to the operating engine while simultaneously lowering the aircraft's nose to increase forward airspeed. After initially settling to within a few feet of the surface, the underpowered aircraft staggered into a gradual climb.

When McGirt looked back through the cabin he saw a peppering of dime-sized holes that ran the full length of the helicopter's right side. It was clear to him what had happened: They'd been struck by small arms fire, and the bullets had probably trashed the aircraft's starboard engine.

McGirt then turned his attention back to the rescue winch, where he saw Bud Lammers's bald head finally emerge in the doorway. He helped the crew chief haul Bud's soaked body to a spot next to Karlena Brandt, on the aircraft's black, non-skid decking.

Bud propped himself on an elbow, turned to one side and coughed up a briny mixture of seawater and vomit. He collapsed back onto the deck, then managed a sad, grateful grin.

McGirt bent down to say something when he a felt hard slap on his back.

"Sir, I think we could use you up front!" Psycho shouted into his ear. "Bruiser, I mean Lieutenant Moseley, took one and looks like he's about to pass out."

When McGirt got to the cockpit he found that the copilot, seated in the left seat, was flying the aircraft. He then turned toward the flight's aircraft commander. He recognized the pilot as one of the guys he'd played cards with after evening meal the night before. Once he'd learned that, like himself, the big, jovial fellow was from the Midwest and had also played college football, he'd taken an instant liking to the man. McGirt had forgotten the pilot's name, but had agreed that the man's squadron mates had tagged him with a fitting call sign: *Bruiser.*

Bruiser sat motionless, his head tilted back against the seat's headrest. McGirt gently raised his helmet's dark-shaded visor and saw a pained, bewildered look in the man's eyes.

Bruiser turned his head slowly and stammered, "Sir, it's my…it's my arm." He pulled a bloody, gloved hand away from his right arm and exposed the wound; blood flowed freely from the gaping hole and saturated the side of his olive-green flight suit.

McGirt saw that at least one bullet had passed through the pilot's side window, torn completely through Bruiser's bicep and shattered the center of the aircraft's instrument panel. A tangle of broken glass and metal shards rested in the sticky blood that now began to pool around the pilot's flight boots.

Bruiser looked up at McGirt and tried to speak again, but he passed out before the words could escape his quivering lips.

McGirt watched as Bruiser's swarthy complexion began to pale from the rapid loss of blood. He quickly undid the pilot's five-point harness and hollered back into the cabin to get Pyscho's attention. The two of them lugged Bruiser's sagging body out of the cockpit. They deposited him on the deck, alongside Lammers and Karlena.

"He needs a tourniquet on that arm—fast!" McGirt shouted at Psycho; he glanced back at Bruiser's empty, blood-soaked seat. McGirt pulled the belt from his cargo pants and tossed it to the crew chief.

Psycho gave him a thumbs-up and quickly wrapped the belt tightly under Bruiser's arm, above the wound. The gushing blood ebbed to no more than a trickle.

Confident that Bruiser, Lammers and Karlena were stable, McGirt turned his attention back to the cockpit. The sight of Bruiser's blood gave him a chill, but he knew full well that the only proper action for him to take at this moment was to strap himself into that vacated pilot seat. Psycho returned with a headset. McGirt plugged in its connections and slid the soundproofing cups over his ears. He adjusted the rig's boom-mike and keyed the ICS.

"Comm check," he said. Until now, McGirt hadn't paid much thought to the junior aviator who'd taken over the controls after Bruiser had been hit. He'd seen the man randomly during his and Bud's brief stay on *Lansing*, but hadn't formerly met him. McGirt noted an ensign's bar embroidered on the shoulders of the pilot's flight suit and located a name emblazoned across the front of the fellow's helmet. It read *Squeaker*. Once the young pilot had keyed his mike and spoken, McGirt understood the odd moniker.

"Got you five-by-five, sir," the early-twenties looking guy said in his high-pitched voice. Squeaker lifted his helmet's visor and wiped down his dripping brow with a trembling hand.

"How you doin', son?" McGirt spotted the same indecisive "look" on Squeaker that he'd seen on Lt. Tim Worley's face that day they'd been forced to land on a crowded San Diego beach.

"I'm hangin' in there, I guess, sir." The fear on the young aviator's face was clearly palpable. "How's Lt. Moseley?"

"Bleeding pretty bad, but I think the crew chief's got it stabilized for now. He'll need some serious medical attention, though." McGirt looked outside and saw that the chopper had lost altitude. "Better watch your altitude, son," he said as he made a quick scan of the cockpit's gauges. He noted that most of the helicopter's pitot-static, or air-driven, instruments, including the airspeed and altitude indicators, had failed. Surprisingly, the bullet's trajectory hadn't influenced the electronic gauges that monitored the aircraft's rotor systems and lone operating engine; they all appeared normal.

"Looks like you've been flying pretty much by the seat of your pants, Squeaker," McGirt said, hoping that his encouraging words might help settle down the ensign's nerves.

"Bruiser did a great job of keeping us in the air after the right engine shit the bed. It's been a challenge after losing all those flight instruments, though."

McGirt let his own hands drift closer to the control as Squeaker fought to maintain a constant altitude; the ride began to feel like being on a roller coaster.

McGirt concluded that, all things considered, the young pilot was doing an adequate job of flying the crippled machine.

"Hey, what do you say I give you a break on the controls so you can rest your hands a bit?" McGirt said. "I've got a few hours in this beast."

"That'd be great, sir. Thanks. We never got a chance to follow up with the emergency checklist." He quickly reached down into his flight bag and pulled out a blue, pocketbook-sized manual, then thumbed through its yellow pages until he found the section he wanted. Within thirty seconds he'd completed all the steps.

"You made contact with the ship yet?" McGirt asked. He thought about digging out the high-tech contraption that Bill Draper had given him, but decided against taking his attention away from the cockpit.

"No sir, but we should be in radio range by now. Let me try." Squeaker removed his sweaty flight gloves before re-tuning the ship's frequency into the aircraft's radio. He rubbed both hands on his thighs to dry them, then keyed the trigger switch at the top of his stick.

"Spartan, Spartan, this is Skymaster One-Zero. Do you read? Over."

"Roger, One-Zero, we've got you at three-five miles on radar. Negative visual contact yet. Say your state?"

Squeaker reported the aircraft's remaining fuel endurance as "four zero 'til splash", or approximately forty minutes until engine flameout. He then gave the ship a synopsis of what had happened: hostile fire; loss of an engine and three souls on board in need of medical attention—one of them in serious condition.

McGirt estimated another calculation in his head: At the much slower single-engine speed, they'd have enough fuel to safely reach the ship with a slight reserve. It would be close, he figured, but not critical.

"You ready to take 'er back, Ensign?"

Squeaker shifted nervously in his seat. The indecisive "look" had returned to the ensign's face as he unassertively placed his hands on the flight controls.

McGirt flashed back to what had been his unexpected final flight in the Navy—a comprehensive check ride during which he'd practiced a myriad of abnormal maneuvers, including simulated single-engine landings to a ship. He was hesitant to assume control of the flight, even though he knew he had ten times more experience than the "newbie" sitting next to him. Technically, he now considered himself a civilian. Nevertheless, it was a no-brainer for him: If Squeaker screwed up this approach to the ship, he'd have to take control of the aircraft. He knew that they'd have enough fuel for at least two approaches: one for the ensign and—if necessary—another one for him.

With Squeaker flying the aircraft again, McGirt acted as the copilot; he reconfirmed their emergency status and souls on board to the ship, gave the cabin crew a "five minutes out" call, and completed the landing checklist.

*Lansing's* navigator had computed a heading for the ship that provided the best winds for a left seat landing—just off the ship's starboard bow.

"Looking good, Ensign," McGirt said as Squeaker rolled the chopper into a shallow bank angle and lined up on a final approach course, three miles directly behind the ship. *Lansing's* second aircraft had broken off from its delta pattern and now assumed a high-perched, hovering position off the stern and to the right.

McGirt reiterated the single-engine power settings that he'd memorized during his two decades as a CH-46 driver. The ball-park, or "gouge," instrument settings would assure that the aircraft maintained sufficient rotor revolutions, or "turns," to remain airborne. The helicopter's airspeed was equally critical: too fast or too slow a speed could cause the rotor turns to decrease, or "bleed off," to a point where the aircraft would lose lift, no longer be controllable, and would fall from the sky. But the cold fact that the helicopter's airspeed system had been rendered unusable presented the pilots with the added challenge of relying on their own raw sense of motion and eyesight; in aviator lingo, they'd be flying by the seat of their pants.

"Okay, that's good," McGirt said. "Now reduce power a little bit and hold the deck in that exact sight picture in your windshield."

Squeaker lowered the collective lever and the helicopter entered a slow descent toward the ship's landing area. About one hundred feet long and eighty feet wide, at first glance, *Lansing's* "helo deck" appeared comfortably adequate in size. Yet, as both McGirt and Squeaker knew, if they were to come in too fast, or touch down too far forward, they'd risk the calamity of the chopper's rotor blades colliding with the superstructure that towered over the flight deck's forward boundary.

The familiar smell of the ship's diesel-oil exhaust spilled into the cockpit as the aircraft descended below 100 feet. Squeaker pulled back on the stick and began slowing down.

"No...no, not yet," McGirt said calmly, like a first base coach holding back an overanxious runner itching to steal second. He nudged the stick forward with his right hand and lightly gripped the collective with his left, ready to take over.

But it wasn't necessary. Squeaker did precisely what was required to maintain the aircraft on speed, and on glide path. The helicopter touched down with a firm "thump," squarely in the center of the landing zone.

Spider grappled to put on a lifejacket while at the same time keeping his eyes fixated on the corpse floating beside him. The flurry of bullets that had ripped his boat to pieces had also riddled his comrade's body into a perforated, bleeding mess. Spider had literally felt the compressed rushes of air against his skin as the projectiles had whizzed past him. But not a single bullet had even grazed his body—not one. The fact that he'd survived the Americans' vicious onslaught had only served to strengthen his belief that he'd been chosen for a higher purpose and his work was not yet done.

He'd been in these waters often enough to know that eventually sharks would probably pick up the scent of his partner's blood. He zipped up the jacket and smoothly paddled away from the dead man's body. He prayed that the motion of his arms and legs didn't create too loud a sound: The sizzling and grinding of the boat's motor as it sank had already made plenty of racket.

Spider's lean body bobbed with the rolling swells as he tried to remain calm. The vision of smoke and fire spewing from the damaged helicopter had given him a moment of satisfaction, albeit short lived. Although the American girl had escaped, he was hopeful that the conspiracy had played out long enough for the ransom money to be sent.

After several minutes of swimming, the wreckage and bloodied water had disappeared from his view, and he felt safe enough to rest. He rolled onto his back and let his body drift with the waves. As he tilted his head back into the water, a faint buzzing sound began to ring in his ears. At first, he assumed that his mind was playing tricks on him: He was exhausted and hadn't had any food or drink since the early morning. He raised his head and shook it. But when he leaned back again, the buzzing sound returned—this time louder.

Spider looked down at his feet and began searching frantically in all directions. *Could something be coming after him?* Just then a swell lifted him, and from the corner of his eye, he saw a white blur. The image sank below his view as quickly as it had appeared. But when his body rose again with the next swell, he had sufficient time to focus on the object as it skirted over the surface.

He thought he was hallucinating, but after several more dips and risings, it was clear what he was seeing: It was the twin-engine boat that he and his men had been chasing. He'd watched as Karlena and its other occupants had been hoisted aboard the helicopter and flown away. But during the melee, he'd never considered that their boat—the very boat that he and Blister had used to commandeer the girl—could still be anywhere near him.

Spider felt a glimmer of hope. Every time he'd rise with a swell, he was able to locate the driverless craft, and after a few minutes, he concluded that it was tracing a continuous circle around him. He remembered how that particular speedboat had a habit of always drifting to one side—to the right—whenever he'd taken his hands off its steering wheel. Blister had explained 'why' one time—something about the way the props rotated—but at this point, he didn't care about the reason; he only wondered how much longer the motors could keep going before running out of gas. He was confident that, if they stopped while there was some daylight, he'd be able to swim the distance and to climb onboard. In the meantime, he would conserve his energy and simply wait.

# CHAPTER 27

When Ensign Jim "Squeaker" O'Leary made his flawless landing, only required personnel were present on *Lansing's* helo deck: the enlisted signalman, or LSE; two sailors tasked with installing wheel chocks and tie-down chains; and a half-dozen sailors outfitted in spaceman-like, metallic-coated fire suits. After the aircraft's engines and rotor blades came to a stop, the ship's helicopter hangar doors flew open. A flood of sailors rushed out toward the aircraft, most importantly *Lansing's* medical doctor and his staff.

Lieutenant Moseley and Karlena Brandt were immediately carted away to the ship's sickbay for treatment, while a headstrong Bud Lammers insisted that he be allowed to walk off the aircraft by himself. He stumbled once but vehemently pushed away any assistance and trudged to sickbay under his own power. The damaged chopper was quickly rolled into the hangar. Ten minutes later, *Lansing's* other CH-46 was recovered and was secured safely on deck.

Bill Draper had been on the hangar deck when McGirt's aircraft had landed. "I think the Army may have age limits for new recruits," he said in a lame attempt to shed some levity in the wake of the exhausted captain's terrifying ordeal. McGirt simply shook his head and followed Draper through the hangar bay. "You probably want to clean up before meeting with Captain Torres. I'll rustle up a fresh set of khaki's for you."

"Yeah, that might be a good idea," McGirt said. Bruiser's blood had dried to a dark, caked consistency and his own perspiration had drenched the olive-drab tee shirt that Banks had given him to wear on patrol. He dug out the radio that Draper had given to him. He stared at the device for several seconds before handing it over. "Here, you can have this back. And thanks—it probably saved our lives."

The shower's hot water felt good on McGirt's aching muscles. Between carry-ing Karlena, contorting himself under their "borrowed" boat's console while hotwiring it, bouncing over the waves, and then being hoisted in the horse collar, his body had taken a beating. He considered himself in good physical shape, but what he'd gone through over the last couple hours had been a much greater strain than his usual regime of jogging and doing a circuit around the base gym's fitness equipment. But he felt a deeper concern for Bud Lammers, who at more than a dozen years older and saddled with the inevitable paunch of a sixty-two year old, must be feeling even worse. When he'd seen Bud's gasping expression after being dragged through the seawater and then yanked up to the helicopter, McGirt had feared that his old pal might suffer a stroke.

He'd been summoned to meet with Captain Torres, but first, he wanted to check up on Lammers. He found Bud tucked in and sound asleep on a bed in sickbay. The surroundings felt the same as all the other Navy medical facilities McGirt had encountered during his career: stark fluorescent lighting, bland pastel-green walls and the lingering aroma of rubbing alcohol.

"Doc gave him a shot," a voice from behind said.

McGirt turned to see *Lansing's* head corpsman, a stocky, mustached chief petty officer whose nametag read HMC ALVAREZ.

"Mr. Lammers was pretty wound up when we got him down here," Alvarez said while scanning the clipboard that hung at the foot of Lammers's bed. He looked at his watch. "I'll be surprised if he wakes up before reveille tomorrow."

McGirt was curious as to what had been written on Bud's medical report, but the chief picked up the clipboard and held it against his chest before he could take a peek. Alvarez glanced over at Karlena Brandt, who was sitting upright in a bed across the room. He leaned in to McGirt and said quietly, "Her, on the other hand...she's another story."

McGirt saw that Karlena, freshly showered and dressed in an antiseptic-looking, government-issue nightgown, was devouring a small bowl of ice cream while paging through a fashion magazine that a female corpsman had given her. She spotted McGirt, waved daintily, and then went back to eating and reading.

"She's lost nearly a third of her body weight, so we put her on an IV," Alvarez said. "Got to bring her along slowly on the solid food," he added. "But overall,

I'd say she's doing pretty well, considering what it appears she's gone through." He shook his head as if astounded by Karlena's rapid improvement. "The young ones...they always seem to bounce back faster."

By the caring smile on the chief's face, McGirt guessed that Alvarez might have a daughter about Karlena's age.

"None of us down here know much about what you and Mr. Lammers were doing on that island, but we're all glad that everyone got back okay."

"Thanks, Chief. How's the lieutenant doing?"

Alvarez motioned to a bi-fold door that led into the ship's operating room. "The Doc's just finishing up with his arm inside the O.R. I've got to tell you though, sir, the way that crewman, Psycho, applied the tourniquet, I don't think me or any of my staff could have done it any better. Moseley lost some serious blood; he might not have survived the flight back without the immediate help he got on that helicopter."

McGirt squeezed Alvarez firmly on the shoulder. "When Lt. Moseley comes around, please tell him that I send my best regards, will you Chief? I'll come back later tonight to check on my running mate." The two men shook hands, and McGirt departed for his long climb up to Captain Torres's office.

The news of Karlena's rescue quickly found its way to Malik Abbas. No phone calls had been made. The news came via a brief exchange of words between him and an informant inside the *Basilan Betterment Foundation's* office. Malik shrugged off the bizarre coincidence that the girl had been saved on the very day that his shipment was scheduled to arrive. But the odd timing didn't matter; when Mitchell Castella had approached him with the elaborate plot, Malik had made the decision to hold Karlena indefinitely in hopes of maximizing her financial value to the Movement.

The rapidity at which events had developed, however, had forced him to activate another extreme action sooner than he'd anticipated. He and Spider had discussed the potential consequences of their actions and they'd agreed to accept the results, good or bad.

Malik gathered his paltry personal effects from the office, bound them to the back fender of his motorbike and sped home.

Ramon sat at his dockside workstation with his heart in his throat. He'd never been asked to do something like this, and despite reassurances from Malik Abbas, his sense of intuition told him that he might be involved in an illegal act. But Malik had been the one who had pulled strings to help get him the job at the Zamboanga Seaport pier—by far, the best job that he'd ever had. After long, grueling days working as a stevedore, he'd moved quickly up the freight company's ladder, and with Malik's help, had wormed his way into the cushy position of "pier-side inspector." The advancement had allowed him, his wife and their infant son to move out of his in-law's place and into the privacy of their own apartment.

Ramon was responsible for observing ship's cargo as it was offloaded and then making a visual inspection to ensure that the shipment's contents matched those on the freight's bill of lading. He would then fill out a form, documenting that the receiving agent had signed for and taken custody. No more time spent in rank-smelling cargo holds, surrounded by sweaty dockworkers. Ramon now spent the majority of his day seated at a shaded dockside workstation, where the heaviest thing that he lifted was a pencil.

When the sputtering, old flatbed truck came to a creaking stop next to him, Ramon's heart raced even faster. The vehicle matched Malik's description, as did its two occupants. He rose from his seat as a pair of wiry, longhaired Filipinos got out of the vehicle and approached him. Their stark attire immediately caused Ramon concern: starched black work pants and fresh-out-of-the-package look-ing white tee shirts. They both wore military style high-laced boots.

"This note is for you, mister. I think you know why we're here," the driver said.

Ramon unfolded a legal-sized yellow sheet of paper and read the brief message: *These two men have generously offered their services. Please allow them to take delivery. —"M"*. Ramon nodded and then tucked the note in his shirt pocket. He stepped out from the shade, unlocked a metal gate and waved them through. The driver pulled inside the pier's secured zone and stopped while Ramon locked the gate behind them.

"It's the red-hulled one, over there on the left," Ramon said as he pointed to a medium-sized vessel moored a few dozen meters away. "I'll ride with you."

The driver told his partner to hop in back while Ramon rode up front.

The ship was a one hundred eighty-five foot freighter of Libyan registry. Stenciled across her stern was the name *City of Da Nang*. Ramon had scanned the vessel's itinerary and noted that it had arrived earlier that morning from Jakarta, Indonesia, and was scheduled to depart in three hours for Manila. Malik's shipment and a single automobile were the only cargo slated for offloading in Zamboanga.

"This is good, right here," Ramon said as the truck approached the ship's boarding ramp. The driver held out some other documents. "Oh, of course; the purchase order and invoice," Ramon said as he grabbed the papers. He got out and walked up the steep incline, where he was met by one of *Da Nang's* crew.

The seaman studied the papers, then hollered to a boom operator who swiveled a long-necked crane over an opened hold and lowered the rigging's hook and cable. A few minutes later, a tightly wrapped pallet containing two rectangular wooden crates was deposited on the pier. The boom operator leaned back in his seat, lit a cigarette and waited for the signal to hoist the cargo back up and onto the truck bed.

"I'll have to look inside the crates. Did you bring a crowbar?" Ramon asked the driver. Malik had instructed Ramon to use those exact words.

The driver looked over at his partner, gave the man a faint smile, then handed Ramon the tool.

Ramon detached the boom's cable hook and peeled away the thick lattice of netting that shrouded the waist-high crates. He carefully pried off the first crate's lid, taking pains to not damage the wood so that the container could be resealed. He shined a flashlight over the tightly packed contents and then carefully slid his hand farther inside; he saw cases of baby formula and bundles of personal hygiene items. Satisfied that he'd gone through the motion of doing his job, he pressed the lid back into place.

Ramon's hands shook as he moved to the second crate. When he looked around, he noticed that there wasn't another city employee in sight on the big pier. He then glanced up at the boom operator and saw that the man had gotten down from his workstation and was involved in conversation with the crewman who'd reviewed the shipment's paperwork. Both men had their backs turned away.

When Ramon's sweaty hands lost their grip, he dropped the crowbar on the pavement. The driver quickly retrieved the tool and helped with prying the crate's cover halfway open. Ramon took a deep breath, composed himself and began looking inside. At quick glance, the contents looked no different than the first. He glanced up again, and saw that the boom operator had returned to his station and that the other crewman was now gazing down at the truck. He ignored the man's stare, and as he'd done with the first crate, pushed the top layer of contents aside for a deeper look. His arm was at elbow depth when he felt a thick padding of foam material, but he was unable to see what was below the foam without prying the crate's lid completely off. He chose to blindly feel what was beneath the padding.

Ramon Mindara, in his twenty-eight years, had never even touched any type of weapon, but when his fingers brushed over the cold, smooth metal of a rifle barrel, there was no doubt in his mind what had been packed in the lower half of the box. He removed his arm slowly from the crate and stood up. He tried looking directly at the truck's driver, but couldn't face the man; his eyes drifted down to the ground as he said "Okay, that's fine, you're good to go." He helped the two men reattach the cargo netting to the cable's hook, and then waived to the boom operator, who promptly raised the load and placed it on the truck bed.

After the vehicle drove away, Ramon sat back down under his umbrella. He felt driblets of perspiration flowing from his armpits; his hands were still shaking. When he tried pouring a glass of iced tea from a thermos bottle, he spilled half of it on himself.

A half-kilometer away from Ramon, at the foot of the Zamboanga-Isabela Auto Ferry Terminal pier, Malik Abbas stood next to the small Toyota sedan that he'd purchased earlier in the week. He'd bypassed haggling with the car's owner and had offered the man full price in cash. The sale amounted to just a fraction of the total he'd withdrawn from the *Basilan Betterment Fund's* bank account. Inside the Toyota's trunk—wedged beneath several suitcases—was a large satchel, stuffed full with a combination of U.S. dollars and Philippine pesos.

Malik had met little resistance from his mother when he'd informed her that they should take a break from their cramped, urban living conditions in Isabela City. She became uncharacteristically energized when he'd told her that he'd made arrangements for them to stay in Central Mindanao, close to where their family farm had been located. The old woman had sprung up from her easy chair and had insisted on packing for both of them.

"What are we waiting for, Malik?" his mother asked from the back seat of the sedan. "Shouldn't we get going so that we arrive before dark?"

Malik lowered the binoculars and held them at his side. "Just checking on the delivery of the supplies I ordered, Mama. You know, the ones my business is donating to those people on the other side of the island."

"Oh, of course," his mother said. "I remember now." Satisfied with her son's explanation, she went back to gently swaying her head and humming a soft, lilting melody.

Malik had booked a spot on the early afternoon auto ferry in order to personally view the final phase of the operation. After that, he planned to disappear for a few weeks, until the commotion of Karlena Brandt's rescue blew over. He raised up the binoculars and sighted his contact, Ramon, standing next to the two men that he'd hired to make the pickup. Everything appeared to be going as scheduled as he observed the two crates being hoisted onto the truck and Ramon walking toward the pier's security gate. As Malik got back inside the car, the front passenger's door flew open.

"Hold it. You're not going anyplace!" the man said as he abruptly sat down and yanked the keys from the car's ignition. His voice sounded familiar, but Malik didn't recognize the face until the intruder removed his hat and dark sunglasses: It was Colonel Felix Romolo. Malik had noticed a sloppily dressed man, wearing work clothing and a wide-brimmed straw hat, sitting alone on the ferry. He'd never suspected that it was somebody he knew.

Malik glanced across the harbor at the Libyan freighter, then traced the path that his delivery truck would travel before exiting the confines of Zamboanga's cargo pier. He no longer needed binoculars to understand what was happening. As the truck approached the pier's end and prepared to merge onto a city street, two military vehicles surged out from inside a warehouse and blocked it. A swarm of police cars followed up by converging on the scene with blaring sirens and flashing lights.

Romolo waived a signal with his hand; a half-dozen plain-clothed men quietly surrounded the car. "Let's make this as peaceful as we can for everybody," he said.

Malik turned to his mother. She had stopped humming and stared aimlessly out at the water. Her normally cheerful expression had changed to one of sadness.

"Don't worry, we'll be kind to her," Romolo said in a low voice. "Now say your goodbyes and get out of the car."

Several hundred miles to the north, at a store in Manila's posh Power Plant Mall, Ling Chin handed the store clerk a third, and her final, credit card. The two previous ones had been rejected.

"Sometimes our computers bog down and just can't get through to the banks," the girl behind the counter said as she swiped the card again. "I remember seeing you in the store last week, Miss Chin, and there wasn't any issue then. I'm sure it must be a problem on our side."

Ling had taken a break from her desk at *Quality Expeditors* in hopes of catching some bargains at her favorite women's clothing store. She checked her watch. "I don't have much more time to wait. Let me see if I have enough cash." She pawed through her wallet and saw that she barely had enough to pay for the cab ride back to her office.

Sensing her embarrassment, the clerk offered, "I'd be happy to hold these items for you. Perhaps you can come back after work. Hopefully, our computer system will be up by then."

"Thank you; that would be so nice of you," Ling said. What she failed to tell the clerk, however, was that the same thing had happened when she'd attempted to pay at another store twenty minutes earlier. Three cards swiped; all three rejected.

A cold streak of anxiety ran through Ling's body. She'd kept meticulous financial records for both her and Ahmad, and despite her recent shopping binges, could nearly quote verbatim their credit card balances and the bottom line of their company's bank statement. She wondered if Ahmad—who had negotiated a flurry of new business for their firm—had somehow forgotten to make a deposit and their line of credit had been frozen.

During the taxi ride, Ling replayed in her mind the week's financial transactions. *Could there have been a glitch with a wire transfer?* She continued to rack her brain for the reason of the foul-up. She was confident that she'd be able to pinpoint the error once she logged on to her computer.

As the elevator door opened on her floor, the elderly man who ran an accounting firm across the hall stepped on as she got off. The usually polite fellow brushed passed without saying a word; he acted as if he didn't know her.

When Ling rounded the corner, she was confronted by a stern-looking man, dressed in business clothing. He introduced himself as a detective with the Manila police department while holding up an identification badge that displayed his grim-faced picture. Over his shoulder, Ling could see a cluster of uniformed men in the process of literally disassembling Ahmad's office. Ahmad was sitting on the carpet with his head in his hands; a heavyset policewoman appeared to be questioning him.

"We'll need to speak with you also, Miss Chin," the detective said. "Do not leave the premises until you are excused."

Ling saw that one of the policemen had stationed himself in front of the office's lone exit to the hallway.

Ling's mind flashed back to the day when Ahmad had first presented the news that their fledgling import-export business had received a windfall, and that his college friend, Malik Abbas, would be their link to additional lucrative contracts. She'd reluctantly gone along with Ahmad's plan, even though her gut had warned her to do otherwise.

As she walked through the doorway that separated her office from Ahmad's, she watched as another Manila cop detached the wires from her computer, and then placed it inside a large, clear plastic bag, labeled—in bold letters—with the word EVIDENCE. The man gave her a disgusted look as he carried it out of the room.

Ling Chin sat down and methodically opened each desk drawer. Her heart sank when she realized that everything had been hauled away, even the pictures of her family. As she began to stand up, the wheels of her chair jammed on something. Ling bent down to retrieve the shiny, brass nameplate that she'd had specially made.

# CHAPTER 28

While making his way through *Lansing's* myriad of passageways and deck levels, McGirt had time to reflect on the day's dizzying array of events, plus one other unrelated topic: how many steep ladders he had to climb from the bowels of the ship, where sick bay was located, up to Captain Torres's office.

Both of his scarred, worn-out knee joints throbbed by the time he reached her office. He made a mental note to track down the ship's doctor later and plead for some off-the-record medication to alleviate the pain. *If I'd known I'd be hurting like this in older age, I would have taken up golf rather than playing football in high school and college,* he lamented.

He knocked on Torres's door, announced himself, and expected to hear her voice instructing him to enter. But instead, the door flew open, and Torres greeted him with a bear hug.

"Welcome back! We're so glad that you all made it out alive!"

McGirt had received plenty of "guy hugs"—an awkward embrace; the perfunctory back slap; and then a concluding, quick separation—but this hug was different from the rest, and his first from a senior female officer. The smell and feel of Torres's firm, athletic physique against his own body felt odd—something for which he wasn't prepared, especially after the icy reception she'd shown toward him and Bud Lammers when they'd first arrived onboard.

After embracing him for several seconds, Torres backed off abruptly; her face reddened with embarrassment. The pair stood eye-to-eye, speechless, and then simultaneously burst out laughing. McGirt suspected that they shared the same notion: *How did that just happen and I'm glad nobody was here to see it.*

"Come in, come in," she said enthusiastically, motioning him toward the long leather sofa positioned adjacent to her desk. "You know, Mr. McGirt,

I'm not sure how we should address each other. Considering that we've both achieved the same military rank, I'm comfortable with first names if you are. Please call me Kathy."

"Okay, *Kathy.* My given names of Johnny Jack usually confuse people, so I'm fine with just plain McGirt. That's what my wife, Gina, usually calls me."

"Fine, McGirt it is," she said. "We can discuss the details of what happened on Basilan in a moment, but before I forget, my chief yeoman wanted me to tell you that he still has not received any documents for either you or Dr. Lammers. You gentlemen showed up without formal travel orders—only a short, classified message directing us to pick you up in Subic, drop you off on Basilan, and then to loiter in the area until further notice. Have there been any advance arrangements made to get the two of you back to the States?"

McGirt suddenly realized that he'd come all this way lacking anything that resembled written orders—only Bud's verbal assurance about what their mission was to be. Likewise, he'd left Admiral Truckee's office without a DD Form 214, the Navy's official discharge certificate. "Well, I'll be honest; I haven't a clue. Without Bud here, I'm in the blind. We'll have to wait until he wakes up tomorrow morning and discuss it together."

"Sure, I understand completely," Torres replied. She looked down at her bad arm and rubbed its jagged scar self-consciously.

McGirt pictured Admiral Truckee and how the man stoically struggled with the handicap of a crippled arm. He wondered if Katherine Torres would suffer the same destiny as she grew older.

"Did the ship's doctor talk to you about Bud's condition?" she asked.

McGirt saw that a look of apprehension had filled her otherwise confident eyes. "No, he didn't. Chief Alvarez gave me the basics and said that the doc had given Bud a shot to help him relax. That's all."

"Well, you need to know, so I'll tell you now. Seems that on initial examination, Lammers exhibited the symptoms of someone who'd suffered a heart attack—actually, Doc suspects that Bud may have had several over the last few days." McGirt saw worry creep into Torres's eyes.

"I was not aware of that," he said. He felt a chill is his veins. He'd experienced the same fears during his tour as a squadron skipper. Like Torres, McGirt knew that the most dreaded event that could occur during one's command was a death. *Lansing* had come within seconds of nearly losing a helicopter and its crew, plus three civilians.

"I'm sorry that I had to be the one who told you, but as you probably surmised, Doc Murphy was tied up in surgery with Lt. Moseley, who, thank God, is out of critical status. Also—good news—Miss Brandt appears to be doing fine and on the road to recovery."

McGirt reflected on how wretched Karlena had looked when the Special Forces had extracted her from the hostage shack. "Yes, considering the shape she was in when we found her. Chief Alvarez told me that she perked up pretty quickly after a hot shower and some nourishment." The vision of Karlena Brandt's weak, depleted body seemed to have triggered his own sense of fatigue. He yawned deeply. "Sorry about that." he said.

"No worries, you've had a rough day." Torres reached for a clipboard that held a ream of classified messages, donned a pair of unglamorous horn-rimmed glasses, then paused to scan the most recent communiqués. "Seems this affair has taken on a very high priority back in D.C., and by what's been pouring into my communications center, I can understand why." She shrugged her shoulders and added, "Way above my pay grade."

"Yes, mine too." McGirt replied. "One thing that I learned from my tour as an attaché at the Philippine embassy is that, once news of this type of event reaches the Pentagon and Congress, the follow-ups will snowball exponentially." He hesitated before going any further, but ultimately decided to elaborate. "I think that's why Bud sought me out for this trip: He knew that, together, we had the best chance to cut to the chase and gain intel about the girl; and we were well on our way to that end." He shook his head at the irony of how things had actually unfolded. "But from the moment the chopper dropped us off at the AFP camp, our original plan took a few unexpected twists and turns."

Torres laughed. "McGirt, that has to be the understatement of the year." She set down the clipboard and removed her glasses. "Reading between the lines, I suspect that the issue of where the ransom money might eventually end up is what's shining the big spotlight on all of this." She raised her eyebrows as if anticipating him to expand on her assumption.

He flashed a sly grin. "Probably best to wait until Bud's able to join us in that conversation...*Captain*."

Torres returned the grin. "You're absolutely right, *Mr. McGirt*. Let's wait until then." She reached for another document. "Chief Pescotti delivered this just before you got up here. We've established communications with the State Department about Miss Brandt, and her father has been notified. He agreed with Doc Murphy's recommendation that she continue resting onboard for several more days before she begins her journey home. With that in mind, my fleet commander has directed me to set course for Pearl Harbor. We'll offload you, Bud and the girl at that time."

"Sounds good by me," McGirt said. He fought back another yawn.

"Okay, *great*. Glad that's settled." They both stood up and began walking to the door. "Oh, one more thing before you go," Torres said. "I'm not sure what the cooks are serving tonight in the wardroom, but I'll be having steak." She touched him gently on the shoulder. "Would you care to join the XO and me for dinner?"

Considering all that Katherine Torres had done for Lammers and him since they'd come aboard, there was no way that McGirt could turn down her invitation. He now understood more clearly why Bill Draper held such high admiration for the lady; she was a true professional and came across as a genuine, caring person once you got to know her. McGirt had a hunch that she'd be a valuable contact after he started his new job in Washington; plus, he really loved steak.

"Sure, Kathy, that'd be wonderful," he said. "Thanks."

Jameel "Spider" Abijon's first sign that he was still alive was when he heard the squawking call of a seagull as it flew overhead. His harrowing night in the South China Sea had unfolded in the same miraculous manner that he'd survived the wrath of the Americans' bullets. He was convinced that he'd been spared by an act of divine intervention.

After the sun had set, he gave up any hope of ever locating the boat that he'd watched circling him for hours. He tried to pray for his survival, but the nauseating rhythm of lifting and falling with the waves distracted him from remembering the appropriate verses. He eventually surrendered to the thought that he'd either die from starvation and dehydration or be eaten by sharks.

But just as the coal black sky seemed at its darkest, a brilliant full moon crested over the eastern horizon. Its glowing brightness struck him as another omen that, once again, Allah had not yet given up on his soul. The rising moon cast a ghostly luminescence over the ocean's surface and enabled him to spot a shimmer of light as it reflected off the abandoned boat. Somehow, by a combination of the boat's circling track and the ocean's current, his body had been carried to a position within only a few dozen meters of the idle vessel. He paddled the short distance, gathered his strength while hugging one of the boat's motors and, then, used the force of a rising swell to help hoist himself aboard. As he collapsed to the deck, a half-full water bottle rolled against his head. He blindly opened it, and gulped down the contents. Exhausted, he passed out and slept soundly through the remaining nighttime.

The next morning, Spider felt the sun's heat baking down on his wet clothing and salt-crusted skin. He rose up from the deck and stumbled his way toward the boat's cockpit, where he discovered another water bottle. He splashed a handful onto his face and eyes, then squinted to read the compass.

He saw that the wind had caused the craft's bow to weathercock in a west-northwesterly direction. However, Spider quickly deduced from the boat's orientation and the prevailing wind that it was actually drifting to the east. He stood up and scanned the horizon: The morning haze had lifted sufficiently for him to see the peak of a landmass in the distance. He was familiar enough with the region to know that what he had sighted was either Basilan or one of the many small islands that comprised the Sulu Archipelago, to Basilan's south. He felt the boat surge with the wind as the following seas continued pushing him closer to land.

Spider dropped to his knees and gave thanks to Allah for the graces that had been bestowed upon him. Though he felt responsible for Karlena's escape, he was determined to make up for his failure by rededicating himself to the Movement. He'd lost the battle but had survived to fight another day.

Bud Lammers's irregular heartbeat was brought into check by medication prescribed by the ship's doctor. He was able to check out of sickbay, and rejoined McGirt in their stateroom soon afterwards. Sadly, though, Bud was forced to confront the reality that he'd need additional care upon his return stateside.

Karlena, along with Bruiser Moseley, remained under the supervision of Chief Alvarez and his staff in sickbay. Their conditions were stable and improving.

The weeklong journey from the South China Sea to Pearl Harbor turned out to be an unexpected pleasure for McGirt. The voyage had provided him with the opportunity to further develop his friendship with Katherine Torres as they discussed a multitude of topics centering on the challenges demanded of a commanding officer in the modern, fully integrated Navy. After Bud was able to join them, his acerbic humor had only added to their engaging conversations.

Commander Bill Draper had worked financial magic by convincing the money keepers at the State Department to fund three first-class airline tickets from Honolulu International to San Diego's Lindberg Field.

*Lansing's* lone functioning helicopter, with Ensign Jim "Squeaker" O'Leary occupying the copilot's seat, shuttled the threesome directly to the Honolulu airport tarmac.

Dr. Gina DeCarlo greeted her husband and Bud Lammers when they touched down in Southern California. She'd taken the initiative to schedule Bud for a full cardio work up at San Diego's Veterans Administration Hospital and offered him the use of a spare bedroom in Coronado while he convalesced. Bud gratefully accepted.

After landing in San Diego, Karlena Brandt was whisked away to the corporate aircraft terminal, where she boarded Congressman Clayton Gantry's private jet, destined for Midland-Odessa.

# CHAPTER 29

"You're out of uniform, Mister!" Tarzan Truckee barked.

McGirt had toyed with the idea of wearing a civilian suit for the meeting, but without official discharge papers in hand, had decided against it. He instinctively lowered his eyes to conduct a quick self-inspection of his summer khakis, and suspected that jet lag had caused him to forget a belt or, worse yet, that he'd neglected to attach the service ribbons and gold aviator wings to his shirt.

Exasperated, he finally relented. "Okay, Admiral, I give. What is it?"

"These," Truckee said as he flung a small box across the room.

McGirt snatched the box with one hand and opened it. He saw a set of silver star collar devices that signified the rank of a Rear Admiral. He laughed loudly. Over the years he'd grown fond of the old warrior's practical jokes. "Yeah, right," he said. "What else you got for me, sir, an all-expense-paid trip to Tijuana?"

Truckee's feigned angry expression quickly changed to that of a proud, happy father. "No, Johnny Jack, it's for real. While you and the CIA were in the Philippines saving the world, the O-7 selection board met—and you made the cut. Congratulations, Admiral McGirt."

"But seriously, sir, I submitted my letter of resignation to you before I left for the P.I. You told me that you'd take it from there and expedite my request."

"Yes…and that's *exactly* what I did," Truckee replied. He reached over to the corner of his big mahogany desk where a three-tiered correspondence file sat. The file's "baskets" were labeled: IN, OUT, and HOLD. "I took your resignation letter from my *IN* basket and *expeditiously* placed it in my *HOLD* basket." He dramatically mimed the act in slow motion. "And that's where your request has been sitting for the last three weeks."

McGirt was flummoxed. "So…I'm still on active duty?"

"Yup, never left it. After you turned over your command to Frank Taswell, I had the Navy detailer assign you surreptitiously to my staff as a 'special projects officer.' Never had anything in writing; we deliberately kept you on verbal orders."

"Oh," McGirt said. He stared at the silver stars as he rolled them between his fingers. "Admiral Truckee, I think you know how much respect I have for you. And this is such a tremendous honor for me—your confidence in my abilities and all, but..." McGirt felt a lump rising in his throat, and his eyes began to well.

"But you're not sure if you want to accept the promotion, is that it?" Truckee's rough and tumble demeanor had switched to that of a kind parent who'd realized that their child was struggling with an important decision. "Well, no need to give me an answer now. Take a few days and talk it over with Gina. No hurry. In the meantime, your letter of resignation will remain parked in my HOLD basket, and you'll continue to report directly to me. Will that arrangement be suitable?"

"Yes, sir, it is. Thank you."

Truckee shuffled across the office floor with hands tucked inside pants pockets and his head lowered. His face was comically contorted as if he were straining in deep thought. "There's one other issue that might help with your decision: Rumor has it that, if you decide to pin on those stars, there just might be a spot for you on the president's National Security Council staff. So, whether you follow in Bud Lammers's foot steps back to Spookville or you accept the promotion, one way or the other, an eastbound moving van may be showing up outside your house pretty soon." Truckee shrugged and winked. "Just saying..."

"Got it, sir," McGirt said with a muted chuckle. "You'll hear from me as soon as possible."

"Oh, and one final thing," Truckee said as he plunked himself back behind his desk and began pawing through paperwork. "I'm still waiting for that case of San Miguel you promised."

McGirt hopped on his Harley and drove across Coronado's North Island Naval Air Station to a concrete, windowless building that served as the base's communications center. The tightly guarded facility was the hub for all classified correspondence coming and going to and from the air station. He'd dropped off Bud Lammers at the fortress-like compound earlier, before his scheduled meeting with Admiral Truckee. Lammers was sitting on a bench, under the shade of a eucalyptus tree, when McGirt eased his big two-wheeler into the "O-6 and above" parking spot. Lammers had made use of the facilities encrypted telephone network to speak with people at CIA headquarters in Langley, Virginia.

"How'd it go?" McGirt asked as he handed Lammers a helmet.

"Well, to be honest, I'm damned pissed after what I just learned," Bud said while cinching the helmet's chinstrap. "On the other hand, I'm feeling pretty strong this morning. You want to take a walk on the beach?"

"Sure, as long as you're up for it."

"Yeah, I think that will help clear my head so we can discuss things better." Lammers straddled the motorcycle's rear seat and said, "Okay, ace, let's go."

McGirt gunned the bike's engine and headed for the air station's back gate that emptied onto Coronado's scenic Ocean Boulevard. The flow of surfer dudes, tourists, and daily beach walkers was relatively light—it was a weekday, and the morning marine layer of thin clouds still blanketed Coronado's coastline. McGirt parked parallel to the curb, draped his and Bud's helmet over the seat, and then secured them to the bike's frame with a chain lock.

"Just in case they grow legs and wander off; you know what I mean?" he said after eying a dilapidated van as it parked nearby.

A pair of grungy looking wave riders got out and began unlashing their boards from a rack on the van's rooftop. They glared at McGirt.

"Must be the uniform," he joked while staring them down. "They're not sure if I'm a cop or the Border Patrol." He and Lammers removed their shoes and socks, then rolled up their pant legs a few turns.

"How far you want to go?" McGirt asked.

"I'll let you know if I need to stop. The doc at the VA said walking is good for me."

"Okay, just let me know."

They plodded through the soft, beige-colored sand for about one hundred yards before reaching the water's edge. The tide was low, so it was a comparatively easier walk over the shore's wet, harder packed surface. McGirt heard Bud's labored breathing, so he slowed down the pace.

"Thanks," his friend said. "That softer stuff was a little much for me at this stage." They walked in silence for the first couple of minutes. The sun began to break through as the low, early-morning clouds started to dissipate, revealing the sparkling blue skies for which the region had become famous.

McGirt and his wife had grown accustomed to the beautiful views. Seeing them every day, though, he'd actually begun to take them for granted—the crashing waves, ships gliding in and out of the bay, and the shoreline's most prominent feature: the iconic, red-shingled Hotel Del Coronado. Built in the late 1800's, the original white, wooden Victorian structure had endured San Diego's rapid growth with the grace of a cherished family elder, who, despite his or her age, seemed to always bring a sense of peace and dignity to a gathering.

Bud was the first to speak. "I never get tired of seeing that grand old lady," he said of the hotel. "Harkens me back to an easier time for all of us."

"Sure does," McGirt added.

Bud casually turned to look behind him and saw that there wasn't another person within a hundred feet. "Well, I guess this is as good a place as any to talk." He paused as if trying to find the right words to begin, but finally just spoke his mind. "We were had, pal. What we went through trying to get that girl her freedom was unnecessary."

McGirt stopped in his tracks. "What do you mean?"

"Felix Romolo knew where Karlena was the whole time. They were using her as bait—long enough to let the ransom get paid so they could gain intelligence on how and where the money trail flowed."

"You gotta be shitting me." McGirt shared in Bud's enraged disbelief.

"As mad as I am, though, from a different point of view, I can understand Romolo's motives," Bud said. "He had an insider, who was working both sides of the fence, and decided to go with it. Fortunately for him, and us, his strategy worked. I wasn't quite sure of all this until I got off the phone with my people back in Langley. When I questioned Karlena on the ship, there was only so far I could go with the interrogation because of her condition; you know, she was pretty vulnerable after all she'd been through."

"Yeah, I understand. So what was it that that convinced you about Romolo?"

Bud started walking again, but much slower and with shorter strides. He folded his hands behind his back, like a college professor pacing in front of students during a lecture. "Remember that dirt-bag-looking guy that drove into the AFP camp just after we'd arrived on Basilan?"

"Yeah...I think so. Old pickup, ripped jeans and the big, dark shades. Him?"

"Yup. Name's Omar Ascero, code name of Blister. A Muslim that the P.I.'s National Intelligence Coordinating Agency paid a ton of money to flip and go deep under cover. Apparently so deep that, for several years, NICA had assumed they'd lost him. He'd gone off the grid."

"Wow. So what did it? How'd you piece it all together?" McGirt asked. He'd unconsciously mirrored Lammers's hands-behind-the-back gait.

"Karlena had mentioned a couple names when I spoke with her: Spider and Blister. They were the ones who'd intercepted the small boat she'd hired to transport her from an island in Indonesia to Mindanao. She was supposed to meet a Filipino friend she knew from college and, together, they'd planned to take pictures and submit them to a travel magazine for publication. My sources confirmed that Spider was probably the one who led the chase after us, in the speedboat, when we were escaping."

"So Romolo knew all the time? I just can't believe that."

"I doubt if he knew her whereabouts from the beginning, but I'm damn certain that he knew the day we found her."

"Jesus Christ, we could have all gotten killed!" McGirt said. He noticed a middle-aged couple approaching them from the opposite direction and lowered his voice. "So, what was in it for Romolo?"

"Like I said, he wanted to let it play out long enough for their NICA to track down the money."

"Okay, I got that part. Now what about that guy we met when we first flew in—the one that Romolo drove us to see at the charity office?"

"Ah, Malik Abbas; that smart little bastard. Apparently, he must have started a path to radicalization sometime after he'd gotten shot in the leg by that Communist group, the New People's Army, the same shitheads that downed Rayburn's helicopter twenty years ago. Didn't matter that it had been some of his own countrymen that had nearly killed him. He bought into the whole idea that Westerners and Christian Filipinos were the one's depriving his people from their just rewards."

Lammers stopped walking; his breathing had become labored again. "Sorry. Walking and talking at the same time is taking a toll on me." McGirt pointed to a bench, a few yards away, at the foot of a condominium complex that overlooked the ocean.

"Whew, thanks," Bud said as he sat down. "Anyway, Abbas went on to get a law degree and then took up the worthy cause of helping poor Muslims in

Mindanao and on Basilan Island. He eventually partnered up in a symbiotic relationship with the Abu Sayyaf Group. Nice tidy arrangement: He'd concoct a convoluted laundering scheme—like the one that bilked Karlena Brandt's old man in Texas—then ASG would carry out the kidnapping. The two groups would split the ransom money for their respective uses. Abbas's charity could then provide food, medicine and what-nots to needy Muslims; the ASG got shiny new rifles and funds to help them recruit new members."

"My heads spinning, Bud. Are you sure of all this?"

"Let me tell you: After twenty years in Langley, I've seen similar ploys—many on a much grander scale."

Just then, a formation of three Navy H-60 *Seahawk* helicopters thundered overhead on their approach to the air station. Both men tilted their heads back to enjoy the spectacle as the flight descended gracefully and landed on the end of the air station's westerly runway.

Lammers looked over and saw the smile on McGirt's face. "You're gonna miss that, aren't you? After all these years, I still do."

McGirt nodded his head. "Yeah. The H-46 was a blast to fly, but not nearly as advanced as those fancy Seahawks. Maybe I can scam a little stick time in one of those new machines someday."

"Oh, yeah? And how you gonna pull that off?"

"Well, it may not be completely out of the picture," McGirt began. "Believe it or not, Tarzan Truckee informed me that I got picked up at the O-7 selection board."

Lammers's jaw dropped. "No way. You told me that you were retiring. For Christ's sake, I even greased the skids with the director for your job with the Agency." Bud started laughing and slapped McGirt on the back. "What the hell?"

"I know; I can't believe it either. But here's the kicker, if I accept the promotion, my orders will be to the staff of the National Security Council in Washington. Either way, looks like you'll have me and Gina as neighbors."

Bud didn't hesitate. "Damn, McGirt, take the promotion. You'll be a lot better off walking around that town with stars on your collar rather than dressed in a cheap suit, shuffling papers at the Agency. That's a no brainer, if you ask me."

"That's the way I'm beginning to see it too. Just need to run it by Gina."

"Oh, *bullshit*. Gina's not going to hold you back, and you know it. I've known her for as long as you have."

McGirt laughed. "Yes, you have. Hell, Jill was the one who introduced us."

Bud nodded and leaned forward, resting his elbows against his thighs. He stared blankly out to sea. A long, silent pause followed as they both absorbed the warm sun and the sound of crashing waves.

McGirt understood the man well enough to know that the mentioning of Bud's deceased wife had triggered a painful memory. Jill Lammers had stood by her husband through it all: his wartime service in Vietnam; the humiliation of being forced to resign his Navy commission; and, finally, Bud's incredible rise from the ashes and subsequent distinguished career at the Central Intelligence Agency. But Jill had passed away before either of them could enjoy the fruits of his labors. Bud still had his children to fall back on, but that wouldn't be the same; they'd be busy building their own lives. McGirt felt guilty knowing that his life was on an upswing while his friend's seemed to be headed in the opposite direction. He and Gina would be moving on to another exciting chapter in D.C., while Bud retired as a widower.

Bud looked down and swiped the tears from his eyes. "We were damn lucky weren't we, McGirt?" he said in a quivering voice. "We both married *up.*"

McGirt wrapped an arm around Bud's shoulder and gave him a firm, guy hug. He held it tightly and said, "Yes, we did, pal. Yes, we did."

# EPILOGUE

Otto Brandt tiptoed past Karlena's room on his way to the ranch house's east porch. As he did each morning, he carried a teeming mug of strong, black coffee. He opened the door slowly, walked out into the crisp West Texas air and found his favorite chair: a bent-wood rocker that his daddy had made.

Otto checked the time: The glowing hands of his wristwatch read 6:05—still eighteen minutes before sunrise. He took a small, slurping sip from the mug and watched as a tiny plume of steam rose around his lips. He leaned back and gazed at the sliver of faint, coral-shaded light that hovered over the horizon.

The past two weeks since learning of his daughter's release had been a whirlwind. Congressman Clayton Gantry had personally phoned Otto to deliver the news, and Gantry's staff had followed up with an update on Karlena's status at least once per day. When Gantry's private jet had gotten airborne from San Diego, the congressman had offered to chauffeur Otto to the Midland-Odessa airport for her arrival. Brandt had graciously turned him down, preferring instead to drive his pickup truck. He'd choked up on the phone while thanking Gantry. "I just can't thank you enough, Claytie. Only one thing that I ask, and that's if you could keep those reporters away from us for a while?" Gantry promised that he would.

When Karlena stepped off the jet, Otto Brandt had stood alone on the tarmac, dressed in a pair of starched jeans and a freshly pressed shirt that Maria had set out; he wore his best-loved string tie. Gantry had kept his word: the only ones present for her arrival had been Otto and a couple of airport workers who'd directed the plane to its parking spot.

The twenty-minute drive home had been a peaceful one. Keeping in form with his stoic German-American upbringing, Otto chose to be mostly quiet, asking only if Karlena was hungry. When she'd replied 'no,' he'd simply added, "Well, Maria stocked the fridge with all your favorites. Just help yourself."

Otto checked his watch again: five minutes to go. He glanced over at the bulky crate that had been delivered to his property after its long journey from the Philippines. After one of his hired men had jimmied opened its lid and removed a useless-looking chunk of metal, he'd held up the rusty part and turned to his boss, bewildered. Otto had emphatically waved his hand down, signaling the man to put it back inside and to reseal the crate's lid. Since then he'd ignored the box of junk that he'd "purchased"—until just now. He made plans in his head to backhoe a deep hole, far away from the house, where he'd bury the rotten thing, along with all of the unpleasant memories it represented.

Otto heard the door creak open behind him. "Good morning, Daddy," Karlena said as she stepped out onto the veranda and sat next to him. Although she'd regained nearly half of the weight she'd lost, Otto still flinched at the young woman's thin, haggard image.

"Couldn't sleep much, so thought I'd get up. I knew you'd be out here." She hugged the thick bathrobe up close to her neck to stay warm and joined her father as he gazed out over the flat, Texas plain. Karlena let out a soft gasp. "Oh, there it is!"

"Yup, right on time," Otto replied. "Welcome home, little girl."

Karlena reached out for his hand as the two of them watched the rising sun—in all of its red-orange, blazing glory—as it crested the new day's skyline. Its beams of light radiated a brilliant, starburst pattern against a thin strand of high clouds. The magnificent sight truly was *Biblical.*

# AUTHOR'S NOTES

Writing *Verbal Orders* presented a unique set of challenges. It was developed as a sequel to my book, *Rotorboys,* which was set in the Philippine Islands during the height of the Marcos regime (1965-1986). Updating the storyline and characters to a post 9/11 scenario required not only a review of Philippine current events, but more significantly, research into the turbulent history of the country's Muslim-dominated southern provinces.

The following is a suggested list of references for those readers who wish to learn more about Philippine history and the quest for autonomy by Filipino Muslims:

*A History of the Philippines from Indios Bravos to Filipinos* by Luis H. Francia. Overbrook Press, 2010.

*Imperial Grunts. The American Military on the Ground* by Robert D. Kaplan. Random House, 2005.

*In Our Image. America's Empire in the Philippines* by Stanley Karnow. Random House, 1989.

*Muslim Rulers and Rebels. Everyday Politics and Armed Separation in the Southern Philippines* by Thomas M. McKenna. University of California Press, 1998.

*On the Palms of My Hands. Ghosts of the Forgotten: Echoes of the Crusades in the Philippines* by A.E. Amaral. AuthorHouse, 2007.

*The Contemporary Muslim Movement in the Philippines* by Cesar Adib Majul. Mizan Press, 1985.

*The Marcos Dynasty* by Sterling Seagrave. Harper and Row Publishers, 1988.

*The Philippine Response to Terrorism: The Abu Sayyaf Group* by Eusaquito P. Manalo. Thesis at the Naval Postgraduate School, Monterey, CA, 2004.

Larry Carello
www.larrycarello.com

**THERE IS DUTY. THERE IS JUSTICE.
AND THERE IS VENGEANCE...**

# GEORGE GALDORISI

His orders: assassinate the strike group commander...

# WHO IS HUNTER?  WHO IS PREY?
# WHO WILL SURVIVE?

# ROBERT BIDINOTTO

**In a world without justice, sometimes
you have to make your own...**

www.braveshipbooks.com

**HIGH OCTANE AERIAL COMBAT**

**KEVIN MILLER**

Unarmed over hostile territory...

www.braveshipbooks.com

# A VICIOUS DRUG CARTEL IS ABOUT TO LEARN THE HARD WAY...

## TED NULTY

...there's no such thing as an ex-Marine.

www.braveshipbooks.com